HEART
OF THE STORM

HEART
OF THE STORM

*A Novel of
Men and Women
in the Gulf War*

L.H. Burruss

Writers Club Press
San Jose New York Lincoln Shanghai

Heart of the Storm
A novel of Men and Women in the Gulf War

Published by Writers Club Press
an imprint of iUniverse.com, Inc.

For information address:
iUniverse.com, Inc.
5220 S 16th, Ste. 200
Lincoln, NE 68512
www.iuniverse.com

This is a work of fiction. While some of the characters actually exist, their actions and dialogue are products os the author's imagiation.

ISBN: 0-595-12025-3

Printed in the United States of America

to four brave American soldiers:

▼

Dick Malvesti

"He always looked after us," a soldier said. "He'd go to bat for us every time."

"I've never known him to do anything unfair," another said…

One soldier came and looked down. He said out loud, 'God damn it!'"

That's all he said, and then he walked away…

(Ernie Pyle—Brave Men)

Pat Hurley

"…I have no regrets about becoming close to the men it was my honor to command. I had the sort of kindred feeling for them that the magnificent ancient warrior Sun Tzu must have felt when he said, 'Regard your soldiers as your children, and they will follow you into the deepest valleys; look on them as your own beloved sons, and they will stand by you even unto death.'"

(Burruss—Mike Force)

Otto Clark and Eloy "Rod" Rodriguez

When a soldier was injured and could not get back to safety, his buddy went out to get him, against his officer's orders. He returned mortally wounded and his friend, whom he had carried back, was dead.

The officer was angry. "I told you not to go," he said. "Now I've lost both of you. It was not worth it."

The dying man replied, "But it was, sir, because when I got to him, he said, 'Jim, I knew you'd come.'"

(Leslie D. Weatherhead, on comradeship)

and to those they left behind

▼

"Also I heard the voice of the Lord, saying Whom shall I send, and who will go for us? Then said I, Here am I; send me."

(Isaiah 6:8)

▼

Flash

17 January 1991

Almost as a living thing would do, the Tomahawk cruise missile's artificial brain saw the city of Basra directly ahead.

A few seconds later its electronic memory recognized the image of a highway intersection just southeast of the city, and the stubby-winged bird of war rolled slightly, turned right toward a Republican Guards corps headquarters just east of Basra, and obeyed its computer program's suicidal order to arm its explosive payload.

At the same time, the Tomahawk switched from the program which had enabled it to fly flawlessly from the deck of the battleship Wisconsin in the Persian Gulf, up the Khor Zubayr waterway to the highway from Kuwait City to Basra, then north to the outskirts of that ancient, ill-fated town near the Iran-Iraq border. The missile now began obeying commands from its target program, which displayed the image of a large building topped by an array of radio antennae. The sensors in the Tomahawk's nose recognized the building ahead and below, aligned it with the image of that same building stored in its memory, and aimed the missile at the center window on the second floor of the structure's southwestern side. It streaked in through the window and crushed its detonating fuze against the office wall of the Iraqi corps commander. The monstrous explosion of the Tomahawk's half-ton warhead muffled the sound of the air raid sirens which were just beginning to wail.

The liberation of Kuwait had begun.

Along with dozens of other Tomahawks speeding toward critical targets throughout Iraq from their launchers aboard American surface ships and submarines in the Persian Gulf and the Red Sea, the giant air armada of the American-led Coalition forces was taking to the dark skies of the Middle East.

U.S. Air Force Stealth fighters were the first to follow the Tomahawks into Iraqi airspace—dark, angular shapes as invisible to Iraqi radars as the bats which darted away from the air raid sirens' belated wailing.

Right behind the Stealth fighters were F4-G "Wild Weasels," their Vietnam era airframes now fitted with state-of-the-art electronic equipment to deceive and confuse enemy radars while the HARMs—Highspeed Anti-Radiation Missiles—they carried were launched to home in on the source of Iraqi radar emissions. Few of the enemy radar operators were wise enough to shut off their radars or flee their sites. As a result, most of them joined their equipment as early casualties of the overt phase of Operation Desert Storm.

The earlier, covert phase of the operation had been equally success-ful, surgically opening an incision in the defensive skin of Iraq's intended empire, enabling General Schwarzkopf's instruments of war to enter the guts of Saddam Hussein's doomed nation. That incision became a gaping wound now, and Iraq's blood began to gush into the Cradle of Civilization.

High above Baghdad, U.S. Air Force Major Billy Boyd laid the crosshairs of his Stealth fighter's infrared targeting system on the center of a tall building five miles below. For the third time, he checked the electronic display to ensure that the building was, in fact, his target—the headquarters of the Iraqi Air Force. Satisfied that it was, he illumi-nated the top of the target with the infrared laser and released a pair of laser-guided bombs, both equipped with delay fuzes to enable them to penetrate deep into the building before detonating. As he watched with fascination, Boyd saw the bombs streak to the intersection of the crosshairs and disappear. A split second later, all four sides of the enemy headquarters erupted in flame and smoke.

"Poor bastards," Boyd muttered, then turned his hellish aircraft toward the south. Behind him, the night sky was torn by streams of tracers from anti-aircraft weapons, reaching blindly and vainly for the invisible invaders who were ravaging Saddam's command, control, and communications systems.

The ancient capitol city shuddered, and Boyd imagined its soul cursing friend and foe alike. He crossed himself as he saw the Tigris and Euphrates rivers joining together far below, and thought, "…the Valley of the Shadow of Death…"

Two hundred miles to the southwest, Hassan al Ahwabi was awakened from a deep sleep by his section sergeant and told to get ready to move immediately. Hassan was the driver of an Al Husseini surface-to-surface missile erector/launcher, known by the Coalition—and soon to be known by the world in general—as a Scud.

Hassan's Soviet-built vehicle carried one of the big rockets and a mobile launch crew of eight men—seven Iraqis and one Russian.

Until a few months earlier, the Russian, Warrant Officer Anatoly Vasilnikov, had been a member of the Red Army assigned as an advisor to Saddam's Republican Guards rocket forces. When the United Nations resolutions demanding Iraq's withdrawal from Kuwait had been issued, Vasilnikov and his fellow advisors had initially been told that they would remain, then that they would be withdrawn, and finally that they could volunteer to remain, if they so wished. About a hundred of the Soviet soldiers, well compensated by the Iraqi government, elected to stay. For Vasilnikov, the folly of that decision was not yet apparent.

He hopped into the cab of the big missile carrier and poked Hassan in the ribs with his elbow. In badly-accented Arabic, he said, "All right, Hassan, you old camel humper, let's go kill some Jews."

Abir bint Hamad bin al-Sabah was already awake when she saw Mara enter the spacious bedroom of her villa on the outskirts of Kuwait City, the small candle Mara shielded with her hand softly lighting the room. Abir had been stirred from her deep sleep moments before by the rumbling of distant thunder. Mara glided silently across the room to the big bed, placed her hand on her friend's bare shoulder and whispered, "It has begun," then turned and left the room as quietly as she had entered.

Abir lay still for awhile, listening. Of course, she thought, that isn't thunder—not this early. Mara—formerly Abir's servant, but now her most trusted comrade in their underground resistance cell—was informing the Kuwaiti sheik's beautiful wife that the war to liberate their ravaged nation was beginning.

Abir turned to the naked man sleeping soundly beside her, kissed his cheek, and reached down to stroke him. He became awake and erect at the same time, and when he rolled over onto her, she said, "It has begun."

Again a sound like thunder rumbled in the distance, and as he gently entered her, Bill Kernan whispered, "Yes, I know."

Major General Wayne Wilson barely noticed the noise made by the incessant stream of warplanes that poured through the hole his men had ripped in the wall of Iraqi air defenses a short distance north. He was looking at the bodies of seven of his men lying side-by-side on the desert floor.

Wilson was the commander of the United States Special Operations Task Force—USSOTAF, as it was called for short—the multi-service task force which had been assembled for the conduct of special operations during operations Desert Shield and Desert Storm.

The seven dead men had been some of the several thousand special operations personnel under Wayne Wilson's command. There were Navy SEALs, and squadrons of Air Force special operations aircrews with their sophisticated helicopters and aerial gunships. There were Army Special Forces units, supported by their own highly skilled Blackhawk helicopter crews. There were soldiers from the highly selective and multi-skilled Delta Force, and their British counterparts of the 22 Special Air Service Regiment.

The secret operations of Wilson's task force were the key to the opening through which allied aircraft were now swarming over a confused and almost impotent enemy, his air defenses blinded, his generals afraid to surface for fear of a "smart bomb" or a sniper's bullet, his every move seemingly seen and reported and responded to with quick, precise strikes by fire.

Yet knowledge of that fact did nothing to lessen the deep sorrow Wayne Wilson felt as he looked at the pitifully torn, twisted remains of his fallen warriors. Four were the crewmen of the helicopter in which all seven had perished, and two were medics who had volunteered to go with them to evacuate an injured comrade from deep in enemy territory.

The seventh was the soldier they had gone for, and his death tore hardest at Wayne's soul. Yes, he had been a superb soldier and an outstanding sergeant major, but he had been more than that to Wayne Wilson. They had been young Rangers together; they had suffered together the derision of a confused, thankless nation after the cauldron of Vietnam had forged them from boys into men. Time and again they had served together: in Vietnam, Grenada, and most recently in the liberation of Panama. They had grown to share not just mutual respect and close friendship, but brotherly love—the sort of pure, raw, soldierly love that only the battlefield can make so strong that it has no need for such warnings as, "What God hath drawn together…"

Wilson sighed heavily, remembering the last time he had heard those words. It was at his now-fallen comrade's wedding years earlier, when he had served as the best man.

Now he looked from one to the other of the bodies. He couldn't tell which of them was his oldest true friend, and he thought, Just as well. It would have made him feel that body was more important than the others, and that would have been wrong. In the darkness, with only his command sergeant major nearby, he gazed at the fallen seven and wondered aloud, "Why? Why like this, in a damned accident? He deserved better—they all did."

Matt Jensen, Wilson's sergeant major, knew all seven of the men. He had served with three of them for many years. He, too, wondered why

God would take them now, like this, instead of at least letting them die in combat. He thought about it for awhile, then said, "Maybe it's because no enemy was good enough to kill them, sir."

Wilson nodded. "Maybe so," he said, then saluted the bodies and said, "See you in Valhalla, you wild Irish warhorse."

He wiped his slightly runny nose—for he had long ago learned not to weep at the sight of dead soldiers, but he had not learned how to keep the unshed tears from running down his nose. Then he and his sergeant major moved toward their waiting helicopter.

There was a war on now, and they still had men deep in enemy territory, and many more waiting with the impatience of untested warriors to get into the fray.

Army Lieutenant Larry Redmond, just south of the border of Iraq, east of the Saudi town of Shubah, didn't hear the first sorties of allied aircraft en route to deliver their devastating bolts of lightning at Iraq's heart. He could hear nothing except the whine of the turbine engines of his tanks. Redmond was maneuvering his platoon of Abrams main battle tanks, just ending a rapid road march from far to the east, into the positions he had chosen for them during an earlier reconnaisance. His tanks were to be the point of a spear formed by the combined arms team of his company's tanks and an attached platoon of mechanized infantry in Bradley fighting vehicles—designated Team Charlie.

When his tanks were in position, he used hand and arm signals to order his subordinates to shut their turbine engines down. Their whine was replaced by a distant roar, as allied fighter-bombers flooded the skies over Iraq.

Redmond's platoon sergeant, standing beside him, said, "My God, sir. Listen to that!"

Just then a pair of British Tornados streaked low over the tankers' heads, bound for an Iraqi airfield. The lieutenant watched the hot glow of their engines disappear, then said, "Yeah, zoomies, give 'em hell! Wake the bastards up for us. We'll be along shortly."

There was no way Kuwait would be retaken without a ground assault to defeat Saddam Hussein's formidable army, of that Larry Redmond was certain. And he damn well intended to lead the way.

▼

Darkness

▼

One

five-and-a-half months earlier: 2 August 1990

"Mara!", Abir called. "Mara, if you cannot make the children behave, then take them elsewhere!"

"Yes, Mistress," Mara answered from the patio pool of Abir's living quarters. Little devils, she thought, but in a kind voice said, "Akil, Khalid, come now, you two. Let your mother have some peace and quiet."

The boys would be wild for the next two days, Mara knew, and there was little she could do about it. She only wished that Madame Abir had waited until they were ready to leave to tell them they were going to America. Oh, well. It would be worth it to spend a couple of weeks in the West. They hadn't been out of Kuwait in months, and Orlando was her favorite of all the places in America they had ever gone: Disney World, the Florida Mall, the new Universal Studios theme park she had heard about from the servants of other households. She could hardly wait either, and now she smiled at the boys and sang, "Who's the leader of the club that's made for you and me?"

As most other priveleged children their ages from around the world would have done, the young Kuwaiti sheiks chanted, "M-I-C...K-E-Y...M-O-U-S-E!"

Abir smiled at the sound of their voices. They were good boys, really. It was a shame that their father didn't know them as well as she did, she thought. But it seemed he was too busy increasing his already immense fortune. Of course, the more he amassed, the more legitimacy would be given in the West to the title "Prince" by which he and the other Kuwaiti sheiks were increasingly desirous of being addressed. Their cousins in Saudi Arabia had for some time been addressed as princes, as a result of their oil-fired fortunes. Such a title would only benefit her sons in later years.

Akil would be a young man soon. Perhaps then his father would pay more attention to him, although it was more likely Akil would learn most manly things from Mustafa, the young Army captain already assigned as the boy sheik's aide.

She remembered that Mustafa was to have returned to the emirate that afternoon with the family's new airplane, a Gulfstream IV jet of which they had only recently taken delivery to replace their aging Lear jet.

God, I hope nothing's wrong with this one, Abir thought. Two of the American girls with whom she had attended Columbia University were supposed to meet her in Orlando, and they were the only ones with whom she felt she could ever let her hair down—have a few drinks, catch up on the latest risque jokes, and gossip about the former American boyfriends she'd had during her university years.

She pressed a button on the intercom beside her lounge chair, and one of her handmaidens answered immediately.

"Madame?" It wasn't Mara, who would have called her "Mistress," as she had done since they were little girls in her father's house.

"Salome, is Captain Mustafa here yet?"

"Yes, Madame. He's waiting for you in the reception suite."

Abir started to tell her to have him come to the pool, then laughed at herself. He had seen her in bathing suits many times since shortly after she married into the family ten years earlier. But not here. In Nice and Miami and Santa Barbara, yes. But not in the Arab world. And not without at least two other adults present.

"Tell him to call me on the phone, then, Salome."

"Yes, Madame."

Mustafa rang up two minutes later, and after exchanging Allah's blessings with him, Abir asked, "How is my husband?"

"Very well, Madame, God be thanked. And his children?"

"Little hellions, at the moment," she replied. "If we don't get them to Disney World soon, they'll drive us all mad. Is the aircraft ready?"

"It will be by tomorrow, God willing. I'm told to inform you that you are to be prepared to leave before dark tomorrow evening."

"You mean the day after tomorrow, don't you?"

"I mean tomorrow, August second, as our master has directed me to inform you." There was irritation in his voice at being questioned by a woman, although he would gladly have died for this one, if Allah willed it.

"Oh, why in the name of…Mickey Mouse would he do this to me? We haven't begun to get ready yet. I haven't even told the servants what clothing to prepare for us. Damn! What reason did he give?"

The irritation still showed in Mustafa's voice. "He has his reasons, Madame. We're to meet him in Vienna, and spend the night there."

His Austrian whore must be starting her period, Abir thought. Or maybe his Florida friend can't wait for him to wallow his soft, fat belly all over hers.

She tried not to even think such things, for fear she'd slip and say them aloud. But she was angry at having such little warning to prepare to leave.

And anyway, they were probably true. Her husband showed little sexual interest in her anymore—although that was fine with her. She shuddered at her thoughts.

"Of course he has his reasons, Mustafa. We shall be ready."

At least the airplane was ready. She hated to think how wild the boys would become if they had been delayed. And how disappointed she would be, if it caused her to miss a session with her chums from Columbia.

She left the side of her lovely marble pool and went into her chambers to dress. One of the gilt-framed mirrors showed her reflection, and she stopped to survey herself. Her long, dark hair draped over her shoulders, framing a face that was, by the standards of any culture, beautiful. And the body within the Dior bathing suit was, for a woman with two children—for any woman, for that matter—trim and firm, yet shapely. She pulled the bathing suit down, and stepped out of it. It was as lovely a body as she had possessed during those years at Columbia, when she had first allowed it to be touched by any man. And touching was all she had allowed.

"What a waste," she sighed as she studied her naked form, then grabbed a silk robe and shouted, "Mara! Mara, come here! We've lots to do!"

Bill Kernan placed the crosshairs of the fat-barreled rifle's scope on the silhouette two hundred meters to his front. His aim was as steady as it had been more than two decades earlier, when he was in the U.S. Marine Corps Platoon Commanders' Course at Quantico, undergoing marksmanship training. He inhaled deeply, then exhaled half way and slowly squeezed the trigger of the .223 caliber rifle. It fired with a barely audible phhht.

"I'll be damned," he muttered, clearing the weapon and handing it to one of the three men standing over him. "You're right, Winnie. It's as quiet as a nun's fart!"

Winnie's partners in Whisper Weapons, Incorporated, were smiling broadly. They had waited a long time for someone from the Central Intelligence Agency—someone who knew what he was hearing—to come to their little company in rural Ruther Glen, Virginia, and test their products. They made the best silencers in the world, and they knew it. But they had so far received few orders for their fledgling company's wares. They sensed that Kernan might be the key to open the door to a big order.

"But let's see where the round hit," Kernan said, moving down the range toward the silhouette target.

The one named John, who had invented the built-in silencer, strode confidently beside him and said, "Wherever you aimed it, Mr. Kernan. Guaranteed."

He was right. The subsonic round had pierced the center of the bulls-eye. Kernan arched his eyebrows and nodded. He was greatly impressed.

"Let me fire a few more rounds," he said, feeling he had found a rare thing—a weapon that worked as advertised.

When Kernan had fired another half-dozen rounds through the cleverly-designed rifle, they went down range again. All seven bullet holes were within an inch-and-a-half circle. Bill Kernan was convinced. Now, as he explained to the trio from Whisper Weapons, all he had to do was convince the bureaucrats in CIA procurement that the Agency needed to place a healthy order. "And of course," he added, "I've got to get suppressed weapons procurement cleared by the lawyers. We've got to get everything cleared by the goddamned lawyers these days."

The one called Nat laughed aloud. "I can probably help you with that, Bill," he said. "I'm a goddamned lawyer."

Kernan's pager began beeping, and he checked the sender's number. "I'd better answer this one, gents. Use your phone?"

Nat had a cellular phone in his car, and Kernan dialed his boss's office at CIA headquarters in Langley, Virginia, a hundred miles away.

His boss answered the first ring. "It looks like the sonofabitch is going in at anytime, Bill. Better get up here right away. And stop by your house for anything you need to take over there for the next, say, few months."

"It's in my car," Kernan answered. "But listen, this stuff I came to look at—it really works. Make sure somebody else gets down here and checks it out while I'm gone. And tell 'em to bring a company checkbook."

He turned to the three men and said, "Sorry, fellows, but I've got to get up the road. Sure wish I had one of those things to take along, but…"

John sensed that it would be well used and held the rifle out to him. "Take it," he said. "I can make another one."

Bill smiled and waved it away. "Without paperwork? They'd throw us all in the slammer."

"Take it," Nat said. "I can handle that. I'm a goddamned lawyer, remember?"

Bill grinned and said, "All right, then. Put a couple of boxes of that subsonic ammo in the case with it, will you, Winnie?" Let the bureaucrats sort it out later, he thought. While I'm in Kuwait.

During the two hour drive to Langley, Kernan tried to figure out how the intelligence agency alleged to be the world's best could have failed to anticipate Iraq's invasion of its little neighbor, Kuwait, until it was too late to do anything about it. It was almost criminal. But it wasn't the analysts who would catch hell. It was the President. And poor bastards like himself who would now be expected to go in and organize a resistance force, if the lefties in Congress didn't pass a law prohibiting it. He would at least, he knew, be going to Saudi Arabia to train Kuwaitis there how to organize an underground force to resist the Iraqi invaders.

"Well," he muttered to himself, thinking of other places he'd been sent since he joined the Agency, "at least I've been to Kuwait! And at least I'll get rid of this beer belly."

Captain Mustafa was terribly worried when he entered Madame Abir's room after sending Mara ahead of him to ensure that she was covered. He wasn't frightened of the Iraqis, but of what would happen to him if he didn't keep Abir and the young sheiks safely beyond their reach.

Fortunately, her husband had been sensible enough to have an underground safe haven built into the villa, in the event that terrorists ever tried to get to him or his family. Mustafa had already sent the two boys there.

"You must go to the safe haven immediately, Madame."

She came fully awake. "Terrorists? Where are the boys?"

"Already there, Mistress," Mara said. "Come quickly. It's the Iraqis. They'll be in the city soon."

"I'm going to make a run for the airport, to make certain the crew is ready," Mustafa announced. "If it's safe, I'll telephone the safe haven. A van will be waiting at the gate to take you to the airplane. Don't tarry."

He disappeared at a run.

It was the last they saw of the captain until several days later, when Mara spied his body hanging from a construction crane.

▼

Two

7 August 1990

Bill Kernan strapped himself into the seat of the little, sand-colored Defender, the McDonnell Douglas helicopter that was to spirit him into Kuwait. It was already cranked and running, although it was so quiet that one could barely hear it whir. Kernan was damn glad of that, because the CIA mission planners weren't certain of the locations of all the air defense systems the Iraqis were still moving into Kuwait. And he was damn glad that Claude Owen was flying the helicopter. If anybody could get him to his landing zone undetected, Owen could. In case they had any problems, though, the Defender was armed with a rapid-firing 5.56mm minigun for self-defense.

Kernan pulled on his helmet, looked over at Owen, and over the intercom said, "I'd rather have a sister in a whorehouse than a brother who flies helicopters."

The pilot laughed. "Conan the vulgarian! I wish you did have a sister in a whorehouse! What have you got us into this time?"

Owen had flown Kernan into—and out of—several hairy assignments over the years. At first the two CIA men had thought it was only coincidence, but after one particularly dangerous situation, they determined that it was due to the fact that neither of them ever questioned their assignments—at least not on the basis of the personal danger they were put in. That made their superiors, the sort of men who sent people on such assignments instead of going on them, feel less uncomfortable than they felt when other subordinates protested being sent. But that suited Kernan and Owen just fine, because the operative was confident that Owen would do whatever it took to get him into and out of the situation, and the pilot was confident that whatever Kernan might be up to on his strange missions, it was worth the risk of getting him there and back. They were a good match.

The quiet little chopper lifted gently off the concrete pad at the isolated base—actually a small villa at an artificial oasis amid the sea of sand of the Arabian Peninsula. It had been borrowed by the CIA from one of Saudi Arabia's hundreds of minor princes. With its skids nearly dragging the ground, Owen nosed the defender over and picked up speed, making the dash into Kuwait at an altitude of ten feet and a speed of 150 miles per hour. The only persons aware of their presence were some of the crew aboard the big Airborne Warning and Control System—AWACS—aircraft several miles above them. The AWACS crew had been forewarned only to track the helicopter, and report it to no one else, unless it happened to crash.

Owen's destination was an empty spot of ground on the desert floor miles from any known habitation. Had it not been for the twelve Global Positioning System satellites in orbit thousands of miles above, there would have been no way of locating the barren spot. But the GPS, as it was known, could tell anyone with one of the tiny receivers the system employed, exactly where he was. A couple of computer chips was all it took to make the calculations, and a digital readout told one the receiver's precise location. There were tens of thousands of such receivers in the hands of the U.S. military and other agencies of the government, and they would prove indispensible in fighting a war in a desert where few landmarks existed.

The GPS enabled Owen to speed Kernan to his featureless drop off point in only a few minutes, and it seemed to Bill that they had just lifted off when Claude said, "One minute, old buddy."

Bill Kernan said, "Have a safe trip back, then, Claude," and pulled the helmet off his head. He didn't even bother to check the GPS readout on the chopper's instrument panel, because he knew Owen would put him down in the right place. The little bird touched down, and Kernan extended a hand to the pilot. "Holler if you need me," Owen said, shaking it once, firmly.

Bill unstrapped the harness, hopped out and grabbed the heavy rucksack and the silent rifle from the back of the doorless helicopter. Without looking back, he walked a few yards away and laid down on the rocky desert floor. The helicopter lifted a few feet off the ground, turned, and flew quietly away.

Quiet as a nun's fart, Kernan thought, remembering what the men who had given him the rifle had said about their product. The Whisper Weapons men had also sent him a new, .45 caliber Glock automatic pistol the day after he had been to their range. It arrived by Federal Express at the accomodation address he used in Reston, Virginia. Inside, with the pistol and its screw-on silencer, was a note from Nat McClanahan: "August 2, '90. Saw the news. We thought you might prefer this in case you go to town. Don't worry about the paperwork." It was signed, "God damned lawyer."

Kernan patted the pistol in the shoulder holster beneath the Arab robes he was wearing, then looked in the northern sky and found Ursa Major. Following the two stars which pointed to Polaris, he determined true north, then turned right and started walking. There was no glow of light from his objective, somewhere over the horizon. Kuwait City was dark.

Abir was weeping again, and Mara had had enough of it. Seeing his mother distraught made Akil start to whine and cry, and Mara said, "Hush, Akil. Sheiks don't whine. Now, go play with your brother and be quiet." When he had gone into the other room, she looked at Abir and said, "You can sit there and sob all you want to, Mistress. But that doesn't accomplish anything. The food is running low, and the boys are hungry. All you're doing is making things worse, damn you."

Abir's face paled, and she looked at her servant of many years. "How dare you speak to me like that! I'll have you...I'll have you deported!"

Mara stared at her, eyes narrowed. "Ha! We've already been deported—all of us. Or haven't you heard? We're in Iraq, now, remember? The Nineteenth Province."

Abir swung an open hand at her, but Mara saw it coming and grabbed her wrist, then slapped the sheik's wife sharply across the face. Abir stood there, stunned for a moment, then screamed, "Get out! Get out of my house now, you bitch! If my husband were here, he'd have you killed!"

"If your husband were a man, he'd be here by now," Mara said, glaring at her mistress. "Yes, I'll get out, Mistress Abir. I'll get out, and you can go to hell!"

Salome, in the next room with the children, heard the heated exchange. She pushed the boys toward the door of the room where their mother was now sobbing again and said, "Go on, now. Go and comfort your mother." When they had left, she looked around to be certain that Mara was gone. Salome was in Abir's dressing room, and she went to the long mahogany dressing table. She knew what she was looking for, and pulled the top right drawer open. Looking around again, she scooped up all the jewelry she could hold in both hands, dropped it into the small wastebasket beside the dresser, then picked it up and hurried from the room, out the back of the villa, and away.

When Abir finally let her anger overcome her self-pity, she hugged her sons to her and quieted their sobbing. "Salome?" she called. "Salome, the children are hungry."

She walked into dressing room, then out through the huge house to the kitchen. "Salome?"

There was no one there. She opened cupboard after cupboard, mentally inventorying the meager stores of food. Abir had not prepared a meal since her marriage, but she opened a few cans of food for the boys and herself, and while the ate there in the big kitchen, she tried to figure out how she was going to get out of Kuwait to safety.

Bill Kernan was approaching the outskirts of Kuwait City. He would have to hurry to make it to the rendezvous point on time. He was bone-tired, the heavy camper's rucksack he carried biting into his shoulders. But he could rest later, after he had made contact with the Kuwaiti who was to provide him a safehouse. The man would also put him into contact with other Kuwaitis who were anxiously awaiting his assistance to form an underground organization to resist the occupying forces of Saddam Hussein. He swallowed a half pint of water from the plastic jug in his hand, then plunged ahead into the darkness.

Two hours later he was near his rendezvous point, a construction site at the edge of the rapidly-expanding city. He checked his watch. Two-twenty AM, local time. His contact time was to be between three and four o'clock.

Kernan moved to a partially-constructed building a hundred yards away and climbed to the second floor, where he could overlook the construction site. After mentally selecting primary and alternate escape routes, he leaned his back against his rucksack, the silent rifle across his knees. He finished the plastic bottle of water, chewed a piece of beef jerky, and waited.

At ten minutes to three, he heard an explosion somewhere in the city behind him, followed by several bursts of automatic weapons fire. That was followed, during the next few minutes, by scattered bursts of fire here and there, and by a helicopter buzzing over the city with its searchlight beaming down.

Kernan doubted that there was any actual fighting. It was more likely that some nervous Iraqi was shooting at shadows. That would cause other nervous soldiers to see things in the shadows and open fire on them, as well. He had seen the same thing happen in a dozen places across the world.

He made a mental note to exploit that nervousness when the time came.

Three o'clock passed, then three-thirty. By ten minutes to four, he was increasingly certain that his primary rendezvous was a no-go. But a minute later, a car came speeding down the unfinished street to the construction site, one headlamp burning. It stopped, the light went out, and the engine died. Kernan slowly raised the rifle, switched on the little Litton night sight atop it, and peered through the aperture at the driver. The man looked nervously about the site, then took a small rag and shoved it into the center of the chain link entrance gate.

Kernan nodded. "That's him," he whispered to himself. The Kuwaiti would leave, to return in exactly twenty minutes. If the rag was gone— the sign of Kernan's safe arrival—the man would move to the far side of the construction site, where he would exchange verbal bona fides with Kernan, and the linkup would be complete.

The man got back into the car and cranked the starter. The car failed to start, but the driver continued to grind the starter until the battery ran down.

Well, damn, Kernan thought. Another wonderful contact plan gone to hell. They seldom did go exactly as they were supposed to, so it didn't worry him much. He would simply sneak down to a point near the man and initiate the bona fides exchange from the shadows.

In the darkness of her huge, but nearly-abandoned villa, Madame Abir bint Hamad bin al-Sabah's two sons were asleep in the small safe haven built into the basement. It was cramped, but it contained two beds, a toilet and sink, several storage cabinets, and a telephone. And it was safe from intruders.

Abir had moved their remaining food there, and also the two pistols of her husband's which he always kept in the dresser of his sleeping chambers. She had never fired a pistol, or even held one before, but she had seen it done a thousand times on television and in films. She examined them, trying to determine which one suited her best. When she figured out how the revolver worked, she chose it. The other was an automatic, and she had no idea how it operated, so she put it away, out of reach of the boys.

She tried the telephone again, but it crackled and refused to accept the numbers she dialed. She prayed a silent prayer for her children, then lay down beside her baby, Khalid, and tried to sleep. She couldn't. Her world had turned to one of utter chaos, and Abir did not know what to do—how to handle it. How, she wondered, had she ever allowed herself to be lured back into this world of archaic, male-dominated values? Why hadn't she stayed in the States? In civilization, instead of this phony world of double standards and values, where everyone of means, except perhaps the elderly ones, lived two different lives in two separate worlds: the Arab one, in which they amassed their great fortunes and pretended to thank Allah for it; and the Western one, where they spent those fortunes as lavishly as they could and pretended that their wealth somehow made them superior to those who took their money.

What good was that wealth doing her now? She touched her son's cheek, and wept, and finally fell into an exhausted sleep.

Bill Kernan was almost to the place from which he would call out to his contact man, when he heard voices. They were speaking Arabic, and he had no idea what was being said. He ducked back into the darkest shadows, silently put his rucksack down, and crept to a position from which he could see the men.

They were at the beat up car of his contact man, and he could see through his night scope that there were three men there now: his contact, who was in Arab dress, and two men in uniform—Iraqis. One of them had the Kuwaiti up against the car, his rifle pointed at the civilian's chest. The other was rummaging through the car. The one with the rifle was speaking heatedly to his captive, and Kernan saw him smash the man in the ribs with the butt of his assault rifle, causing him to double over in pain.

Kernan lifted his silenced rifle to his shoulder, took it off "safe", and placed the crosshairs of the Litton scope on the Iraqi's head. He squeezed the trigger and the rifle kicked, barely audible. His actions were almost automatic, leaving his mind free to think, Why does it always come to this? When will the killing ever stop?

The man crumpled to the ground, and before he was completely down, Kernan had cycled the bolt and was ready to fire again, waiting for the other Iraqi to appear from the car.

He saw the Kuwaiti stand there stunned for a moment, then reach beneath his robe and withdrew a dagger. Turning to the car, he plunged it several times into the back of the soldier who was still rummaging in the car. Then he used the deadly dagger to slit the throat of the one Kernan had already killed.

From his hiding place, Kernan called, in English, "Do you know if the Hilton is still accepting guests?" He shook his head as he issued the contact phrase, thinking how ridiculous it sounded under the circumstances.

The response was supposed to be, "I don't know, but the Meridien is never full." But the man faced the direction of Kernan's voice and said, in nearly accentless English, "Fuck the Hilton, it's full of Iraqis. Go to the Meridien—or something like that. Did you kill this one?" He was gesturing with his bloody dagger to the man on the ground.

"Yes," Kernan replied, walking out of the shadows toward him. He liked the man already. From the dossier he had studied, he thought he would. Abdul al Rahman was one of the new breed of Arab middle class. He had worked in Houston for several years during the oil boom, not as an oilman, but as a builder. He had then returned to Kuwait to start his own construction business and to help modernize the wealthy emirate, not materially, but intellectually. His efforts in that regard, particularly his advocacy of greater participation by Kuwaitis in their government and increased rights for women, had put him on the bad side of Emir al Sabah's authorities. But they had all fled. This man had not.

Kernan introduced himself simply as "Bill," and the Kuwaiti repeated it and said, "I am Abdul. There is much to do."

Five minutes later, as Kernan stood guard, Abdul had stripped the Iraqi corpses of their uniforms and weapons and stashed them beneath a pile of concrete blocks at the construction site. He managed to get the old Chevrolet started, and Kernan dropped his rucksack in the back seat, keeping the rifle up front with him, and holding the Glock pistol in his lap.

They arrived at the safehouse by a circuitous route ten minutes later. It was a service station, now without gasoline, with a small residence behind it. There was a basement, and that is where Abdul took Kernan.

A boy of about twelve was there, and Abdul introduced him as his son, Yassir. The boy had an AK-47 assault rifle across his knees. He spoke no English, so his father said, "Yassir will be your bodyguard for now. There is food and water on the table there, and here is your bed. I will bring others for you to meet sometime tomorrow."

He disappeared up the stairs, followed by Yassir. Kernan heard someone drag a chair to the door at the top, and figured that it was Yassir, establishing a guard post there.

Kernan dug into his rucksack and pulled out what looked like two video cassettes, although they were much heavier. He connected them together with a small cable, then flipped one of them open. From inside he took a small antenna that had four telescoping radials. He extended them into a cross shape and held them horizontal to the ground, then pushed a button inside the open cassette and placed his face near it.

"Wiseguy, wiseguy," he said softly, and a moment later a small speaker in the little satellite radio answered, "Roger wiseguy, out." That was all that was required for him to inform his case officer, as his CIA handler was called, that he had successfully infiltrated Kuwait City and was in contact with the Kuwaiti resistance.

He collapsed the antenna, returned it to the cassette, and closed the cover, then placed both of them back into his rucksack. After he ate a small amount of the food on the table—sardines, cherry tomatoes and goat cheese on bread—Kernan took off his boots and Arab robe, and got onto the hard bed. He fell asleep almost immediately.

▼

Three

10 August 1990

Young Sheik Akil was awake, and heard the noise first. He went to the other bed, shook his mother awake, and whispered, "There is someone out there."

Abir held him to her and listened carefully. Yes, there was someone outside the safe haven, tapping at the hidden door. Heart pounding, she pulled the revolver from beneath her pillow and went to the door. Who would know the location of the entrance to the hidden chamber? From the outside, it looked just like the rest of the inlaid mahogany panels of her husband's office. It must be him! She put the pistol down and swung the door open, then recoiled. It was a veiled woman, a submachine gun in her hands.

"It is only I, Mistress. It's Mara. I've brought the boys and you some food, and some news."

Abir rushed to her servant and threw her arms around her, sobbing, "Oh, Mara, my Mara. You've come back." She gave no thought to the words they had when Mara had stormed out several days before, nor did Mara mention the incident. Instead, she gestured back to another veiled woman in the shadows of the sheik's office.

Mara introduced her as Sanaa, adding, "She has already killed many Iraqis. And some Palestinian traitors, as well."

Instead of giving Abir a bow of deference as she would have done before the Iraqis arrived, the woman extended her hand. Abir reached timidly for it, thinking, The world has changed now, Abir. Kuwait will never be the same. And these women will never be servants again.

∗   ∗   ∗

Lieutenant Larry Redmond spent the tenth of August trying his best to get reassigned from his duties as a support platoon leader in the 24th Infantry Division Support Command, back to a tank platoon in one of the fighting battalions. The 24th was assigned, along with the 82nd Airborne and 101st Airmobile Divisions, to the XVIII Airborne Corps, and the corps was in the midst of a rapid deployment to Saudi Arabia. Their mission was to assist the Saudis in the defense of their desert nation against further Iraqi aggression.

Redmond's duties as a support platoon leader were important ones, especially during the deployment of the division, with its 16,000 men and women and more than 600 tracked combat vehicles and thousands of wheeled vehicles. He had done extremely well as a tank platoon leader, but after two years in that capacity, he had been reassigned to DISCOM—Division Support Command—to get some additional experience and to "broaden his perspective," as his battalion commander had put it. Redmond had made the mistake of referring once too often to those who supported the combat units as "support pukes," and he had been sent to DISCOM to gain a greater appreciation for their invaluable role.

It hadn't taken him long to get a genuine feeling of respect for the importance of the service support troops he had for so long denigrated, and to build for himself a reputation as one of the best support platoon leaders in the division. It was that fact which, as much as any other, was now keeping him in that job. No commander ever wants to lose his best men, and many are selfish enough to refuse such men's requests for reassignment to duties for which they are best suited. He made personal requests to every officer in his chain of command, including one of the assistant division commanders, who well knew Redmond's reputation from his platoon's high scores in the annual tank gunnery competition. The assistant division commander even went so far as to call up the DISCOM commander, but was told that the request had already been considered and disapproved by Redmond's battalion and group commanders. Besides, his present duties, during the deployment of the division's personnel and equipment, were more vital than commanding a tank platoon.

After Redmond made one final plea to the ADC, the brigadier general said, "Larry, you don't need to be so impatient. In the first place, we'll probably just sit there in the desert for months on end, losing our training edge. And in the end, the Iraqis will give in to the sanctions and go home. But even if they don't, and it turns into a shooting war, there'll be plenty of time for you to get into it—for all of us to get into it. Your job now is to help ensure that our equipment and support materiel get there in good order, so that if there is a fight, the troops will have what they need to fight with."

My ass, the impetuous lieutenant thought, then said, "With all due respect, sir, the way I see it is, my job should be to prepare a tank platoon to kill as many Iraqi tanks and crews as possible. I'm an armor officer, not a damned quartermaster."

The old general, who had seen much killing during two years with the armored cavalry in Vietnam, scowled. He was getting impatient with the boy, and he reverted to a more formal tone of voice.

"Lieutenant," he said, "killing is something you really know nothing about." He shifted uncomfortably in his chair, then went on. "You know, you claim to be a student of General Patton, but you seem to forget that his strength as a logistician was as important to his success as his strength as a tactician. I'd suggest that, when you get a chance to do so, you go back and study him a little more closely."

"I'm well aware of his abilities as a logistician, sir," the lieutenant replied. "But he let somebody else do that for him. He was up front with his troops, where the killing was being done."

The brigadier had heard enough. He stood, walked toward the door, and said, "Lieutenant Redmond, you just make sure our fighting troops are supplied with what they need. They'll do the killing that has to be done. They'll win the battles, and—if officers like you and I do our jobs—they'll win the war. Now, I'm sure we both have a lot to do tomorrow, so I'd suggest you get to your quarters and get some sleep. And let this be the last I hear of you whining about getting reassigned."

Redmond shot the general a hateful glance as the older man opened the door in an unmistakable signal that the discussion was over. The disgruntled lieutenant gave a quick but sharp salute and stepped out into the night without another word or a backward look. He hopped into his car, slammed the door, and drove off toward his bachelor officers' quarters.

"Damn it all!" he said aloud. "Damn it, Georgie Patton, old mentor spirit, don't let them do this to me. Don't let them take away my chance to fight. It's the reason I'm here, the reason I've worked so hard. Don't let them do this to me!"

▼

Dawn

Four

▼

15 September 1990

Colonel David Ames had his ID card checked by a corporal guarding the entrance to the headquarters of the British Forces, Middle East, then climbed the stairs to the office of the Commanding General, Lieutenant General Sir Peter de la Bretaigne. He entered the outer office and saw two British soldiers sitting at uncluttered desks, reading newspapers. One was a major—Scots Guards, Ames correctly surmised from the man's uniform insignia. The other's face was hidden by the paper she was reading, but Ames noticed her well-turned ankles beneath the desk. Dave Ames had an appreciation for such qualities.

Neither of the Britons noticed the American walk in.

"Excuse me, major," Ames said. The Guards officer looked up, but before he could speak, the woman said, "Da...Colonel Ames. How are you?"

He looked in the direction of the familiar, lilting English voice and saw a pretty face lighted by a bright smile, and ignoring the major, grinned broadly and walked toward her with his arms open.

"Jane? What in the world are you doing here?" he said, as she rose and held out her hand to him. He ignored the hand and took her by the shoulders, then kissed the cheek she offered. The woman blushed slightly and glanced at the major who was now looking curiously at the couple.

"Uh, Major Howard," she said, "this is Colonel Dave Ames, American Special Forces. We met some years ago, in Hereford."

The British officer smiled and stood. "Ah, yes, of course," he said, rising from his chair and walking around his desk to shake the American's hand. "How do you do, Colonel?"

"Very well, thank you, major. I'm kinda early for my appointment with DLB, I guess."

Major Howard raised an eyebrow at Dave's use of de la Bretaigne's initials, then checked the appointments calendar on his desk, pursed his lips, and in an icy tone replied, "General Sir Peter de la Bretaigne, if it is he to whom you refer, doesn't have you on his schedule, colonel." He pronounced it "shed-ule."

Ames grinned and gave Jane a quick wink. "Sorry," he said sheepishly to Major Howard. "I guess I shouldn't refer to the Commanding General of the British Forces, Middle East, as 'DLB.'"

"I don't see why not," a voice said as the door behind the major opened and the general stepped out. "It's a damned sight less offensive than 'Dirty Lying Bastard,' as you used to call me in the officers' mess in Hereford… How are you, David?"

De la Bretaigne shook Ames's hand warmly, clasping the American's shoulder as he did so. "I presume you've met my aide-de-camp, Arthur Howard? And you know Jane, of course."

The attractive young woman blushed again and looked down. The general was well aware that they had met years earlier, when Ames was an exchange officer with the 22 Special Air Service Regiment in Hereford, England, which then-Lieutenant Colonel de la Bretaigne had commanded. Jane Parry had been attached to the intelligence section of the regiment, and had distinguished herself as an undercover operative in such places as Belfast and Beirut. She and Dave Ames had been strongly attracted to each other from the moment they met, and the relationship had quickly developed into one of public companionship and private passion.

Dave Ames's guts stirred at the thought of those memorable days, and he and Jane exchanged a quick look so charged with remembered passion that it was almost electric.

"Yes, sir," he said. His face felt ablaze, but it wasn't from embarassment.

Turning to his aide, de la Bretaigne said, "I'm afraid I forgot to mention that Colonel Ames would be popping in, Arthur. He's the ops officer of the U.S. Special Operations Task Force, Wayne Wilson's command."

He gestured toward his inner office for Ames to go in, then turned to the woman and said, "Would you be good enough to brew us a cup of tea, Jane?"

"Of course," she replied, then the general closed the door behind Ames and himself.

Dave waited until the Briton sat down, then took a seat and said, "General Wilson sends his best regards, sir. The reason he sent me to see you is to ask for your assistance in getting General Schwarzkopf to let us employ our Special Forces assets."

General de la Bretaigne was one of the world's premiere Special Forces officers. During his career, he had commanded Britian's elite Special Air Service at every level from troop commander through the senior Special Forces position in the British armed forces; Director, SAS. His successes included operations in Malaya, the Oman, Northern Ireland and, as Director, the daring and brilliantly successful operations of the SAS in the Falkland Islands campaign.

He was absolutely convinced that the early and proper employment of Special Forces behind enemy lines would greatly increase the probability of success of conventional forces if open hostilities began.

Unfortunately, General Schwarzkopf did not appear to share that belief. His previous experiences with special operations forces in Vietnam and the invasion of Grenada had apparently left him with a bad taste in his mouth, for some reason. Or perhaps it was the fact that he was uncomfortable with the degree of risk such forces faced in their missions deep behind enemy lines. He had been directed to make the minimization of allied casualties a top priority, and operations in enemy territory made the avoidance of casualties a difficult task to accomplish.

Schwarzkopf's attitude toward the employment of special operations forces was reflected by most of his staff. The United States Special Operations Command—the headquarters responsible for the selection, training and equipping of all of America's special operations forces— had made an effort to attach one of their general officers as a principal member of Schwarzkopf's staff in order to improve the likelihood of their prompt and proper employment. But the proposal met fierce resistance from some members of the CENTCOM—Central Command—staff, who were reluctant to give up their seat at the table to an outsider.

Central Command had a small staff cell, designated Special Operations Command, Central, or SOCCENT, which was there to plan and coordinate special operations for General Schwarzkopf. But the SOCCENT commander was just a colonel, and colonels were a dime a dozen around CENTCOM headquarters. To date, as far as Ames could tell, about the only thing SOCCENT had accomplished was to give the Central Command staffers an excuse for keeping Wayne Wilson and his US Special Operations Task Force, with its broader and more sophisticated capabilities, out of the theater of operations.

"But we already have a special operations cell," they would say.

Whether such resistance was the result of a clash of egos or a genuine concern for the avoidance of allied casualties, it was a disservice to the men who were prepared and waiting to do the job on the ground. They were ready—anxious—to conduct the missions for which they had trained themselves so long and hard. And, like their British counterparts' commanding general, they knew that those missions could prove invaluable to the success of conventional forces in the event an all out war became necessary.

De la Bretaigne knew the frustration that Ames and Wilson and the other American special operators were experiencing. He had already been as forceful in his arguments to bring them in as he dared be in the highly-political arena of the allied coalition's headquarters. But all he had been able to garner was Schwarzkopf's eventual if still reluctant authority to send a handful of small British SAS patrols into Iraq and Kuwait to gather intelligence on Saddam's critical field installations.

He explained all of this to Dave Ames, and finished his explanation by saying, "So, with the exception of the few patrols he's agreed to let us expendable Brits put in, I'm afraid that's all he's going to allow—at least for the moment. It seems that some of his principal staffers have convinced him that satellites can tell him all he needs to know, without putting any of your men at risk."

"But damn it, boss," Ames said, reverting to the familiar form of address which SAS officers were often called, "You know as well as I do that there's no substitute for a pair of Mark One, Mod One eyeballs on the ground, reporting exactly what's going on."

Those staff officers to whom the general referred seemed to have no sense for the fact that no electronic system could give the element of human evaluation to the situation on the ground in enemy territory. How could a satellite evaluate the morale of the men in the bunkers it was able to photograph? How could electronic devices tell whether or not the equipment they detected on their sensors was being maintained by its crews, or was even operational?

The British commanding general nodded in agreement, and said, "You're preaching to the choir, David. But I think once our patrols prove they can deliver things that you Yanks' electronic wizardry can't, then perhaps he'll reconsider. Meanwhile, though, I think we'd be well advised to do some advance planning for joint operations when the day comes."

Jane walked in just then with two steaming mugs of tea, and each of the men accepted one with, "Thanks, Jane."

Dave's eyes met hers for a moment, and her full lips parted in the same smile he remembered from the first time they had met.

"You know Ken Hammer, don't you?" the general said, interrupting the couple's unspoken communication.

"Yes, sir," Ames answered, tearing his mind away from Jane. He had known the quiet, capable Ken Hammer since his days in Hereford, years earlier.

"Ken is our special forces liaison officer with Central Command headquarters. Jane will take you to see him and arrange the necessary credentials to get you into the SAS operations center."

The woman's smile broadened and she nodded slightly to each of them, then disappeared from the room.

"OK, boss," the American said, then stood to leave. "I'll get Jane to take me to see Ken as soon as possible, then. Meanwhile, I'll let General Wilson know where things stand."

"Good," de la Bretaigne said. "And feel free to pop in here daily and let me know how it's going."

"Will do, sir," Ames replied, then threw the British commander a salute and left his office.

His brow wrinkled as he stepped into the outer office. He hadn't gained any more from his visit with de la Bretaigne than he had from his visit with the Director of Operations at Central Command, except the authority to do some contingency planning with the British Special Air Service.

He was getting increasingly irritated by his inability to find any immediate missions for the highly skilled forces of the US Special Operations Task Force. There were a lot of promises of missions for special forces teams "if the war starts," as the Central Command staff usually put it: search and rescue of downed pilots, raids on key installations not within the sectors assigned to conventional forces, and that sort of thing.

But, damn it, that wasn't good enough, Ames felt. There was so much more they could do, and do now, if only the conventional military thinkers would give them a chance.

They should be all over Iraq and Kuwait, keeping tabs on Iraqi air bases, armored forces, and air defense networks. They should be conducting strategic raids to destroy the enemy's nuclear, biological, and chemical warfare capabilities—or at least maintaining surveillance on them.

And they should be in Kuwait City, organizing, training, and equipping resistance forces. There had been reports of resistance activities in the press, and Dave Ames hoped that the Central Intelligence Agency at least had someone in the occupied city to help the resistors.

Jane was waiting for him in the outer office, and when Major Howard stepped into the general's office, she said to Dave, "Shall I get a car and driver to take us to the operations center?"

"No need to," he replied, "I have a car."

"Good," the British woman said. "I'll leave Arthur a note to say I'll be on my pager tonight if I'm needed for anything."

*   *   *

As Dave Ames hoped, the Central Intelligence Agency did have someone in Kuwait City; they had Bill Kernan, and he was indeed helping organize resistance against the occupying forces of Iraq.

It was not a difficult thing to do, because many Kuwaitis were more than willing to join the resistance once they saw the brutality of the invaders. Rape and plunder were the order of the day in the city. Psycopathic torturers of Iraq's intelligence apparatus, the Mukhabarat, began to employ such methods of "interrogation" as tearing out fingernails, burning genitals with cigarettes, inflating intestines with air, and drilling through kneecaps with electric drills. For some reason, instead of hiding the evidence of their brutality, the Mukhabarat were collecting the bodies of torture victims in hospitals, until the hospital morgues became overloaded. Then an ice skating rink, its electrical power still intact, was used as a temporary storage facility for many of the bodies.

During the month since his arrival in Kuwait City, Kernan had taken advantage of this macabre mortuary system by having members of the resistance with access to those places take photographs of the torture victims. Some copies he put away for future war crimes trials. Others, he circulated throughout the city for the purpose of drawing additional embers into the underground resistance apparatus he was building. In several cases, he even had videotaped evidence of murders and rapes, including one in which a young Kuwaiti mother was gang raped and then beheaded in front of her children, who were being made to watch by those awaiting their turn at violating the woman. Kernan made many copies of that particular video, and it resulted in the surfacing of many enraged Kuwaiti resistors who might otherwise have simply remained in hiding until they were liberated.

The biggest problem Bill Kernan was having was trying to keep the members of his underground organization compartmented into cells, so that if one member was caught and tortured into revealing what he knew about the organization and its activities, he would be able to give the enemy only a small amount of information. But everyone, it seemed, had a cousin or a friend in a different cell, and they invariably ended up learning the names of just about everyone else in the other's cell. Still, he had some success at compartmentation.

It was not very difficult for members of the underground to move about the city. All they had to do was wear a Saddam Hussein or a Palestine Liberation Organization T shirt, or display Saddam's or Arafat's photo in their car, and they were generally left alone. Kernan even found it easy to move around the city himself, by wearing traditional Arab clothing, carrying a small Iraqi flag in his hand, and pretending to be a partially crippled, brain-damaged Arab. He always carried the suppressed Glock .45 pistol beneath his robes, though, just in case.

Communication within the resistance organization was not difficult, either inside Kuwait or with organizations in the US and Saudi Arabia.

Some members of the resistance still had functional satellite-link telephones, a few of them portable versions of the device. They also had some facsimile machines, and messages were regularly being faxed between elements of the resistance inside and external to the occupied city.

For voice communications security, Kernan had taught his cadre how to employ "open code" techniques, whereby innocuous sounding phrases could be used to pass orders and intelligence.

There was even one fax machine available to Kernan which had a signal scrambler on it, and he regularly used this to transmit detailed maps of the disposition of Iraqi forces to Saudi Arabia, after getting the CIA station there to take control of the terminal.

An organization as large and as loose the one Kernan was attempting to maintain was likely to be penetrated by enemy agents, so as a matter of policy, he and his key Kuwaiti resistance chiefs moved occasionally to avoid being "rolled up" by the Mukhabarat.

On September 15th, Bill Kernan's command cell undertook one such move. After checking the location of their new hiding place on the map with Abdul, the resistance leader, Kernan put on the dirty robe he used when moving about the city posing as a lame, moronic Kuwaiti. He checked the Glock pistol in his concealed holster, then limped out into the enemy infested streets of the dying city.

*   *   *

That same day found First Lieutenant Larry Redmond aboard the USS Williamson, a roll on, roll off, or "RORO" ship, so named because of the design which enabled vehicles to quickly embark and disembark it and similar vessels. Through a number of huge hatches on the side of the vessels, tanks and other large vehicles could simply drive on and off at dockside, instead of having to be lifted on and off by cranes, as was the norm for cargo vessels.

Redmond's coveralls were smeared from collar to cuff with grease and oil. He had spent the previous eleven hours working with maintenance specialists on an M1A1 Abrams main battle tank which was undergoing a shipboard overhaul.

The crusty old chief warrant officer who had spent much of that time with him said, "It's a damned pleasant change to see a young officer with so much interest in maintenance,sir. But I've sure as hell had enough for one day."

"OK, chief," Redmond replied. "I'll just take this maintenance manual on the thermal imaging system up to the mess with me, if you don't mind."

"Suit yourself, lieutenant," the chief said. He had been maintaining tanks since shortly after the Korean war, and he had never before seen an officer with such a keen interest in the nuts and bolts of a machine—especially an officer of the combat arms.

On the way topside, he asked Redmond, "What's an armor officer like you doing in a support job anyway, sir? I'd have thought you'd want to be commanding a platoon of those damn iron coffins, not maintaining them."

Redmond stopped and looked back at the chief.

"Actually, I'd rather be commanding a regiment of them," he said. "And one day I will. That's why I'm trying to learn every little nuance about how they work, and what's likely to break in the desert, and how to fix it."

"You going to try to get back in a line job when we get over yonder?" "Line job" was an archaic term to describe duties with a combat maneuver element.

"Damn straight I am," Larry said. "But I really am glad I'm in this job right now. I've learned a hell of a lot this past week, chief, thanks to you."

"Well, at fourteen or fifteen hours a day, you're bound to have learned something." He was impressed with the way Redmond would pick up on the smallest of details, then remember it without prompting days later.

"See you in the mess, chief?" Larry asked when they had gotten to the deck on which they were quartered.

"Yes, sir. As soon as I get a shower."

"Uh, would it be possible to bring along the chief who's in charge of Bradley maintenance?" Redmond inquired. "I'd like to get with him for a few days and see what I can learn what makes an M-2 tick."

"Be glad to, lieutenant," the chief warrant officer said. "But, sir, I thought you were supposed to be doing fuel and ammunition forecasts during the trip over."

"Oh, but I am, chief. I'm just doing this maintenance stuff during my free time."

"Damn," the chief said. "Don't you ever sleep?"

"I'll sleep after I win my first tank battle," the would-be warrior answered.

*   *   *

The villa of Madame Abir bint Hamad bin al-Sabah in the western Kuwait City suburb of Al Jahrah was now an aid station for resistance force members and a storehouse for some of their weapons and munitions. It was ideally located for such facilities by virtue of the fact that it was surrounded by many partially finished buildings which were of little use to anyone, including the Iraqi military. The fact that electrical power to this part of the city had been disrupted during the invasion six weeks earlier and had still not been restored precluded the Iraqis from having much use for establishing a presence there.

They were not aware that the villa was equipped with its own emergency generators.

Major arteries leading west and north from the city passed near there, so vehicular traffic was common just a block away. And the open desert to the northwest was an ideal site for the clandestine delivery of equipment for the rapidly expanding Kuwaiti resistance forces.

Abir's former servant, Mara, and her friend Sanaa—a nurse at the Mubarak hospital—helped Abir run the small underground aid station. Sanaa was the only one with any medical training, and she was required to spend most of her time at the hospital which was now under Iraqi control. But she spent each night at the villa, usually managing to steal a few bits of critically needed medical supplies and medicines to bring to the aid station with her.

There was a Kuwaiti medical doctor who tried to make daily rounds to the villa, but he was required to spend most nights in the hospital. The Iraqi doctors preferred the day shift, and left the night duties to the Kuwaiti physicians.

"I'm worried about Dr. Hussalam," Sanaa said to Mara as she arrived at the villa on the evening of September 15th.

Mara was bathing the only patient they currently had at the little aid station, a Kuwaiti torture victim whose fingernails had been torn out and whose nipples had been sliced off during interrogation. The girl was only a teenager.

"Worried? Why?" Mara asked.

"Because they suspect he has been killing Iraqi soldiers with lethal doses of narcotics."

"Has he?"

"No," the nurse replied. She hesitated, then added, "But I have."

Mara looked up at her friend and saw a face that was expressionless at first, then turned to one of sorrow when she saw the hands and breasts of the girl Mara was bathing. Mara said nothing.

"I don't know what to do," Sanaa continued. "I can kill several each evening, and if they do suspect that Dr. Hussalam is the one doing it, they'll probably kill him sooner or later, anyway. Then I'll stop, and that will reinforce their belief that he was the one."

"But can you just let them do that?" Mara asked. "Don't you think that, if the killing stops, they'll leave Dr. Hussalam alone?"

"Perhaps," Sanaa replied. "Or perhaps not. He should be killing them himself, anyway. Together, we could kill twice as many. Maybe I should tell him that."

Mara had finished bathing the girl, who was now looking at Sanaa with undisguised admiration. The girl said softly, "I hope you kill them all."

Sanaa stroked the teenager's cheek with her hand and smiled. "There is a major with a badly broken leg there," the nurse said. "Tomorrow, I will kill him for your sake."

Abir, standing at the door of the room during most of the conversation, found herself awed by these women. She had been raised to believe they were far inferior to her, yet these last weeks, since Mara returned, she had seen in them degrees of strength and self reliance and selflessness that no man she had ever known came close to matching.

It has all been lies, she thought for the hundredth time. Lies to keep women meek and subjugated, and to maintain the myth that money somehow makes one person superior to another.

"Sanaa, my dear friend," she said, "just make certain that they don't find you out. Dr. Hussalam is only one man. If you can kill many and the Iraqis kill only him for it, then it is a worthwhile exchange. From what I've seen here, he's not a very good doctor, anyway."

She was referring to the lack of care and concern he showed for the women patients that he had treated since the underground clinic had been established. "So don't worry about the loss of Dr. Hussalam, if it happens."

"Oh, I'm not worried about his loss," Sanaa said. "I'm just worried that he'll break under interrogation and tell the Mukhabarat about this place—about you and Mara and your sons."

Abir's younger son, Khalid, was asleep in the safe haven of the villa. The older son, Akil, had been given the duty of standing watch on the roof of the villa, and although he was just a boy, he sensed the importance of his assignment. He came rushing in just then, and said, "Mother, there are some men coming. They're at the front gate now!"

"Come," Mara said to the girl she had just been bathing. "We must hide you in the safe haven."

"Wait," Abir said. "It's all right. I'm expecting several men to come this evening—members of the resistance." She had been told by her niece's husband, who was her contact with the rest of the resistance organization, that there would be three men arriving there to stay for a few days. She had prepared the dressing rooms behind her husband's swimming pool, far at the back of the compound, for the three men.

"How will we know them?" Sanaa asked.

"One of them, with a boy, will come to the front and ask to use the telephone. I'm to reply that the telephones haven't worked for two weeks, and the man will say, 'I would rather have some water anyway.'"

"I'll go to meet them, then," Sanaa said.

"But mother," young Sheik Akil said, "it isn't a man and a boy. It's Salome, and four soldiers!"

▼

Five

It was a quarter of an hour later that Bill Kernan arrived at the address where he was to meet Abdul, the man with whom he had first made contact after his infiltration of the Iraqi-occupied emirate. Abdul was now the chief of the American sponsored element of the resistance, the strongest in Kuwait City. To the north, Kernan had learned, the Shia muslims, supported by the government of Iran, were becoming a formidable force, as well.

Kernan limped past the gate of the villa, expecting to be hailed by Abdul's son, Yassir. Abdul and Yassir were to have arrived first to make certain that it was safe, and as Kernan passed, the boy would call to him to let him know it was all right for him to enter.

Oh, well, Kernan thought. It's not quite sunset, when I was supposed to show up anyway. He decided to make a wide circle around his new headquarters to check out the surroundings and choose his primary and alternate routes of escape, so he limped on.

He heard a scream from deep within the villa before he had gone ten yards. He stopped, listened carefully, then proceeded to limp on until he reached the corner of the compound in which the villa was situated. He looked around, turned the corner, then climbed over the four-foot high wall into the compound. There were two shots from somewhere inside, then a short burst of automatic weapons fire.

Jesus, he thought, have they got Abdul and his boy, or is it something else? He considered whether he should flee the place, or go ahead and find out what was going on. He decided to go on.

It was a well-landscaped villa. Or rather, it had been before a month of neglect. The shrubs and other greenery were badly dried up now, in need of water and a trim. But it still afforded a reasonable amount of concealment for movement around the grounds of the compound.

The main building was shaped like a large H, and as Kernan moved past one of the wings, he saw that a swimming pool occupied the open space between the two large wings on this end of the building. He heard voices from the other side of the pool—a mixture of men's voices and laughter, and women's voices pleading and sobbing. Kernan reached beneath the Arab robe and withdrew the silenced Glock .45 pistol, then slid along the wall, now well shaded from the setting sun, toward the sounds of the voices.

The first person he saw was Mara. She was face down on the tile deck beside the pool, naked, her hips raised. The second person Kernan saw was the Iraqi soldier who was raping her from behind.

Beyond them, another woman sobbed as two more Iraqis tore at her clothing, laughing and kicking at a young boy who was crying and struggling to try to pull the men away from her. Lying beside the building were what appeared to be two other women. One was motionless, while the other was writhing, perhaps trying to crawl.

Kernan backtracked to a door in the wall along which he had crept to the pool. He tried the knob. It was unlocked, and he entered the building, pausing to listen for the sounds of anyone else who might be there. Hearing nothing except another wail from the woman who was being assaulted by two men, he moved on along the wide corridor toward the center of the H-shaped villa. He was almost there when he heard grunting from a room ahead and to his left. He froze, listening carefully. The grunts became closer together and louder—the animal grunts of a man finding sexual release. Kernan crept carefully to the door of the room and, pistol at the ready, peered in. The man was standing over the woman with whom he had just finished—a woman whose hands were tied to the leg of a heavy table, her glazed eyes staring with unmasked hatred at the man above her. The woman was Sanaa, and she saw Kernan in the doorway, or sensed his presence, and her eyes moved to him without changing expression, then back to the Iraqi soldier, who now raised a pistol and pointed it toward her face.

Bill Kernan killed him with a single shot to the back of the head, then put another round through his temple as soon as he hit the floor, just to be certain. The loudest sound from both rounds was that of the bullets smashing bone.

Quiet as a…He erased from his mind the metaphor he had used earlier to describe the silencer. It didn't seem funny anymore.

Sanaa stared at Kernan for a long moment, then gestured with her head toward the sound of the others. Kernan produced a small knife from beneath his robes, cut the belt the Iraqi had used to bind the woman's hands, asking softly, "How many?"

"There are four," the woman whispered, then watched the American disappear quickly, silently out the door.

There was a large, open window overlooking the pool area from the corridor, and Kernan paused there, remaining in the deep shadows on the far side of the corridor, looking and listening.

The woman whom he had first seen—Mara—was still in the same position, a different man now behind her. The one who had been raping her before now had the boy, his hand across the struggling child's mouth. They were watching as another man knelt between the knees of the sobbing woman whose clothes had now been torn from her body. He held a pistol in her face with one hand. His other hand held his penis, which he was trying unsuccessfully to get into the struggling woman. He raised the pistol to smash her in the head, but Kernan killed him before he could do so, the bullet blasting out of his forehead, spraying the woman's bare chest with brain tissue. Two.

He killed the one holding the boy next, just as he released the child to try to figure out what had caused his comrade to pitch forward onto the naked woman. Three.

The fourth Iraqi died before he realized that anything was amiss, slumping forward onto the woman behind whom he had been kneeling, when his head exploded from the heavy .45 caliber slug of Kernan's whispering pistol. Four. Good.

Kernan went to the boy. He knelt beside him and said, "Are there any more of them? Can you understand English? Are there any more Iraqis?"

Mara, ravaged by two of the men Kernan killed, was standing now, hugging her naked body with her arms as she studied the strange American man in the filthy robes.

"There is one inside," she said.

Kernan turned to her, amazed by her calmness as he was by that of the woman in the room. "I've killed four," he said, "including one inside. Are there any others?"

Mara pointed to one of the clothed women lying on the tile deck—the one who was struggling in a pool of her own blood, trying to crawl away. "Just that one," she said. "Salome. She brought them here. The girl shot her, and the Iraqis killed the girl."

The boy was hugging his sobbing mother now, and Marawent to them as Kernan said, "I'll be back in a few minutes."

He went to the front of the villa, and could see the last of the sun disappearing over the horizon in the distance. The resistance chief, Abdul, was just arriving at the entrance gate, his son Yassir beside him.

Bill and Abdul gave the women twenty minutes to compose themselves before they went back to see how they were faring after being brutalized by the Iraqis. They left young Yassir to guard the entrance. Neither of the men knew what to do or to say to the women after such an awful experience, but they reckoned that they should go to them.

Only Mara was there, dressed in jeans and a Hard Rock Cafe T shirt. Even the dead girl and the former servant Salome, who had led the Iraqi soldiers there, were gone. The bodies of the three that Kernan had killed there by the swimming pool were gone, as well.

Mara was on her knees, mopping up pools of blood from the tile deck.

"We put the bodies in the Cherokee," she said in English after glancing up at them. "It's in the back garage. You will have to get rid of them, somehow."

"We will," Bill Kernan said, then asked, "What is your name?"

"Mara."

"My name is Bill, and this is Abdul. His son, Yassir, is here, too, guarding the gate. What happened here, Mara?"

Without looking up, she said. "Some people came. We thought it would be you. Mistress Abir said she was expecting you. But it was Salome, a Palestinian who used to be a servant here. She brought four soldiers with her." She looked at Kernan and said, "The four that you killed," then went back to scrubbing as she talked.

"We went to the safe haven, but Salome led them there. They said they only wanted some jewelry and things, but that if we didn't come out, they would burn the place. Abir was afraid for her sons, so she let them in. They left the baby there, and made the rest of us come out by the pool."

She threw the bloody sponge into the pan of water and wearily stood up, looking at Kernan. "You know the rest," she said, then slumped down onto a deck chair.

"You said the dead girl shot Salome. How did that happen?" Kernan asked her.

"Oh," Mara said. "She brought the revolver from the safe haven under her robes. When she saw what they were about to do, she shot Salome in the spine. She shot at one of the Iraqis, too, but missed. They killed her."

Those were the shots that Kernan had heard.

"Do you know if anyone else—any other Iraqis or traitors—know they were coming here?" Abdul asked her.

"No one else knows," Mara said. "Sanaa made sure of that."

"What do you mean?"

"I mean that she got the information from Salome before she finished her off. They were going to rape Salome, but she told them she was bleeding, and that she knew where a sheik's wife was hiding, and that there was a lot of jewelry they could take, as well. They came immediately here."

"You're certain that's true?" Kernan asked.

Mara looked up at him, her eyes seeming to ask, How dare you doubt me? Then they softened, and she said quietly, "Yes, I'm certain it is true."

"Where are the others now?" Abdul asked.

"Abir is in the safe haven with the boys. Sanaa has gone to Mubarak hospital to—well, to get something to make certain we don't become pregnant, and to take care of some unfinished business for the girl they killed. There is no one else but you three."

"How is Madame Abir doing after…is she all right?" Bill asked her.

"Sanaa gave Akil and her something to calm them. They will be all right." Now Mara's composure collapsed, and she hid her face in her hands and sobbed.

Bill and Abdul looked at each other, unsure of what to do to comfort her. Finally, Kernan said, "It will be all right now, Mara. I'm sorry that we didn't get here sooner, that we didn't stop them before they…did what they did."

The lousy bastards, he thought. It suddenly struck him that the four men he had killed half an hour earlier were the only ones about whom he felt no remorse—the only human beings he had ever wanted to see dead, instead of just gone. Well, almost. There were a few terrorists he wouldn't have minded killing, but he had never caught up with them, in spite of his best efforts.

Mara wiped her dark eyes and looked at him.

"Thank God you came when you did," she said. "They would have killed us all if you had not come. Sanaa said that she would be dead if you had arrived only a moment later."

Bill Kernan looked at her with eyes as full of sorrow as her own, and they said nothing more. But their eyes spoke for them, and there was a bond of some sort between them now.

Then Abdul said, "I will take Yassir and get rid of the bodies later. There will be four more of my men arriving at midnight, and we can go after that. Meanwhile, I need to get out some of the weapons we have stored here, in case more Iraqis come."

"I'll help you, then," Mara said.

"No, you show Bill around the villa," he said.

An hour later, Kernan had chosen the spot he wanted for his small headquarters and hiding place. It was a little attic above the water pumps and filters for the pools, in one of the outbuildings beside the back wall of the compound. It was hot, but it was probably the last place that might be searched on the whole compound, and it offered quick escape over the back wall and into a block of unfinished buildings.

The four men who were coming at midnight were to bring his radios and the facsimile machine which worked through a satellite telephone, giving Kernan the ability to transmit and receive worldwide through commercial circuits. It amazed him that, if he wanted to, he could make a phone call from his little attic in the occupied city to almost any telephone in the world. It was a fact that the resistance force and its sponsors were putting to good use.

Mara came to the little building to bring him several bottles of water to keep there, and a battery operated lamp.

"Abir would like to see you, sir, when you have time," she said.

"Please just call me 'Bill', Mara," he said, "not 'sir'. Where is she?"

"In the safe haven."

He walked with Mara to the sheik's office into which the safe haven had been built. She left him there with Madame Abir. Her boys were in the little vault, asleep. Abir was sitting across the room in the dim glow of a desk lamp.

"Please sit down," she said, gesturing to the chair across a low table from the sofa on which she was sitting.

First he leaned over and offered his hand, which she shook briefly as he said, "My name is Bill." Then he sat down and said, "Thank you very much for allowing the resistance force to use your home, Madame Abir."

She said, "It is my husband's home, not mine. But I'm the one who should be thanking you. Let me assure you right now that my husband will reward you handsomely for what you did today."

His eyes narrowed. You money grubbing bastards are all the same, he thought. You think everything and everyone's for sale. But he said, "My reward, Madame Abir, will be in seeing Kuwait—and everyone in Kuwait—free."

She looked at him for a long moment before saying, "I didn't mean to say that you would expect to be rewarded materially, Bill. I know that men such as you are above that. But when my husband finds out what happened—what you did—he will insist on rewarding you substantially, nevertheless."

Kernan thought, Yeah, to soothe his guilt for not being here to take care of his family himself, no doubt.

Again Abir seemed to sense what he was thinking, and said, "He'll think that makes up, somehow, for not being here."

"Is your husband in the resistance?" he asked rhetorically.

"Ha!" she said derisively, "Only if there's a resistance cell in Vienna or London or wherever the hell he is."

"Then there's no reason that he should know what has happened here," Kernan said. "I would prefer that it remains the business of the resistance."

Abdul had briefed him about her husband while they were waiting for the women to compose themselves after the Iraqi soldiers' assaults on them. He told her what he knew about Abir, as well—her degree from Columbia University, the fact that she had volunteered the use of her villa and whatever material goods she had there for use by the resistance. And he had learned, too, that she had taken considerable risk upon herself by going about the western part of the city, observing the location and activities of Iraqi forces and reporting what she had learned to her neice's husband for use by the Coalition. It was no mean feat for a priveleged woman such as she, and Kernan was favorably impressed by this Madame Abir al-Sabah.

"And speaking of the business of the resistance, Madame al-Sabah..."

"Let's just drop the 'Madame' bit, why don't we?" she interrupted. "I don't think they have 'Sheiks' and 'Mesdames' in the Nineteenth Province of Iraq, do they? Call me Abir, please."

He smiled. "All right, then, Abir. You know, you're a remarkable woman, for going around checking on the Iraqis for us. I know it's risky."

"Compared to the other women here, I've done nothing. Do you know what the girl did? The one they killed?"

"You mean, shooting the woman who brought the Iraqis here?"

"No. I mean before they took her in for interrogation. She went down on the beach and took two of their mines. Why she wasn't blown up, I have no idea. But she took the mines and put them in plastic bags, then laid them at the entrance to Dasman palace. The Iraqis are using it for a headquarters building, you know. A car carrying an enemy colonel ran over one of them. It killed the driver and the man beside him, and blew the colonel's leg off. I think he died later."

She frowned, wondering something, then said, "I wonder if Sanaa killed him?" She looked at Bill and said, "Did you know that she's gone to the hospital now? She's gone to kill an Iraqi major. Revenge for the death of the girl."

She sat there looking at the floor, shaking her head, thinking about how much her life had changed, her whole environment, her values.

Kernan was thinking much the same thing. He would never have believed it—not if he hadn't actually seen these women and others like them, and seen the things they were doing to the enemy occupying their country. And he had always thought that Arab women were so submissive.

Once more, Abir seemed to know what he was thinking. She looked at him, studying this American agent who had happened upon a mass rape in a strange country, and had ended it so coldly and ruthlessly and efficiently.

"This must be about the ultimate in culture shock for you, what you've seen here, Bill. Especially the things you've seen from Arab women."

"It's mind boggling, to be honest with you," he said. "I had hoped to be able to recruit a few women—Filipinos and other non-Arab women—to be couriers, or perhaps underground nurses. But I never expected…" he let his comment end there. He didn't want to say 'assassins' or 'killers' or something that would offend her.

Abir stood up, and for the first time, Kernan noticed that she was wearing jeans. Tight jeans, and a little sleeveless silk blouse. He couldn't avoid the image of her lying naked beside the pool earlier, struggling with the man who was trying to rape her. She was beautiful, and he tried not to imagine that he was that man, and how it would have been, but he did. Then he remembered the man's head exploding, and his brains being splattered on her lovely breasts, and a wave of nausea surged through him.

Abir looked at her watch. "It's eleven o'clock. I haven't even offered you anything to eat," she said. "Come, and I'll fix us something."

"No, thank you. But go ahead. I have to relieve Abdul at the gate. Perhaps he and his son would like something."

She smiled. "Has someone told you that I never fixed a real meal in my life, before last month? Are you as afraid of my cooking as I am?"

He laughed. "No, really, that's not it. I do have to go relieve Abdul, until the other four men get here at midnight."

"Very well, then. I'll fix something and feed Abdul and Yassir. And Mara and Sanaa, if she's back from Mubarak hospital. They may feel like eating something by now. You and I will wait and have dinner together after the others get here."

He watched her walk away, and the scenes of debasement that he had witnessed earlier in the day seemed like something that he had only dreamed—something that couldn't really have happened. Then he felt the weight of the Glock pistol at his waist, and he knew that it not been a dream. But it was so strange, so alien to what he wanted reality to be.

"I hate this fucking job," he whispered to himself. Then he pulled the pistol out, changed the magazine he had used earlier with the full spare he carried in the belt beneath the filthy Arab robe he still wore, and went to the front gate to relieve Abdul.

▼

Six

16 September 1990

Jane Parry got out of bed, pulled on a hotel bathrobe, and opened the sliding glass door to the balcony. Riyadh was quiet except for the sound of jet engines as allied aircraft landed and took off. The airbase had been busy almost constantly for the last several weeks, pouring men, equipment and supplies into the Saudi kingdom to ward off the threat of Saddam Hussein's powerful army.

Jane stared up at the broad, white sweep of the Milky Way, then sat down, drew a pack of cigarettes from a pocket of the robe, and lighted one. She was not a nicotine addict, but she enjoyed an occasional cigarette, especially after a satisfying session of lovemaking. This was the third cigarette she'd had tonight.

She sighed and looked in at the dark figure of Dave Ames lying naked and asleep on the bed, and she wondered whether it was a mistake to become involved with him again.

It had been an on and off relationship since that first summer in Hereford eight years earlier, when they had both been attached to 22 Special Air Service Regiment. After those months of weekend trips to little hotels in the English countryside, and nights of uninhibited passion, he had returned to the States and duty with the Delta Force, a job which kept him out of the country much of the time. Neither of them was much of a letter writer, and the several attempts each made to contact the other by telephone in the months after that had failed. The following summer, she did arrange to meet him in Washington, only to have him fail to show up. She didn't know until she returned to England and found a message from him on her answering machine, that he had been sent away unexpectedly.

They saw each other briefly in London the following year, and renewed the affair, but again the chance to build a meaningful relationship was missed when she fell in love with an SAS soldier. She spent several months in Belfast with him, posing as a married couple while working undercover against the Irish Republican Army.

By the time that affair had cooled—the man decided, in the end, to return to his estranged wife—Dave Ames had become engaged to marry. Shortly afterward, Jane went overseas on an extended tour to Hong Kong and Singapore, only to learn later that Dave hadn't married after all.

It seemed that their love was not to be, and although they had managed to see each other a few times since they had resigned themselves to that fact, they had not been together in more than three years.

She sighed again and thought, Oh, well. I'll enjoy the fact that fate has thrown us together once more, no matter how briefly, and not pretend it's more than that.

Still…

Her pager, on the table beside the bed, began to chirp. Before she could get to it, Dave was awake. He turned on the light, and when she reached for the pager, he caught her, pulled her to him, and kissed her warmly.

"Here we go again," he said, as she looked at the readout of the telephone number she was to call.

"DLB," she said, then picked up the telephone to call Lieutenant General de la Bretaigne.

Ames looked at the clock on the table. It was just after three AM.

When the general answered, she said, "It's Jane, Sir Peter. You paged me?"

After a moment, she said, "Yes, I know where he's staying. I'll get hold of him, and tell him you want to see him right away. Shall I come in, as well? No? Very well then, sir. See you tomorrow."

She hung up the telephone, then lowered herself onto Dave's muscular chest and said, "He wants to see you right away—at the ops center."

"Right away?"

"Yes."

He kissed her softly. "Will you be here when I get back?" he asked.

She smiled. "God only knows," she said, and rolled off of him.

Colonel Dave Ames arrived at the Special Air Service operations center fifteen minutes later. De la Bretaigne, Major Ken Hammer, and Warrant Officer Rover Harvey, an old SAS hand whom Ames also knew well, were studying a map of western Kuwait.

"What's up, boss?" the American said after he was admitted to the secure environment of the operations center and greeted the trio.

"Nothing good, I'm afraid, David," the British commander replied. "We've got a bit of a hiccup with one of our patrols."

He gestured toward a small tape recorder on a nearby table and said to Warrant Officer Harvey, "Play the tape for him, Rover."

Harvey punched the "play" button on the tape player, and a scratchy British voice said, "Ah, Christ. I'm afraid we're buggered, Base. They're after us in vehicles, now."

There was a pause before the voice continued. "We may have to break up soon and try to evade to our war RV, but I don't see how we'll be able to lose them even then. There's just no bloody place to hide out here."

"That's the last we heard from them," Rover Harvey said, turning the tape recorder off.

Dave Ames looked at the British officers one at a time, then asked Harvey, "How long ago did they send that, Rover"

Harvey checked the clock on the wall and said, "Nearly an hour ago. We've been trying to get permission to send a reaction team in a helicopter to try to find them, but we're getting a lot of resistance from Central Command. And a lot of 'I told you so's.'

"I thought perhaps you might have something in your bag of USSOTAF tricks that we could use to pull the patrol's nuts out of the fire," General de la Bretaigne explained.

"Do they have anything cached at the war RV?" Dave Ames asked. The "war RV" to which the trooper had referred is a preselected rendezvous point to which the team would attempt to evade, there to reassemble and either wait for pickup, or continue to evade as a team.

"Afraid not," Harvey replied.

Sometimes the patrols would establish a cache site near their war RV with emergency equipment and supplies, unless they felt that the establishment of such a cache site might compromise their mission.

Ames shook his head, then asked, "What was their exact location?"

Ken Hammer led Ames to the situation map and pulled back the curtain covering it. He pointed to one of a number of small blue map pins. It was located just east of the big, normally dry riverbed named Wadi al Batin, which formed Kuwait's western border with Iraq. Several miles north of the patrol's location was an Iraqi-occupied airfield. Hammer pointed to a black pin in the wadi and said, "This is where they'd be trying to go."

Ames studied the map for awhile, then said, "I've got an idea that just might help."

During his brief time in Saudia Arabia, Ames had run into an old friend at Hafir al Batin airbase named John Rains. He learned that Rains, now retired from the Army, was working for a company that produced unmanned aerial vehicles, or UAVs. UAVs are small, remotely controlled aircraft which are capable of flying over enemy territory carrying a variety of surveillance equipment, including television cameras which can transmit live pictures back to friendly territory.

The company for which Rains worked was under contract to the Kuwaiti government-in-exile to fly such surveillance missions over their occupied country. Rains had mentioned to Ames that they had one of their little spy planes over Kuwait much of the time. He had given Ames one of his company business cards, and had written on the back of it the number of the secure telephone in the office they occupied at Hafar al Batin, not far to the south of the borders of Kuwait and Iraq.

"You ever need to take a look at something up close and personal over there, Dave, just give me a call," Rains had said. Dave Ames figured that now might be a good time to call.

He explained Rains's offer to the British officers and said, "I could give him a call now, and see if he has anything in the area to go have a look."

"Yeah," Ken said. "Yeah, that might work, Dave. At least he may be able to tell if there are any vehicles still in the area."

Ames knew that most of the UAV missions were flown at night, using infrared sensors to locate enemy positions. He dialed the secure telephone number John Rains had given him. Someone else answered, but got Rains to the phone.

"John? Dave Ames here. Look, you know that offer you made about taking a look at something, if I needed to? Well, I need to. Now. Badly."

Rains explained that they were preparing to launch one of their little aircraft in about half an hour, to take a look at some activity in one of the oil fields.

"But we can do that later," he said. "What did you want us to check out for you?"

Ames gave him the coordinates of the SAS patrol's last known position, and Rains looked it up on his map. "Got it," he said. "What's supposed to be there?"

"People. And maybe some vehicles," Ames said. He didn't want to be too specific, because of the sensitivity of having Coalition troops in Kuwait. He was taking a big risk anyway by asking Rains to send his UAV to go take a look.

"Good people or bad people?" Rains inquired.

"Don't ask. Just sent that magic little bird to go take a look, will you, buddy?"

"Hey, gimme a break!" Rains said. "If they're good guys, I can stick something in the cargo bay for them—bullets or something. If they're bad guys, I've got a few things I can deliver them, too."

"What kind of things?" Ames asked.

"Well, things like smoke markers, or firefight simulators. Or anything else of about forty pounds or less that can fit in a cylindrical container fourteen inches in diameter and two feet long."

The smoke markers could be used, Ames correctly surmised, to mark targets located by the drone for attacks by fighter aircraft.

The firefight simulator was an improved version of an old trick used in the jungles of Vietnam to deceive the enemy. When activated, it ignited fireworks that sounded, from a distance, like machine guns and hand grenades going off. It had proved useful for confusing the enemy, especially when dropped from helicopters during attempts to rescue downed pilots or reconnaisance teams who were being pursued. It might be just what the SAS patrol needed to enable them to break contact with the Iraqis, if they hadn't already been rolled up.

"How many firefight simulators can it carry?" Ames asked.

"Two, unless we take off some of the fuel," Rains replied.

"Then shove two of them suckers in there and get it in the air, Johnny boy. How long will it take?"

"It'll take about ten minutes to rig the simulators, a couple of minutes of run up before we launch, and about—oh, let's see—about a hundred and fifty klicks to the target. At two hundred KPH, that would be about forty minutes of flight. It'll take about an hour from now to get the bird over the coordinates you gave me, Dave. But at least it's within the launch and recovery window we already have from Air Defense Command. Without clearance from them, they'd shoot the damn thing down."

An hour was an awfully long time to expect a patrol that was being pursued by enemy vehicles to successfully evade. But the men of the patrol deserved whatever help they could get. And right now, the unmanned aerial vehicle was the only help available.

"OK, Johnny," Ames said. "Go for it. You sure your bird's got that much range?"

"It's got four hours of fuel," Rains said. "That'll let us spend about two hours over the target—unless you want me to crash the thing into something for you."

"What I mean is, can you control it, and can it send video back from such a long range?"

"Oh, hell yeah," Rains answered. "That's where we're so much better than our competitors. The flight commands and the video both go through a satellite link. It's about a half-second delay, but it lets us fly low, and we can control the bird from half way around the world if we have to. Fuel's about the only limiting factor. But if I don't get off the phone and get it into the air, it'll never get there."

"Right," Ames said. "Call us when you have any news. And good luck." He passed John Rains the number. Now there was nothing to do but wait.

The general left to freshen up and get some breakfast before his early morning meeting at Central Command, and the other Britons busied themselves reading the latest intelligence reports.

Ken Hammer passed Dave a folder of reports to read and the American opened it, but stared blankly at the top page. His mind was on Jane Parry.

Why was it, he wondered, that they never seemed able to get their lives in sync? At one time, he had decided to ask her to come to the States to live with him. But when he saw her soon after he made that decision, she had just returned from duty in Northern Ireland. She had found someone else, a soldier with whom she had worked there, she said. They were going to be married.

That news stung him badly; hurt him more deeply than anything in his romantic life. For a time after that, he had looked for someone to replace her, and when he found a girl who reminded him of Jane, he asked her to marry him. But she turned out to be a poor substitute for the British woman, and when he realized his mistake, he broke off the engagement.

Thank God for that, he thought now, then turned his attention to the intelligence reports on the movements of Saddam Hussein's armed forces.

Fifty minutes later, the secure telephone in the Special Air Service operations center rang. Rover Harvey answered it. It was John Rains for Dave Ames, with news about the unmanned aerial vehicle mission.

"The bird will be there in a few minutes, Dave," Rains said. "Now, exactly what do you want me to be looking for?"

"People or vehicles," Ames said. "I'm not exactly sure how many or what kind of vehicles. But they're Iraqi."

"OK, I'll tell you what," Rains said. "When the bird gets to the target, I'll pop it up to get a wider view of the area, then put it in orbit and take a look for any vehicles within a few miles of the grid you gave me. Then I'll call you back and tell you if I see anything or not."

"All right, Johnny. We'll be waiting to hear from you," Ames said, then hung up the telephone. He sat back down between Ken and Rover and said, "I still can't believe CENTCOM would hang those guys out like that without letting you make provisions for a reaction force to get them out of this kind of trouble."

"I can't either," a voice behind him said. It was General de la Bretaigne. "I should have bloody well pulled them out when they refused to do so. They're going to allow us to send a helicopter for them, but not until after dark tonight—if they're still there. Now, what's the latest on the drone you sent out to look for them, David?"

Ames stood, went to the map, and explained to the British lieutenant general what he had asked Rains to do with his remotely piloted aircaft.

De la Bretaigne's brow wrinkled and he said, "Yankee technology. Do you think the thing can actually do it?"

"Don't know, boss," the American replied, "but it's better than just writing them off, or waiting until tonight to do something."

The secure phone rang several minutes later. Ames answered it. It was Rains, who said, "All right, buddy boy, I found your vehicles. Three trucks, moving slowly west, around two miles west of the location you gave me, with about, oh, forty guys dismounted, walking ahead of them. Now what?"

Ames passed the information to the general and his SAS officers, then asked Rains, "Have they detected your bird?"

"I doubt it. It's at eight thousand feet, and it's not daylight, yet. Hard to hear it up that high, much less see it, even with night vision equipment."

"OK," Ames said. He was getting excited by the idea that the unmanned aerial vehicle might actually be able to do the evading patrol some good. "John, can you drop the firefight simulators, one at a time, to the east and north of them?"

"Roger that," Rains said. "How far north of them, and how far east?"

Ames thought for a moment. If he had the first firefight simulator go off, say, a half mile east, then that should draw the Iraqis' attention away from the direction in which the patrol was attempting to evade. Once the enemy force was on their way toward the place the first one was dropped, he could then have the second one dropped well to their north, to make them think the patrol was running in that direction. He explained the plan to Rains.

Rains had been having one of his assistants fly the UAV to this point, but rather than try to explain what he wanted done, he took over the controls.

The controls consisted of what looked like the cockpit of a fairly simple airplane. The only big difference was that the airplane itself was more than a hundred miles away, connected to the controls by a satellite radio link. Instead of looking out of a cockpit window, the pilot watched two video screens. One showed what the camera in the UAV saw. The other was a computer-generated diagram showing the attitude of the airplane in relation to the ground. Superimposed on that screen were airspeed, altitude, and other critical data relayed to the computer through the satellite link. At the flick of a switch, the computer would also display a map of the terrain over which the UAV was flying. It was a technological masterpiece, and, fortunately, it worked.

Rains put the distant little aircraft into a dive to the east of the Iraqi vehicles, and when it was about fifty feet above the ground, he leveled it off. He flipped on the map display, and when the crosshairs showed that the UAV was about eight-tenths of a kilometer east of where he had spotted the vehicles, he armed the cargo release and remotely jettisoned one of the firefight simulators. It would drop to the ground by para-chute and begin its simulated firing and detonations in about one minute. Rains turned the bird north and had it climb back up to watch the Iraqi reaction to the phony firefight a half-mile to their east.

It was obvious to Rains when the simulator initiated. The infrared camera in the drone showed the dismounted troops suddenly hit the ground and face toward the east, and the vehicles halted. He continued to watch for awhile, until he saw the Iraqis hurry off in the direction from which they thought they heard firing. He turned the controls over to his assistant again and got back on the secure phone with Dave Ames.

"By gosh, Dave, it worked!" John Rains announced gleefully. "They've headed off in that direction as hard as they can go. When they get a ways toward the east, I'll drop the other one a mile to their north, like you said."

Ames reported the news to the British men, and General de la Bretaigne said, "Well done, David. That should help the lads evade the bastards now." Turning to Ken Hammer, he said, "We'll certainly have to see about getting one of those for our own use, won't we, Ken?"

The second firefight simulator had a similar effect on the pursuing Iraqis as the first one. They went for cover when it was initiated, then turned in that direction, advancing cautiously toward the source of the noise they assumed to be gunfire.

After Rains had reported that fact, he told Ames, "I'll take it back to a higher altitude again, video the surroundings, then send you a copy of the tape we're making here."

"That would be great, Johnny," Ames said. "How about taping the terrain between where you first spotted the vehicles, and west to the wadi, if you could?" If the SAS patrol was somewhere in that area, perhaps a careful study of the video tape might show them.

"Can do easy," Rains said. "And, uh, let's just keep this little mission to ourselves, OK, Dave? And if there's anything else I can do for you with this thing, just give me a holler. By the way, where should I send the tape?"

Ames had another idea just then, and said, "Wait one, John." He turned to the general and said, "Sir, if I can get him to fly another mission later, what would be the possibility of getting a radio to drop to the patrol? That is, if we can locate them."

De la Bretaigne thought about it a moment. He had to do something for the patrol, and until he could send a helicopter to try to rescue them during the coming night, the UAV seemed to be the only thing they had going for them.

"Certainly, David. Damned good idea, actually. Rover, get an emergency radio to drop in to them. Even if we can't find them, we can have it dropped at the war RV. If it's near enough, they should be able to spot the parachute."

"Will do, boss," Harvey replied. "How much can he carry in the thing, colonel?"

"Forty pounds," Ames recalled being told by Rains. "It has to fit in a two foot by fourteen inch cylinder."

"Right, then. I'll get some other emergency kit to put in with the radio, as well. We'll need to use your heli to take it up to the launch site, general."

"Of course, of course," the general said. "I'll not need it for awhile. I'm going to Central Command and make bloody well certain it's understood that, as long as we have patrols out there, we're going to have the proper means to get them out of trouble when they need help."

With that, the Commanding General of British Forces, Middle East strode out of the operations center, determined to have a showdown, if necessary, with those who were standing in the way of seeing that the special operations forces of Operation Desert Shield were properly employed and supported.

The unmanned aerial vehicle made another flight that afternoon. It flew to the missing patrol's emergency rendezvous point in the dry riverbed called Wadi al Batin, located them with its television camera, and dropped them a two-foot long cylinder by parachute.

Included in the package was a small emergency radio, and just a few minutes after the UAV had dropped it, the patrol used it to contact the Special Air Service operations center.

The British patrol leader reported that he had lost one of the four men of his patrol, killed by enemy fire shortly after the last radio contact they had made. Their long range radio had been destroyed by the same burst of fire that had killed the man carrying it.

Because the radio that had been dropped to them was unsecure, their reports were encoded using brevity code formats which would be meaningless to the enemy, even if they were intercepted.

The activity that they had been observing when they were discovered by the Iraqis near the airfield in northwestern Kuwait was, they felt certain, of vital importance. They had seen a convoy of three large, tarpulin-covered trucks arrive and move into one of the hardened aircraft shelters at the airfield. There was an unusual amount of security around that particular bunker, so the SAS patrol moved in closer to a position which would enable them to see into it when the shelter doors were open. They had just moved to a position from which they could see into the bunker when they were discovered. What they had seen was that the men in and around the bunker were wearing gas masks and protective suits. They had taken photographs, they reported, of the bunker and the enemy vehicles and soldiers.

Major Ken Hammer made a secure telephone call to Central Command headquarters as soon as the patrol's report had been decoded, and passed the information to General de la Bretaigne. He hung up the telephone, turned to the American and said, "He said that it was just the bit of information he needed as a final selling point. And he said to tell you that, if he gets the answer he now expects, we'd better get on with the joint planning we're meant to be doing."

When the British general returned to his headquarters two hours later, he called his special operations staff, including US Army Colonel Dave Ames, to a meeting.

"All right, lads," he said when they had gathered, "thanks to the help of Colonel Ames, and the information our patrol has sent back, we're now to begin planning, with US Special Operations Task Force, to conduct extensive long range reconnaisance and surveillance operations in both Kuwait and Iraq. It seems that the vehicles and the suspected chemical weapons activity our patrol reported were picked up by neither the air recce missions that have been overflying enemy positions, nor by satellite.

"The target list will be forthcoming; however, our initial mission is to get a patrol back up to the airfield where the chemical kit apparently is. We can do that at the same time we go after the patrol at the war RV. You know what to do, so get on with it."

He turned to Ames and said, "David, you come with me. We're going to see this friend of yours with the magic drone and inform him that he now works for the joint US-UK special operations center that Wayne Wilson is being despatched out here to run."

Ames grinned at the British general and said, "Well done, boss."

"No," de la Bretaigne said, "well done you, David. Now we'll show the bastards what we can do."

Jane was gone when Dave Ames returned to the hotel room that would serve as his lodging only until the arrival of his commander, Major General Wayne Wilson, and the other members of the US Special Operations Task Force. Once the rest of USSOTAF arrived, they would establish a base far to the northwest of the Saudi capital.

And once again, a moment that Dave Ames and Jane Parry had managed to seize and share would end.

He flopped down onto the bed, stared up at the ceiling, and thought, Well, such is life.

Perhaps he would see her again, perhaps not. The important thing now, though, was to deal with Saddam Hussein. There might well be a war with his formidable forces, and war had a way of affecting personal lives as normal times seldom did.

*   *   *

The special operations forces were not the only ones en route to the Arabian Peninsula as the American-led Coalition gathered its strength.

The roll-on, roll-off transport ship that US Army Lieutenant Larry Redmond was aboard continued its slow journey to the Persian Gulf throughout the remainder of September, 1990. And Redmond continued to use every waking moment to increase his knowledge of the intricacies of every piece of military equipment aboard the ship—the M1A1 Abrams tanks he now knew as intimately as any man aboard the ship, Bradley infantry fighting vehicles, self-propelled howitzers, the various configurations of the "Hummvee" utility vehicle, and every weapons system that they carried.

When he was not up to his elbows in grease and oil in the maintenance bays of the big ship, he was studying the maps of Kuwait, Iraq, and northern Saudi Arabia that he had brought with him, analyzing each ripple in the vast stretches of desert.

He went to the colonel who was the commander of troops aboard the ship and requested permission to conduct map exercises for the officers and senior non-commissioned officers aboard. He gained permission to do so, and ran several such exercises, using the combat arms officers—those in the fighting branches such as armor, infantry and artillery—to make the tactical decisions, and the combat support and service support officers to do the administrative and logistical planning and decision making.

The exercises were a great success, for not only did they generate a considerable number of good ideas and potential shortcomings of modern desert warfare, they did a great deal to ward off the boredom of the long sea voyage.

Once, during a satellite radio conversation with the chief of staff of the division, the colonel mentioned the map exercises, and the tactical and logistical lessons they were deriving from them. He gave Lieutenant Redmond full credit for coming up with the idea and the scenarios they wargamed, and in addition, mentioned Redmond's enthusiastic involvement in the maintenance effort taking place aboard ship.

"His company and battalion commanders should be advised of the fine job he's doing," the colonel said.

"Yes," the chief of staff agreed. "And that's just the kind of thing the commanding general loves to hear about, too."

Several hours later, the colonel summoned Lieutenant Redmond to the mess. There was a message for him from the Commanding General, 24th Infantry Division.

"The outstanding manner in which you have conducted yourself en route to Operation Desert Shield," the message began, "has contributed significantly to the readiness of those aboard the ship and to the preparation of the fighting equipment of the Victory Division for war.

"It is my understanding that you desire a combat leadership position, and your past record indicates that you are well trained for such duties. As a result of the fact that you have now proven yourself to be a well-rounded warrior who fully appreciates the indispensibility of combat support and combat service support elements, I have, on the advice of your present and previous company and battalion commanders, directed that you be reassigned as a tank platoon leader upon the arrival of your ship in the Central Command theater of operations…"

The message went on to encourage the young officer to continue his efforts until the arrival of the ship in Saudi Arabia, and further stated that the division commander intended to use the map exercises that Redmond had generated to assist in preparing the remainder of the 24th Infantry Division for battle.

"I'll be damned," Redmond muttered as he reread the part about his reassignment to a tank platoon. "There is a God, after all."

"Yeah," the colonel said, "but I don't envy you one bit, Lieutenant. You'll be known as 'the general's boy' from now on. Every son of a bitch in the division will be watching you now, waiting for you to make just one mistake."

Redmond thought about it for a moment, then said, "Well, you're probably right, sir. I'll just have to try to make certain I don't screw up. But at least now I'll have a tank platoon to lead into combat."

▼

Seven

17 September 1990

Bill Kernan sat across the small table in his attic hideaway looking at Abir as she picked at the meager meal she had brought there for them to share.

"You look awfully thoughtful," he said.

She glanced up at him and smiled slightly, then flipped her long, dark hair back with one hand.

"I was just thinking," she said. She dropped her fork into her plate, pushed her chair back, and looked at her hands for awhile before continuing. "I was thinking about how strange it is that we're sitting here like this, eating this so-called meal together. I mean, I had never met you until two days ago. I've never been alone with a man, except for my husband or my father, for the last ten years or so, until tonight. It just feels kind of, well, strange, that's all."

Kernan nodded, watching his fork stir the bits of lamb and potato in his plate. "Of course it feels strange," he said. "Your country's been invaded, you haven't seen your husband in six or seven weeks. You've been subjected to…well, to all sorts of things."

The image of the Iraqi soldier attempting to rape her came back to him, and again he saw her as she had been at that moment. He looked at her until her eyes raised to meet his.

"I'm glad I killed that son of a bitch," he said.

"I'm glad you killed all four of those sons of bitches," she replied, looking at him with an expression that left no doubt that she meant it. She stood, and began collecting the plates they had used.

"What makes you do it, Bill?" she asked.

"Do what?"

"Do this," she replied. "Come to strange places, help the people you consider to be friends, kill the ones you consider to be enemies. You could be anything. Why this?"

Kernan watched her scrape and stack the dishes before he answered.

"That's a pretty heavy question," he finally said.

"Yes," she said as she picked up the dishes, "I suppose it is. Life is pretty heavy, these days. I'll be back in a few minutes. Think about it. Why do you do this?"

Abir climbed down the pull-down staircase with the dishes and Bill watched her as she did. She was wearing the jeans she had on when they had first met, and a T shirt with a big Minnie Mouse on it. He wondered if there was any significance to the fact that she wore a Minnie Mouse shirt in this part of the world where women had no status.

"Heavy," he muttered, then checked his watch. It was almost ten PM.

In four hours, Kernan was to meet an American telecommunications technician who was still in hiding in the city. Like thousands of other westerners, the man was unable to leave—a "guest" of the Iraqis, as Saddam Hussein referred to the foreigners he held as virtual hostages.

The man had agreed to assist the resistance effort by helping them tap into the telephone circuits the Iraqis were using, and by trying to repair some of the circuits critical to the resistance effort. In return, Kernan would see to his exfiltration to Saudi Arabia by helicopter—the same little chopper of Claude Owen's which had been used for Kernan's infiltration.

At some point, he would have to get with Abdul and decide who else they would send out at the same time, since the helicopter was capable of carrying three passengers, or even four, if they weren't unusually large.

Abir returned just then, knocking three times, pausing for a second, then knocking a fourth—the Morse code for "V" which the members of the resistance used as a recognition signal. She climbed up to the attic carrying a decanter, two glasses, and a bottle of Perrier water.

"Scotch," she said, holding the decanter out toward Kernan. "It's legal here now, you know, since we're now in Iraq's Nineteenth Province."

She put the bottles and glasses on the table, poured a large shot into each glass, then sat down.

"Now," Abir said, "tell me what made you decide to make your living this way."

Bill picked up one of the glasses and smelled the scotch. It was good stuff. He held the glass up to her and said, "Cheers."

She clinked his glass with hers and said, "To the resistance," and they each took a sip.

Christ, she's beautiful, Kernan thought as he looked at her in the dim light of the little battery-operated lamp. When the sight of her, nude and sobbing beside the pool two evenings earlier came into his mind again, he stood and turned away from the table.

"Please don't, Bill," she said.

"What?"

"Please don't do that. Everytime you look at me for more than a moment, you turn away. Why?"

He turned back toward her. Kernan was a frank and forthright person, and he seldom lied or was evasive when confronted with uncomfortable issues.

"Because everytime I look at you, Abir, I see you about to be raped. And because you're beautiful, and that frightens me."

"Frightens you? What do you mean, it frightens you?"

He took a swallow of the scotch and said, "Because I'm supposed to be here to organize and help run a resistance organization. Because I'm supposed to be working with a bunch of backward, unsophisticated ragheads, sneaking around and sabotaging equipment and leaving little encoded messages in dead letter drops.

"Instead," he continued, gesturing toward his equipment on a shelf in the corner, "I'm making calls on a satellite phone, sending secure fax messages, and bargaining with Americans about tapping telephones in exchange for a free ride out of here. And drinking scotch with a sheik's beautiful wife—and a Columbia graduate, at that."

He shook his head and Abir laughed.

"Well, I don't see why that would frighten you," she said. "But it is rather bizarre, isn't it?"

Kernan nodded, smiling at her. "Sure as hell is."

"A lot has changed," she said, then downed a large swallow of scotch.

"In Kuwait, you mean?"

She poured herself another shot of the whisky. "In Kuwait. In the people of Kuwait. In me." She took a swallow and said, "Did you know that, if the Iraqis had come in just a day later, my sons and I would be in Orlando? We'd be sitting in the Grand Cypress, on the Regency Club floor, where we had the whole wing reserved. Mara would be there, too. And Salome. Poor Salome. I still can't believe she would do what she did."

"She was a Palestinian, wasn't she?" Kernan asked.

"Yes."

"Then you can't really blame her."

Abir looked at him curiously. "What do you mean?" He sat down across from her and said, "I mean, if I were a Palestinian, I'd embrace Saddam, too. He's the first ray of hope they've really had for a long time."

"Oh, what a bunch of bullshit," she retorted. "He's just come up with that to try to provoke the Israelis so the rest of the Arabs won't join Bush's coalition. He doesn't give a fuck for the Palestinians."

Kernan raised his eyebrows at her profanity. He took a sip from his glass and said, "Well, nevertheless, if I were a Palestinian, I'd side with him."

Abir glared at him, shaking her head, then thought about it a minute and said, "Hmmph. Yes, I suppose so. I guess I should be a lot more understanding these days about what its like to lose one's country." She drained the second shot of scotch from her glass and poured herself another, then held the bottle out to Kernan.

"No, thanks," he said. He still had half of the first shot she had poured for him. "You're downing that stuff pretty quickly, Abir," he said.

She shrugged, gulped another swallow, and looked at the glass, then at Kernan. "Yes, I guess I am." She set the glass down and smiled to herself, thinking about something as Kernan studied her. After a time she said, "Actually, if we were in Orlando, the boys would be with Mara and I'd be out on the town with Sharon and Brigette, my two pals from Columbia. We had big plans this time." She stuck a finger in the glass and stirred the liquor with it, staring absently at it, still smiling.

"Big plans," she said, looking up at him with glassy eyes. "We were going to one of those male strip joints—there's a Cuban place there where they do that, Brigette says. We were going to stick dollar bills down into their G strings." She threw her head back and laughed. "Maybe even hundred dollar bills." Then her mood darkened and she said, "Now I'll probably never have the chance to do that. Or anything else, for that matter."

Kernan looked at her in disbelief and thought, This is not real. This woman is not an Arab—not a shiek's wife. Things can't have changed that much.

"You don't believe me?" she asked. He said nothing, but looked at her with a furrowed brow and shook his head.

Abir nodded and threw back another swallow of scotch. "You don't believe it. You think this is 1950, and that Arab girls still get their clits whacked off, like Egyptian peasant girls, is that it?"

"I think you'd better go now, Abir. You've had too much to drink."

She put her glass down and grasped her T shirt at the bottom. "I'm not going anywhere until you make love to me," she said with a slur.

"That's what I came here for." Then she pulled the shirt off over her head to reveal her flat, tanned stomach and creamy breasts.

*   *   *

The debriefing of the three surviving members of the SAS patrol which had been discovered by the Iraqis near the airfield in northwestern Kuwait was disturbing to Lieutenant General de la Bretaigne and the others who heard it. The three tarpulin-covered vehicles they had seen going into the hardened bunker were, there was no question in the men's minds, Soviet-built MAZ-543 missile erector/launchers.

The film the men had brought back with them proved that their identification was correct. They were still in the debriefing when one of the British intelligence officers entered to tell the general and the others in the room, including US Army Colonel Dave Ames, that he had examined the negatives. The vehicles were definitely MAZ-543s.

That information was not itself particularly disturbing. But the fact that the Iraqi soldiers in the photographs were wearing chemical protective clothing and masks was, and the general said so.

"You think it's particularly disturbing to you, boss," one of the patrol members said, "how do you think we felt, what with no bleedin' respirators or chem suits!"

The other surviving members of the patrol laughed nervously.

"Yes," D.L.B. said. "It's also damned disturbing to think that they weren't picked up by satellite or by high level recce flights."

Turning to the officer who had brought in the report about the film, he said, "Make me some enlarged photographs of the most dramatic shots you have of the things, will you, Captain? I want to take them over to Central Command and shove them up the arses of certain members of the staff."

Rover Harvey dug through a drawer full of charts and produced one depicting the MAZ-543 missile erector/launcher. It showed detailed drawings of the big vehicle, and of the missile it was designed to carry and launch, the inertial-guided SS-1 surface-to-surface missile, known to NATO forces as the Scud.

"Well, gents," Warrant Officer Harvey said, "it looks as if we'd damn well better be taking this chemical threat seriously. It appears that old Maddas-spelled-backward has all the range he needs to reach out and touch us with whatever nasty gas he's got the things loaded with."

"Where is the patrol we sent in to go back up to the airfield, Rover?" de la Bretaigne asked.

"At last report, which was almost, oh, four hours ago, they were still southwest of there some eleven kilometers," Harvey replied. "They should be there and dug into their hides before first light. If not, they'll wait to close in tomorrow night."

"Bloody Scuds," the British general said to no one in particular. Then to Rover he said, "What do the lads have with them that they could use to disable the things, if they have to?"

"M-16 rifles, two of which have grenade launchers. But they'll attack the effing things with bayonets, if you tell them to, boss," the Special Air Service warrant officer replied.

✳　　　✳　　　✳

Bill Kernan tore his eyes from Abir's body and locked them on her face as she undid the button at the waist of her jeans. "Leave, Abir!" he said forcefully.

She glared at him a moment, then said, "It's my house," and unzipped the fly, sliding the jeans down over her hips.

Kernan softened his voice and said, "Abir, you're a lovely, attractive woman. But you're drunk. You're also someone else's wife. And I'm a representative of the American government, for Christ's sake. Don't do this!"

She pulled the waist of her jeans back up over her hips, and Bill Kernan experienced a twinge of disappointment and relief at the same time. Without putting the T shirt back on, she sat down, crossed her arms on the table and put her face in the crook of one elbow.

He thought she was weeping, but then she looked up at him with dry eyes and said, "We could be killed at any time, you know. They could surround this place and walk in here at any time and kill us all."

"Yes," he said. "But they probably won't. And then what? What would you tell your husband when Saddam pulls out, or when the Coalition forces come, and things go back to the way they used to be? How would you feel? What would Abdul say, and Mara, and the others?"

She reached over and picked up the T shirt, and looked at the picture of Minnie Mouse, then shook her head and looked at him.

"Abdul? I don't know. Mara? She'd say 'Good for you, Mistress.' What would I tell my husband? 'Fuck off,' that's what I'd tell my husband."

She stood up, pulled the T shirt over her head, and fastened the front of her jeans, then picked up her glass of scotch and drank the rest of the warm liquid.

She squinted as it burned down her throat, then she looked at Kernan again and said, "You just said something about 'when things go back to the way they used to be.' They never will, you know. Not all the sheiks and all their oil and their money and their Koran and the American army can ever make things the way they were again—not even you, Bill. And thank God for that."

She started down the staircase of the little hideaway but stopped and spoke to him once more.

"I apologize for imagining that you might make love to me. You're just too cold for that, aren't you?"

She disappeared down the stairs. Kernan watched her go, then drained the scotch from his glass and cursed under his breath. He was seething with anger inside, but he wasn't sure whether it was because of the difficulty he feared Abir might cause, or the fact that he had nearly given in and taken her.

"God knows, I wanted to," he muttered, then asked himself the question Abir had posed earlier: "Why do I do this for a living?"

▼

Eight

18 September 1990

Sergeant Lofty Morrison peered through his night vision goggles at the empty hangar two hundred meters to his front. Seeing nothing, he raised his lanky frame to a kneeling position and looked all around the Iraqi-occupied airfield. At the far end were two Mi-8 Hip helicopters and four aging, Chinese built J-7 fighters. There was no activity at the airfield that he could observe, other than two rotating radar antennae and a light in the headquarters building.

Morrison was the leader of the four-man British SAS patrol that had been sent back to the airfield to confirm the presence of the Iraqi Scuds that an earlier patrol had been observing when they were discovered.

"There's sure as hell no chemical Scuds here now, mate," he whispered to the trooper beside him.

"No surprise, I reckon, Lofty," the man said. "They knew they'd been seen by the other patrol, they know it was a British patrol because of Scouse's body, and they know the rest of the patrol escaped. They wouldn't be stupid enough to just sit here and wait for the Royal Air Force to come calling."

"Yeah," Morrison agreed. "Well, let's get back to the RV and get a signal off to Dirty Lying Bastard. He won't be at all pleased to hear this."

* * *

Bill Kernan and the American telecommunications expert had a successful night tapping into several of the telephone circuits the Iraqis were using. In one instance, they were able to tap into a line used for communications between a Corps headquarters in Kuwait City and the Ministry of Defense in Baghdad.

All of the circuits were now electronically routed through a terminal in the basement of a resistance-controlled residence in the center of the city, where shifts of underground members listened to the conversations and recorded them on tape.

Now the man was with Kernan in the kitchen of Abir's villa, having some coffee and discussing his coming exfiltration from Kuwait via helicopter.

"So, who will the other passengers be, Bill?" the man inquired after learning that the little helicopter could carry three or possibly four passengers.

"Don't know yet," Kernan answered. He had an idea of who they should be, but he hadn't spoken to Abdul about it yet, and he wanted to clear it with his Kuwaiti counterpart before deciding.

Abdul's son, Yassir, came in just then with a fax for Kernan. He handed it to Kernan, who took it, said "Shukran, Yassir," then looked at the sheet of paper. It was a page full of five-letter groups of what appeared to be random letters. Kernan would need his code book to decipher it.

"Make yourself at home," he said to the American. "I've got a little work to do."

When he got to the attic above the pumping and filter equipment at the back of the compound, he found Mara there. She was cleaning the place up for him, and he said, "Mara, you don't have to do that. I can clean it up myself."

"You have more important things to do," the woman replied. She stopped dusting and looked at him with worry on her face. "Sanaa didn't come back last night," she said.

"Oh, no," Kernan replied. Like Mara, he was worried that the Iraqis might have discovered that the resistance force nurse had been killing Iraqi soldiers in their hospital beds. "I'll get Abdul to have someone check on her right away."

"Abir has already gone to Mubarak hospital to do so," Mara said.

The sheik's attractive wife seemed to be taking more and more chances, doing things that others were better placed to do. It worried Mara. If they found out who Abir was, God knows what she would be subjected to.

"May I ask you a very personal question, Bill?" Abir's former servant asked.

"What's that?"

"Why did you reject her?"

"Reject her?"

"When a woman bathes, then takes a bottle of liquor and two glasses and goes to see a man, only a fool would fail to realize what she has in mind," Mara said. "And when she comes back a short time later and goes to her bed to weep, only a fool would fail to realize that the man rejected her."

Kernan nodded. "She's another man's wife, Mara," he said.

"She's a piece of property to him," Mara retorted. "You know, don't you, that in the world of Islam, all he would have to do would be to walk around her three times saying, 'I divorce you,' and they would be divorced?"

"Yes," he said. "I also know that he hasn't done so."

Mara threw the dust rag onto the table. "Do you? What has he done? In six weeks, what has he done for her? Did you know that her niece's husband has received a message from him?"

Kernan raised his eyebrows. He wasn't aware that the sheik had been in contact with the resistance, although he had wondered why not. Many other Kuwaitis who were out of the emirate when it was invaded had made contact with their families through the resistance.

"I didn't know that," the CIA agent said.

"Yes. And do you think he even mentioned Abir? No. He only mentioned his sons. He offered a lot of money to Abdul if he would smuggle Akil and Khalid safely out of Kuwait. But not one word about Abir. That's how much her husband is concerned about her."

She went back to her dusting, and Kernan thought about what Mara had just told him.

"When did he contact Abdul, Mara?"

"About a week ago, I think," Mara said.

He wondered why Abdul hadn't mentioned it to him. He would ask his Kuwaiti counterpart as soon as he saw him.

And then he thought about Abir, a—a what?—a pampered piece of property, until six weeks ago. He recalled her having said that, if she had left Kuwait a day earlier than she planned to, she'd now be sitting in the Regency Club of the Grand Cypress hotel in Orlando. She'd be surrounded by servants—Mara would be one of them—and by members of the hotel staff, sucking up to her and her entourage in hopes of receiving one of the gigantic tips for which Arab royalty was famous at such places. He still didn't really believe she'd be out with her school chums from Columbia at a Cuban strip club. That was only the scotch whisky talking.

But she wasn't in Orlando. Instead, she was in an occupied country, her once elegant villa now a deteriorating haven for members of the resistance, her former servant now a peer in the underground. Instead of being escorted around Disney World with her children, she had gone off by herself to an enemy-occupied hospital to check on another woman, whom they feared had been discovered killing hospitalized enemy soldiers. She had nearly been raped, as her former servant had been, and would certainly have been tortured afterward, and probably killed.

But he had stopped that from happening, and so she felt obligated to him, he supposed.

"Mara, she only wants me because I happened to come along at…to come along when the Iraqis were here."

Mara looked at him, shaking her head slowly.

"No," she said. "No, that's why I want you—that's why I—and Sanaa as well—would do anything for you that you ask us. Abir wants you because you are the kind of man she has always really wanted."

Neither of them spoke for awhile, then Mara said, "Do you have a wife?"

"No. I had one, once."

It was a part of his life that he would have preferred to forget, a marriage that had robbed him of trust in women and respect in the institution and, somehow, of belief in the idea of love.

He said, "Too bad I couldn't have just walked around herand said 'I divorce you' three times. I'd be a lot better off."

Mara gave him a hostile glance. "Yes," she said, "I suppose that's the price of living in a free society where women are considered to be human beings."

She finished her dusting and said, "I'll leave you now. And I hope you will think about what I said. She is taking too many risks, trying to show you that she's worthy of you, or some such thing."

"Thank you," he said. He sat down with the encoded message to decipher it, but found himself staring at the empty wall, thinking about what Mara had said.

*   *   *

"Do you think we'll really have to fight, sir?" Private Luther Anderson said as he stood on the fantail of the USS Williamson, watching the sunset with Lieutenant Redmond.

"Yes," Larry Redmond replied. "If he doesn't pull out of Kuwait, we'll throw him out, Anderson."

"But what about the hostages?" the young tanker asked. "Won't he kill them if we attack?"

"I don't think so. Right now, all he has to do is leave Kuwait. If he starts killing hostages, he knows we'll turn Messopotamia into a damned parking lot."

"Messopo-what?"

"Messopotamia. The Cradle of Civilization. It's where the first recorded history of man was found," the lieutenant said, unsure if that was exactly correct. "You remember the land between the Tigris and Euphrates rivers from the map exercise we did yesterday?"

"Where you said we might need to do a river crossing after the 101st establishes a bridgehead?"

Redmond looked at the teenaged warrior and smiled.

"Very good, Anderson," he said. "Yep. That's Messopotamia."

"Messopotamia," the boy repeated. "Hell, I never even heard of Kuwait, or Saddam Hussein either, for that matter, until he invaded it. Now I'm going there. To fight."

"You scared, Anderson?" Redmond asked as they watched the last orange bubble of the sun disappear below the empty horizon.

"No, sir. I mean, I ain't scared scared, just scared a little bit. Scared of that damn gas he's got."

"Well," the lieutenant said, "I wouldn't be worried about that. The air filtration system on the Abrams tank will keep out any chemical agent known. Just make sure you take care of it, and it'll take care of you."

"What about you, sir? You scared?"

"No. Not yet, anyway," Redmond answered honestly. "But I guess I will be, when the time comes." He didn't really think he would, but he felt obliged to say it.

"George Patton used to say there was nothing wrong with feeling fear," he continued. "But controlling fear is what you have to do—you know, not let it interfere with getting your job done—with getting the mission accomplished."

"Yeah," Private Anderson said. "I seen the movie. Hell of a good flick. I'd follow George C. Scott anywhere."

Redmond chuckled and glanced up into the darkening sky.

"Look at that," he said, pointing overhead.

High above them, the sun was still reflecting off the contrails of a number of aircraft. There were about a dozen contrails visible, all but one headed in the same direction as the USS Williamson—east, toward the Suez canal and the Persian Gulf and the Arabian Peninsula.

"That's some sight, ain't it, sir?" Anderson asked. "All them damned airplanes up there at once, probably headed for Messopotamia."

Redmond elbowed the youngster and laughed.

"Could be, Andy," he said. "Could very well be."   .

★   ★   ★

Colonel Dave Ames of the United States Special Operations Task Force stood on the concrete apron at the end of the huge Dhahran air base, watching two American F-15C Eagle air-superiority fighters take off into the night sky.

He was awaiting the arrival of Major General Wayne Wilson and the staff of USSOTAF. They were to establish a combined Anglo-American forward operations base at King Khalid Military City. Once the base was established and operating, the task force would begin infiltrating American Special Forces and British SAS reconnaisance and surveillance teams into Kuwait and Iraq.

General Sir Peter de la Bretaigne and Warrant Officer Rover Harvey arrived in a staff car and joined Ames just as the first of the huge C-5B Galaxy cargo planes touched down, bringing Wayne Wilson and his staff, and the helicopters and crews of the 160th Special Operations Aviation Regiment.

Ames saluted the general, pointed at the aircraft and said, "That's the bird General Wilson is on, sir."

"Have the Pave Lows arrived yet?" the general asked. He was referring to the big US Air Force MH-53 helicopters which were to support the combined US-UK operations. The Pave Lows' precise navigation, electronic countermeasures and communications capabilities would enable the reconnaisance teams to be infiltrated deep into enemy territory with little risk of detection.

"I don't know, sir," Ames replied. "They're self-deploying direct to KKMC, I think."

"KKMC," Rover repeated, snickering. "You Yanks abbreviate everything, don't you? I guess it easier than saying King Khalid Military City all the time, though."

"Have Lofty and his team seen anything of the Scuds?" Ames asked him.

"I'm afraid not, boss. God only knows where the damn things are now."

"Well, we'll find them once we get the recon teams in," Ames said.

"We'd better," the general commented. "Too bad we have only two of those magic drones working for us."

The big Galaxy cargo plane taxied toward them behind an Air Force "follow me" truck with a flashing light atop its cab. The lumbering giant of an aircraft turned in a wide semi-circle and the moaning engines shut down. The crew door opened and an airman exited, followed by Major General Wayne Wilson and his command sergeant major, Matt Jensen. They walked directly to Ames and the two Britons.

Salutes were exchanged and Lieutenant General de la Bretaigne said to Major General Wilson, "Welcome to the Big Sandpile, as your lads call it, Wayne."

✴   ✴   ✴

Abdul returned to the villa the evening of September 18th and went to Bill Kernan's attic headquarters.

"The Mukhabarat came for Doctor Hussalam this morning," he announced, "but before they took him away, he took a lethal poison. He's dead."

"Oh, no," Kernan said. "What about Sanaa?"

"Sanaa is safe, but she didn't know about Doctor Hussalam. She killed three more Iraqi patients after they took him, so they must know there is someone other than Hussalam doing it."

Kernan had attempted to get the hospital murders stopped soon after he had learned of them, but Sanaa refused to cease her vengeful actions.

"You saw what they did to me, and to Mara," Sanaa had said when he questioned the wisdom of the killings. "You know what the bastards did to the girl who killed Salome and what they would have done to Abir, and even Akil. Yes, I'll stop killing them. When all of them are dead, I'll stop."

Now Kernan said to Abdul, "Abir went after her. Is she back?"

"Yes. And she brought a report about a new piece of equipment near the souk—the marketplace. Some kind of anti-aircraft missile, I think. And speaking of Abir, Bill, I want to send her and her sons out on the helicopter tonight."

"Abdul," Kernan said, "why didn't you tell me about her husband contacting you?"

"Why should I?" the Kuwaiti resistance chief said. "It was not about an operational matter. It was only about getting his family out of Kuwait."

"I see," Kernan said. "but the use of the helicopter is an operational matter, isn't it?"

"Yes. But it has nothing to do with Sheik al-Sabah's message to me. He wanted to pay me a lot of money to smuggle his sons out, but I don't want his money. I want him to feel that he remains obligated to the whole resistance organization. If he paid me for getting them out, he would feel as if his debt to us—those of us who are still here, fighting for our country—was paid. But I can tell you, my friend, when this is all over, they are going to be shocked at our demands for what we've done. And it won't be money."

It was the sort of statement of which Kernan had been hearing more and more from the Kuwaitis in the resistance force. They were becoming increasingly disenchanted with the ruling family and their lack of leadership and active participation in the underground movement to retake the heavily-pillaged emirate.

"What will your demands be, Abdul?" Kernan asked.

"Democracy," the Kuwaiti replied. "Restoration of the parliament the Emir suspended in '62, but a real parliament this time—real democracy. And something for the women—some rights."

Democracy, Kernan thought. Yes. And really, isn't that is why I do this job, after all? He suddenly wished that he had said that to Abir when she had asked him why he did what he did. As corny as it might sound if said in a classroom, or in an interview, it was nevertheless the truth. And these days it seemed that the whole world was coming to realize that it was the best thing for mankind.

"Yes," he said aloud. "Democracy. Very well then, Abdul. We'll send Abir and the boys out tonight."

When Kernan told Abir, she looked at Sanaa and said, "Sanaa should take them out. If you don't leave, Sanaa, they are bound to catch on to you. And that will be the end. You have done enough, dear friend."

"No," the nurse replied. "You are their mother. They need you. Especially Akil, after he saw what happened to you at the hands of the Iraqis."

Bill said, "And as you said, they could come back at any time. They would be brutal."

Abir glared at him, then her eyes brimmed with tears and she said, "And this time, there might not be an American around to stop them? Or he might not care to?"

It was a childish thing to say—a response to her perception that he had rejected her, Bill supposed. So he ignored the comment and said, "We'll have to leave for the pickup zone in an hour or so. I'm afraid you'll be able to take only a small bag with you."

He went to his attic to make a satellite radio call to the CIA station in Riyadh to confirm the pickup and to advise them of who the passengers would be. There was no change in the planned time and place of pickup. Yassir and one of the older men in the resistance had gone to the area the day before to maintain surveillance on the pickup zone and to make certain there were no Iraqi forces nearby. They had reported to Abdul by radio that there was no one to be seen in the vicinity.

When it was time for her to say goodbye to the children, Mara wept quietly. She had, until the invasion, at least, spent more time with the two young sheiks-to-be than their mother had. She kissed the baby, Khalid, and handed him to her mother, then knelt and drew Akil to her.

"You are the bravest sheik in all of the Arab world," she said to the boy. "When you are grown, you must remember what people such as Abdul and Yassir, and especially women such as Sanaa and your mother did for Kuwait, when the other sheiks left them here."

The boy said, "But now I'm leaving, too, Mara."

"Yes," she said, "but you have already done more than any other sheik. And you have seen what evil men the Iraqis are. You must tell your father what you saw them do to me and to the girl who shot Salome, so he will know how bad they are."

"And what they did to Mother," he said, then started crying.

"No, Akil. That is not for you to tell," she said, wiping his tears with the back of her hand. "That would only hurt your mother. Do you understand that?"

He nodded several times, then shook his head to indicate that, no, he didn't really understand.

"Do you love me?" Mara asked the boy.

"Oh, yes, Mara."

"And do you love your mother?"

"Yes. As much as I love you."

"Then you must make me a promise. A promise to tell no one what the Iraqis tried to do to your mother. You must forget about that."

He nodded, although they all knew that he never would.

"Promise?" Mara asked, and he said, "Yes. I promise."

She hugged him and said, "Goodbye, my brave young sheik. Take care of your brother for me."

"We're going to ride in a helicopter," he said, "all the way to the Saudi kingdom!"

"Yes," she said, "I know. But you had better get started, or you might miss it."

They left then, in the Cherokee station wagon of the elder Sheik al-Sabah. Sanaa went with them, taking her nurse's kit in case there were any medical problems during the trip into the desert and back. One of the men in the resistance led the way out of town on a bicycle to warn of any enemy along the way.

There were none, and soon Kernan was driving across the empty desert toward the pickup zone, guided by his small Global Positioning System receiver.

✶   ✶   ✶

Major General Wayne Wilson entered the briefing room of his newly-established forward operations base in King Khalid Military City, Saudi Arabia. He walked to the front of the room where a number of his staff and two twelve-man American Special Forces teams stood at attention.

"Be seated, please," he said.

As soon as the men had done so, Wilson reached into the canvas container strapped to his hip, pulled his chemical protective mask over his head, and yelled a muffled, "Gas!" as he moved his clenched fists back and forth toward his temples, the signal for a chemical agent attack.

The other men in the room quickly repeated his actions, although some of them fumbled with their masks somewhat. When they had all finished donning their masks, Wilson removed his and called, "All clear!"

As he did, his subordinates removed their masks and returned them to their carriers.

"Not bad, not bad," he said to them. "Remember, the standard for donning the mask properly is eight seconds. And remember, too, that exposure to the skin of some chemical agents is just as deadly as breathing them, so we'll be issuing eveyone chemical protective suits as soon as they're delivered here.

"Now, all of you, I'm sure, have seen the film we're about to see, but I wanted to show it to you again, because it bears directly on our initial mission here for Central Command. OK, run it, Sergeant Major."

He sat with the others as the lights dimmed and an Army training film was projected onto a screen in front of them. It began by showing several sequences of animals—rats, goats and monkeys—as they were exposed to nerve agents. The animals, in each case, fell, writhed in agony, then died, twitching and voiding themselves as they did so. When the gory scenes ended and the narrator began an elementary explanation of chemical warfare, Wilson stood and said, "Cut it there, Sergeant Major."

When the projector had stopped and the lights were back on, Wilson said, "That's just a reminder of what chemical weapons do to their targets. Now, here's another reminder…"

Sergeant Major Jensen handed out copies of several photographs from news magazines. They were pictures of chemical agent casualties from the eight-year Iran-Iraq war, and of Kurdish civilians—men, women and children—killed by chemical agents used against them by their own countrymen.

"In case any of you have forgotten that Saddam Hussein has chemical agents, has used them, and has even used them on his own countrymen, I wanted you to be reminded of that fact.

"I also want to remind you that he has artillery, aircraft and missiles capable of delivering those munitions. And the reason that I want to remind you of all these things is because what we are going to do is infiltrate Iraq with reconnaisance and surveillance teams, find these weapons and their means of delivery, and, if ordered to do so, destroy them."

The twenty-four Special Forces soldiers sitting there in front of the staff reacted to Wilson's news in various ways. Some nodded, others looked at each other with nervous smiles, and some shifted uncomfortably in their seats. Most assumed expressions of greater seriousness than had been on their faces before.

One of them, Staff Sergeant Walter Shumate, smiled broadly and said, "Shit hot!" All his life he had wanted to take part in a reconnaisance mission deep in enemy territory, and he was at last going to get his chance.

*   *   *

Claude Owen spotted the triangle of tiny infrared lights on his forward-looking infrared screen, or FLIR as it was commonly known, before the people at the pickup zone even heard his remarkably quiet helicopter approaching. He flew straight to the lights, flared the little Defender, and touched softly down on the rocky desert floor.

Bill Kernan went to the pilot and reached in to shake his hand. "How's it goin', ol' rotorhead?" he said.

"OK, buddy," Owen replied. He handed Kernan a book-sized package. "Something from headquarters," he said.

"Thanks. I'll put the American up front with you, and the mother and her kids in back."

Owen nodded, and the passengers, whom Kernan had briefed earlier, were already climbing into their assigned places in the little helicopter.

He saw that Abir had pulled her robe across her face, and wondered if it was to keep the swirling dust stirred up by the helicopter out of her eyes, or to hide tears. He reached in and buckled Akil's seat belt as she held the baby in one arm and buckled herself in with the other.

Kernan reached for her hand and squeezed it, then gave Owen a thumbs up and stood well back from the Defender. It lifted off, pivoted half a turn, then nosed over and disappeared into the darkness. By the time the dust settled, he could no longer hear the helicopter.

"They'll be safe now," he said to Sanaa, whose face was buried in her hands.

"Yes," the woman said. "Thank God, they will." But it was Abir's voice, not Sanaa's, that he heard.

Kernan lifted the woman's face and looked closely at it in the faint light of the desert night.

"Abir. Why?" he asked.

"Because I wanted to. Because Sanaa agreed to take good care of the boys. And because Abdul just ordered her to do it."

Abdul was picking up the tiny infrared lights they used to mark the landing zone, and Kernan walked over to him.

"How could you do this, Abdul, without asking me?" Kernan said to the Kuwaiti resistance chief.

"I am terribly sorry to have to deceive you like that, Bill," he said. "But it was the best thing."

"Why do you say that? Why the hell do you think you had to lie to me?" Kernan asked, the anger obvious in his voice.

"If you had told your people in Riyadh that Abir was not coming out, they would have asked why, wouldn't they?" Abdul asked.

"So what?" the CIA man responded.

"So, they would have told the sheik. He would have demanded that she be sent out—and not because he really gives a damn if she stays or not, but only because he thinks that's what he would be expected to do. Your people would have ordered you to send her. Would you have disobeyed?"

Kernan said nothing, so Abdul answered for him. "No, of course you wouldn't have. I need her here, Bill. Kuwait needs her here to experience the horror of this occupation. When it ends, we'll need someone of her stature to lead the women of this fucked-up little country out of the Sixteenth Century and into the Twentieth. She couldn't do that if she left. If she stays, she may be able to help us become a democratic country."

"And when did you decide all this, Abdul?" the American asked.

"I didn't," he said. "Mara and Abir did."

"What?"

"I said, Mara and Abir did. And I agreed. Sanaa didn't want to do it at first, but I convinced her that the Mukhabarat would kill her if she ever went back to the hospital again. And I explained to her about why we need Abir to stay. So she agreed to go, and to make you and Akil believe that it was his mother who was getting on the helicopter."

Bill Kernan stood there, shaking his head.

"The Middle Eastern mind," he muttered. "I guess I'll never understand it."

He was reminded of a fable he had heard once, long ago. It was about a frog and a scorpion on the bank of a river.

The scorpion said, "Frog, I need a ride across the river, and I can't swim. Give me a ride across on your back."

"No," the frog said. "You might sting me, and I would die."

"Don't be silly," the scorpion said. "If I stung you, and you died, I would drown."

So the frog took the scorpion on his back and started across the river with him. Halfway across, the scorpion stung him.

"Why did you do that?" the frog asked before he died. "Now we will both die."

"Because," the scorpion said, "this is the Middle East."

"Democracy, huh?" Kernan said to the Kuwaiti resistance leader. "That would be a pleasant change in this part of the world, all right." He shrugged his shoulders in resignation and said, "Well, let's get back to the villa, Abdul, and let me try to explain all this to the station in Riyadh."

▼

Storm Clouds

▼

Nine

9 November 1990

Bill Kernan watched the erotic scene with fascination, as if he were outside his body, observing from a distance.

He was nude, lying on his back, his hands bound above his head and tied to the same heavy table that Sanaa's had been when he had killed the man who raped her.

The lovely young Sanaa let the robe she was wearing drop to the floor, and stepped out of it. She was beautiful, and her lithe body glided gracefully to him. She straddled his bare belly and lowered her body to his. He felt the warmth of her flesh against his as she leaned forward and kissed him sensuously. She raised her hips above him and took him in her hand, guiding him into her as she pressed down onto him. He lay there, unable to move as her maddeningly sensual movements drew them both toward sexual satisfaction.

Then Mara appeared, just as Sanaa reached orgasm. She stabbed the the Kuwaiti nurse in the back with a hypodermic needle, and Sanaa slumped forward onto Kernan's chest, dead.

Mara threw the needle aside and untied his hands. She stepped out of her gown as Sanaa had done, and he saw again the full, curvaceous body that he had seen during the Iraqi soldiers' violation of her. She drew him to a kneeling position, then got on her hands and knees in front of him and pressed herself back against him. He took her hips in his hands and pushed into her as she desired, and together they began to move, slowly at first, and then with increasing energy.

As they neared the peak of their lovemaking, Abir came into the room. Her beautiful body was draped in all of her jewelry—rings and bracelets and necklaces of gold, diamonds and emeralds. She wore nothing else.

Kernan's Glock pistol was in Abir's hand, and she pointed it at Mara and pulled the trigger. It made no sound, but the bullet blew Mara's head apart, her brains splattering back onto Kernan's chest. He pushed Mara's body aside and grabbed the sheik's bejeweled wife, wresting his pistol from her and throwing her to the floor in front of him.

He got between her knees, holding the pistol at her face, and tried to enter her. Abir looked at him with eyes filled with terror and sorrow and deep, deep sadness. She closed them, then stopped struggling and spread her knees wider for him, and he thrust into her.

She opened her eyes again, and they were blank—totally without expression or feeling, as if they were dead.

Bill Kernan turned the pistol from Abir's face to his own. He put the fat silencer in his mouth, and pulled the trigger.

He awoke with a jump, perspiring profusely, the bare sheet under which he slept on the hard little cot sticking to his sweaty body. He looked at his watch. It was almost four AM. He stumbled into the adjoining room where Abdul slept when he was there. The resistance chief was gone, Kernan knew, but his Marlboro cigarettes were on the table beside his cot. He felt for them, and when he found the pack, he took one out, broke off the filter, and struck a match.

He lit the cigarette and inhaled deeply, the images of his dream still vivid in his mind.

"Do you always smoke after sex?" he said aloud, then broke into a mad giggle.

"I don't know. I've never looked!" he answered with the punchline of an old, mindless joke. Again he giggled, but this time it died quickly away, and he found himself shaking his head, trying to clear his mind.

He inhaled another deep breath of smoke from the cigarette, then snuffed it out.

"You're losing it, boy," he whispered to himself. "You're really starting to lose it, now, Bill Kernan."

*   *   *

"We've got to locate the bloody things, Wayne," Lieutenant General de la Bretaigne said to the US Special Operations Task Force commander.

Wayne Wilson, standing beside him studying the map, nodded. "Yes, I know we do."

The chemical warhead-tipped Scud missiles that the British reconnaisance patrols had seen in northwestern Kuwait almost two months earlier had disappeared. Exhaustive intelligence collection efforts had so far failed to turn up any sign of them. The reconnaisance and surveillance patrols which the American and British Special Forces had been conducting throughout Iraq and occupied Kuwait had seen no further indication of their presence.

Satellite surveillance and high altitude aerial reconnaisance aircraft had located a number of Scud launchers and support facilities, but patrols sent in to determine whether they were conventional or chemical all reported that the missiles which had been spotted were apparently equipped with conventional high-explosive warheads.

John Rains and his unmanned aerial vehicles had been called upon on several occasions to check out suspected locations, but had no luck, either. On the last mission, one of his two drones had crashed inside Iraq, and until additional ones arrived from the little Texas factory where they were built, the decision was made to hold the remaining UAV in reserve.

Human intelligence reports had been no more productive. The agents of the Coalition intelligence networks in Iraq and Kuwait had produced a lot of rumors and little else.

"All I can figure," Wilson now speculated, "is that when they learned they'd been discovered at the airfield by your patrol, they took the damn things back to the production facilities."

"I just don't think so, Wayne," the British general said. "As much as MI-6 and CIA know about those places, they should know if that happened. But I wouldn't be surprised to learn that they've taken them into the cities and hidden them in schools or other public buildings."

They stood there, studying the map and thinking about the problem, and trying to determine what to try next.

Locating the chemical-filled rockets was the primary mission USSOTAF and the British Special Air Service had been given by Central Command, and there was a growing amount of grumbling from the CENTCOM staff that the special operations forces had failed to accomplish that mission, even though the patrols deep inside Iraq and Kuwait were producing a bonanza of other valuable intelligence.

"How are the preparations for emplacing your—what do you call them? Selective mines?" de la Bretaigne asked.

"Discriminating mines," Wilson said. "The first patrols to use them will be taking them in tonight. Maybe they can spot the damned things."

The discriminating mines to which Wilson referred were an ingenious combination of miniature television cameras and remotely-detonated mines which American Special Forces patrols were preparing to emplace along several of the main lines of supply being used by the Iraqis. Some of the mine systems operated through satellite links, much as John Rains's unmanned aerial vehicle did. The mines, with their tiny, radio controlled firing devices, would be emplanted beneath the roadbed. The little solar powered, all-light-level television camera and the satellite-linked receiver/transmitter would be placed well back from the road. It would be aimed at the mined road, and covered with a shapeless fiberglass shell colored to blend in with the surroundings. Once the camera was actuated by remote control, it would transmit a video picture of the road and the traffic on it through the satellite, back to a control room in USSOTAF headquarters. There, the traffic on the road would be monitored for intelligence purposes, twenty-four hours a day, if necessary.

If a lucrative target—a Scud missile erector/launcher for example— came into view, the mine could be remotely detonated from the control room to destroy it. The capability the system had to discriminate between civilian or low-priority traffic, and lucrative, high-priority military targets was the reason it was known as a discriminating mine.

The less sophisticated systems the Special Forces teams also had in their arsenal worked much the same, except that they operated through a direct radio link instead of through a satellite. A team could employ a number of the systems, linked to the TV camera and mines several miles away by radio, enabling them to engage targets entering their minefields from a safe distance.

Staff Sergeant Walter Shumate was the primary operator of the discriminating mine system for the six-man Special Forces team of which he was a member.

The team had not taken the system with them during their first mission into Iraq a month earlier. That mission had been to maintain surveillance on a remote airfield in the Syrian Desert region of western Iraq.

During two weeks of surveillance on the seldom-used airstrip, they had seen nothing of significance. But they had learned a great deal about the rigors of living hidden in a harsh desert deep in enemy territory, and after several weeks of waiting for another mission, they were more than ready to go back in.

Shumate and his team leader were waiting for the rest of the team to arrive so that they could rehearse the briefback they would be giving the 5th Special Forces Group commander and staff in a couple of hours.

"Well, at least we'll actually be doing something this time, sir," Shumate said to the team commander, Captain Jack Marsh. "That last mission was about as exciting as midnight at a nursing home."

"Yeah, but it was sure useful for working the bugs out of living like a scorpion—no pun intended," Marsh said. "And this time, we might have to sit out there until the real shooting war starts."

"You really think so, sir?" Shumate asked. "I'm still betting my money that they'll pull out of Kuwait before it comes to that."

"I'm afraid I'm not so optimistic, Shu," Marsh said. "It doesn't look like the President is, either, or he wouldn't have ordered another quarter of a million troops over here."

President Bush had announced the previous day that he had decided to double the number of American forces in the theater of operations. When that was accomplished, it was clear to all, the allies would have enough military might facing the Iraqis to forcibly expel Saddam's army from Kuwait, if necessary.

"Anyway," Marsh said as the other four team members arrived, "as Sergeant Major Jensen said, we'd damn well better plan on it being that way."

When the rest of the team was seated, Marsh stood before them. He always began his team meetings with a quotation that he felt was appropriate to the subject of the meeting. He pulled a piece of paper from the pocket of his desert camouflage trousers and looked at it.

"Today's quote," the Special Forces officer said, "is from Michael Scharra's superb book about the battle of Gettysburg, Killer Angels:

> '...He could not retreat now. It might be the clever thing
> to do, but cleverness did not win victories; the bright com-
> binations rarely worked. You won because the men thought

they were going to win, attacked with courage, attacked with faith, and it was the faith more than anything else you had to protect; that was one thing that was in your hands, and so you could not ask them to leave the field to the enemy...'

When Marsh finished reading the quotation, the assistant team leader, Al Schwarbacher asked, "Has that book been translated into Arabic, sir?"

Marsh looked at him curiously and said, "Arabic? I doubt it."

"Good," Al said, smiling.

Another member of the team quipped, "Not bad, sir. But where we're going, I'd have thought your quote would begin, 'Yea, 'tho I walk through the valley of the shadow of death...'"

"...I will fear no evil," Shumate added, reciting the rest of the irreverent Vietnam-era version of the Psalm, "'cause I'm the baddest motherfucker in the valley."

The six-man team was going into Iraq's western panhandle again. But this time, instead of maintaining surveillance on a seldom-used airstrip, they would be planting discriminating mines along the busiest road in Iraq these days—the Amman-Baghdad highway, near Rutba, Iraq, the biggest town in the region.

✳   ✳   ✳

"Dead camels?" Bill Kernan asked Abdul. "And goats?"

"Yes," the Kuwaiti replied. "Not a mark on them, but their eyes are all bugged out."

"But no sign of people?"

"That's right. Just the animals."

Abdul had just come to Kernan with a report from the Rumaylah oil-field in northern Kuwait. A member of the underground who worked there reported that a number of dead animals had been found two days earlier, near a warehouse in which oil drilling equipment was stored.

"Which side of the building were they on?" the American asked, "and how far from it were they?"

"Which side? Why do you ask that?" Abdul wondered aloud.

"Because we can find out which direction the wind was blowing the day before yesterday," Kernan said. "Maybe there was a leak from some chemical weapons the Iraqis have stored in there, or something such as that."

"I'll have to find that out," he said. "But the man also said that he didn't think there was anything in the building, because there was no security on it."

"Strange," Kernan mused. "Of course, if there was security, it probably wasn't visible anyway. They'd want to keep it out of sight of the satellites. Or it could be that there was an accident there, or—hell, I don't know what might have happened. But we have to try to find out."

"I'll go up there myself and have a look around, if you think it's that important," Abdul said.

Kernan thought about it. The location of chemical and biological weapons had the highest priority on the list of intelligence requirements the CIA had given him, and this was the first indication that anyone in the resistance had learned of the possible presence of such weapons in Kuwait.

"What cover would you use?" Kernan asked.

"The same as the owner of the animals," Abdul said, "a Bedouin goatherd."

"Well, it is important. Or at least it could be. Let me radio Riyadh with the information we have first, though, and see what they say."

He did so, and while they waited for a response, Kernan cleaned the Glock .45 pistol that was always with him.

Everytime he did so, he was reminded of the only time he had used it in anger, when he killed the four Iraqi rapists at Abir's villa in mid-September.

That was almost two months ago, he thought. He hadn't seen the beautiful wife of the Kuwaiti sheik in more than a month.

Except in that damned dream last night, he recalled, a chill coursing through him.

He and Abdul had moved their headquarters in early October, a routine move to avoid being rolled up by the Mukhabarat. It was now in two small rooms above an electrical appliance repair shop in the northern part of Kuwait City. The shop had long since been looted by the Iraqis.

He had seen Mara once, when she had brought some new photographs of torture victims she and Abir were treating at the aid station in Abir's villa. But he had not seen Abir, although he thought of her often. And not just when he cleaned the deadly, quiet pistol.

"How are things at Sheik al-Sabah's villa these days?" he asked Abdul as he reassembled the handgun.

Abdul studied him a moment. "Abir is fine, if that's what you mean," he said. "She always asks about you. Why don't you go to see her?"

"Is she still taking more risks than she should?" the American inquired.

"Yes. I spoke to Mara about it. She told me about you and Abir."

Kernan squeezed a dab of grease into the back of the silencer, then screwed it onto the threaded barrel.

"What about me and Abir?"

Abdul waited until Kernan put the pistol down and looked at him, then said, "It's over between her husband and her. You know that, don't you?"

Kernan arched his eyebrows. "What did he do, walk around her photograph three times, and divorce her?"

Abdul glared at him. "After she was raped by the Iraqis, it doesn't really matter. He'll never touch her again."

Kernan wiped a spot of grease off the weapon and looked Abdul in the eye.

"They didn't rape her," he said. Holding up the pistol, he added, "This thing made sure of that."

"That's not what the sheik thinks," Abdul said. "Sanaa will tell him they raped her. And Mara will agree, as will Abir, herself."

Kernan narrowed his eyes and shook his head. "I'm missing something here, old buddy. Why would you say they raped her? I was there. I know they didn't."

"Because it will make people that much more sympathetic toward her. It will add a lot to what they feel she has suffered. It will give her more credibility in her demands for democracy and for rights for women, when the time comes."

Kernan shook his head again. "You baffle me, Abdul," he said. "Are you a Moslem, or not?"

"Of course I am," the Kuwaiti said.

"You don't sound like it," Kernan muttered. "You sound like a damned women's libber."

"You don't look like a Christian monk, either, Bill," Abdul said. "But you sure act like one."

Kernan looked at him with narrowed eyes for a moment, then chuckled. "You wouldn't think so if you'd seen this dream…" he mumbled, then added, "Oh, never mind."

"It would be a big help to us if you would go to her," the resistance chief declared. "Maybe then she'd stop taking too many risks. At the rate she's going, she won't be around by the time Kuwait is free again. And if she's dead, she won't be of much use to Kuwait, except as a martyr."

"I thought Islam put a lot of stake in martyrs," Kernan said.

Abdul stood up. He walked to the window, then came back to the table where Kernan sat waiting for an answer to his earlier radio call to the CIA station in Riyadh.

"Bill, you sound as if you really don't care whether Abir gets herself picked up and tortured or not. She's already given up a lot for this fight, you know—a hell of a lot."

The resistance leader opened a pack of Marlboros and lit one. Inhaling deeply and blowing out the smoke, he said, "You act like you don't believe in what we're doing, or that you don't care what sacrifices people like her are making. If that's the case, why don't you just call for the helicopter and go home? If you don't want to help make Kuwait a free, democratic country, then just turn the resistance effort over to the Iranians. They believe in what they're doing, at least."

Kernan rubbed his eyes with his hands, thinking about Abdul's remarks. After awhile he looked up at his Kuwaiti counterpart and said, "I guess maybe I had that coming, Abdul. It isn't true, though; I care a great deal about all of you and what you're doing. They couldn't pay me enough to do this damned job, otherwise."

Abdul walked over to him and put his hand on the American's shoulder.

"Ah, I know that," he said. "But I don't understand your aversion to Abir. If she wasn't a beautiful woman—a gorgeous woman—that would be one thing. If there was some other woman, which you say there isn't, I suppose I might understand. But, damn it, Bill, otherwise...Ah, never mind."

He removed his hand from the American's shoulder and walked away, then turned back and mumbled, "I won't mention it again."

The radio broke the silence that followed as each man thought his separate thoughts. Kernan answered the call.

It was the chief of the CIA station in Riyadh.

"Bill," he said, "we need one of those animals. Do you think you can get one?"

Kernan looked at his Kuwaiti counterpart, who nodded and said, "Yes, I can get one, unless they've been taken away, or disposed of by the vultures."

"Affirmative," Kernan said into the radio.

"Good," the voice from Riyadh radio replied. "All right, I'll let you work the plan. We'll sling it out with the Defender. But listen, you'd better use protective clothing and a mask when you're handling it. Owen can bring it in to you before he picks up the goat."

"Is that really necessary?" Kernan asked. "I thought chemical agents dispersed fairly quickly after they did their dirty work."

"They do," the distant American said. "But we think these might be biological agent casualties."

"Oh, Jesus. I hope to hell you're wrong," Kernan said.

"So do we, Bill. But that's what we need the carcass to determine."

✶   ✶   ✶

Lieutenant Lawrence Redmond stood atop his Abrams tank surveying the empty expanse of desert before him.

"Perfect," he said, then climbed down from the turret onto the hull of the tank and jumped to the ground.

"Perfect tank country, Anderson," he said to his driver. "If they want to fight in this terrain, we'll go through 'em like shit through a goose, as Patton used to say."

"Boy, sir," the young enlisted tanker said to his platoon leader, more concerned with his machine than the terrain, "this dadburned dust is rough on the filters, though. Look at that."

He held the air cleaning intake filter out to Redmond, who studied it a minute.

"Cover it with a piece of ponch liner," the lieutenant said. "If it doesn't cut off too much air, maybe that'll help."

That evening, at his platoon meeting, Redmond discussed the dust filtration problem with the rest of the platoon. The big gas turbine engines of the Abrams battle tanks would soon be ground up by the dust particles if a solution wasn't found to filter them out.

"We tried a poncho liner, but it cut off too much air," he informed the others.

His platoon sergeant interrupted the meeting to discipline one of the tank crewmen.

"Stokes," he said, "get that damn thing off your head. You look like a—a streamlined A-rab!"

The black soldier grinned sheepishly and pulled off the piece of nylon stocking he was wearing over his hair. "It makes my CVC more comfortable, sarge. Didn't realize I still had it on."

It wasn't unusual for African-American soldiers to wear stockings—"do rags" as they called them—on their heads beneath their combat vehicle crewman's helmets, because it did make them more comfortable over coarse hair. But it was obviously not acceptable for wear with the uniform at other times.

Another black soldier said, "At least he didn't call you a sand nigger, Stokes."

Redmond glared at the man who had made the comment. To the entire platoon he said, "I'd better never hear anybody use that term again. Ever. Do, and you'll be low-crawling across the desert to division headquarters for reassignment."

The look on their platoon leader's face made it plain that his threat was a serious one, but then that look turned suddenly into a grin.

Lieutenant Redmond looked at Stokes and said, "By damn, Stokes, you're a genius!"

There were curious looks from everyone until he explained himself.

"Nylon hose! That will probably make the perfect filter for the air intakes. If it works like it I think it will, Stokes, I'm going to see that you get a medal."

They tried the nylon "do rags" as improvised filter on two of the Abrams tanks the next day. They worked like a charm.

When Redmond showed the results to his company commander, the captain slapped him on the back and said, "All right, Lieutenant Redmond, here's your mission: get your ass back to Division, find every female soldier, Red Cross lady, and transvestite you can. Beg, borrow or steal their pantyhose, and once you have enough for the company, with spares, go to General Almueti—he's the new Assistant Division Commander for Support—and show him how well it works. What did you say the troop's name was who came up with this idea?"

"Private Stokes, sir. Willie T. Stokes."

"All right. I'll put him in for an Army Achievement Medal, for inventing the…what should we call the damn thing? We can't call it the 'pantyhose filter.'"

"You're right there, sir. George Patton would roll over in his grave. Let's call it a, uh, a Stokes filter."

"Yeah. Stokes filter. Sounds good."

Redmond laughed aloud, and his company commander gave him a quizzical look.

"I was just thinking, sir," Redmond said. "I never got to go on a panty raid at the Citadel. But here I am, a commissioned officer sitting in the middle of the desert, and my company commander sends me on one."

The captain chuckled. "Yeah, Larry, fate works in some strange ways, doesn't it? Now, get yourself moving and go round us up some Stokes filters."

▼

Ten

11 November 1990

Captain Jack Marsh looked at the other eleven members of his Special Forces A team and thought, "I will fear no evil."

They were, Marsh was convinced, the finest group of soldiers a young officer could ever hope to lead. In their charcoal-impregnated chemical protective suits and camouflage face paint, they all looked much the same. But they weren't.

They were a mix of everything that was America.

There was Francis X. Nicholas, a Passamaquoddy Indian from the woods of Maine and the best heavy weapons man in Special Forces. His young counterpart, Lew Merletti, was fast becoming one of the best, too, thanks to Nicholas.

There were the medics, Brown and Atkinson, the former an unabashed redneck, the latter a quietly competent African-American from the District of Columbia. They were both superb medics and, as disparate as their backgrounds happened to be, the best of friends.

There was Al Schwarbacher, full of dry humor and professional competence, unflappable in any situation and the best operations and intelligence specialist that Marsh had ever worked with.

One of the radio operators, a Puerto Rican staff sergeant named Jorge Torres, was an electronics wizard who knew more about new communications technology than most electrical engineers whose salaries were ten times that of his.

The other communications specialist on the team was Leroy Carter, a second generation Special Forces radio operator who still wasn't too sure how radios worked, but who seemed to know every page of the operations and maintenance manuals of the team's commo gear.

One of the team's engineers was a Cajun named Baribeau whose knowledge of engineering was confined to how to blow things up. But his courage, fieldcraft and sixth sense about the enemy were irreplaceable.

The other engineer was Walter Shumate, Jr., a Vietnamese orphan who had been adopted as an infant by a legendary Special Forces sergeant major of the same name. The elder Shumate had enlisted his son in the Army as soon as he graduated from high school at age seventeen. Young Walt Shumate knew almost as much about the other military occupational specialties of Special Forces as he did his own.

The team sergeant, Master Sergeant Reeve Whitson, was a bagpipe-playing Scotsman who demanded absolute loyalty to the team, and who thought that raw courage was the only real requirement to being a soldier. He had a chest full of medals from Vietnam and Panama to back up his theory of soldiering.

And finally there was the executive officer of the team, Chief Warrant Officer Wade Herrington. His strength was a practiced belief that sticking to the basics and working hard could accomplish any mission. Marsh would command half of the twelve-man A team on the mission to interdict the Amman-Baghdad highway with discriminating mines. Herrington would command the other half.

Jack Marsh smiled as he looked at each of them. With subordinates like these, he could he think of no job he'd rather have.

The big Pave Low helicopter which would deposit the team onto two landing zones deep in enemy territory rolled forward, then shuddered and lifted off the runway.

Jack Marsh closed his eyes and thought, "for thou art with me..."

✱   ✱   ✱

Abdul howled at the sight of Bill Kernan trying to ride the camel. Mounting the animal had been easy enough, but when the thing rose, hind legs first, Bill tumbled forward off its neck into the dust.

Kernan got up and scowled at the camel, his Arab headdress all askew. The camel returned his scowl, snorted, then released a long, loud fart. That caused Abdul and his son Yassir to laugh so hard that they were afraid someone in the distance might hear them, so they tried to stifle their laughter. The attempt caused them to giggle and wheeze, while the American stood there glaring at them momentarily, then joined their fit of giggling.

They were in a wadi with a Bedouin who had supplied the camels. They would ride them a short distance north to the landing zone where Claude Owen was to land his little Defender helicopter. He was bringing an Arab-American with him to provide security, and a pair of protective suits, containers, and respirators for Kernan and Abdul. The plan was that Owen, his guard, and Abdul's son would remain with the helicopter, camouflaging it in the wadi while Kernan and Abdul rode the camels to a point near the warehouse where the dead animals had been found.

There, they would don the protective gear, recover one of the goat carcasses, seal it in a protective container, and prepare it for slingloading beneath the helicopter. They would then radio Owen to bring the helicopter to the pickup point, where the container would be slung beneath the chopper and flown back to Saudi Arabia for autopsy.

When their giggling subsided and the men got their minds back on their serious and dangerous mission, Abdul drew one last chuckle from Kernan when he said, "This is supposed to be a Bedouin operation, not a bedlam operation, Bill. Now, get back up on that damned camel and let's get out of here."

*   *   *

Captain Jack Marsh shook hands with each of the six members of his Special Forces A team who comprised the split team commanded by his executive officer, CWO Wade Herrington.

"Keep your head down, Wade," he said.

For security purposes, Marsh had not been told exactly where along the Amman-Baghdad highway Herrington's half of the team would be located. That way, in the event that anyone on either of the reconnaisance and surveillance teams was captured, he could not be tortured into revealing the location of the other team. One glance at his Global Positioning System receiver, though, told Marsh that the other half of his team would be deposited about twenty kilometers west of his own landing zone.

"Good hunting, boss," Herrington responded as the crew chief of the Air Force Pave Low helicopter called, "One minute!"

The ramp at the rear of the big helicopter opened as it slowed for landing. Holding onto the nylon seats along the sides of the cargo compartment, Herrington and his men struggled to their feet with their heavy, bulging rucksacks. The burdensome packs were crammed full of the things the men would need to survive in the desert for at least two weeks, and with the discriminating mine systems they were to employ along the enemy highway.

The helicopter touched down in a swirl of dust, and Herrington and his men disappeared off the ramp and into the darkness. A few seconds later the aircraft shuddered and lifted off the desert floor. The crew chief came immediately to Marsh and announced, "Five minutes to your L.Z., sir."

Marsh nodded, then looked to make certain that the other five men were watching him. He pointed to his watch and held up five fingers. The others each gave him a thumbs up, and he sat back in the nylon troop seat.

It was hot in the chemical protective suit, and Marsh was glad he would be out of it soon. Once they had cleared the landing zone, he and his men would remove the suits and attach them to the outside of their rucksacks for easy access.

He thought again of the horrible deaths of the animals in the film General Wilson had showed them at the beginning of their first mission briefing. God, it would be a horrible way to die.

His greatest fear had once been burning to death in a helicopter crash, but now, when he was unable to prevent the thought from creeping into his mind, Marsh imagined death coming in the form of one of the terrible chemical agents the enemy was known to possess, and to have used.

But the thing which bothered Marsh most was that his young wife, an Army Reserve nurse who was scheduled to deploy to the theatre of operations soon, might be just as vulnerable as he to chemical attack. He shuddered at the thought, then remembered what she had said to him the night before he left Fort Campbell for Saudi Arabia.

"I'm going to volunteer to come over there as soon as possible, Jack," she had said. When he asked why, she said, "Because I love the same things that you do. And not just freedom and the flag and those nebulous things, either. But people—people like those crazy characters in your team, and the women who support them. One of them might need me, and I'm a darn good nurse. So, I'll be there, just in case."

They had made love after that with the desperation of young lovers who might be together for the last time, though neither of them had said that.

He said a silent prayer that it would not be the last time they were together, then looked at his men. Shumate was the first one he saw, and he recalled what the young staff sergeant had told him about his departure from his own young wife—his bride of only two months. She was gone when he went home to get his gear and say goodbye, attending class at the local college. And she had not returned by the time the team departed. He had said goodbye to his wife on the answering machine of their telephone.

Marsh wished now that he'd violated security and advised the team the night before that they were going to be alerted the next morning, and that they would be able to go home only briefly that day to get their gear.

Shumate was returning his gaze in the dim, red light of the cargo compartment, and Marsh leaned over to him.

"We're going to be all right, you know that don't you, Sergeant Shumate?" he said to the Vietnamese orphan turned American Green Beret.

"Yes, sir," Shumate said. "I knew that as soon as the President said this wasn't going to be another Vietnam."

*   *   *

Claude Owen's McDonald-Douglas Defender—tiny in comparison to the Pave Low which deposited Jack Marsh's team in the panhandle of western Iraq—sat beneath a camouflage net at the bottom of a wadi just south of the Rumaylah oilfield near Kuwait's northwestern corner. Owen was sitting on the ground in the dry streambed beside it, awaiting a radio call from Bill Kernan.

Standing guard nearby on the banks of the six-foot deep wadi were Abdul's son Yassir and the Arab-American CIA man Owen had brought with him for protection.

While he waited, Owen considered the complaint he was going to make to the Inspector General at CIA headquarters when he returned to the States, though God only knew when that might be.

The veteran pilot was not a complainer, especially not on his own behalf; if it ever came to something he disagreed with to the extent that he felt the risk wasn't worth the mission results, he would just say "Screw you," and quit. But he was furious about the fact that his friend Bill Kernan was out in the middle of a Kuwaiti oilfield recovering an animal carcass suspected of having been killed by a biological weapon.

When he had first been briefed on the mission, Owen had told the station chief that he felt it was unnecessary to risk sending Kernan all the way from Kuwait City to recover the carcass. After all, he argued, his friend Bill Kernan was not an Arab, and didn't even speak the language. It was common knowledge around the station that Kernan was doing an outstanding job of organizing and running the resistance forces in the city, and would be irreplacable if something happened to him.

Kernan wasn't even trained in the correct use of the protective gear he would have to wear to recover the animal. The first time he would ever put it on would be when it was brought in to him aboard the helicopter. There were plenty of Arabs, and Americans of Arab descent who could be trained in its use and taken by Owen to the wadi to join up with Abdul without risking Kernan.

But Claude Owen had been overruled, and Kernan was now out there somewhere riding a camel, of all goddam things, to recover a dead goat.

Suddenly, in response to a feeling of impending danger, Owen got up, pulled on his night vision goggles, and checked the small but deadly 5.56 millimeter minigun in the chin of his aircraft. Satisfied that it was loaded and ready, Owen sat back down beside his bird and waited for his friend to call.

Upwind of the warehouse beside which the dead animals lay, Kernan peered through the night sight of the .223 caliber silenced rifle. It was the one he had used three months earlier to save the life of the man who now stood beside him, holding the camels they had ridden to the oilfield.

"It looks clear to me, Abdul," he whispered. He was peering at the warehouse and its surroundings, looking for signs of any human presence.

"You stay here," he said to Abdul. "There's no sense in both of us going to get the goat."

He handed the Kuwaiti the rifle and began to don the protective suit Owen had brought him. After a struggle, he got it on, pulled on the respirator, then helped Abdul into the other suit and mask. When he had finished, he took the sealable container in which to place the dead goat and moved to the dozen or so carcasses lying on the floor of the desert.

Getting the goat into the container was not an easy task. Sweat burned Kernan's eyes as he perspired in the hot, awkward suit. The gloves were far too large, and it was difficult to handle the decomposing animal as he tried to stuff it into the container.

He finally accomplished the task, though, hefted the container onto his shoulder, and carried it back to where Abdul waited. They loaded it into the cargo net they would sling beneath the helicopter, then Kernan radioed Owen that the animal was ready to be lifted out.

"The sooner the better, pal," Kernan added. "These damned suits are wearing us out."

It took only a couple of minutes to remove the camouflage net from the helicopter and start its blades turning.

"Lifting off now," Claude Owen advised as the almost silent little chopper lifted out of the dry riverbed in a swirling cloud of dust. He would be at the pickup site in just a few minutes.

Abdul took the camels well upwind of the spot where Bill Kernan waited with the corpse and tethered them to a disused wellhead. He still had the American's suppressed rifle with him, and now used its night sight to look to the southwest, the direction from which they expected the helicopter to come. Abdul saw nothing.

Had he looked to the north instead, he would have seen an Iraqi foot patrol roaming through the oilfield in response to threats of Kuwaiti sabotage reported by the Mukhabarat. The Iraqis spotted the camels first, then the curious sight of two men in hazardous materials protective clothing. The patrol leader halted his men and crept forward with one other man to see what it was all about. They were fifty meters away when the little Defender helicopter appeared out of the darkness, flaring to a hover above one of the alien-looking men.

Kernan hooked the sling shackle to the cargo hook beneath the helicopter, yanked it hard once to make certain it was firmly attached, then dashed out from under the hovering aircraft. He gave Owen a thumbs up, and the chopper slowly lifted until the pilot felt the weight of the dead goat come off of the ground.

The Iraqi patrol leader was desperately trying to raise his headquarters on the radio, but to no avail. Finally, he decided that, if this was a friendly operation, he would have been told about it, or would have at least been prohibited from entering this area of the oilfield. Anyway, the helicopter was not one of the types in the Iraqi inventory. He motioned the rest of the patrol forward and as the helicopter turned and started south, ordered them to open fire.

One of the first bursts of fire struck Bill Kernan. He felt something slam into his shoulder and spin him around. Even as he spun, another blow knocked him from his feet and he knew that he had been shot.

Abdul escaped the first burst of fire, and used Kernan's suppressed rifle to shoot back. He needn't have bothered. By the time he got the first round off, Claude Owen's spinning minigun was spitting a stream of steel into the Iraqi patrol at fifty rounds per second. All six of the men were dead or dying by the time Abdul realized that the loud rattle and groaning which filled the air around him was the noise of the deadly little weapon in the nose of the helicopter.

Owen made a second pass over the Iraqi patrol, looking for any signs of life. One of the men moved, so the CIA pilot unleashed a two-second burst into the midst of the enemy soldiers. Another hundred rounds ripped through the men and nothing moved after that.

Bill Kernan realized that he was not terribly hurt, because he had been badly wounded before and knew what it was like. His left arm was numb except for a dull ache at the shoulder, and the flesh of his thigh burned. But he could move the leg, and his mind was clear. He pulled the mask and hood off his head and tossed them aside, then got on the radio to Owen. Claude was about to drop the container attached to the hook beneath his helicopter before landing to check on his old friend.

"Hold what you got, ol' buddy," Owen heard Kernan say over the radio. "You better get that damned goat back to the lab guys."

"You all right?" Owen asked. "I thought I saw you go down."

"Nothing to worry about," Kernan replied. "Just a scratch."

"Let me land and take a look," Owen said.

"Negative, negative!" Kernan said. "If this area's contaminated, it's too risky. We'll see what happens to me. If it is something really devious, we'll know soon enough."

"Ah, shit, man," Owen said. "OK, I'm going to take this damned cargo back, but I'm coming straight back here after I drop it off. I'm not leaving you out here with a bullet hole in you, Bill."

"The bullet hole isn't a problem, Claude—honest. But if there's some bug out here, Saddam would like nothing better than to have a couple of Americans pick it up and spread it all around for him."

Owen felt a deep wave of frustration. It was certainly true that they needed to know what had caused the deaths of all the animals around the isolated storehouse. Saddam Hussein and henchmen were capable of anything. But it was also true, in Owen's mind at least, that it was wrong for Bill Kernan to have been sent to recover the carcass, and wrong to leave him, wounded and with a camel as his only means of escape, in the midst of enemy territory. Damn it, why was it always the same ones who were made to take the risks for everyone else?

"All right, Bill, here's what I'm going to do; I'll take this thing back, I'll make damned sure they test it immediately, and if whatever it is has an antidote, I'll bring it right back. If they can't figure out what it is, or they don't have an antidote, I'm coming back anyway. So, I'll see you back at the hide site. Out."

Kernan knew better than to argue with Owen at the moment, so he just said, "Roger. OK, we're going to get the hell away from this area. If anybody else is around, that firefight is bound to have gotten their attention, so we're heading back to the hide site. And thanks, rotorhead, for hosing those bad guys for us."

Owen had already switched frequencies to advise his base station that he was en route with the animal carcass and that he needed a word with the chief of station as soon as he landed. He wasn't aware of what his superiors had in mind for him when he arrived.

*   *   *

"So, what words of wisdom for today, boss?" Staff Sergeant Walt Shumate, Jr. asked Captain Jack Marsh. The two men were lying together in a rocky depression in the desert of western Iraq. A short distance away, in two other locations, were the other pairs of their teammates. Dawn was just beginning to lighten the sky to their east. Marsh pulled his desert poncho more tightly around him to keep out the cold, dry air of the desert night.

"Well, let's see, Shu," he said, trying to think of some quote appropriate to the time and place. "How about this: '…if they mean to have a war, let it begin here!'"

"Humph," Shumate mumbled, his brow wrinkling with concern. "How about adding, 'as soon as the US Air Force arrives.' I could go for it then. Who said that, anyway? Some admiral at Pearl Harbor?"

Marsh chuckled. "A little before that. One of the Minute Men at Lexington at the beginning of the Revolutionary War."

The radio handset between them relayed the voice of Lew Merletti. Merletti and Atkinson were in a shallow hole they had dug into a slight rise about three hundred meters east of Marsh and Shumate's position. "Blacked out vehicles approaching from the east," the young weapons expert reported. "Can't tell the type or number yet."

"Roger that," Marsh replied. "Let me know as soon as you have them identified." He scooted up to the edge of the depression so he could see over it to the highway a quarter of a mile to the north. The fact that the vehicles were running without lights made it probable that they were military. The trucks which normally ran this road between Amman, Jordan and Baghdad were commercial trucks carrying goods from the Jordanian port of Aqaba into Iraq, since the United Nations embargo and blockade of the Persian Gulf had made this the only route by which most goods—particularly those of a military nature—could be shipped there.

Once the vehicles were near enough to be seen with night vision goggles from Merletti's position, he reported to Marsh in a voice pitched high with excitement.

"I've got an ID. Be advised, these are eight-wheelers with missiles aboard. Can't tell whether they're Frogs or Scuds yet, but they're definitely missile carriers. A couple of Zil six-bys, too."

The remaining members of the team could picture in their minds the vehicles Merletti had named. They had spent countless hours committing to memory photographs and line drawings of Soviet-built military vehicles, and the recognizable characteristics and NATO codenames of each.

Both the Frog and Scud missile carriers were somewhat similar in appearance—big, eight-wheeled vehicles with a single missile atop each. Once they were close enough, though, it would be fairly easy to tell whether it was the Frog missile, with a range of only seventy kilometers, or the much longer ranged Scud, capable of reaching out to 300 kilometers, which had entered the team's area.

The six-wheeled Zil trucks Merletti had mentioned were probably support vehicles. He called a moment later to confirm his findings. "These are definitely Scuds, sir—three of them," he said. "The wheels are evenly spaced, there's a door between the center two, and the missile hangs over the back. They're Scuds all right."

"Roger, roger," Marsh acknowledged. "What's their speed?"

"Speed, about one zero miles per hour," Merletti answered.

Shumate had scooted up beside Marsh and opened the cover on the little, flat-screened monitor of the discriminating mine system he was responsible for employing. The monitor was radio-linked to a small, camouflaged television camera overlooking the road. The controls of the keyboard beneath the monitor enabled him to tilt, pan, and zoom the all-light level camera, and to select and detonate any of the five powerful anti-tank mines the team had set beneath the roadway during the night.

Captain Marsh was on his satellite radio to the United States Special Operations Task Force war room at King Khalid Military City in Saudi Arabia.

"Zone Plato, three Scuds, ETA one minute. Permission to engage, over."

Marsh didn't really expect to gain permission to destroy the missile carriers, but at least his request would get the USSOTAF staff energized. When and if hostilities began, it would be imperative that procedures were in place to have such decisions rapidly made and relayed to the teams in the field. A half-minute later, Lew Merletti's voice came over the handset of the team radio. In muffled tones, he said, "Enemy crew is in chemical protective gear! I say again, enemy is wearing gas masks. We've masked here. Recommend you do the same, over."

Before he answered Merletti, Marsh nudged Shumate and said, "Mask, Shu!" as he pulled his own protective mask from the carrier at his side. He pulled it on, then picked up the radio handset and said, "Schwarbacher, this is Marsh; mask, mask, over!"

From the position where he and Jorge Torres were, several hundred meters west, Al Schwarbacher's muffled reply came over the radio immediately. "Roger, roger. We heard Lew, and we're already masked, over."

Now Marsh turned his attention back to the satellite radio to his headquarters. He reported the fact that the Scud missile crews were wearing chemical protective equipment, imagining as he did so the sudden scrambling around that it would cause among the staff officers who heard the report.

The base station radio operator acknowledged his report, then a new voice, full of authority, came over the radio.

"Do not, I say again, do not engage the enemy vehicles at this time. Acknowledge, over."

"This is Plato One," Marsh answered. "I copy and will not engage."

Just then Shumate tapped him on the shoulder and pointed to the monitor linked to the TV camera near the road. The Iraqi vehicles were moving into the camera's field of view. Shumate pressed the "record" button, then skillfully panned and zoomed the remote camera's lens to scan the vehicles. Led by a cargo truck, three missile carriers came into view. Shumate zoomed in until one of the Scud vehicles filled the screen of the monitor. Once he confirmed Merletti's earlier identification, he zoomed in on the cab of the carrier and saw that the crew was indeed wearing gas masks.

Jack Marsh was filled with a sudden sense of dread.

He wasn't afraid for his own safety, but he imagined his young wife at work in a field hospital. He pictured a Scud missile streaking out of the sky toward her, then exploding and engulfing the hospital in a cloud of deadly vapor. The images he had seen of nerve agents doing their cruel work on labratory animals were transformed to a picture of Barbara, helpless and confused, writhing and screaming and voiding herself as she died a horrible death.

He was breathing hard through the filters of his mask, sweating profusely inside it, until Shumate's voice dispelled the image of terror when he said, "Sir, are you all right? You're breathing awfully hard."

Marsh shook his head to clear it, inhaled deeply and held it for several seconds, then exhaled.

"Yeah, I'm OK, Shu," he replied to his teammate. "I was just thinking too much."

"Look at this," Shumate said, pointing to the monitor.

The last truck of the five-vehicle convoy was passing. Shumate zoomed in on it. It was a Zil cargo truck similar to the one at the front of the convoy, except there was a large cylindrical tank mounted on the back of it.

"Water tanker?" Marsh asked.

"Maybe," Shumate said, then zoomed in on the tank and hoses which ran from it. "Or it could be a decon vehicle." Marsh searched his mind for the characteristics of Soviet built decontamination vehicles.

"ARS-12," he said as he recalled a picture of one of the trucks. "Rounded cab, spare tire right behind it. Yeah, I'd·say it's an ARS-12 decon vehicle. Figures it'd be with chemical Scuds."

He fumbled with the satellite radio handset, trying to get the microphone to the voice transmitting diaphragm of the mask's "voicemitter," and to position the earpiece against his ear. It was difficult to do with the cumbersome protective mask on.

"Zeus, this is Plato One," he said. "Be advised, the targets are passing the mines. We no longer have a target, over."

"Roger," a voice replied over the radio. "Stand by, Plato."

A moment later a voice came over the radio that Marsh recognized as that of the USSOTAF commander, Major General Wayne Wilson.

"Plato, this is Zeus," he said. "Good job out there. Did you get pictures?"

"Affirmative," Marsh said. "We got video tape."

"Can you retransmit it to us?" Wilson asked.

"Negative, sir," Marsh answered. "The satellite link transmitter is with the other half of the team—RT Plutarch."

Each of the Special Forces A teams involved in the long-range recon and surveillance missions inside Iraq had one of the satellite-link video transmitters, which were capable of sending immediate images—"real time" images, in intelligence corps parlance—back to the headquarters base station. But the one Marsh's A team had been issued was with Wade Herrington's half of the team, somewhere well to Marsh's west.

"If Plutarch is where I think he is, though," the young Captain added, "he should be able to send you real time video about an hour from now."

Shumate, monitoring the intra-team net while Marsh was on the satcom to headquarters, answered someone with, "Wait one," then looked over at Marsh.

"Al says the vehicles are pulling off the road just west of his position, sir."

In the growing light of the approaching sunrise, Marsh could see Shumate's eyes through the eyepieces of his mask. They were wide with anticipation.

"How far west, and which side?" he asked.

Shumate asked Schwarbacher, then relayed the reply. "They're about 350 meters to his west, about a hundred meters off the far side of the road."

Marsh stood slowly and looked in that direction. He couldn't see that far across the slightly rolling desert floor, although there was enough light now that he would have been able to see the vehicles if they hadn't been masked by the terrain.

Shumate was listening to another report from Schwarbacher. Into the radio handset he said, "Roger, wait," then to Marsh, "He's going to move their position about a hundred meters west, where he can get a better view of the vehicles. He says it looks like they're laagering up there for the day."

"All right," the captain said. "Just tell them to be real careful. It's getting awfully light."

There was a slight breeze blowing from the southwest. Marsh picked up a handful of dust from the desert floor and tossed it up into the air to verify the direction of the wind, then removed his protective mask. "You can unmask now, Shu," he said, "and tell the others they can, too. The way the breeze is blowing, we're not in any danger from those warheads." Thinking aloud, he added, "I guess they just travel with protective gear on in case of a wreck or if they hit a big bump, or something."

"Yeah, well it's too bad we couldn't give them a real bump with those damned anti-tank mines they just rode over," Sergeant Shumate commented.

"It ain't over yet," Marsh said, then picked up the satcom handset to send a situation report to the USSOTAF war room.

As he did so, he heard Shumate repeat the quotation he had used just before the Scud convoy showed up: "...if they mean to have a war, let it begin here!"

▼

Eleven

12 November 1990

Claude Owen sat in the sealed, sterile trailer in the middle of the desert fuming with anger as he listened to the cold, emotionless voice of the CIA station chief on the telephone.

"If you insist on quitting once you get out of quarantine, Owen, then so be it. But you're not going to leave that isolation facility until we make absolutely certain that you're not carrying some biological warfare agent. As for Kernan, we'll handle that situation as we see fit. It's not a matter for a member of Air Branch to be concerned with."

"God damn it, Ralph," Owen said, "at least you can tell me what you've heard from him since he got hit, can't you?"

"I'm sorry, Owen, but as I said, that's not a matter of concern for Air Branch."

"You son of a bitch! When I do get out of here, I'm…Hello? Hello!" The line had gone dead. The helicopter pilot slammed the telephone down on its cradle so hard that a piece of it broke off. He picked up the phone again and listened for the dial tone. It was completely dead.

"Good!" he muttered, then slammed it down again and turned to the Arab-American who had accompanied him on the flight to recover the goat carcass that his old friend Bill Kernan had risked his life to acquire.

"Gimme a cigarette, Majid," Owen said, running his hand through the stubble of graying hair atop his head. The other man tossed him a

pack of unfiltered Camels, then a Bic lighter. Kernan lit one of the cigarettes, inhaled deeply, coughed, and stubbed it out.

"Might as well sit down and relax, Claude," Majid said. "Looks as if
we're going to be here for quite awhile."

Owen looked out of the window of the small, two room trailer. A
man in a protective suit was filling the fuel tank of the generator which
provided power to the trailer. Beyond him, just outside the razor wire
which ringed the quarantine site, was another man—an armed guard,
also in full protective gear.

"Bill, old buddy," he mumbled toward the north, "they'd better be
taking care of you."

"It's bleeding again, damn it," Bill Kernan said as he lifted the bandage and looked at the torn skin on the inside of his thigh. It didn't hurt
much—not nearly as badly as the throbbing wound through the meat
of his shoulder did. But he couldn't get it to stop bleeding unless he
applied considerable pressure to the pressure point on the top, inside of
his thigh.

"It must have nicked an artery," he said.

Abdul put down the items he had taken from the pockets of the Iraqi
patrol members whom Owen had killed with the minigun of his helicopter. He walked over to Kernan and looked at the wound in the early
morning light. A small but steady stream of bright red blood trickled
from it.

"I should have kept the Bedouin and his camels here," Abdul said. As
they had planned, the Bedouin tribesman who had supplied the animals they rode to their mission the night before had taken his camels
and left as soon as Abdul and Bill returned to the hide site in the wadi.
Now, it would be around midnight before one of Abdul's resistance
force members returned to the wadi in the Cherokee to pick them up.
Abdul was beginning to worry that, with the amount of blood Kernan
was losing, he might not be able to make it that long.

"I'm going to burn it," the Kuwaiti said to his American comrade.

"What? Burn what?" Kernan asked.

"The wound," Abdul said. "I'm going to cauterize your wound before you bleed to death."

Kernan stared at him awhile, then said, "You've been watching too many cowboy and Indian movies, old buddy."

"No," Abdul replied, drawing out his knife. "Too many combat first aid videos, maybe. But that's what they say to do for bleeding wounds that won't stop when you keep pressure on the pressure point. You've lost a lot of blood already, Bill." Kernan was frighteningly pale.

Kernan knew he had lost a lot of blood, and although Abdul kept making him drink water, he was growing weak, passing into semi-consciousness from time to time. There was no sign of the rapid onset of illness in either of the men which they expected might occur from a biological warfare agent, but they still had no idea whether they might have been exposed to some insidious germ.

Kernan wished that he had brought the little satellite radio hidden inside two video cassettes, but he hadn't wanted to risk the loss of it in case he was captured.

Abdul was whittling shavings of wood from the stock of one of the rifles he had taken from the Iraqi patrol. When he had a small pile of shavings, he tore the paper from several cigarettes and used it to set the shavings afire, then propped the blade of the knife just above the flames.

"Let me examine the wound," he said, and the CIA operative removed the bandage from the inside of his thigh to let Abdul look at it.

"You sure this is a good idea?" Kernan asked, wincing from pain as Abdul spread the wound open in an attempt to see where the blood was coming from.

"Do you have a better one?" Abdul asked.

"Guess not," Kernan replied, thinking that, even if it didn't staunch the flow of blood, it would be of little additional harm.

"I think I see where it's coming from," the Kuwaiti said after his examination of the gunshot wound. He picked up the knife, and Kernan lay back and wadded up a corner of his robe to bite on.

"Make it quick," he said as Abdul leaned over him and spread the wound apart with the fingers of his left hand.

Abdul located the spot from which the blood was flowing, and quickly pressed the searing hot blade of the knife against it.

A wail of pain came from deep in Kernan's throat and his body stiffened. Abdul continued to press the hot blade hard against the wound, the smell of burning flesh causing a wave of nausea to wash through his guts. Then Kernan's body went limp. He had passed out from the pain and loss of blood. But Abdul saw, when he removed the knife, that the flow of blood had ceased. He cut a piece of cloth from Kernan's robe and fashioned a bandage from it, then used the captured rifles to prop his own robe over Kernan's face and chest to shield him from the rising sun.

Now there was nothing to do but wait until midnight, when one of his men would arrive at the hide site to take them back to Kuwait City.

Sergeants Schwarbacher and Torres, the westernmost element of Captain Jack Marsh's six-man reconnaisance and surveillance team, had moved their position to a spot from which they could observe all five of the Iraqi vehicles which had passed them earlier.

The three Scud missile carriers and the decontamination truck were parked side by side, and the crews had covered them with sand-colored camouflage netting. Now the men were gathering around the cargo truck, which was parked just off the side of the highway upwind of the other vehicles. Two of the Iraqi soldiers were erecting a small tent beside the truck. As the crewmen arrived at the tent, they removed their chemical protective suits and masks and placed them inside it. One of the men, the tallest of the lot, pulled off his mask to reveal a head of blonde hair. Al Schwarbacher noticed, and handed his binoculars to Jorge Torres.

"Look at that one," he said. "The tall one with the blonde hair."

Torres scanned the group of men with the binoculars and found him.

"That's no Iraqi, I'll tell you that," he said.

"I don't think so either," Al Schwarbacher agreed.

"Russian?"

"Could be," Al said. "According to the intel briefing, there's still a bunch of them here, in spite of what Gorby claims."

"Damn!" the Puerto Rican sergeant said. "I've always wanted to shoot a Russian."

"Why, Jorge," Al quipped, "that's mighty un-glasnostish of you. Anyway, I saw him first."

Anatoly Vasilnikov threw his protective gear inside the tent, then drew a Turkish cigarette from his shirt pocket and lighted it. He offered one to Hassan al Ahwabi, who took it and said, "Shukran, Anatoly. Praise God we don't have to wear those damn masks for awhile."

"If you pig pricks followed procedures the way we taught you, you wouldn't load the warheads until you were in firing position. I still don't see the purpose in dragging loaded missiles all over the country."

Hassan scowled at the Russian. But he had to agree this time. They had been moving from place to place with the nerve-agent-charged Al Husseini missiles for almost two months now—first to an airfield in Kuwait, where they were discovered by an enemy patrol, and since then, moving every few days from one site to another. At one location—a large warehouse in the oil field at Rumaylah, Kuwait—one of the warhead's seals had ruptured, and the eight crewmen in the warehouse at the time had been killed, along with a Bedouin family and their animals who had been passing a short distance downwind. Only by a stroke of luck were Hassan and Vasilnikov spared; they had been at a supply point picking up rations for the crewmen of the missile battery.

Still, the Iraqi soldier couldn't bring himself to voice agreement with the Russian mercenary.

"Well, now that the devil, Bush, has decided to bring more soldiers to occupy Saudi Arabia, war could break out at any time," Hassan declared. "Our missiles have to be immediately ready, because at the first hint of an attack, we'll rain them down on the Jews, and all true Arabs will see the chance to rid the world of them forever. And when that happens, the Islamic soldiers who have been sent to Saudi Arabia by their misguided leaders will turn on the Americans, and while they slaughter them, our forces and the Jordanians and Palestinians can drive the Zionists into the sea."

The Russian gave a scornful laugh and tossed his cigarette away. "The way you drove them into the sea in '56 and '67 and '73?"

"Things were different, then," Hassan replied. "That was before the time of Saddam Hussein." He threw his cigarette down. "You, of all people, should appreciate the power of Jihad, Vasilnikov, after what the true believers in Afghanistan did to your army."

The Russian glared at him a moment, then spat on the ground at the Arab's feet. "Go suck a camel's dick, Hassan," he said, and walked away.

In his surveillance position a quarter of a mile away, US Army Special Forces Captain Jack Marsh was on the radio with the USSOTAF operations officer, Colonel Dave Ames.

"If it's possible to get some good photos of any numerals or markings on the erector-launchers, and the missiles themselves, it would be a great, great help, Jack," Ames was saying. "Just make damned certain you don't get anybody compromised."

"We'll get the photos for you, Colonel," Marsh promised. "Meanwhile, keep pushing for permission for us to destroy the damned things. We'll get photos of the Russian or whatever the big, blonde guy is, too."

Marsh put the handset down. "All right, Shu," he said to Staff Sergeant Shumate, "I'm going to Schwarbacher's position. He and I will circle around behind the missiles and get some photos of them. I'll have Nicholas and Merletti move over here, too, to cover us, just in case."

"Bad idea, boss," the young staff sergeant said. Marsh gave him a quizzical look, and Shumate continued, "Schwarbacher and I should go. You need to stay here with the satcom and talk to headquarters. Anyway, I'm the smallest guy on the team—the easiest to hide."

Marsh thought about it a moment. It was true that, as the team leader, he should stay with the satellite radio. And since Schwarbacher was the second in command of the six man patrol, it would be improper for both of the patrol leaders to go.

"Yeah, I guess you're right," he said. "OK, Sergeant Shumate; it'll be you and Al. I'll get Merletti in here with me to man the video camera, and Nick can link up with Torres over there."

He picked up the intra-team radio handset to issue instructions to the other members of the team, just as Torres called to report that most of the Iraqi missile crewmen had loaded onto the cargo truck and headed east down the highway toward Rutba. It appeared that only four had remained behind, two of whom were lying in the shade beside the tent. The other two were seated on the ground nearby.

That was good news, for it made it that much more likely that Shumate and Schwarbacher could move around and get photos of the vehicle and missile markings without being discovered.

Marsh issued his orders, and half an hour later, Shumate and Schwarbacher departed the hide site to make a long, looping arc around to the far side of the camouflaged Scud missile carriers.

✶   ✶   ✶

It was noon by the time the US Special Operations Task Force commander, Major General Wayne Wilson, got to General Norman Schwarzkopf's Central Command Headquarters in Riyadh, Saudi Arabia. The commander of British Forces Middle East, Lieutenant General Sir Peter de la Bretaigne, was there also, as was the commander of the Arab coalition forces, Lieutenant General Khaled bin Sultan bin Abdulaziz al-Saud. In addition, there were the commanders and principal staff members of two major corps of the growing army; the XVIII Airborne Corps, and the newly arrived members of VII Corps, the most powerful armored corps ever being assembled for war. The French, Italian, and other Coalition forces were represented at the gathering, as well. It was a council of war which had one single purpose; to prepare to wreak havoc and destruction on the forces of Saddam Hussein.

The British commander saw Wilson enter the conference room and walked over to him.

"I just spoke to the Bear," he informed Wilson. "He wants to have a word with us before the planning conference begins."

Five minutes later, the Central Command commander-in-chief had the two Special Forces trained generals in his office.

"What's the latest from the team that spotted the chemical Scuds?" the portly, four-star general asked Wilson.

"They were moving into position to photograph the markings on them, at last report," Wilson said.

"So, we still don't know if these are the same ones that Sir Peter's men spotted in Kuwait a couple of months ago?"

"No, sir," Wilson replied. "We may not even know that with any certainty after we get the photographs."

"Well, I know we'd all like to take the doggone things out while we have them located," the Coalition commander said. "But the political situation just won't allow us to do it—not yet. This is still an awfully fragile coalition. And I'm also concerned that, if we start dealing with his chemical weapons piecemeal now, Saddam will launch them to try to expend what he's got before we get all of them. One Scud into Israel—especially one carrying a chemical warhead—and this whole thing could come apart."

De la Bretaigne nodded in agreement, and Wilson said, "I understand completely, general. I think, though, that we should do our best to try to maintain contact with them, and to have people in position to neutralize the things in case he does try to sling a few of them at Israel."

The general's brow furrowed in thought and he rubbed his chin, pondering Wilson's comment.

"Your boys have any sort of beacons or transponders they could try to attach to the missile carriers, to try to keep track of them?" His question was directed to both of the other men.

"I don't think they have any with them," Wilson answered. "But they damn sure will from now on."

"All right," the big man said, rising from his chair. "We'd better get this conference started." He headed for the door, then paused and looked at the others.

"Oh, one other thing—a bit of good news. The goat that the CIA got out of Rumaylah was killed by nerve agents."

"That's good news?" the British general said.

"Well, compared to the fact that we thought it might have been killed by anthrax or some other biological agent, it's good news."

"I see your point," Sir Peter responded as the three men left for the council of war.

Staff Sergeant Walter Shumate was soaked with perspiration as he crept slowly and cautiously toward the net-shrouded missile carriers. He was wearing full chemical agent protective gear—"MOPP four," as it was known in army parlance, for "Mission Oriented Protective Posture four," the highest level of chemical warfare readiness, which required the wearing of charcoal-impregnated overgarments, protective gloves and overboots, and mask with hood.

Sweat burned the young NCO's eyes, and his target, now just fifty meters away, appeared as a blur. He stopped a moment to rest, breathing with difficulty through the hot, sticky mask.

He had never felt so utterly alone in his life, even though he knew that Al Schwarbacher was watching him from a hundred meters away, his rifle at the ready in case any of the four Iraqi soldiers beside the tent at the far side of the target happened to move toward him. He was aware, too, that his other teammates were in a position to engage the enemy soldiers, if required. But he still felt totally and absolutely alone.

Shumate's own weapon was with Schwarbacher. After donning the protective gear and attempting to move with the radio, rifle and a plastic bag containing the camera and several other items, he had abandoned all but the bag. The mask and bulky rubber gloves made it impossible to operate his weapon or the radio efficiently anyway. It would be difficult enough to try to operate the camera.

He withdrew a canteen of water from the bag, plugged it into the drinking tube of his mask, and sucked in a couple of mouthfuls of the warm water.

He wondered if all the protective gear was a waste of time, anyway. If they could have seen the markings on the vehicles from a distance, it wouldn't have been necessary to wear it; he and Schwarbacher could have remained upwind and photographed them from a considerable distance away. But the camouflage netting made that impossible, so it was necessary for him to crawl all the way up to the weapons with their deadly warheads.

He thought, better safe than sorry, unhooked the canteen from his mask, and continued his low, slow crawl toward the Soviet built missile launchers, now anxious to just get there, take the photos, and get out of the area.

Jack Marsh was beginning to worry about the amount of time it was taking Shumate to take photographs of the markings on the Scud carriers and withdraw to safety. It had been twenty minutes since Schwarbacher reported that the young sergeant had disappeared beneath the camouflage netting which covered the vehicles. Marsh called the assistant patrol leader on the radio again.

"Any sign of him yet, Al?" he inquired.

"Nothing yet. I don't know what could be taking him so long. If he doesn't show soon, I'm going to move up there and see what the problem is."

Both men were beginning to worry that the heat-retaining chemical protective gear, combined with the strain of the mission, had caused Shumate to pass out. Or worse, that he had somehow been exposed to the agent in the missiles' warheads.

Also, they had no way of knowing how long the other enemy crewmen would be gone. If they were to return and move back onto their vehicles, Shumate would surely be discovered.

"He's coming out now!" Schwarbacher announced over the radio.

"Thank God," Marsh muttered. He would wait until Shumate had linked up with Schwarbacher to find out if he had gotten photographs of any markings before reporting to USSOTAF and arranging for a helicopter pickup of the film. Meanwhile, the team would continue to cover the unarmed sergeant as he made his way slowly away from the missiles, crawling backwards and using his gloved hands to brush away the marks his crawling made in the sandy desert floor.

At mid-afternoon, the cargo truck carrying Hassan al-Ahwabi, Anatoly Vasilnikov, and the other Scud missile battery crewmen returned to the area of the small tent where their four comrades had been waiting.

By then, Shumate and Schwarbacher were well on the way by a long, circuitous route back to the positions of their other teammates. They had already called to confirm the fact that the missiles and their launch vehicles did indeed bear various distinguishing markings and numerals on them, and that Staff Sergeant Shumate had photographed everything he thought was significant.

Jack Marsh had relayed those facts to USSOTAF headquarters, and arrangements were being made to send a helicopter in to pick up the film. In addition, Marsh had been told, the chopper would bring a number of small electronic beacons for his team to attach to the enemy vehicles, if possible, so that they could be tracked and, eventually, destroyed by airstrikes.

By late afternoon, though, it became apparent that Marsh and his team would not be able to get to the vehicles again to attach the beacons. As the sun fell near the horizon, the missile crewmen again donned their chemical protective gear, moved to the vehicles, and began removing and folding the camouflage nets. At sunset, just and Schwarbacher and Shumate finally arrived at the patrol base, the deadly enemy vehicles pulled onto the highway and headed west.

"Damn," Marsh said when Torres reported the vehicles' departure. "If they had just stayed here for another day, we could have gotten beacons on the things. Now we'll probably lose them again, unless they happen to stop somewhere that Wade and his half the team can get to them."

Shumate, guzzling a pint of water to ward off the dehydration he felt from spending much of the day in the hot chemical protective suit, looked at his team leader and said, "Beacons? What do you mean, sir?"

"They're sending some beacons in to us tonight when they come to pick up the film you took. We were supposed to try to attach them to the Scud carriers, so they could track them."

Schwarbacher and Shumate exchanged conspiratorial looks.

"Might as well tell him now, Walt," Al Schwarbacher said.

Marsh looked from one to the other. "Tell me what?"

"I put something on them better than beacons, sir," Shumate said. He took another swallow of water as Marsh gave him a questioning look, then said, "I attached soap dish charges on remote detonators to all three of them."

The Special Forces Captain glared at him, then at Schwarbacher. "You put soap dishes on the Scuds? Without even asking permission? What the hell's wrong with you, Shumate?"

The so-called soap dish charge is a small explosive charge so named because the ideal container for it is a plastic soap dish. In addition to plastic explosive, it contains a quantity of aluminum or magnesium shavings. When detonated against a fuel tank, the explosion bursts the tank and sends superheated shavings into the fuel, ensuring its instant ignition. Attached to a remotely activated detonator, such as the ones the discriminating mine system employed, the charges can be command detonated by a coded transmitter from anywhere within range of the transmitter.

"If I'd had the radio with me, I would have asked permission," Shumate said. "But I didn't. And once I got up under them, it seemed like too good an opportunity to pass up. So I put them up between the chassis and the fuel tank. If I screwed up, well, I'm sorry. But I thought we were going to war with these bastards."

Marsh's expression changed from one of anger to one of concern, and then to amusement. He put his hand on the young staff sergeant's shoulder and said, "Well, it's done now. And you're either a hero, or a damned fool—maybe both.

But you did what good American troops have always done—you showed initiative. I don't know how they're going to feel about it back in the rear, but I'm proud of you."

✶   ✶   ✶

The CIA physician who examined Claude Owen before he was released from the quarantine site found nothing wrong with him except higher blood pressure than the pilot's medical records indicated he normally had.

"Probably just because I'm pissed off," Owen said as he finished dressing.

"Pissed off?" the doctor asked as he signed the medical report. "I've just informed you that you haven't been exposed to biological or chemical agents, and you're pissed off?"

"Nothing to do with that," Owen replied. He looked at the physician a moment, then asked, "What do you know about Kernan's condition, Doc?"

"You know I'm not supposed to discuss other company employees, Claude. But I know he's your friend." He sighed, handed Owen a copy of the medical report he had just signed, and said, "The last we heard about Kernan was what you told me when you got back with the goat carcass—that you saw him go down, and that he said it was just a scratch. The station has been unable to make radio contact with him or anyone in the resistance who knows about his condition."

Claude Owen scowled, shaking his head as he looked at the CIA physician. "I told him I was coming back for him. And then you idiots..." He cut himself off there. "I didn't mean that, Doc. I know the quarantine was necessary. And I know it's not your fault that the station didn't send another chopper in after him. But, Jesus Christ, the Army has hundreds of medical evacuation birds over here now. And those guys would love nothing better than to go into Kuwait for a live pickup."

"I told Ralph that," the doctor said. "But by the time he got around to making the request to Central Command, it was daylight. They couldn't fly in there in daylight. We both know that."

He stood, walked to Owen, and put a hand on his shoulder. "Listen, Claude. There's probably no reason to worry about him anyway. We know the goat you brought back was killed by a nerve agent, not a biological bug. And it was a non-persistent agent, so unless he got exposed to some from a different source, he should be all right. I'm sure we'll hear from him, or from somebody in the resistance, soon. Meanwhile, you'd better get over to the ops room. They wanted to see you as soon as I cleared you—unless you were serious about wanting to quit flying for the Company."

Owen looked at the doctor and smirked. "You're OK, Doc," he said. "In fact, they should make you the chief of station of this damned place."

"Ha! And put up with whiners like you and wild men like that damned Kernan? Not for a million bucks!"

In the operations room, Owen learned that USSOTAF had requested the Central Intelligence Agency's assistance in delivering a small amount of equipment and picking up a roll of high value film from a Special Forces team in the western panhandle of Iraq. The little McDonnell Douglas Defender was much better suited to the clandestine mission than the military's much larger and louder Blackhawk and Pave Low helicopters.

Claude Owen was glad to oblige USSOTAF's request, except for one reason; it would deny him the opportunity to fly to the hide site in Kuwait where he figured Bill Kernan might still be. He had told his old friend that he'd back, and he had meant it. But the Special Forces mission was to be flown hundreds of miles from Kuwait, providing him no opportunity to try to find Kernan.

Thank God, he thought, that at least now we know he wasn't exposed to any biological agent. He only hoped that his old friend had been telling the truth after Owen saw him go down from an Iraqi bullet, when Kernan had declared that he wasn't badly wounded. Owen was glad that he had still been in the area when the patrol opened fire, and that he had been able to destroy them with his rapid-firing minigun. If only he'd seen them before they opened fire…

"If, if, if," he muttered as he went to the big air operations map on the wall of the Air Branch operations room.

Sometimes, he thought as he began to plan his flight to the Iraqi pan-handle, life seem to be nothing but a long string of goddamned "ifs."

At exactly 0210 hours, Owen saw a flashing light directly ahead of him through his night vision goggles. He flipped the goggles up momentarily to be certain that it was an infrared light—invisible without the aid of a night vision device—that he saw. With the naked eye, he saw nothing. He flipped the goggles down again and triggered his radio transmitter.

"Plato, this is Rosebud," Owen called.

Lew Merletti answered. "Rosebud, Plato. Winds calm, negative hostiles, clear to land." He and Atkinson had been at the remote landing zone for several hours. The barely audible sound of the approaching Defender was the only thing they had heard since arriving there.

"Plato, Rosebud. Roger," Owen replied as he homed in on the light. After one final check of the digital readout of the helicopter's Global Positioning System, he slowed the little aircraft, then settled gently and quietly down onto the light.

He looked to the left and saw a figure appearing out of the darkness almost immediately.

"Morning, sir!" Merletti said. He held a zip lock bag out to Owen. "This is the film. There's also a sheet of paper in there. Make sure the paper gets to Colonel Ames."

Claude unzipped the leg pocket of his flight suit and shoved the bag into it, then zipped it shut as he said, "Will do. One of the boxes in the back is marked 'Plato.' That's for you."

Merletti used his pen light to ensure that the box he unstrapped and removed from the back of the chopper was the correct one. The other box, he noticed, was marked "Plutarch"—the code name of the other half of Captain Marsh's team, temporarily under the command of Chief Warrant Officer Wade Herrington.

Rather than announce over the radio the fact that Shumate had concealed remotely activated explosive charges on the enemy Scud carriers, Marsh had decided that he would send that information straight to the USSOTAF operations officer, Colonel Dave Ames. The information would be more closely held if it went straight to Ames than if it was received by the radio operator at the base station, the watch officer on duty at the time, and God knows who else. Wiring enemy chemical weapons systems for destruction without permission—especially when it wasn't yet certain if there would actually be a war—was not the sort of thing one wished to be known by too many people.

Less than a minute after he had landed at Merletti's pickup zone several miles south of the patrol base, Claude Owen lifted the quiet little helicopter off the ground and turned west. He would deliver the other box of electronic beacons to Team Plutarch, then head for King Khalid Military City to deliver the film and the sheet of paper accompanying it.

▼

Twelve

13 November 1990

When the fog in his head dissipated enough for Bill Kernan to realize
that he was conscious, he had no idea where he was or what had happened. His hazy thoughts consisted only of surprise that he was still
alive, and awareness of a burning pain in his thigh.

The lights were too bright for his barely-opened eyes, so he closed
them and passed into unconsciousness again.

Mara had seen his eyes open, though only slightly and for a few seconds, but she went straight to Abir and Doctor Singh to tell them so.

Francesca Singh was Abir's latest recruit in the underground resistance force. Doctor Singh was the Spanish-born, American-educated
wife of an Indian oilfield engineer who had disappeared in the early
days of Iraq's occupation of Kuwait. She had been gone from Kuwait
when the Iraqis invaded, attending a pediatrics seminar in London. The
day after the invasion, she had reached her husband by telephone. He
assured her that he was safe, and that he had made arrangements to
leave Kuwait in a few days. That was the last she heard from him.

She waited in London for almost two months, until all efforts to contact him or learn of his fate had yielded nothing. Finally, traveling on
her Indian passport, she went to Jordan, volunteered her medical skills
to the Red Crescent in Iraq, and made her way to Basra. From there it
had been a simple bus ride to get into Kuwait City using her Red
Crescent credentials.

It took Francesca Singh a week to learn from a Kuwaiti friend she eventually encountered, that her husband had been picked up by the Mukhabarat and tortured to death after trying to arrange to have himself smuggled out to Saudi Arabia.

That same friend had informed Abir of Dr. Singh's presence and situation, and Abir had gone to her, told her that she was a member of the resistance whose home was being used as an underground hospital, and invited the physician to join her.

Dr. Singh thought about it for a few seconds, took a Red Crescent smock from her suitcase, and told Abir to pull it on over her robe. When Abir asked her why, Dr. Singh replied, "Because on the way to your house, we're going to go to the government hospital and steal some supplies."

Now the resistance force's new physician smiled at Abir and said, "See? He'll be fine. I told you there was nothing to worry about. Let's go check on him."

It had been obvious to her that Abir's interest in the American was more than just a friendly one, and when she had discovered that Abir's blood type matched Kernan's, she had made a direct transfusion from the sheik's wife to the CIA operative.

Abir had wept as she watched the flow of blood from her own arm into Kernan's, and Francesca Singh said, "Are you all right, Abir? Is anything wrong?"

"All right? Yes, I'm all right. For the first time since my younger child was born, I feel as if I'm doing something worthwhile."

Bill was still unconscious as Dr. Singh checked his vital signs, but the return of color to his skin made it obvious even to Abir that he was improving. Francesca smiled at her as she removed the stethescope from her ears then said, "Perhaps you'd better prepare him some food, Abir. He's going to be awfully hungry when the medicine wears off and he wakes up."

Abir smiled and reached over to stroke the stubble on Kernan's cheek, then left to get some food for him while Francesca checked the gunshot wounds in his shoulder and thigh. She had debrided both wounds, but had not yet sutured them, as she needed to be certain, first, that she had removed all of the dead tissue.

The shoulder wound looked clean. The wound in his thigh, cauterized by the blade of Abdul's knife, was messy. She would have to trim the muscle tissue again before she closed it, and it would leave an ugly scar. But at least, thanks to Abdul's knife and Abir's blood, he had survived.

"Wh-who are you?" she heard Kernan ask weakly as she closed the dressing on his thigh. She looked at his face and he asked, "Where am I?"

She raised his eyelids with her fingers to check his eyes as she replied, "I'm Doctor Francesca Singh. We're in Madame al-Sabah's home. Abdul brought you here. You have a couple of wounds. You nearly bled to death before he got you here, but you'll be fine now."

He stared blankly at the ceiling for a few moments before a look of near-panic came to his face and he said, "The goat. I was exposed to a germ warfare, uh…"

He couldn't think of the correct terminology, but Dr. Singh said, "Abdul explained about the goat you recovered. But we haven't seen any of the symptoms one would expect from a biological warfare agent such as anthrax or bubonic plague or botulism."

He looked at her with dull eyes, the look of panic gone from them. "Thirsty," he mumbled. "Can I have some water?"

"Of course," she said, pouring some from a plastic bottle. "Drink all you can. And let me know if you can urinate. If not, I'll have to put in a catheter."

As Kernan sipped from the glass, she said, "Abdul said that, as soon as you feel up to it, you need to radio your headquarters. They will know for certain whether or not the goat was contaminated."

He nodded. He was weak, but his brain was clearing now, and he remembered Abdul's knife searing the wounded flesh of his thigh. He reached down and touched the bandage.

"Is this thing going to heal, Doctor…what did you say your name is?"

"Singh. But just call me Francesca. Yes, it'll heal. It's going to take a while, though."

He tried to prop himself up on his elbows, but the wound to his left shoulder prevented it.

"How long have I been out?"

Singh looked at her watch. "Twenty-six hours, more or less," she replied. "Loss of blood was your biggest problem. You're fortunate that Abdul decided to cauterize the wound. You're also lucky that Abir's blood type matches yours. I suppose I transfused about a liter of it to you."

There was a wail from somewhere nearby, and Singh saw Kernan's eyes open widely.

"Nothing to worry about," she said, smiling. "Another of our patients. Mrs. Kawash is about to have a baby. How's your appetite?"

"I could eat a horse," he said. "Or maybe a goat, anyway."

She smiled. "I'd have thought you'd had enough to do with goats for awhile." She checked the bag of fluids dripping through a tube into his arm, then handed him a bedpan.

"See if you can get some of that fluid running all the way through you, and we'll let you have something to eat. Now, I'd better go get this new baby off to a good start."

He smiled weakly. "Life goes on, in spite of all this mess we humans cause, doesn't it?"

"Yes," she said, thinking of her husband, tortured to death not far from where she was about to deliver another woman's child. "Somehow, life goes on."

She left, and Bill Kernan lay staring at the ceiling, his mind racing with thoughts about life and people and death and near-death.

He had nearly died this time. But so what? Who would miss him? His former wife was the closest thing to family that he had, but the bitter fight that two greedy lawyers had caused over the division of half a lifetime of accumulated savings and material possessions had turned a fairly amicable separation into a bitter divorce. He wondered if, had he been killed, her lawyer would get any of the life insurance money she would collect. Those thoughts disturbed him, so he turned his mind to the handful of real friends he had. Had it not been for one of them, Claude Owen, he would be dead now. He wondered why Claude hadn't returned to the hide site, and hoped it wasn't because something had happened to him on the flight out of Kuwait, or back in. He'd have to get someone to get his radio so he could check in with his headquarters.

He was fortunate, too, he realized, that Abir's blood matched his. Without it, he might well have died anyway. He looked at he needle in his arm, through which other life-sustaining liquids were now running. Abir's blood. He would have to remember to thank her.

Perhaps he should get the agency to evacuate him to a hospital in Saudi Arabia, he thought now. Not only would they be able to provide better care, enabling him to heal more quickly, but it would be less of a strain on the staff of the little underground hospital, and their limited supplies. But what would that say about his confidence in the resistance? And whom would the agency send in to replace him?

He thought long and hard about these things, his mental debate centering on two things: his own self-interest, and his role in the resistance effort alongside men and women whom he had grown to respect and admire, against the brutal occupation of Kuwait by Saddam Hussein and his thugs.

"You've done enough," one part of him said. "You've pushed your luck to the limit. You've nearly died, and you're bedridden, and you need to get away and heal your wounds and think about whether this is all worth it."

And then he thought about the things that had happened since his arrival in occupied Kuwait three months earlier.

He thought about Abdul, alive only because of Kernan's skill with his whispering rifle. Abdul. What was it he had said about freedom? About democracy? About dragging Kuwait into the Twentieth Century? About the women of Kuwait?

He remembered the horrible scene he had discovered when he first arrived in this villa, and the remarkable calmness and continued courage of the women whose brutal assault by Iraqi soldiers he had ended with equal brutality.

Abir and Mara and Sanaa. And now this Doctor Singh. She was obviously not Kuwaiti, and he wondered how she had come to be in the resistance.

Nearby, the sacred agony of a woman in childbirth gave way to the wail of a newborn infant, and Bill Kernan listened for awhile. Was it a boy or a girl, he wondered. It made such a difference in this part of the world.

His thoughts turned to Abir, her own children gone from her. Why had she stayed? Was it because of him, or because of the higher things Abdul had spoken of, or a combination of both? Abir. What had she done that caused him to push her away? Was it other things that had made him shy away from her? Professionalism—that was the excuse he had used for rejecting her. He was there to work for the interests of the United States government, of a free Kuwait. Professionalism? What the hell did that mean?

He recalled the scene in his little attic hideaway when she had brought a bottle of scotch, when she had wanted him to make love to her. What had he said? Something about things going back to the way they used to be.

She had replied that they never would; that they might be killed at any time. She had spoken from the heart, and he had replied with some drivel that sounded like a politician. He wasn't a politician. Politics. Professionalism. People.

People. That's what really matters. Good guys versus bad guys. People making sacrifices for something other than their own self gratification. People wanting the freedom to make their own choices, to change their minds, if it seemed a better thing to do. People trying to make things better for other people. And, yes, for themselves, too, when it didn't cause the oppression of others.

He heard the newborn child's wail again, and wondered if he would ever have a child of his own. He had been involved in so much death; justified death, he believed, but always death. Bad guys killed by good guys, but always death, nevertheless. And nothing to offset it.

He was so tired, so empty, so alone.

He closed his eyes, and listened to the baby cry. Tears spilled out from beneath his eyelids, and he let his pain and exhaustion take him away from consciousness once more.

✶   ✶   ✶

Colonel Dave Ames sat at his desk in the U.S. Special Operations Task Force headquarters and read the note from Captain Marsh again:

Sir,

Enclosed is the film of the markings

on the three Scud missile carriers we

reported. During the course of taking

the photos, we seized on the opportunity

to doctor the vehicles with M-122 remote

firing device detonators and "soap dish"

explosive incendiary charges. I realize

this goes beyond the limits of our

assigned reconnaisance and surveillance

mission, but I fully support the initiative

of the NCO who, being without a radio to

ask permission to do so, seized on the
opportunity to hide the devices on the
enemy weapons systems so that, in the
event hostilities commence, they can be
remotely destroyed. The code numbers of
the firing devices are on the enclosed
sketch which shows exactly where on the
vehicles they are attached.
I felt that, under the circumstances,
it would be best to inform you directly
of this action. As our Brit buddies
would say, "Who dares wins."

Marsh

Captain, SF, USA

Commander, RT Plato

The sketch showed that the devices had been attached up under the fuel tanks of the carriers, where a close inspection of the vehicle would be required to discover them. Also on the sketch were the code numbers of the remote firing devices. Ames knew from his own Special Forces demolition training that the M-122 transmitter sent a coded radio signal which, when received by the detonator on the proper frequency in the correct sequence, would cause the detonator to send an electrical impulse to the blasting cap inserted in the explosive charge. Because each receiver had its own specific coded signal, it was necessary to punch a particular code into the transmitter to cause it to fire a certain receiver.

The problem was that the transmitter had a range of only a few kilometers. If the receiver was out of range, it would fail to receive the signal telling it to detonate.

For the moment, though, that was a moot point. Not only were the Scuds in all probability out of range of Marsh's transmitter, but unless the decision was made to commence hostilities, it was unlikely that an attempt to destroy them would be made.

"Well," Ames mumbled to himself as he got up from his desk, "at least they're out there trying."

The thermal imaging system of Lieutenant Larry Redmond's M1A1 Abrams main battle tank picked up the other tank from two miles away, and Redmond's gunner reacted with practiced speed, engaging the distant vehicle before its crew was even aware of their presence.

"Driver, halt," Redmond ordered over the intercom. The big war machine lurched to a stop, and Redmond swung open the hatch of the commander's cupola, lifted his seat until his chest was level with the top of the turret, and raised his binoculars to his eyes. He saw another Abrams tank on the desert horizon.

"Damn it," he muttered to himself, then over the intercom said to his gunner, "You just killed another friendly, Pete."

Redmond's company commander, following the platoon as they ran through the movement-to-contact exercise, saw what had occurred and made it known over the secure voice radio.

"Charlie One Six, this is Charlie Six. Isn't that a another friendly you just engaged?"

"One Six," Redmond answered. "Affirmative." It was the third time that day that one of his platoon's gunners had simulated the engagement of a tank which turned out to be a friendly one. They had been conducting offensive maneuvers all day, racing through an area dotted with formations of American, British, French and Soviet-made armored vehicles, the latter belonging to units of the Syrian and Egyptian armies. The intent was to give the crews the opportunity to practice identifying the kinds of vehicles they might encounter in a war to expel the Iraqi army from Kuwait, while at the same time practicing offensive maneuvers.

Now the company commander's tank pulled up beside Redmond's, and the captain yelled across to his subordinate above the whine of the tanks' turbine engines, "What the hell's the problem, Lieutenant Redmond?"

Redmond knew the other platoons of the company and the other companies of the task force had been encountering the same problem all day. He pulled off his combat vehicle crewman's helmet, climbed out of the turret, and met the captain on the ground between their tanks.

"Damn, Larry," the captain said, "what is the problem? I thought your crews, above all others, wouldn't be having problems like this."

Redmond took it as the offhand compliment it was meant to be. Both men knew that Larry had drilled his crews harder than the other platoons in vehicle recognition, and the captain had said before the exercise even began that he expected Redmond's training to manifest itself in the best platoon score of the day.

"Well, there seem to be two problems, sir," Redmond said, accepting the bottle of Evian water the captain held out to him. "The first is that the thermal imaging system is just too damn good. I mean, the TIS isn't really a problem, but it's picking up the other vehicles long before we can recognize what the hell they are."

The men subconsciously glanced at the turret of the high-tech tank, where the lenses of the thermal imaging system clustered above the tube of the main gun.

"The other problem—the real problem—is this idea that, in order to win, we have to kill Iraqis from the full range of the gun."

The company commander looked down and stirred the sand of the desert with the toe of his boot, then looked at Redmond.

"What are you trying to say, Larry?" he asked.

"I'm trying to say that it's bad doctrine, sir. We're going to have these troops shooting at anything they can see as soon as it gets in range. Hell, sir, I've never been in combat, but I've read enough, and I've been on enough exercises to know that confusion reigns when you start trying to maneuver a company, much less a couple of corps. Nobody's sure of where anybody is—where they are, for that matter. If you tell people to start shooting as soon as they see something, instead of as soon as they are sure it's an enemy—well, you're going to have friendlies shooting friendlies."

Redmond watched his commander stir sand with his toe again, then continued. "I guess what I'm trying to say, sir, is that, instead of saying we should kill the enemy at max range, we should say 'as soon as you're sure the target is an enemy, kill it.'"

The company commander nodded, thinking. He had learned, as had other superiors in Redmond's chain of command, that the young armor officer seemed to have a sixth sense about war fighting.

He scratched his head, looked at Redmond, and said, "You've got a point, Larry. But you've forgotten about GPS. With GPS, everybody knows where they are all the time. And even if there are a few casualties from friendly fire, that's to be expected in fast moving tank warfare. Compared to the number of casualties we'd take if we hesitated—if we sat there and waited until we were sure the target in front of us was the enemy—they won't amount to much."

"Unless you happen to be the one hit," the lieutenant said. "Then it'll amount to a whole hell of a lot. I mean, we have GPS. But who pays any attention to it when you're hauling ass toward an objective at forty miles an hour?"

He, too, stirred the sand with his boot. It was a real problem, as evidenced once more by the Abrams tank which Sergeant Peterson had just "killed." The superior sighting system and range of the Abrams gave the Americans a great advantage over the Soviet built T-72 and older tanks. They could shoot the enemy tanks before they ever came into range of the enemy tank guns, and it made perfectly good sense to use that advantage. But would it work? Would it turn an attack which needed to be one characterized by speed, shock and firepower, into a cautious, slow creep forward? If so, the advantage of a superior tank would be offset by giving the enemy time to bring other weapons—conventional or chemical artillery, or airstrikes—to bear on the Coalition formations. And it would give him time to maneuver; to discern where the main Coalition efforts were, to mass and counterattack at critical points.

This wasn't going to be any cakewalk, even though the Coalition could be expected to quickly gain air superiority. The standard doctrine of modern warfare dictated that one should enjoy a three-to-one advantage in numbers over the enemy to ensure a successful attack, yet the Iraqi army had more tanks than the Americans facing them. The Abrams was, of course, a much better tank than the ones it would face, and with superior air support, the Coalition had another great advantage over their enemy. But the enemy was dug in, protected by mines and anti-tank ditches, and his artillery pieces had a greater range than those of the Coalition. He had chemical weapons, which would require his enemy to attack "buttoned up," with all his hatches closed to protect him from those weapons.

It was going to be the biggest tank battle in history, if Saddam Hussein knew how to fight.

Both of the young American Armor officers knew it was going to be tough, and they looked around at the dozen-and-a-half tanks of their company. They would be responsible for them and, more important, for the crews in them.

"Jesus," the captain said. "I sure hope we get assigned the flanking attack."

His platoon leader looked at him. "Everybody wants the flank, sir."

That was generally true. It was almost certain that the Coalition assault would involve the maneuver the greatest tanker of all time, General George S. Patton, had so succinctly described when he said, "We're going to hold 'em by the nose, and kick 'em in the ass!"

Now Larry Redmond echoed his mentor spirit. "Well, somebody's gotta hold 'em by the nose while somebody else kicks 'em in the ass. And Seventh Corps has the biggest boot."

There was no doubt of that. The American Seventh Corps, still pouring in from Germany, was the most powerful armored corps ever assembled on earth. The speculation among the young officers of the US Army maneuver battalions was that VII Corps would do the ass kicking, while the lighter XVIII Airborne Corps' only mechanized division, the 24th Infantry Division to which Redmond and his captain were assigned, would be used—probably with a Marine division—for the nose holding. XVIII Corps' other divisions; the 101st, with its helicopter-borne troopers, and the 82d Airborne's paratroopers, were expected to be used to strike quickly in the enemy's rear areas to seize critical installations and terrain, such as the bridges over the Euphrates River.

The captain nodded his agreement with Redmond's belief that VII Corps would be the main flanking force. But he hoped to join them, and he said, "Maybe the Marines and the Brits and other allies will be used to fix them, and we can be used as VII Corps' reserve. Or maybe there won't even be a war."

Redmond stared at his company commander with narrowed eyes. It was sounding more each day as if he didn't want to fight. To Redmond, that was a dangerous, contagious attitude which could detract from preparation for the great battle he felt was certain to come.

"Oh, there'll be a war, sir," he said. "I just hope we get to lead the attack—whether it's into the Iraqi's teeth, or up his nasty ass. But when the time comes, I'm not going to take the chance of killing my buddies by shooting at things as soon as I see them. I'm going to take my tanks in where I can be sure who I'm killing. And I'm going to send every Iraqi son of as bitch I see to Allah-land."

With that he saluted, slapped his captain on the back, and climbed atop his big tank.

*   *   *

Although his mind had drifted into drug-assisted unconsciousness, the tears on Bill Kernan's cheeks had not yet dried when Abir walked in and looked at him.

She stood at the door of the room a moment, her hands holding a tray of bean soup and pita bread, her dark, sad eyes surveying him.

His breathing was strong and regular now, his bare chest rising and falling in a slow rhythm. The arm into which her own blood had flowed some hours earlier still held the needle Dr. Singh had inserted, now taking other life sustaining fluids into him.

And then she saw his tears. She knew somehow that they were not from the pain of his gunshot wounds. What, then?

She put the tray on a table near the door and went to his side. She used a gauze pad to wipe his cheeks, then leaned down and lightly kissed his forehead. When she raised her head, his eyes were open, studying her face.

His hand raised slowly to hers, and he took it and drew it to his mouth.

His lips parted in a weak smile. "Hi," he said softly.

"Hi," was all she could think to say in reply before she leaned her face to his again and kissed him lightly on the mouth. Tears fell from her eyes onto his cheek when his hand moved to her hair to hold her there. She withdrew her face from his and wiped her tears.

He took her hand and said, "I was thinking, a little while ago, that if I had died, I'd never have seen you again.

I didn't know, 'till then, how much that meant. I'm such…"

His voice trailed away, and she said, "We'll talk later.
I've brought you something to eat."

She pulled a chair beside his bed and brought the food to him. He devoured the soup in silence, then munched on the bread as she watched.

"Do you want something to drink?" she asked.

He looked at her, and she saw his eyes twinkle and his lips curl in a mischievous smile.

"Still got that bottle of scotch?" Bill Kernan asked.

*   *   *

The general plan was laid now, and as Wayne Wilson rode toward the airbase outside Riyadh where his helicopter waited, he was as confident as any of the general officers who had taken part in the council of war. The Coalition would prevail if it became necessary to drive the Iraqis out of Kuwait.

The President of the United States had made it plain that only the decision of whether or not to use force would be left to him and his partners in the Coalition. If force were to be used, it would be left to General Schwarzkopf and his subordinate officers and their Coalition counterparts as to how it was done. He had also made it plain that the objective of driving Saddam's forces out of Kuwait did in no way exclude Iraqi territory and neighboring waters and airspace from being used to accomplish that mission.

Wilson thought back to his first war, Vietnam, and the ridiculous restrictions which gave the enemy the unchallenged use of sanctuaries in neighboring countries during most of that war. There would be no such restrictions this time.

It was an elegant plan based on the tried and tested principles of modern warfare, with a few twists to exploit the technical superiority of Coalition weapons systems.

Air superiority would be gained and maintained to deny the enemy use of the skies for either weapons delivery or reconnaissance, and to enable the Coalition to destroy or disrupt Iraq's command, control and communications links.

Once the allies had free reign of the air, supply lines would be cut to strangle enemy forces, and precision air attacks would concentrate on the methodical destruction of Saddam Hussein's war fighting machinery and weapons production capabilities—particularly those facilities at which he was developing and producing weapons of mass destruction. Earth trembling, terrifying attacks by formations of B-52 heavy bombers, each capable of dropping twenty tons of bombs, would be used to destroy and demoralize the vaunted Republican Guards divisions, and to obliterate concentrations of enemy supplies and equipment.

An aggressive psychological operations campaign would target the conscripts manning the enemy's forward defenses to encourage them to surrender or desert, and to draw defectors to Coalition territory for intelligence exploitation purposes.

A major effort would be mounted to deceive Saddam and his generals into believing that the ground offensive was to consist of a massive amphibious assault from the Persian Gulf combined with a frontal assault into Kuwait.

When General Schwarzkopf was satisfied that the air attacks had blinded and deafened Iraq's intelligence collection and communications capabilities to an adequate degree, and had crippled his ability to maneuver large formations, the real ground assault plan would be put into place. It would be the most massive and rapid move of an army in the history of warfare, with the equivalent of three corps of troops, tanks, personnel carriers, helicopters, and other equipment—including supplies and ammunition to support them for a period of months—moving hundreds of miles across open terrain in the face of the enemy.

While two divisions of US Marines, the US Army's 1st Cavalry and 2nd Armored divisions, and an Arab force of several divisions would mount an assault directly into Kuwait, the huge formation to the west would strike deep into Iraq and then turn east—a massive left hook of a knockout punch directed against Saddam Hussein's Republican Guards divisions.

There was no question that the assault would be successful. The only question was what the cost would be.

Much of the answer to that, Major General Wayne Wilson knew, would depend upon the success of the secret operations conducted by the United States Special Operations Task Force, some of which were already underway.

It had been difficult to convince the CENTCOM commander and staff of the great value special operations forces could be to the success of the operation, if they were given adequate time in the enemy's back yard. But thanks to the success of the few minor operations they had been allowed to conduct so far, and to the persuasiveness of General Sir Peter de la Bretaigne and himself, the argument for aggressive, pre-assault special operations had prevailed.

Wilson had his orders, now. He knew his mission, and how critical his task force's operations would be to the early success of the increasingly likely war.

One thing above all else made Wayne Wilson supremely confident that the covert phase of the operation would be successful; the fact that he had the best men on the planet to prepare the way for success in the gathering desert storm.

▼

Thirteen

23 December 1990

"I just can't believe he'll really stay in Kuwait, Jack," Barbara Marsh said to her husband. "Not when the United Nations have finally agreed on something and authorized the use of force to get him out."

Jack stared for a moment at the glass of beer in his hand, then looked at her.

"I hope you're right, hon," he said. He took the last swallow of beer from his glass, then poured the rest of the bottle into it. "But even if he does, he's going to have to be dealt with sooner or later. He's a madman—a madman with an arsenal of chemical weapons and maybe even nuclear and biological ones."

"Well, thank God we've at least had enough time to train everybody on treating chemical casualties," the Army Nurse Corps lieutenant replied. "If we'd had to start right in, it would have been terrible. We'd only given chemical training lip service before we got over here."

Jack watched her stir the glass of Campari and soda, thinking as he did of the chemical-tipped Scud missiles he had seen six weeks earlier. His team had remained in their surveillance positions overlooking the Amman-Baghdad highway for more than two weeks before they were replaced by another Special Forces team. They had monitored the road, awaiting the authority to employ their discriminating mines the entire time, and had counted more than twenty Scuds moving west—

although the three that Sergeant Shumate had photographed were the only ones which appeared to have chemical warheads.

He shook his head now, still unable to understand why there had been no effort to detonate the remote firing devices Shumate had placed on them and destroy the chemical Scuds.

Barbara reached her hand to his. "What's wrong, Jack?" she asked.

He looked at her and forced a smile. "Oh, nothing," he said. He hadn't told her about the missiles, or even about the mission into Iraq. He had led her to believe that he had been in Saudi Arabia training Kuwaiti refugee recruits the four months since they had seen each other.

He stood and took her by the hand. "Well, whether it comes to a war or not, I'll be damned if we're going to waste the chance Uncle Sam has given us to spend some time together. Let's go play doctor and nurse some more."

When Jack Marsh's battalion commander had learned that Barbara volunteered for duty in the Persian Gulf and was now at a field hospital in Saudi Arabia, he called her commander and arranged to have her released for a few days of R & R—rest and recuperation—pointing out that he knew Lieutenant Marsh had only recently arrived, but that her husband had been in theater for months. The hospital commander was glad to comply.

Jack Marsh was at first reluctant to go without the remainder of his team having the opportunity to do so, but then he recalled the awful vision he'd had of his wife under attack by chemical weapons, and decided to take whatever opportunity he could get to see her.

They were now at a luxury hotel in Manama, Bahrain. US Central Command had taken over most of the hotel to give American servicemen a place to get away from the harsh desert for awhile. Here, they could get alcoholic beverages, and the women could wear bathing suits—the reason, many said, that the causeway between the little island emirate and the Saudi Kingdom had been built.

Most of the rooms not taken over by Central Command were used by the large number of European prostitutes who had rushed to Bahrain when they learned it was to be used as an R&R center for American servicemen.

Staff Sergeant Michelle Myers was at the hotel also, on R&R from her duties as a radio intercept operator.

She watched two of the hookers walk past in string bikinis and heard a low whistle from one of the three American men at the table near her. She knew the whistle was directed at the prostitutes, and she was suddenly self-conscious of her dry-skinned arms and legs and cracked lips.

Michelle was a classic, natural beauty, and it was a rare thing for her to feel anything but self-confidence about her appearance. When she did have any such concern, it was usually because she'd put on a few more pounds than she wanted, but that was not a problem this time—Army field rations had made certain of that. This time it was the effects of the Arabian sun and the terribly dry air.

She was lounging around the pool, trying to even out the farmer's tan on her arms and neck which she had acquired during the previous two months in the desert.

She couldn't help overhearing the conversation of the men at the nearby table—three young Army officers, she had determined by their earlier discussion.

"Why couldn't they have this war before AIDS came along?" one of them said as they watched the prostitutes sway past, obviously trolling for business.

The other two chuckled, and one of them said, "Well, I'll take an all-American girl any day—like that pretty little thing lying right beside us."

Michelle smiled to herself. Maybe, she thought, I don't look so bad after all. She rolled over onto her back, glancing briefly at the three.

One of them, the best looking of the three, said to the others, "Probably an enlisted soldier, gents. Better find a donut dolly or something."

Arrogant bastard, she thought. There was no longer any prohibition against single officers and enlisted soldiers meeting socially, unless they were in the same unit, or the officer was in a position to influence the soldier's duties, although many officers sensibly avoided fraternizing with soldiers of the opposite sex. After several years of such permissiveness, there had been too many cases of "date rape" accusations and other complications.

Michelle had been involved in one such incident herself, with a major who had claimed to be single. When she found out he was in fact married, she hadn't reported him; she had gone to him and said, "Sir, if you ever speak to me again, or I hear of you approaching any other female soldier, I'll have your balls cut off…sir!"

She wondered if the one at the table beside her—the arrogant one who had just warned the others to avoid her—was married, or just being sensible. Or maybe he's gay, she thought. He's certainly pretty enough.

Then one of the others said, "How do you know, Larry? Maybe she's an officer?"

"Yeah," the third one said. "The one you've been searching for, to—how do you put it? —'create more warriors'?"

The one named Larry laughed. "Procreation of the warrior," he said. "The sole military duty of women should be procreation of the warrior breed."

Michelle glanced at the three young officers and said loudly, "Oink, oink!"

Larry looked sheepishly at her, a blush visible beneath the deep tan of his face. "Sorry, miss," he mumbled.

"'Mizz,' to you," she replied snidely, then rose and hopped into the pool as his friends laughed at Larry's embarrassment.

When she returned to her lounge chair, the three officers ignored her. They were involved in a discussion about the increasing probability of a war to expel Saddam Hussein's forces from Kuwait. Unlike the generals above them, the young warriors had not been made privy, for reasons of security, to General Schwarzkopf's plan for the destruction of the Iraqi army. Their discussion was based on their speculation of what the plan would entail.

"Aw, come on, Redmond," one of them was saying to Larry, "there's no way you could out flank 'em with enough forces to get in their rear—not armored forces, anyway—unless you're ready to sacrifice more troops than the folks at home would stand for. All they'd need to do would be fix you with chemical artillery and counterattack with those Republican Guards divisions he's holding back for just that reason! Maybe you could drop the 82nd Airborne behind 'em, and airmobile the 101st in, but they're so light that those damned T-72s would tear them apart!"

"You're overestimating the bastards," Redmond argued. "Forget those worthless outfits in the front. All they amount to is a human minefield…"

"Oh, sure!" the other said. "A human minefield with trenches of oil and anti-tank ditches and a bizillion damned anti-tank mines, and more friggin' artillery backing them up than…"

"That's just what I'm saying," Redmond interrupted. "Leave 'em alone! Give them a few feints with the Saudis and Egyptians or somebody, and take the American forces around the flank, cut 'em off, then kick the shit out of the Republican Guards…"

"Easy to say," one of the others remarked.

"Easy?" Redmond replied. "Who the hell said war was easy? You want easy, why don't you get out and go become a stockbroker or something? Look, we have the best damned air force on the planet. You think Stormin' Norman's going to have them sit on their asses? No! He's going to take a few days to gain air supremacy, then bomb the sons of bitches halfway to hell. By the time they pick up the pieces and try to get reorganized, we'll be kicking their butts on the banks of the Euphrates. Come on, guys! You don't seriously think they can hold out for long against our troops, do you?"

·

"Not if we're willing sacrifice enough of them," one of the others said sorrowfully.

"Well, that's not our job to determine," said Larry. "Our job is to make damned sure they, and their equipment, and our own minds are ready to move so fast and hit so hard and accurately, and so goddamned relentlessly, that we'll be in Baghdad before that camel-screwing son of a bitch can say 'Messopotamia'!"

"Baghdad? I thought the mission was to take Kuwait back?"

"Baghdad's where the snake's head is. The troops in Kuwait are nothing but the rattle. You don't kill the snake by cutting off his rattle, you kill it by cutting off his fucking head."

Redmond heard a single pair of hands applauding nearby. He turned to see Michelle looking at him, clapping her hands together.

"Well said," she remarked, smiling.

His look of irritation with his comrades changed to an appreciative smile.

"We'll see...How's the water?" he asked.

"Wonderfully wet," she answered, and watched him rise, walk to the pool, and dive in.

You may be an arrogant bastard, she thought, but you sure are a good looking one.

Michelle appreciated Larry's apparent attitude about soldiering, if not about women. She'd heard far too much whining and wanting to go home and unwillingness to take risks from members of her own unit since they'd arrived in Saudi Arabia. What the hell had they expected when they joined the Army? It was good to hear somebody say that their job was to prepare to go to war and win, instead of second-guessing every decision the President and their other leaders made. She wondered what Redmond's job was, though. Talk was cheap from those far to the rear of the battlefield. She sat up and faced the two men he had left at the nearby table.

"So, what job does young Patton there hold down?" she inquired.

They both laughed, and one of the officers answered, "We're all tank platoon leaders in the 5th of the 64th Armor, Victory Division. And you're right; he does think he's George Patton reincarnate!"

"What about you, miss?" the other one asked. "What are you doing in the Big Sandpile?"

"Oh, I'm uh, I'm with the Red Cross. A donut dolly."

"Yeah? Down here, or up north?"

"Well, just up north. In Dhahran," she lied. "My name is Mickey, by the way."

"Pleased to meet you, Mickey," one of the lieutenants said. "I'm Jim—Jim Locher. And this is Joe Cincotti."

She shook hands with the two lieutenants, and Jim thumbed toward Redmond and said, "The big, ugly one there is Larry Redmond."

She glanced over and watched him swimming powerfully across the pool, then looked at Locher. "He seems to think there's going to be a fight after all, it sounds like."

"Yeah. He's itching for one. But I don't know. It'll be one hell of a bloody mess, if it does come to that."

"Well," Michelle replied, "I know this is easy to say when you're just a support...a donut dolly. But sooner or later Saddam's going to have to be dealt with, and if its not now, when?"

"Ha!" Locher commented. "When the Israelis feel threatened enough, they'll solve that problem."

"As long as they wait 'till we're out of here, that's fine," Cincotti said. "But if they stick their noses in now, we'll be fighting ragheads from every direction."

"Good," Redmond's voice said from behind them. The others turned to see him wiping his broad chest with a towel. "That's more targets for all of us. But I wouldn't worry about the Israelis doing anything foolish. They've only got one friend, and in spite of what they might claim, they'd have been wiped out in '73 if it hadn't been for Uncle Sam's TOWs and tanks and air weapons. Damn near went under anyway.

Uncle Sam's logistical help is all that kept them from going under, if you ask me."

He was, like his idol George Patton, a student of logistics now, as well as tactics, terrain and troops. That was one of the reasons that he had recently seemed to better his peers—and many of his superiors—on the field evaluations and training exercises the division was almost constantly engaging in since their arrival in theater. He finally had developed as high a regard for beans as he had for bullets.

Cincotti introduced him to Michelle as "Mickey, donut doll from Dhahran."

Redmond blushed again, remembering his earlier comment about finding a donut dolly.

He shook her hand strongly. "Pleased to meet you, Mickey."

"No, it's my pleasure," she said, her hand still in his. "I admire your attitude. It's guys like you who are going to get the job done, so we can all go home."

The blush on his untanned forehead appeared again, but a twinkle came into his eyes. "By way of Baghdad, I hope."

"By way of Saddam Hussein's headquarters, if you're lucky, huh?" she remarked, grinning at him. His hand squeezed hers a bit more tightly as he chuckled.

"I admire your attitude," he said.

She suddenly found herself wondering what kind of lover he would be, or if he'd ever even made love. Probably a New York bimbo on a weekend leave from West Point, at least, she thought.

"West Point?" Michelle inquired.

"The Citadel," he said. "They don't..." He'd started to say, "They don't let women in there like they do at West Point," but changed it to, "They don't have as many distractions at the Citadel."

"You mean, they don't have women."

"Yes. I mean they don't have women."

Then the bimbo would have been from Charleston, she decided. She looked at him with raised eyebrows and said softly, "No women, no warriors for the next war." She stretched her arms up and back, and her ample breasts strained at the thin fabric of her one-piece bathing suit. His eyes moved involuntarily to her chest, and she said, "It is hot," then rose and walked to the pool, hiking the high-cut hips of her bathing suit even higher and gliding slowly to the pool with an exaggerated sway.

He watched her. Her uneven tan did little to detract from her shapely hips, firm buttocks, and well-turned legs. As she hopped in, she faced him, her lips in a sensuous, slightly-parted smile, then disappeared slowly beneath the surface of the water, reminding him of a seductive mermaid.

"Men," he said to the others in the voice he saved for his most serious comments, "do me a big favor and let me have a few minutes to see if dollies have donut holes."

Cincotti laughed, "Driver, halt! Gunner, female, front!" he said. He had been ogling a gorgeous hooker at the far side of the pool, and she had noticed. She licked her lips slightly, and pulled the top of her skimpy bikini halfway down.

"Let's go, Jimbo," he said, striding purposefully toward her.

When Michelle returned from her cooling swim, Larry said, "It's getting hungry out here. How about some lunch? The hotel cafe has a nice spread."

She was watching Cincotti approach the hooker with undisguised desire. The woman's back was to them, the back of her bikini bottom little more than a string.

"So does the object of your buddy's attention," she said with a chuckle, then looked at Larry and added, "Yes, thanks. Lunch would be nice. I'll go change and meet you—where?"

"Well, I'm in room 651," he said.

"I see." Clumsy attack, Lieutenant, she thought, then said, "I'll meet you in the cafe in fifteen minutes," and walked away without looking at him.

Poor boy, she thought as she waited for the elevator. Probably been in military schools since he was twelve. She supposed that his only dates had been the Ring Dance, or whatever they have at the Citadel, Regimental formals, and that sort of thing. But a guy as attractive as that must have been seduced by a husband-hungry belle somewhere along the way, or by a general's daughter. Or a female West Pointer who recognized his potential as an officer.

Her thoughts continued to be about Redmond as she showered. It had been such a long time since she'd been with a man. This is a war zone—potentially, at least. He's the kind of overly-aggressive guy they ship home in body bags before they really have a chance to live. And he's so young—certainly younger than she. And so attractive.

What the hell. I want him, and he deserves me. Better than having him pick up AIDS from one of these Dutch whores.

Her only civilian clothes were a long, flowered dress with a high collar and long sleeves for wear in Saudi, where such dress was required for off duty wear. She reached into her AWOL bag for some underwear. Along with the cotton sports bras and oversized drawers she wore with her uniforms was a filmy, peach-colored bra and matching, loose legged panties. She pulled them out, remembering that she had gotten them to wear for the major with whom she'd had a brief affair before she discovered he was married. As she pulled on the underwear, she remembered their times together, and how he had been such a bumbling boy of a lover. She glanced at her watch. It had been twenty-five minutes since she'd told Redmond she would meet him in the cafe in fifteen minutes. As she grabbed the dress to pull it on, she caught sight of herself in the big mirror across the room. She twirled, admiring the way she looked in the pretty underthings, farmer's tan or not. On impulse, she picked up the phone and dialed the three digit number for the hotel cafe.

"Cafe? Would you page Lieutenant Redmond and have him come to the phone, please?"

While she waited, she wondered what he'd say. Something very military, no doubt.

"Lieutenant Redmond, sir," he said.

"Hi, it's Mickey."

"Hi. You're late for LD time. I'm at the Line of Departure now, getting ready to press the attack without you."

Michelle laughed. "Don't do that! But, look…rather than the cafe, how about some donuts up in my room? Number 875."

There was a brief hesitation. "Shot, out!" he mumbled before the line went dead.

Michelle was right about Lieutenant Larry Redmond; he knew little of lovemaking except what went where and when he was finished. So she took charge, slowing him down, expanding the range of his interests and of his senses, teaching him to give as well as take. He was as good a student of love as he was of tactics, and at some point late in the night, when he was thinking of the previous several hours, he remembered what his battalion commander had said to him one night when they had been sitting in the officers' club at Fort Stewart, and a particularly attractive woman walked past: "There are two things which turn boys into men, Redmond: women and war. If you're lucky, you'll know both."

Mickey made Redmond feel like a man instead of a curious boy, and he turned to her soft, naked form lying there beside him in the dim light from the bathroom. He took command then, a creative artist who needed only the slightest hint of what might please her.

In the morning, while she watched him shave with a disposable razor from her AWOL bag, she said, "Why did you tease me for so long? I thought you didn't know anything."

He turned to her. "I didn't, until late last night." He put the razor down, and held out his arms to her. She went to him as if they had been lovers for a long time. He kissed her lightly, then held her at arms length and looked into her eyes. "Mickey, I don't even know your last name. How do I get in touch with you."

Oh, dear God, she thought. I don't want him to know the truth—not now, not yet.

She nestled her head against his chest, afraid to look at him when she lied. "We're getting ready to move, Larry. Give me your unit APO, and as soon as we get settled in our new billets, I'll let you know. My last name is Mitchell."

He went to the telephone table and wrote his military address on the hotel notepad, then handed it to her. "I don't know when the next chance might come, Mickey, but I…Please let me see you again."

Again she went to him, and he wrapped his arms around her. "I'll see you again, Larry. If…" He felt her tears on his chest, lifted her chin in his hand and kissed her softly. She wondered whether her tears were because she was ashamed of her deception, or because she feared for his safety.

Both, she knew as soon as she had thought it.

"Yes," he said with strong voice. "You'll see me again, Mickey. Just get me that new address."

It was time for him to leave, and he didn't miss Line of Departure times. He kissed her forehead and released her, quickly pulling on the shorts and polo shirt he'd worn to the cafe the day before. She watched him, wondering if it was really fair to him to let him continue being misled about who and what she was. If she had been concerned only about him, she would have told him then. But she was afraid for herself, now—afraid that he would be angry and disappointed and would never want to see her again.

"I'll understand if I don't hear from you until this thing's over, Larry."

"I know you'll understand. You're that kind of woman. Meanwhile, you take care of the troops." He displayed a new kind of confidence when he added, with a cocky grin, "Just make sure it's the donuts you give 'em, not the holes."

"Naughty, naughty!" she answered with a smile. He turned for the door and her face became serious. "Keep your head down, soldier boy. And good hunting."

He looked back at her, her words transforming him from boyish lover back into the manly warrior he wanted so much to be, his eyes looking through her. "See you in Baghdad," he said, and was gone.

25 December 1990

"Merry Christmas," Abir said as she watched Bill Kernan come awake.

He pulled her to him and kissed her dark hair, feeling the soft warmth of her naked body against his.

"Strange thing for a Moslem woman to say," he whispered.

She kissed his shoulder near the gunshot wound, now nearly healed, and said, "Strange place for a Moslem woman to be."

They had spent every night together for the past week, dropping all pretenses and seizing the time they had to enjoy the love that they had finally come to share.

Bill had been worried that the other members of the resistance who frequented the villa would resent such a relationship between an American and the estranged wife of a Kuwaiti sheik, but they did not. The appreciative smiles of Mara and Abdul and even Dr. Singh had proved otherwise, and their occasional comments made it plain that they saw the affair as a sort of symbol of the new order they intended to establish in their nation, once it was free.

He slid his legs out from beneath the sheet which covered them and picked up his watch from the table by the bed.

"I've got to meet Abdul and plan the resupply pickup for tonight," he said.

"Francesca wants to see you this morning, too," Abir said as she watched him dress. "The stitches in your thigh are supposed to come out today."

He nodded. It was nearly healed, now, and he barely limped.

"About time," he muttered. He was about to leave the little attic hideaway when the telefax machine beeped, then whirred, ejecting a page of data. He walked to the machine and picked up the page.

It was a routine message from the Central Intelligence Agency station in Riyadh, reminding field officers in the region that the open conduct of Christmas services and other Christian activities was to be avoided, especially in the Kingdom of Saudi Arabia, Kuwait, and other fundamentalist Moslem states.

Kernan shook his head in disbelief. He sat down at the table, scrawled a brief message on a clean sheet of paper, and inserted it into the fax machine. Then he dialed the number of the machine at the regional CIA headquarters in Riyadh, and transmitted it.

It read, "As this is the 19th Province of Iraq, for the time being, where the practice of the Christian religion is protected by the government, I would like to take this opportunity to wish you a thoughtful and meaningful Christmas. As ever, Bill."

Jane Parry sat on the bed beside Dave Ames and watched him unwrap the Christmas present she had gotten for them to share when she learned that he was coming to Riyadh for an overnight stay.

The bottle of champagne she'd managed to get from an acquaintance at the embassy was on top, and he raised it and smiled at her.

"I won't even ask how you managed to get hold of this," he said.

"Not very cold, I'm afraid," she replied. "Let me put it in the fridge." She took it from him and walked to the hotel room's small refrigerator, and put it inside. When she turned around, he was looking curiously at the other two items in the package—a folded plastic shower curtain and a bottle of baby oil.

He looked up at her and said, "I don't get it."

"You will," she said as she began to undress. "Just spread the shower curtain out on the bed and take off your clothes."

▼

Fourteen

14 January 1991

Hassan al Ahwabi turned to the masked Russian warrant officer seated beside him in the cab of the big missile erector/launcher and asked, "What do you think, Anatoly? Will Bush and his cronies attack tomorrow?"

The 15th of January was the date the United Nations had agreed upon as the deadline for Saddam Hussein to withdraw his forces from Kuwait, or face the combined might of the American-led Coalition forces now gathered in Saudi Arabia, ready to expel Iraq with force, if necessary.

Anatoly Vasilnikov laughed in his gas mask.

"I hope the pig pricks try," he said. "We've waited a long time to show them and the rest of the world what a mistake it would be to fuck with the Soviet Rocket Forces. And the Tank Corps troops feel the same way, as do the fighter pilots. If you camel humpers have the guts to use our equipment as we've taught you, we'll run the Americans back into the Persian Gulf."

Hassan wasn't so confident of the superiority of Soviet equipment. The Americans and their allies from Europe had an awful lot of technology going for them.

"They have a lot of airplanes," he said to the Russian.

"And Saddam has a lot of air defense forces," Vasilnikov said, "Russian equipment, with Russian advisors. And Russian fighters."

"But no Stealth fighters," the Arab muttered.

Vasilnikov laughed heartily. "Stealth. It's the biggest hoax the capitalist weapons dealers have ever gotten away with. Don't you read the papers, you illiterate raghead? Even their own congress has found them out this time. Stealth! What pig shit, trying to convince people you can hide a huge airplane—especially one with hot jet engines—from radars and infrared sensors."

The Al Husseini carrier was nearing the Jordanian border in Iraq's northwestern panhandle, and ahead Hassan saw a sign with an arrow pointing to the right, down a dirt track. "National Parks Construction Camp," the sign read. Hassan guided the big vehicle, its chemical-tipped cargo covered with a camouflaged tarpaulin, off the Baghdad-Amman highway onto the dirt road. Ahead of him, he knew, more than twenty other Al Husseini missiles had already infiltrated the assembly area.

Although Hassan lacked full confidence in the superiority of Soviet equipment, he was still not worried about the might of the military forces sitting far to the southeast of his present location, thanks to the genius of his president in Baghdad.

If the Americans did try to expel Iraq from the newly-liberated Nineteenth Province, the rocketeer knew, Saddam had a plan of simple brilliance. He would hammer the Jewish blasphemers in Israel with Al Husseini missiles, and the Jews would, as always, retaliate. That would not only immediately destroy the so-called coalition the Americans had put together, it would vastly add to the Arab forces under Saddam's control, for Hassan al Ahwabi was dead certain that most of the Arabs now in Saudi Arabia would immediately turn their guns on the infidels, and the Arabian Peninsula would be awash with American and European blood.

And then, too, Iraq can rid herself of these arrogant Russian blood-suckers, he thought, looking with disgust at Vasilnikov.

The Soviet warrant officer turned toward him, and Hassan forced a phony smile and said, "I hope the sons of Satan try to attack us as well, Anatoly. But it's not Soviet equipment that will carry the day. It's the unshakability of our faith in Allah and the brilliance of our earthly leader."

"We'll see, my camel humping comrade," the Russian replied with a sneer. "We shall see."

✶ ✶ ✶

"It's a piece of trash—militarily insignificant," the Air Force brigadier general said. "They can't hit a bull in the ass with the thing."

Colonel Dave Ames bit his lip and said evenly, "General, the point is not whether or not the Scuds are militarily good weapons. The point is that they're sitting up in the panhandle, within range of Israel. And Israel's considerably bigger than a bull's ass."

Ames was at Central Command headquarters in Riyadh, trying to convince senior staff members there that the chemical Scuds Jack Marsh's team had encountered were a critical target that needed to be dealt with in the opening phase of the coming offensive.

"Look, Colonel," the brigadier said, irritated with the Special Forces officer's insistence on dealing with such unimportant targets as the inaccurate, obsolescent Scuds. "We only have a limited number of assets to employ in the first strike. Now, we're fully aware that these missiles have the potential of hitting Israel from up there. But that doesn't make them a priority target for D Day. The targets we've selected for the first couple of days are, unlike your Scuds, critical military targets—ones that really matter. Furthermore, the target priorities we've set have been approved all the way up through the Joint Chiefs of Staff."

Ames clenched his teeth. He was getting nowhere with the general.

"But, sir," he argued, "these are chemical warheads we're talking about. Suppose they do hit Israel with them? You know how the Israelis are, general. They'll demand that they be allowed to retaliate."

The brigadier laughed scornfully, then glared at Dave Ames with narrowed eyes.

"You're getting a little above your pay grade, aren't you, Colonel? The Izzies won't do a damn thing, unless we tell them to. Don't you think the administration has considered that?"

He picked up a piece of paper from his desk to signal to the Army colonel that the conversation was about over as he said, "Now, we'll worry about minor targets like single missiles when they show up on the target list. Meanwhile, if you green weenies just carry out the missions we've already given you, the big boys will take care of the rest."

Ames wasn't yet ready to concede defeat. "All right, general," he said, picking up his briefcase. "But can you at least get us the authority to take them out if they show up as targets of opportunity?"

The brigadier rolled his eyes and shook his head. As much to get Ames out of his office as anything else, he said, "Colonel Ames, your Scuds are already included as authorized targets—not critical ones, mind you. But they're already listed as targets. You just make damned certain that they don't become targets of opportunity until after the air offensive officially begins." Wagging his finger at Ames to emphasize his point, he added, "Otherwise, son, I'll have your ass."

Ames saluted crisply and left.

Night had fallen while he had been inside the underground labyrinth that was CENTCOM headquarters. He checked his watch and noted that he still had more than an hour and a half left before the USSOTAF Blackhawk would depart for King Khalid Military City.

He considered giving Jane a call at the headquarters of British Forces, Middle East, then rejected the idea.

It was going to be a busy night for the special operations forces of Wayne Wilson's command, and Ames was anxious to get back to the operations center.

∗   ∗   ∗

Five miles beneath the odd-looking Airborne Warning and Control System aircraft that circled above the desert of northern Saudi Arabia, two MH-60 Blackhawk special operations helicopters in tight formation dashed toward the border of Iraq. One of the radar operators aboard the AWACS interrogated the onboard transponders of the Blackhawks, electronically verifying that the low-flying helicopters were the two which they were to shepherd to two points inside Iraq.

The AWACS radar operator tasked to supervise and control the Blackhawk mission, Air Force First Lieutenant Jeanne Lockwood, called the lead helicopter on secure voice radio to let the pilot know that she had acquired them on her radar. She was, the Blackhawk crews knew, prepared to advise them of their position, if required, although their onboard Global Positioning Systems were fully functioning. The important thing was that she would let them know if any enemy aircraft capable of intercepting them appeared, and she was also prepared to vector American F-15C Eagle fighters, in orbit high above the Arabian Peninsula, to deal with any Iraqi planes that dared to threaten the American helicopters.

The pilot of the first specially equipped Blackhawk helicopter turned to the man in charge of his passengers and advised him that the AWACS had contact with them, and the flight was going as planned. Sergeant Major Pat Healy gave the pilot a thumbs up in acknowledgment, then verbally passed the information on to the other seven men in the cargo compartment with him—half the soldiers of 2nd Troop of D Squadron, 1st Special Forces Operational Detachment—Delta—better known throughout the world as the Delta Force.

When the helicopters reached the first of their two landing zones, Healy and his men would quickly exit the dark helicopter, taking with them the equipment which crowded the cargo compartment. The second Blackhawk would travel several kilometers deeper into Iraq before depositing its cargo—Healy's troop commander and the other half of D-2 Troop.

Meanwhile, Healy nestled back into the equipment as best he could and tried to rest, supremely confident that this mission would turn out better than the last mission he had been involved in near the Persian Gulf—the ill-fated attempt to rescue American hostages from Tehran more than ten years earlier.

This time, there were none of the ridiculous political restrictions imposed upon the men tasked to do the job. This time, the full weight and range of capabilities of the U.S. armed forces, with the exception of nuclear and chemical weapons, could be used. And that would begin with air power. Almost, anyway.

First, there would be a few clandestine activities conducted by special operations forces to improve the allied air forces' chances of quickly and fully gaining air superiority.

The mission on which Healy and his troop were engaged was one of those activities.

The route the Blackhawks were taking to their objectives had been carefully selected. Months of intelligence collection efforts directed against the Iraqi air defense forces had given the Coalition planners detailed knowledge of where they were located, in what strength, with what equipment, and what activities they were conducting. This included the location and coverage of their air defense radars, both sur-veillance radars—the ones which detected incoming aircraft—and those with a much lesser range and sweep which were used to guide anti-aircraft weapons to intercept enemy airplanes.

The Blackhawks' flight route avoided the coverage of these radars, and took the troop-laden helicopters around and to the rear of the sur-veillance radar sites. Healy and the other Special Forces soldiers were to be deposited there, along with their equipment, and would make their way toward the surveillance radar sites some eight to ten kilometers from their landing zones. Once there, they would conduct a careful analysis of the radar installations and determine the best means of attacking them to render them ineffective. They would then back off into hide sites until orders were received over their manpack satellite radios for them to attack and neutralize the radars.

They expected to receive those orders within the next forty-eight to seventy-two hours.

When the orders came, Healy knew that a flight of Army AH-64 Apache attack helicopters would be taking off to attack enemy air defense positions as well. Led by the Air Force's sophisticated MH-53J Pave Low III helicopters, whose onboard electronic devices enabled them to make high speed, low level flights directly to precise points on the ground, even in total darkness, the Apaches would then break off from their Air Force pathfinders and attack their targets. With a mix of Hellfire laser-guided missiles, 30mm cannon fire, and 70mm high-explosive rockets available, there was little doubt that the Apaches would quickly and effectively accomplish their deadly missions.

Before that could occur, though, it would be necessary for the Delta Force teams to eliminate several positions which appeared impossible for the Apaches and their Pave Low shepherds to approach undetected. They would have to be destroyed by a coordinated ground attack to preclude the Iraqis from spreading the alarm that the Coalition air offensive was beginning. The destruction of one of those critical positions was the task which Pat Healy and his men had been assigned.

The roundabout flight of the Blackhawks gave Sergeant Major Healy time to reflect on the long Army career that had brought him once again to a dangerous mission with a handful of other men, far from the comforts and safety and family life of home.

It had begun for Healy twenty-two years earlier, when he had chosen, unlike nearly all of his college classmates, to forsake the safety of the university classroom for the uncertain adventure of an increasingly unpopular war in Vietnam.

He had been disappointed in what he found there. By the time he arrived in the 4th Infantry Division, the rot that is bound to set into a conscript army, declared by its own citizens to be on an evil crusade, was manifesting itself in drugs and indiscipline and carelessness.

Pat Healy had been to Ranger school, though, earning the coveted black and gold shoulder tab that graduates of that demanding course are awarded. Several Ranger companies had been formed in Vietnam to conduct long range reconnaissance for each corps headquarters, and one of them was commanded by the officer who had been his inseparable partner in Ranger school, his "Ranger buddy."

He sought out the orderly room of F Company, 75th Infantry (Ranger), the unit his Ranger buddy, Wayne Wilson, was commanding. Captain Wilson was out on patrol, but Healy explained to the first sergeant that he wanted a transfer, and when the first sergeant discovered that Wilson and Healy had been Ranger buddies, he didn't hesitate; he called the corps sergeant major, who owed him several favors, and got Healy transferred to F Company immediately.

It was during their time together in Vietnam that Pat Healy and Wayne Wilson had been forged from boys into men.

On one occasion, deep inside a North Vietnamese base area, Healy's reconnaissance team had been discovered, and had attempted to beat back the enemy and break contact. The team leader and one other man were killed in the process, and it was left to Healy to try to get himself and the other three members of the team, one of whom was badly wounded, out of the area before they, too, were killed or captured.

Wayne Wilson learned of the recon team's desperate situation and reacted immediately, flying to the area with two more of his teams aboard a pair of Huey helicopters. There was a thick cover of clouds over the valley Healy and his men were in, which not only precluded the use of close air support to assist them, but made it almost impossible to get the Hueys into a landing zone.

The pilots finally found a break in the clouds, though, and landed Wilson and his reinforcements. They rushed toward the sound of the gunfire being exchanged by the North Vietnamese and Healy's men, reaching them just as the enemy was mounting an assault to overrun the four survivors.

Led by Wilson, the two fresh teams beat back the attackers and began moving to the pickup zone with Healy and his dead and wounded comrades. When they got there, Wilson and Healy stayed in the edge of the jungle to cover the loading of the helicopters. The landing zone came under attack from another direction. Barely able to lift the men they already had aboard, the helicopter pilots took off to avoid being overrun, radioing a promise to return as soon as they could find someplace safe to set down and offload some of the other Rangers.

Healy and Wilson attempted to sneak away from the little clearing as the enemy closed in on them, but were taken under fire. Wayne Wilson took a round through one of his lungs and collapsed heavily onto the jungle floor.

Healy thought it was the end of the line for his Ranger buddy and himself, so, with the impetuosity that bold young warriors so often display in such situations, he determined that his best course of action would be to take as many of the enemy with him as possible.

He attacked them single-handedly. Throwing hand grenades and firing his CAR-15 assault rifle as he charged, he killed three of the North Vietnamese and caused the remainder to withdraw, if only temporarily.

Healy ran back to Wilson, plugged the wounds in his captain's chest, then picked him up and started out into the jungle. He carried Wilson for over an hour, stopping to rest only when he was near exhaustion.

He had just spotted a small open patch in the jungle when the helicopter pilots radioed their approach to the area. Healy directed the helicopters to the clearing and soon had Wilson aboard one of the helicopters, flying at top speed for the nearest field hospital.

Wilson was going in and out of consciousness, but once he looked at Healy and said, "You saved my life."

"Yeah," his Ranger buddy replied. "But I wouldn't have been able to if you hadn't already saved my ass!"

The bond between the young officer and the enlisted man was unbreakable after that. Wilson had managed to get Healy assigned to units he commanded several times during the years since, but even when they were at different posts, they took every opportunity to get together for a beer and to catch up on each other's news. And each had served as the other's best man at their weddings.

And now Wilson was a major general, commanding Healy and thousands of other special operators.

When he found out that Healy, presently serving as a sergeant major in the Delta Force, was still going on tough missions such as the one on which he was now embarked, Wilson had sent for him.

"Pat," the general said to his good friend, "Matt Jensen's going to retire soon. I'd like for you to take his place as my command sergeant major."

"We'll see how it goes, boss," was all that Healy had said, but now he thought about what an attractive offer it was. He loved what he was doing, but after all, he had done his share and more. It was time to move on and let one of his subordinates move into the troop sergeant's job. Besides, he owed it to his family to take a job that would keep him at home for reasonable periods of time.

He turned to the master sergeant next to him—the man who would no doubt replace him as troop sergeant.

"Looks like this is my last one, ol' buddy. You ready to take over the troop?"

"What do you mean?" his Delta Force teammate asked.

"General Wilson offered me a job as his next CSM. I've been thinking maybe I'll take him up on it."

The master sergeant grinned, then offered Healy his hand to shake, as much in congratulations to himself as to the man whom he would replace as a Delta Force troop sergeant.

Healy shook it heartily, then leaned back and closed his eyes, concentrating his thoughts on the mission ahead.

*   *   *

Lieutenant Joe Cincotti of Team Charlie, 5th Battalion, 64th Armor (Reinforced), raised the edge of the camouflage netting which concealed Larry Redmond's tank and ducked beneath it.

Redmond looked up from the book he was reading by the light of a red-filtered flashlight and shined it's dull beam on Cincotti's face. "Hey, Joseph," he said. "What's up?"

"Rumors of war," Joe said, dropping down on the desert floor beside his fellow platoon leader and leaning back against one of the road-wheels of the big tank.

Redmond stared at Joe's barely visible silhouette for a moment, then held the light on the book he had been reading and flipped back several pages.

"'And ye shall hear of wars and rumors of wars; see that ye be not troubled: for all these things must come to pass, but the end is not yet...' I was just reading that," Larry said. "The book of Matthew."

Both men were silent for a moment, considering the coincidence, until Cincotti said, "Scary."

"The rumors?"

"No. The fact that you were reading that. Maybe I'm psychic."

"Could be," Redmond said. "Patton was, you know."

"I hope I'm not," Cincotti said. "Jesus, I sure hope not."

Larry closed the little pocket Bible and slipped it beneath the top of his chemical protective suit and into the left breast pocket of the desert camouflage uniform he wore beneath it.

"Why do you say that, Joe?" he asked.

Cincotti said nothing for awhile, but it was obvious to Redmond that his brother officer wanted to talk, so he waited until Joe finally spoke.

"Take this letter for my mom, will you?" he asked, pulling an envelope from the side pocket of his trousers. "In case…well, you know."

"Ah, come on, Joe," Larry said, sensing the fear that his comrade-in-arms was feeling. "We're going to be all right." But he took the letter from Cincotti nevertheless.

The coming war was more than just rumors now. The United States Congress had given the President the authority to go to war if Saddam Hussein failed to withdraw from Kuwait by the deadline the United Nations had set.

That deadline was the following day, and there was no evidence that the Iraqis were doing anything except reinforcing their positions with additional conscripts.

If there had been any doubts among the tankers that the war was about to begin, the looks in the eyes of their commanders the previous day would have dispelled them. The battle plans had been slowly seeping down to the lower levels of command, and the commander of the 5th of the 64th Armor had all but said to his assembled officers the previous day that their next move would be a long-range march to their attack positions somewhere to the west.

And along with the rumors of war had come a deadly seriousness in the attitudes of all but a few, whose anxiousness had manifested itself in nervous joking and laughter.

Larry Redmond was enough of a student of warfare and warriors that he understood the nervousness and fear that had been growing in the soldiers surrounding him. He felt nothing that he could discern as fear himself, but there was a certain anxiousness to get on with it, to finally know what battle really was.

The sense of foreboding that Cincotti apparently had was not uncommon, Redmond knew. No doubt many such letters to parents and wives and sweethearts were being passed from friend to friend in the Arabian desert this night.

He shoved the letter from Joe to his mother into the pocket with his Bible. "I guess I ought to write a letter, too," he muttered, but he didn't really mean it—not one of those "just in case" letters, anyway.

He had wanted to write to Mickey for the first couple of weeks after he had returned to his unit from R&R in Bahrain, but she had never sent her address. At first he had thought it was just the fact that there was so much mail to handle; at each mail call, his platoon was given dozens of letters from strangers in the States who just wanted to express their support for the troops in the Gulf. But after awhile he had decided that Mickey never really intended to write. She had, when he thought about it, been awfully evasive about herself, and he finally came to the conclusion that she had only wanted him for a one night stand. He didn't harbor ill feelings about it. It was, after all, the most memorable night he had spent in his life. But he had hoped the brief relationship might develop into something more.

"I wrote one to Beth, too," Cincotti said, his words interrupting Redmond's thoughts of Mickey. "But I mailed it to her dad to give to her if…"

Larry patted him on the knee. "Nothing to worry about, old buddy," he said. "We'll be home in a few weeks, and you can use all that money we haven't been able to spend on beer to buy a big diamond for her. Then, when she walks down the aisle and sees you standing there with a chest full of medals, you'll say, 'Ol' Larry was right. There was nothing to worry about. We went through the bastards like shit through a goose.'"

Cincotti laughed nervously. "Well, the only problem with that is, I spent all the money I was saving for her diamond on that hooker in Bahrain. Should have done like you did, and found myself a donut dolly. You ever hear from her, by the way?"

"Nah," Redmond said, pushing himself to his feet. "She just wanted to spend one night with a real warrior, I guess. Well, we'd better get some sack time, Joe. Might be the last good night's sleep we have until we get to Baghdad."

"Yeah," the other lieutenant said, standing and raising the camouflage netting to go back to his own tank. "Thanks for taking the letter, Larry."

"No sweat," Redmond said. "I'll give it back as soon as we get to Saddam's headquarters."

Cincotti disappeared from beneath the netting, and Redmond climbed up on the tank and pulled his sleeping bag from the turret bustle. From the other side of the tank, he could hear the soft snores of his driver, Private Anderson, and his gunner, Sergeant Peterson. Specialist Begay, the Native American loader of the tank crew was there as well, but, as always, he slept without making the slightest of sounds.

Redmond threw the sleeping bag to the ground and jumped off the tank. The cold of the desert night was causing him to shiver, even through the two layers of his desert uniform and the chemical protective suit, and he supposed that the Goretex uniforms they were to have been issued to ward off the cold would never get to them. Apparently the only members of the Victory Division who would get them before the war started were the rear echelon troops.

Oh, well, he thought as he unrolled his sleeping bag and unfastened the protective mask from his waist to place it near his head. As long as they get the fuel and ammunition to us when we need it, they can have the damn things. The chemical protective "MOPP gear" was fairly warm, and the body odor absorbing characteristic of the charcoal impregnated suits made them preferable to Goretex anyway.

He crawled into the sleeping bag and drew the protective mask beneath his head for a pillow, and stared at the stars which twinkled through the camouflage netting above him. He hoped Cincotti would be all right, and not just for his friend's sake, but for his whole platoon—and the platoons on his flanks, for that matter.

God, help me to be a good warrior, he thought. And help my crew and Joe and all the rest of this army. We didn't start this war, but, with

Your help, we'll end it—quickly and victoriously. Amen.

▼

Fifteen

15 January 1991

"The radios are the really critical element of the whole complex," Pat Healy said to the other five Delta Force soldiers. "Just remember that. Even if it means ignoring the rest of it—the radars, the missiles, the guards and their weapons—the radios have got to be taken out first. And I mean completely shut down."

The others nodded, examining the field sketch Healy had put together from the drawings that the men had made of the Iraqi air defense complex from several vantage points.

The satellite photographs they had studied so intently during their premission planning had given them the layout of the surface-to-air missile complex, and they knew where such items as the four SA-3 missiles, the target acquisition and fire control radars, and the supporting bunkers were. They even knew where the larger, fixed antennae were located. But until their close reconnaissance of the site, it had been impossible to tell for certain which of the bunkers were sleeping quarters, generator bunkers, and command and communications bunkers, nor had they been able to detect the smaller antennae of the portable radios, and the communications wire that ran between the dug-in radar vans, the firing battery, and the various bunkers.

"What about the commo lines between the bunkers, Pat?" Staff Sergeant Garrett Winston asked.

Healy looked up at him. "Not important," he replied. "They're just internal lines among the various bunkers, not connected to the outside. As long as we take out their radios—all of their radios—we don't have to worry about them telling anybody else that they're under attack. The heart of this whole mission, remember, is to prevent them from alerting Baghdad or anyone else that the air attacks have begun. That's even more important than keeping them from launching a missile."

He looked carefully at each of the five men with him. The other two members of the team were still up near the enemy missile site, maintaining surveillance on the installation and the activities of the soldiers manning it.

"But we're not going to let them launch any damned missiles, either. Now, the second most important thing is to make certain that nobody leaves the place in a vehicle. Since we're hitting this target before H-Hour, we can't let anybody haul ass away from here to some other site to spread the alarm. So if anybody sees someone heading for a vehicle, put him down. If any vehicle cranks or moves, turn your whole attention to it, even if it means you have to stop giving cover to one of our own guys."

Healy went through the remainder of his briefing, prioritizing the tasks and targets involved in the attack, outlining contingency plans, and ensuring that all five of the men fully understood the plan. When he was satisfied, he sent two of them to relieve the men in the surveillance position.

They had just left the hide site to do so when there was the whoop! whoop! sound of an alarm from the enemy air defense missile complex.

The men who were maintaining surveillance on the site with their night vision goggles reported in immediately.

"There's some sort of alert there," one of them reported in a whisper over the radio. "People running all over the place."

"They haven't spotted you, have they?" Healy asked.

"Negative," his teammate replied. "It looks like they're getting ready to engage an aircraft or something. Yeah! One of the missiles is being raised now."

"OK," Healy said over the radio. "Keep an eye on everything that goes on, and keep reporting. Even if they don't fire, it'll be helpful to know what happens when they go on alert."

He passed the radio handset to one of the other men and ordered, "Write down everything significant he reports." Then to Garrett Winston he said, "Come on, Garrett. Let's go have a look for ourselves."

They grabbed their weapons and scrambled to the top of the wadi in which the team had established their patrol base some 700 meters from the perimeter of the missile complex. Healy stood up at the top of the eight-foot-high bank and turned around to say something to the men below him when he stepped on a loose rock. He slipped and fell back into the dry streambed, landing on his back on one of the large stones there. A sharp jolt of pain shot down his spine and through his legs, and he involuntarily issued a low moan.

"Damn, Pat. You all right?" Winston asked in a stage whisper from the bank above him.

Healy tried to rise, but could not. His legs were numb, unable to respond to his brain's command to move.

"My back," he grunted. "Can't move my legs." The sharp pain in his spine was still there, but he had no feeling at all from his waist down.

The team medic scrambled over to him. "Don't try to move, Pat." He felt gently beneath Healy's back. There was a sharp-edged stone beneath the injured sergeant major's back. He had landed directly on it, smashing one of the vertebrae of his spine.

Ten minutes later, the surveillance team reported that the missile had been lowered and the Iraqi crewmen were returning to their bunkers. Apparently, it had been only a readiness drill to test the missilemen's reaction time as the UN deadline for war approached.

It had also become apparent by then that the feeling was not returning to Healy's legs, and the medic was on the satellite radio to Delta's forward operations base near the Saudi town of Ar'ar.

"He wants us to just leave him here until after we make the hit, but I think he needs to be medevaced ASAP, especially with the respiratory problems he's having," the medic reported to the Delta surgeon, Major Curt Rowe.

Rowe turned to Colonel Pete Gerald, the Delta Force commander. "Can we do it?" he asked.

"Dadburn it," Gerald muttered, considering the options before giving Rowe an answer. He studied the map for a moment. The target was not too far inside Iraq—a short flight for the quick Blackhawk helicopters standing ready nearby for just such a mission. Glancing at the clock on the wall above the map, Gerald noted that it was only 2210 hours—10:10 PM. There was still plenty of darkness left to allow the team to move Healy a considerable distance away from the patrol base to preclude the Iraqis from hearing the helicopter make the pickup. If they moved soon, they could have him evacuated and be back in their patrol base long before daylight—the last day before the air war would begin.

In about 27 hours, Gerald knew, there would be hundreds of pilots sitting in the seats of their aircraft, waiting to launch into the dark skies above the Arabian Peninsula and the Persian Gulf to deliver a fatal punch to the Iraqi armed forces. Healy's team, along with others from the Delta Force and other Special Forces units, would be moving to their targets, striking the first blow to blind the Iraqi front line air defenses. That would enable Apache attack helicopters to safely strike the next line of air defense warning systems, opening the way for the swarm of Coalition fighters to hit their targets deep in the interior of Iraq.

It would be a furiously busy night, and there were many more missions for the Blackhawks to perform; search and rescue missions for any allied pilots who went down in enemy territory, the delivery of additional strike teams deeper into Iraq to hit secondary targets, the exfiltration of enemy prisoners of war taken by Special Forces "snatch teams" for interrogation.

He pictured the injured Healy lying in the desert, unable to move, in pain and gasping for breath. He knew the distraction it would be to the others, concerned about both Healy and the need to accomplish their mission. And what if they were discovered? Suppose they got into a running battle with the survivors of their attack on the installation, or with reinforcements coming to their assistance?

The decision was clear; accept the medic's recommendation in spite of Healy's protests.

Gerald turned to Doc Rowe and the operations officer, who had joined the other two men at the radio.

"Let's get him out as soon as possible," he said.

*   *   *

"So, they're going to get him out tonight?" Major General Wayne Wilson said to his operations officer, Colonel Dave Ames.

Ames, who had just been on the secure telephone with one of Wilson's subordinate commanders, Colonel Pete Gerald of the Delta Force, replied, "Yes sir. As soon as the four men who are carrying him get to the pickup zone, they'll bring the medevac in. Pete said he wasn't worried about the choppers getting picked up on radar, because they're going in on the same flight path they used to infil the team."

"Good," Wilson said, nodding.

"Healy's an old mate of yours, isn't he, General?" Rover Harvey asked. The British warrant officer was at USSOTAF as the liaison officer from the headquarters of the Commander, British Forces Middle East.

"Sure is," Wilson replied, thinking back to their days together as young Rangers in Vietnam. He hoped the injury was not something permanent—something which might prevent Healy from taking the job as Wilson's command sergeant major at the US Special Operations Task Force. He made a mental note to try to find time in the next couple of days to get to the field hospital to check on his old Ranger buddy. It was going to get terribly busy, but Wilson owed it to Pat to drop in on him. Hopefully, there wouldn't be others of his command to check on at the same time.

"Well," Wilson said to Ames, "what other changes or loose ends are there to take care of, Dave?"

"Just the remote firing devices on the chemical Scuds," Ames said. "Everything else is pretty well set."

Wilson nodded. He agreed with Ames that the chemical-tipped missiles which had first been sighted in Kuwait by Rover Harvey's British Special Air Service comrades, and later in the panhandle of Iraq by the US Special Forces team of Captain Jack Marsh, should be high on the priority list of targets. But their fear that the Scuds could provoke armed reaction by Israel if they were fired there was not shared by others at Central Command. Israel could not act, even if they decided to ignore the US President's plea to avoid the war, the Pentagon and CENTCOM skeptics declared. The United States had refused to issue them the IFF—Identify Friend or Foe—codes which their aircraft would need to avoid being mistaken for Iraqis. Without those codes, if the Israeli Air Force dared to enter Iraqi or neighboring airspace, they would be engaged by American or other Coalition fighters or missiles, and destroyed. So the "conventional wisdom" of the political advisors to the Pentagon and Central Command was that there was little likelihood of Israel destroying the delicate coalition of the Euro-Arab-American governments aligned against Saddam Hussein.

The unconventional wisdom of the Special Forces men disagreed. They had spent, collectively, too many years training, advising, and getting to know Arabs and Israelis alike. Studying foreign military forces, cultures, and attitudes was one of the things which made Special Forces special. It had made them keenly aware of the deep-seated fears and hatred which so many of those on both sides of the Arab-Israeli issue harbored.

And they had a better appreciation for the psychological aspects of warfare as well, for that, too, was a Special Forces specialty.

While the Scud was, indeed, a relatively insignificant weapon militarily, one needed only to look at the British experience of World War II to understand what a powerful psychological weapon it could be. The dreaded "buzz bombs" and V-2 rockets the Nazis had rained on the civilian population of London were "militarily insignificant" weapons, too.

Well, at least the Special Warriors hadn't been denied the authority to use their own resources against the enemy missiles, once the war began. The only problem now was how to locate and destroy them.

"All right, Dave," General Wilson said, seating himself at the conference table in the USSOTAF war room and gesturing to Rover Harvey to do the same, "review for me what we know about these damned Scuds."

Ames went to his desk and withdrew a folder from a side drawer. He flipped it open and placed several photographs in front of his commander, then read from the top sheet of paper in the folder.

"16 September. British SAS patrol detects several SS-1 Scud missiles under heavy security at an airbase in western Kuwait." He pointed to a red symbol on the map behind him, adding, "right here." Pointing to the top photograph in front of Wilson, he said, "That's one of the photographs from that mission," then glanced at the paper in his folder.

"As you know, sir, the patrol was bumped and had to withdraw. One SAS killed in action.

"18 September. A second SAS patrol returned to the airfield and reported that the missiles spotted by the earlier patrol were gone. It can be assumed that they moved because the Iraqis knew they'd been discovered.

"2 October. A CIA report indicated that a five vehicle convoy, including three tarp-covered MAZ-543 missile erector/launchers, were spotted moving north from Khabra Jalib, Kuwait. The crews were wearing protective gear."

"Do we know if those were the same missiles?" Wilson inquired.

"No, sir, we don't know. But they fit the pattern. "9 November. In the Rumayla oilfield, here in northern Kuwait, Kuwaiti resistance forces reported suspicious activity in a warehouse building, and dead animals outside the place."

Ames looked up at Harvey. "This is codeword stuff, not to be disclosed to foreigners like you, Rover. So close your ears."

The two men grinned at each other, then Ames continued.

"A CIA mission was undertaken on 11 November to recover one of the animal carcasses. Subsequent laboratory tests proved that the animal, a goat, was killed by nonpersistent nerve agent, on or about 7 November. Some other shit happened there, too, but it's immaterial to the Scuds."

He flipped the page. "10 November. Another CIA report indicates a five vehicle convoy with three missile carriers and masked crews pulled off the road near Shithatha, Iraq, just before daybreak, laagered up, and camouflaged the vehicles. They remained there until dark, then departed to the west.

"12 November. A US Special Forces R&S team west of Rutba, Iraq—Jack Marsh's team—spotted a five vehicle convoy, confirmed by photos they took to be one Zil-131 cargo truck, three MAZ-543 SS-1 Scud missile erector/launchers, and one ARS-12 decontamination vehicle. Again, the crews were wearing protective clothing around the missiles, they laagered up the same way the report of 10 November indicated, at daybreak, and departed again at nightfall."

He pointed to the pile of photographs again. "As you can see, sir, the markings on two of the Scud carriers that Shumate's kid took photos of, match the ones that the Brits got shots of 'way back in September."

Wilson and Harvey compared the photographs. Yes, the markings on two of the vehicles in each picture were identical. They looked back up at Ames.

"The other key piece of information, of course, is that young Shumate also attached a soapdish incendiary charge wired to an M-122 remote firing device receiver on the fuel tanks of all three missile carriers."

Wilson nodded, then stood up and walked to the map. "Right," he muttered, "the day before we got the damn electronic beacons to them." He turned back to face Ames and said, "And the Scuds haven't been seen since, correct?"

Ames shook his head. "No, sir, they haven't. I mean, there have been some Scuds picked up on satellite photos since, but there's no way to tell whether they're the same ones or not. None in convoy with decon trucks, either."

All three men studied the map of western Iraq for awhile, thinking their own thoughts until Rover said, "What do you reckon the probability of the dems being discovered, Dave?"

"The demolition charges?" Ames asked, and Rover nodded. "No idea," Ames said. "I even put in a request to DIA to find out whether normal Soviet maintenance procedures would likely lead to the discovery of something attached at the top of the gas tank, but I haven't heard anything. With all the high priority requests they're getting, I doubt if I ever will get an answer."

"Well, even if they didn't find them, the batteries in those detonators are probably dead by now, aren't they?" General Wilson said.

"Oh, no sir. They're in a passive standby mode. They should be good for at least six months, even with the extreme temperature changes you find in the desert. They've only been on there for a couple of months or so."

Wilson's eyebrows raised, and he smiled. "Well, that's it, then," he said. "You've got the firing codes, right? As soon as the air offensive begins, we'll just transmit them through the satellite and back down to the receivers. The things'll be history!"

Ames frowned. "Afraid not, sir. I already thought of that. The satellite frequency range doesn't cover the frequency of the detonators. It won't work."

"How many teams do you have up in that region now, boss?" Rover Harvey asked. "You could give each of them a transmitter. Maybe they'll get lucky, and be within range."

Dave Ames shook his head. "We only have two teams up that way right now, Rover—the two halves of Jack Marsh's A team. They went back in to take out what they can with the discriminating mine systems they planted on the highway 'way back when. We've pulled all the other teams out to hit air defense sites and to keep an eye on the Republican Guards up along the Euphrates. No, all I can think of is to put a transmitter in one of the AWACS birds and hope they're within range. But they'd have to be pretty close, since the receiver is stuck up under the carrier, masked by all that steel."

"What about a helicopter?" Wilson said. "Once things get going, we could send a chopper up that way to crisscross the whole area. That might do it."

"The only problem with that, boss," Dave Ames replied, "is that it'll have to be long after the war has started, after we have air superiority. Otherwise, a chopper won't be able to hang around up there without getting blown out of the sky. It's tough enough making a dash into Iraq away from enemy units, to deliver the recon teams."

The men were silent again for a time, gazing at the map and trying to work out a solution in their minds.

"Bloody hell," Rover Harvey muttered after awhile, and the two Americans looked at him. "I think I've got it," he said, breaking into a grin.

"What's that?" Ames asked.

"Your mate, John Rains, and that magic flying machine of his that we borrowed when our patrol was in trouble. Why the hell couldn't we hook the transmitter to that, and send it back and forth across the panhandle?"

"Yeah," Ames said, slapping the Briton on the back. "By God, Harvey, you're a genius! That just might work, and with no risk to any aircrew. It's sure as hell worth a try, anyway."

Wayne Wilson had no idea what they were talking about, and was looking at the other two with curiosity.

"The unmanned aerial vehicle that we used before you got here, sir," Ames explained. "We can rig up the remote firing device in it and send it up there tomorrow night, once the fighters get their first sorties in."

The USSOTAF commander considered the idea for a moment, then said, "All right, let's do it. One thing, though—how are we going to know if it works?"

Rover Harvey pondered the question and his face took on a serious look. "I guess the best evidence," he said, "will be if the Israelis stay out of the war."

*   *   *

Bill Kernan re-read the message he had just decoded to be sure that he understood it, then burned it to ashes and stirred them. So, that was it. The war was on. In 24 hours, the Coalition air forces would begin to rain fury on the Iraqis in the opening phase of the effort to destroy Saddam Hussein's ability to fight.

Kernan's shoulders involuntarily hunched in despair as he thought of the hundreds, perhaps thousands, of lives that would be lost in the process.

Well, maybe it would be the end of such naked aggression as Saddam had displayed by his seizure and rape of Kuwait, at least for a long time. After all, the Warsaw pact was crumbling into an impotent mess and, more important, the United States, under the banner of the UN, had

managed to pull together a coalition of governments for an unprece-
dented, planet-wide stand against armed bullying. "Enough is enough,"
the world had declared, and Saddam's refusal to heed that warning was
about to lead to his violent destruction. So be it.

The mission the resistance had been given for the opening phase of
Desert Storm was a simple one; assess the damage Coalition airstrikes
did to Iraqi command, control, and communications systems in
Kuwait. The use of armed force by the resistance was to be withheld
until the ground offensive to liberate Kuwait City commenced. Central
Command was convinced that their air offensive would be adequate to
destroy the key targets necessary to enable the ground offensive to
begin, and the resistance could best support the war by waiting until
that occurred, then disrupting and dividing the Iraqi effort to defend
the city by creating confusion and harassment in the enemy's rear areas.

There was nothing in the mission which required Abdul to be forewarned of the opening of the air war, so Bill Kernan turned off the little
lamp in his attic headquarters and climbed down to head for the master
bedroom of the spacious villa. Abir would be waiting for him there.

Colonel Pete Gerald, the Delta Force commander, paced back and
forth across the room, trying to decide what to do.

Radio contact had been lost between the four men carrying Sergeant
Major Healy to a pickup zone for medical evacuation, and the remaining
three members of the team who were still at the Iraqi air defense site.

Two of the three men at the target were continuing to maintain surveillance on the Iraqi position. The third—the master sergeant who had
replaced Healy as the troop sergeant—remained in the hide site, manning the satellite radio which was the team's only direct link to Colonel
Gerald and Delta's forward operations base.

According to the plan the men had made, the evacuation team would move to the general area of the landing zone where they had been dropped off at the beginning of the mission—an empty spot in the vast desert some eight kilometers from the patrol base, identifiable only by the digital readout of the Global Positioning System receiver the men carried. Once they arrived there and ensured that the area was still free of enemy presence, they would call the patrol base on the frequency-hopping FM radio they had with them. The man on the other FM radio at the patrol base would relay their arrival to Delta's war room on the satellite set, and the Blackhawks would launch to recover Healy.

But they had failed to call, and it was now only an hour until the darkness would begin to give way to daylight. Repeated attempts by the men at the patrol base to raise the evacuation team on the FM radio during the preceding hour had failed.

Now, Colonel Gerald's problem was not just the evacuation of Sergeant Major Healy, but the situation at the target, as well. If the team had bumped into an enemy force as they carried Healy across the desert, there was no way of knowing what the result might have been. They might now be evading or hiding in the desert, or perhaps they had even all been killed or captured. The Delta Force men at the missile site had not seen nor heard a firefight, but as they pointed out, if it hadn't occurred nearby, they wouldn't have been able to; the desert sands were being kicked up by a strong wind, obscuring both sight and sound. At least, Pete Gerald thought, it will help hide the noise of the helicopters. And, if the patrol had made contact with the enemy, the storm might afford them some concealment.

It was unlikely that the three remaining men at the enemy complex could neutralize their target before the Iraqis spread the alarm that they were under attack. And taking out the enemy missile position the following night had to be the paramount consideration.

All right, Pete Gerald thought now. It's time to make a decision.

He turned to his operations officer. "Get a backup team saddled up to reinforce the guys at the missile site," he said. "We'll make a run at the LZ where we think they were taking Healy. If there's enemy there, we'll drop the backup team at the alternate. If not, and the others are around, we'll pick up Healy and whatever wounded they might have and bring them out. Tell the new team to hustle. And tell the team leader I'll talk to him at the choppers. We have to launch right away."

He slumped heavily into a chair beneath the operations map, wondering what could have happened to his missing men.

Pat Healy raised his head to listen for the sound of a helicopter above the moan of the desert wind, but a jolt of pain caused him to drop it back onto the desert floor.

His teammates should be back at the patrol base by now, he figured. He wondered if he'd ever see them—if he'd ever see anyone—again.

They had wanted to leave the medic with him, but he finally convinced them that they'd need everyone at the target to be sure it was attacked with enough force to accomplish the mission. Besides, he had argued, there was nothing more anyone on the team could do for him now, and the medic would be needed if anybody was wounded during the attack.

"Damned lousy radio," he mumbled to himself. He should have ordered them to leave him and return to the patrol base as soon as they learned that the radio wouldn't transmit. They could hear the men at the base trying to call them periodically, but it had soon become obvious that the men couldn't hear the litter party returning their calls.

The movement had been slow, primarily because of the fact that each little bump the improvised litter made had caused Healy to gasp or moan from the excruciating pain of his back injury. He'd tried to get the medic to give him morphine or something, but the medic was afraid that it would worsen the considerable difficulty Healy was already having in breathing. Until he finally lapsed into unconsciousness, the continued pain had made Healy delirious, and his teammates had ignored his pleas to leave him where he was.

It was only after they arrived at the intended pickup zone where he now lay, that the pain and his delirium had subsided enough for him to convince his subordinates to leave him. When they got back to the patrol base and the satellite radio, he argued, they could call Delta's forward operations base and dispatch a helicopter for him. And even if he couldn't get out tonight, the team could come back to him after the hit on the critical target. A lot more lives would be dependent on the success of that attack, he'd told his teammates.

He raised the luminous dial of his wristwatch in front of his eyes, and a feeling of despair swept over him. Too late now. It was getting too close to daylight to risk sending a chopper in for him. He doubted that he could last another night. And the longer he lay there, the less likely it was that the damage to his back could be fully repaired. He would probably never walk again. Pete Gerald was about to walk out to the chopper pad to brief the backup team's commander when the Signal Squadron base radio operator turned from his console and called, "Colonel Gerald! I've got them!"

The radio operator acknowledged the team's call, then relayed their message to Gerald.

"They had to leave Pat at the PZ when the radio went tits up. He's there by himself, waiting to be picked up. The rest of the team's at the patrol base."

The Delta commander glanced at the clock above the map and muttered, "Thank God." There was still time, if the choppers departed immediately, to get in, pick up Healy, and get out before first light—though only barely.

"Scrub the backup team," he ordered his operations sergeant. "Send the medevac birds in as we planned to do initially. Do it now!"

In less than five minutes, the two Blackhawks lifted off and disappeared into the darkness, headed north. The lead helicopter was the primary evacuation bird, with two Delta Force medics aboard. The second was a flying spare which could be used for search and rescue if the first went down as a result of enemy fire or mechanical problems.

Major Rowe, the Delta Force surgeon, had intended to go on the flight into Iraq, but one of the medics said, "You just get the OR team ready to work on Pat, boss. You'll have plenty of chances to work on your Air Medal before this war is over." It was good advice, so Rowe heeded it after reminding the two medics of the key points to be remembered when handling back injuries.

Healy again thought for a moment that he heard a helicopter, then dismissed it as wishful thinking. He'd not leave Iraq this night—he was certain of that now.

His arms felt heavy, and he couldn't pull the nylon poncho liner more tightly around him to keep the desert wind from drawing his body heat away. The swelling around his injured spine was numbing the nerves to his arms.

He wondered if he'd make it through the following day. It was all so—what word could he give to it? Strange? Unfair? Disappointing? No, unexpected—that's the word he was looking for. It was just so unexpected, that's all. Everything had seemed to be falling into place. He could retire anytime he wanted to, and there was plenty to do outside the Army to keep a retired Delta Force sergeant major busy. He was going to accept Wayne Wilson's offer to be his command sergeant major for a couple of years—help his old Ranger buddy run US Special Operations Task Force for a while, then hang up his rucksack and enjoy watching his kids mature into adults. Well, the chance to do that was probably gone now. Even if he got his legs to work again, he'd never be able to return to parachute status, and that was a requirement for the USSOTAF Sergeant Major.

But that wasn't the end of the world. Suppose he wasn't able to even walk? At least Congress still hadn't taken disability pay away from the military, as they had done with so many of the other benefits he'd been promised when, as a young recruit, he swore almost the same oath that members of Congress swear. The biggest difference was that he meant his oath. Congress. Hell, maybe he would run for Congress. God knows, he could do as good a job as most of the clowns on Capitol Hill. And whoever the president might be when he got there wouldn't need to worry about his vote for going to war against the likes of Saddam Hussein. The bastards. Here was the whole world, almost, lined up behind President Bush's effort to deter aggression, and those lousy, self-serving sons of bitches had barely passed the resolution to allow America to lead the whole planet, almost, in doing what was right for a change.

Healy's mind wasn't wandering; it was avoiding the thoughts he most wanted to avoid. But he could no longer deter them, and now his mind was flooded with longing for his wife and children, and with the fear that he might not see them again in this life, and with things left undone, unsaid, unresolved.

Tears welled up in the eyes of the tough, battle-hardened sergeant major, and he whispered their names, and said, "I'm sorry. Oh, God, I'm so sorry I have to leave you."

A dust devil—one of those little tornado-like swirls of desert wind—passed over him, and turned his tears to mud. It also blew the poncho liner off of him, and the cold wind seemed suddenly to penetrate to his bones. And then his brain shut down for awhile to try to let his body rest. It would need all the strength it could muster to get him through the coming day—the last before the storm of war was unleashed across the swirling desert around him.

▼

Lightning

▼

Sixteen

16 January 1991

"We'll never see him in this mess," the pilot of the medical evacuation helicopter said over the intercom.

The windblown sand and dust of the desert storm was making it all but impossible to see the ground through the night vision goggles he was wearing.

The bare-eyed copilot, looking at the television-like screen of the Forward Looking InfraRed sensor, added, "Not much showing on the FLIR, either."

"You don't have to see him. Just set us down somewhere near the GPS coordinates they gave us, and we'll get out and find him," one of the medics in the back of the Blackhawk said.

"Roger," the pilot answered. "We'll be there in about one minute."

The Global Positioning System was so accurate—its computerized receiver taking data from several satellites at once, triangulating them, and displaying a digital readout of its coordinates to within 25 meters accuracy—that the Delta Force medics were certain they'd be able to find Healy in spite of the sandstorm. All they needed was for the helicopter crew to put them down somewhere nearby.

The pilot put his machine into a high hover above the coordinates at which Healy was reported to be and began a slow, steady descent toward the ground. They knew the altitude of the ground at that location, and as the helicopter descended, the copilot called off the remaining height above the desert floor. The other crewmen and the medics scanned the ground below through night vision goggles to ensure that there were no obstacles, and to make certain that the Blackhawk didn't land atop the injured sergeant major.

The ground effect from the helicopter's rotors let the pilot know that he was almost down, and he made his aircraft settle to the desert floor with a bump.

"He should be out the right side, no more than fifty meters away," the copilot informed the Delta Force medics after checking the GPS readout again.

They disconnected their helmets from the communications cords and hopped out of the right door.

Sergeant Major Healy was barely conscious, the pain and fatigue and heat-sapping wind numbing his mind as well as his body. He thought the sound was something he was imagining—a desperate ploy of his brain to get his body to hold on a while longer.

"Over here!" one of the medics called to the other. He had spotted Healy, now almost covered by the blowing sand.

They moved to him, kneeling on either side in the howling wind, and began a skillful examination of their injured comrade.

"You'll be OK now, Pat," one of them assured him.

"We're going to get you home," the other said.

Healy recognized the voices of two of his Delta Force teammates, and a weak smile crossed his pale lips.

"Otto. Rod," he said. "I knew you'd come."

"That should do it," John Rains declared, stepping back and surveying the strange-looking little drone. He had just completed the installation of three M-122 remote firing device transmitters in the payload bay of the unmanned aerial vehicle.

The three transmitters were set to send coded signals to the three receivers which Staff Sergeant Shumate had covertly placed on the chemical Scud transporters weeks earlier. If the firing devices received those signals, the tiny battery in each would close a circuit and send an electrical charge to the blasting cap attached to it. The cap would ignite, and set off the explosive in the small "soap dish" charge atop the vehicle's fuel tank. The explosive would superheat the metal shavings in the charge, at the same time blasting open the fuel tank and sending the hot shavings into the fuel, creating a huge, destructive fireball.

"Damn, I hope it works," Dave Ames declared.

"Well," Rains said, "the airplane will take them wherever you want them to go."

Where they wanted them to go was to the panhandle of western Iraq, where the chemical-tipped missiles were believed to be hidden.

The little, twin-winged drone would be programed to start near the Jordanian border and fly north, almost to Syria. Then it would turn east, fly several miles, and head south before turning east again as it neared Saudi Arabia. It would continue that pattern, crisscrossing the whole panhandle during several hours of flight. The remote firing device transmitters were hooked to a rotating switch that would cause each to send its coded signal every few seconds.

Ames stared at the ingenious little aircraft for awhile, imagining it in flight. If its GPS-fed computer brain would just take it somewhere near the things. And if the storm blowing across that area would end, so it could fly. "We'd better get the waypoints for the flight selected, Dave. It's going to take me some time to program them into the computer," Rains said.

Ames yawned and nodded, and they headed for the USSOTAF operations center.

The sun was just beginning to lighten the eastern sky. The last day before the war was dawning.

*   *   *

The storm reached the field hospital before the helicopter carrying Healy did. The pilot made a couple of passes over the hospital, but couldn't see well enough to set his aircraft safely down.

"Maybe we should divert to the alternate," his wingman in the flying spare said over the radio.

That would mean a considerably longer time before Healy could be put onto the operating table—a long, overland drive by vehicle to the field hospital.

"You go ahead. I'm going to give it one more try," the determined medical evacuation pilot declared. "If I can't get in this time, I'll see you there."

It was the last thing anyone heard from the seven men aboard the helicopter.

Command Sergeant Major Matt Jensen woke his commanding general, Wayne Wilson, an hour later. The US Special Operations Task Force commander was getting a good night's sleep before the opening of the air offensive; the last he would get, he knew, for quite some time.

He came awake quickly and sat up, swinging his legs over the side of the cot.

"What's up, Matt?" he asked. His command sergeant major's boyish face looked troubled.

"Bad news, I'm afraid, boss," Jensen said, sitting down on the cot beside Wilson. "The helicopter bringing Pat out of Iraq crashed. All seven men aboard were killed."

The color drained from Wilson's face. "Oh, no," was all that he could manage to say.

Jensen told him what little was known about the crash—who was aboard, what the last radio transmission had been, where the terrible wreckage had been found.

The loss of subordinates, of comrades—even of close friends—wasn't something new to Wayne Wilson. He had known far too much of it during his two-and-a-half decades of soldiering in the combat arms. But not Pat Healy. He had already done so much for his country, for freedom. He had shouldered more than his share of the load.

He looked at Matt Jensen. No, it wasn't right to say of men like Jensen and Healy that they carried more than their share of the burden of freedom. It was a heavy rucksack that they bore, yes. But it was one that they chose, that they carried willingly, even eagerly. And they knew the risks, just as they knew the rewards: the sense of satisfaction, the respect of their peers, of their families, of themselves. And it wasn't just the old soldiers, either. The young ones had volunteered, too, and took the same risks for the same good reasons. They all did. It could have happened to any of them, at any time.

Wayne Wilson had long ago stopped trying to determine why; how one was chosen and another was not. That could only drive you mad. He believed in God, and trusted the reasons to Him. Most soldiers did, whether they were quick to admit it or not.

"He was my Ranger buddy, Matt," Wilson said. "He saved my life in Vietnam."

Jensen clasped the stooped shoulder of his boss and friend.

"I know," he said. "He told me that. And he told me that you saved his life, too."

They sat in silence for a time, then Wilson turned to Jensen and asked, "What's that quote from the Bible they use as a motto in the Delta Force?"

"It's from Isaiah," the former Delta soldier replied. He knew the verse by heart:

"'Also I heard the voice of the Lord, saying Whom shall I send, and who will go for us? Then said I, Here am I; send me.'"

The two special operations warriors thought their own thoughts while Wilson got into his uniform. Then they walked outside into the dying wind.

The war to liberate Kuwait was about to begin, and they had duties to perform.

▼

Seventeen

17 January 1991

At two-fifteen AM on the 17th of January, the seven Delta Force soldiers who had been with Pat Healy at the Iraqi SA-3 surface-to-air missile site made the first incision in the skin of the air defenses shielding Saddam Hussein's military might.

The four men in the assault group opened the attack on the communications facilities, employing satchel charges on the radio bunker, its external antennae, and the radar vans. They followed that with hand grenades and long bursts of automatic rifle fire to eliminate any survivors of the initial blasts.

The missiles were the next target of the team's vengeful fury, erupting in flame as they were ripped apart by 40mm shells from the support element's Mark 19 automatic grenade launcher. Next, the Mark 19 disabled the three Iraqi vehicles at the complex to avoid their being used for escape.

Meanwhile, the target acquisition and fire control radars were converted to twisted junk by explosive charges laid by the assault group, who then withdrew from the complex under the covering fire of the support element.

Their mission was accomplished by 0219 hours—four minutes after it began.

Twelve miles away, the other half of 2d Troop of Delta's D Squadron destroyed a similar site. Now there was a narrow gap through which the special operations helicopters of Wayne Wilson's task force could attack the second line of enemy air defenses.

Healy's teammates spent two more minutes killing the handful of Iraqi soldiers who dared to appear from the untouched bunkers where they had been sleeping, then disappeared into the desert night. Low overhead, a pair of big US Air Force Pave Low helicopters roared past, leading a flight of four Army Apache gunships.

Air Force Major Bob Leonard of the 20th Special Operations Squadron could smell the acrid smoke from the Delta Force attack as he sped over the SA-3 site just fifty feet above the ground. Along with the FLIR system which allowed the Pave Low helicopter pilots to see in darkness and, to some degree, through fog and smoke, the sophisticated helicopter carried terrain-following radar, which would automatically sense the terrain ahead and below, and fly the big chopper at a preset height above the ground. There were also precision navigation devices to tell the crew exactly where the aircraft was at all times, accurate to within ten meters; and communications equipment which allowed the crew secure voice communications over a variety of radio nets.

A short distance past the ruined complex, Leonard spotted seven men ahead and to his left on the FLIR screen. His heart skipped a beat until he saw that they were waving wildly and gesturing the flight on toward the north. It was the team which had destroyed the site he'd just crossed over.

"Good work, guys," Leonard muttered, jigging the tail of his chopper in recognition of the Delta Force soldiers as he swooped past them.

The route to the release point was a twisting one, for unlike the routes the Blackhawks followed when they took the Special Forces teams to remote landing zones well away from enemy forces, Leonard's flight would take him right into the teeth of the Iraqi enemy.

He thought of the irony of his leading a flight of helicopters on a mission which was so important to the safety and success of the fighter pilots who would follow.

Bob Leonard had wanted to be a fighter pilot himself, when he was commissioned in the Air Force twelve years earlier. He had harbored visions of dogfights with Soviet fighter planes in the skies over Europe, a game of deadly tag, with airplanes twisting and turning and loosing bursts of cannon fire at each other. Or diving into a hail of enemy ground fire, blazing away with 20mm guns in support of pinned down foot soldiers.

But Bob Leonard had not been selected for fighters. Instead, he had been relegated to flying helicopters. At the time, he felt it meant he would be nothing more than an airborne taxi driver. Then he had arrived at the 1st Special Operations Wing's Pave Low helicopter squadron. It didn't take him long to change his mind about fighters, for while they had evolved into high-tech, flying video game machines, whose pilots seldom saw their targets except as electronic symbols, Leonard soon found himself flying dangerous missions in the black of night just fifty feet above the ground.

There had been dashes into the coastal jungles of South America, runs to bring covert teams out of the North African desert, rescue missions in weather so bad that none but the Pave Lows dared venture out into it. And now this mission, leading the deadly gunships deep into Iraq to rip a hole in Saddam's defenses so that the fighter pilots whose job he had once coveted could reach Baghdad with the safety of surprise.

Now, Bob Leonard wouldn't trade his helicopter for any of the fighter pilots' flying video games.

A short distance before he arrived at the next echelon of the Iraqi air defense network—the early warning radars which could alert Baghdad of the impending air offensive—he would signal the flight of Apaches behind him that their targets were just ahead. But first he had to lead them there, ducking down into folds in the desert floor to stay beneath the radars, popping up to avoid high tension lines, then swooping down again, so low and fast that dust swirled up from the ground as they passed.

The Pave Lows made their last turn toward the target and began to bleed off speed. Maintaining strict radio silence, they signaled the Apaches with infrared lights, invisible to the naked eye, but showing up brightly on the gunship pilots' FLIR screens.

The deadly Army helicopters broke left and right of their Pave Low pathfinders, boring in on the Iraqi radar site ahead.

The first the enemy knew of the Americans' presence was the explosions of the initial volley of laser-guided Hellfire missiles blasting the radar installation apart. A second volley of Hellfires followed a moment later, destroying secondary targets and the men who manned them. Next, the site was raked by scores of 30mm rounds, the deadly cannon in the Apache's chin slaved to the gunner's helmet, following his eyes as he looked for anything worth shooting.

It took but half a minute to blind the eyes of Iraq's electronic early warning system.

Bob Leonard and his wingman watched the Army pilots make one more run across the site. There was little firing this time, for there was little left to shoot.

Now Leonard broke radio silence with a single codeword over his satellite radio.

"California." Mission accomplished.

To scores of command posts across the Middle East, the word was flashed immediately. To flight leaders circling anxiously with their bomb-laden squadrons at dozens of orbit points over Saudi Arabia, Turkey, the Persian Gulf and the Mediterranean Sea. To lumbering battleships and silent submarines whose Tomahawk cruise missiles waited with inhuman patience for the signal to launch themselves at the targets memorized by their electronic brains. To impatient young Navy pilots waiting on the catapults of carrier flight decks to find out for themselves what war was like.

"California," Bob Leonard said, and a thousand bolts of lightning were unleashed into the skies above Iraq.

Colonel Dave Ames watched in awe as the small, pilotless airplane was catapulted off its launching trailer. It accelerated as its buzzing propeller bit into the cool night air, climbing steadily and disappearing from sight and sound into the starlit sky.

"Well, there she goes," Rains said. "The poor man's cruise missile. Nothing to do now but wait and see if it comes back home."

Ames shook his head in amazement at the thought of the tiny plane flying automatically back and forth over Iraq. It was as if the thing had a brain of its own. The firing device transmitters in the belly of the little craft were already sending a constant stream of signals, calling to the detonators on the hidden explosive charges, telling them it was time do their hellish work.

Dave Ames wondered if he'd ever find out whether or not the desperate ploy succeeded.

"Well," he said to Rains. "Good luck. I've got to get back to work."

The second wave of aircraft bearing their terrible loads filled the sky with noise, and Abir wept softly.

"Thank God my sons are far away from here," she said. Bill Kernan hugged her closely to him.

They were standing, along with Mara and Abdul, and Abdul's son, Yassir, on the flat roof of Abir's villa, watching the flashes and fireballs of the bombs, and the impotent streams of anti-aircraft fire that searched in vain for the aircraft, most well beyond their range.

Now and then, the fiery trail of one of the Iraqi surface-to-air missiles which had survived the initial wave of Coalition air attacks could be seen streaking up into the sky. Each time, Kernan noticed, another missile trail could be seen seconds later, blazing down from above and detonating at the enemy launch site. Highspeed anti-radiation missiles, Kernan correctly surmised.

The Wild Weasel escorts were doing their job, inflicting immediate punishment on any enemy rocketeers who dared to challenge the Coalition's domination of the sky.

Somewhere well to the southeast of the villa, the horizon suddenly lit up with a twinkling line of flashes which went on and on for a long time. Kernan mentally counted off the seconds until a deep rumble of explosions from that direction reached his ears, and the roof trembled beneath his feet.

Eleven, he counted in his mind when the first sound of them arrived. That would mean the explosions were some seven miles away.

"B-52 bombers," he explained to the others, who were staring in that direction. "Probably a flight of three. That means sixty tons of bombs—about fifty thousand kilos. Somewhere near the airport, I guess."

"Fifty thousand kilos?" Abdul asked incredibly. "From only three bombers?"

"That's right," Kernan replied. "They carry twenty tons apiece—something around seventeen or eighteen thousand kilos."

The Kuwaiti resistance chief looked again in the direction of the airport, considering what massive damage such a huge airstrike would do to the Iraqis dug in there.

"Good," he said.

*   *   *

There was a look of deadly seriousness on the face of Lieutenant Lawrence Redmond, Jr. as he stood in front of the combined arms team of American tankers and their attached platoon of infantrymen. The company commander and executive officer were at battalion headquarters, receiving orders for the next phase of Team Charlie's move to outflank the entrenched Iraqis to their north, and it fell to Redmond, the senior platoon leader, to address the men—a duty which he relished.

As darkness gave way to daylight on the first day of Operation Desert Storm, the flashes of light from bombs exploding well to the north were no longer visible, but the distant rumble of their detonations still reached the young men's ears.

Rumors and speculation had given way to reality with the first of what were now the almost incessant sounds of war.

There was no need to call for the men's attention. They were waiting silently for the last few members of the company to gather around the young lieutenant, whom they all regarded, with good reason, as the finest officer in the company.

Redmond looked from one anxious face to another. They looked so young, most of them. They were young, and so was he. But he didn't feel young. He felt as if he'd been preparing for this day for a hundred years.

There were soldiers from southern farms and city ghettos in the company. There were the sons of factory workers, of businessmen and businesswomen, cowboys and Indians, and fellow servicemen. They were black and white and in-between. Tall, and short, and smart, and not-so-smart.

They were they best who ever wore the uniform, as far as Larry Redmond was concerned, and he wouldn't have traded them for any other on the earth.

The first sergeant nodded to indicate they were all there, and Redmond looked them over once more.

"As you may have noticed," he said to them in his strong, clear voice, "the war is on."

They broke into a cheer, most of them, and, as if on cue, two Tornado fighter-bombers streaked low overhead, returning from the north. Several of the tankers dived for cover, uncertain if the aircraft were friendly or not, then stood and brushed themselves off as their comrades pointed at them and howled. Then they grew silent again to listen to their First Platoon leader.

"What I'm going to read you now," Redmond said, "are some excerpts from the speech the President made to the world last night."

He read from the paper in his hand.

"'Five months ago, Saddam Hussein started this cruel war against Kuwait; tonight the battle has been joined…'"

Again, a cheer came up from the troopers, then they quieted.

"'Now, the twenty-eight countries in the Gulf area have…no choice but to drive Saddam from Kuwait by force.'"

The lieutenant looked them over as he quoted the next line without referring to the paper.

"'We will not fail.'"

The men cheered loudly once more. Redmond went on, quoting other lines from the speech of their Commander-in-Chief, drawing frequent vocal acclaim from the young warriors.

The line they cheered the loudest was, "When the troops we've sent in finish their work, I'm determined to bring them home as soon as possible."

When he had finished reading excerpts from the President's speech, Redmond said, "All right, men, we don't know yet when the order to attack will come. But when it does, we're going to be ready. We're going to attack so hard and so fast—with such speed and shock and violence—that before Saddam knows it, somebody will be knocking on his bunker door.

"'Who's that?' he'll ask. And one of you will say, 'Team Charlie, 5th of the 64th Armor, you son of a bitch! Now, get your ass out here and surrender!'"

They roared at that, and Redmond grinned broadly at them, then his face became serious again.

"But first," he said, "we have to make sure our tanks and fighting vehicles are in the best shape that they've ever been. So break out the maintenance checklists, and let's get with it."

He noticed the company executive officer approaching with a bag of mail just then.

"But before we start," he said, "It looks like we're gonna have mail call—probably the last before we get stuck in."

The first sergeant called off the names on the personal letters, then passed out the envelopes addressed to "Any Soldier" to the men who hadn't gotten one.

There was no letter addressed to Lieutenant Larry Redmond, and he was sure, now, that he would never hear from Mickey.

He sighed deeply and looked up at sky. It was streaked with the contrails of another flight of fighters miles above, headed for the heartland of Iraq.

*   *   *

"Come on, come on. Nothing but civilian vehicles, damn it. Give us a military target."

Staff Sergeant Walter Shumate, Jr. was back in the same position along the Amman-Baghdad highway where he had been more than two months earlier, when he planted soapdish charges on the vehicles carrying chemical-tipped Scud missiles.

Shumate, Captain Jack Marsh, and the four other members of their split A team were manning the discriminating mine system they had implanted along the road in mid-November. Shumate was watching the TV monitor of the system, expressing his frustration at the fact that there were only civilian vehicles on the road—most fleeing west, away from the furious aerial assault of the Coalition air forces, toward the safety of Jordan.

The Special Forces team was in a "weapons free" status now, authorized to employ their mines at their own discretion. In addition to the mines, they were also prepared to use their laser target designators to mark targets for aircraft to attack. But so far, they had seen no targets of military value.

"Patience," Marsh remarked at his subordinate's frustration, then added one of the many quotes stored in his memory. "'He that has patience may compass anything.'"

"Hmmph," Shumate muttered, his eyes glued to the monitor. "I don't want to compass something, whatever that means. I just want to blow something up."

*   *   *

Major Niza Al-Shari fired a burst from the 7.62mm machine gun in the turret of his armored personnel carrier over the tops of the vehicles clogging the road in front of him.

"Move over, damn you all!" he yelled.

Major Al-Shari's eight wheeled BTR-60 had been on the road from Al Asad, in west-central Iraq, since daylight.

So badly had the lightning strike of Coalition bombs and missiles disrupted the Iraqi high command's ability to communicate with its units in the field, that it had become possible to talk to only a few of them. In order to pass some of the orders critical to Saddam's war plan, the Iraqis were having to resort to messengers. Major Al-Shari was one of them.

He had been dispatched from Al Asad with a top secret message for the commander of the ballistic missile batteries hidden near Iraq's border with Jordan. It was a simple but historic message he bore: "Initiate chemical missile attacks on the Zionist infidels' cities of Tel Aviv, Jaffa and Haifa."

Al-Shari was the second officer dispatched with that message. The first, speeding from Baghdad in a Gazelle helicopter just minutes after the high command realized it could not communicate with its missile units, was dead. An American F-15C Eagle fighter had spotted the helicopter and wrecked it with a Sparrow missile.

Major Al-Shari fired the next burst from his machine gun directly into one of the vehicles blocking the bridge over the wadi. The others quickly moved out of the way, and his BTR-60 sped on toward the Jordanian border.

On the fourth south-to-north leg of its automatic journey, John Rains's unmanned aerial vehicle passed not far west of the chemical Scud battery. It came close enough that, had the remote firing device receivers not been shielded from the radio waves of the transmitters by the underground bunkers in which the missiles lay hidden, they would have received the electronic command to detonate. But the command failed to reach them, and the little aircraft sped on. Its next pass near the area would be even further away.

Lew Merletti peered through his binoculars, searching the road to his east. He had heard a burst of automatic weapons fire, and was looking for its source.

"There," he said to his teammate, Earl Atkinson, beside him in the easternmost surveillance position of Jack Marsh's team.

Atkinson raised his own binoculars to his eyes and peered in that direction.

"Got it," he said. "Soviet BTR-60 armored personnel carrier, headed this way."

Merletti was on the radio to Marsh and Shumate now.

"Target," he announced. "One Bravo Tango Romeo six zero, moving west on the road at high speed, over."

"Roger," Captain Marsh acknowledged, then relayed the information to Sergeant Shumate, lying in the hide site beside him.

Shumate swung the remote TV camera to the right, using the controls on the console beneath the little monitor, and waited.

"Identity confirmed," Merletti announced as Major Al-Shari's armored personnel carrier came abreast of his position. "One Iraqi BTR-60 APC."

"Take it," Marsh said to Shumate as the vehicle came into the field of view of the remote television camera.

Shumate swung the camera left until the monitor showed a flashing crosshair superimposed on the road. It marked the location of the easternmost mine beneath the roadbed. He flipped up the cover guarding the red button marked "#4," and at the bottom of the monitor a message flashed, "#4 armed."

When the vehicle appeared in the left edge of the monitor, Shumate held a trembling finger above the button, and when the nose of the BTR-60 reached the flashing crosshairs, he pressed it.

Al-Shari's armored personnel carrier lifted off the highway in an instant cloud of flame and dust, then crashed back to earth—a twisted, burning wreck. The Iraqi major, blasted out of the hatch of the vehicle's cupola, landed in the fireball of flaming fuel and burned to death. But it mattered not to him; he was already unconscious from the concussion of the initial blast.

Marsh and Shumate saw it happen on the TV monitor, and neither spoke for awhile. The image of the Iraqi's broken body flopping through the air and into the flame was etched forever into their minds. It was the first time either of them had watched someone die.

Shumate finally broke the silence.

"Holy Jesus," the young sergeant whispered, looking at his trembling finger, still pressing the button which had caused the explosion and death. "Oh, holy Jesus Christ."

*   *   *

The men in Arab robes looked carefully around before stepping out of the entrance of the compound into the street, checking to make certain that there were no enemy soldiers in sight. There were not, so the men nodded to each other and quickly walked away, headed in different directions.

Most of the 300,000 Kuwaitis still in and around the occupied city were in hiding in their homes, fearful of the air attacks which had been underway almost incessantly for hours.

As soon as he was a block away from the villa, Bill Kernan slowed, exaggerating the natural limp he still had as a result of the thigh wound he had suffered two months earlier. He reached beneath his robe and pulled a small Iraqi flag from the holster where his silenced Glock pistol was stored. He would wave the flag at any Iraqi soldiers he encountered as he wandered the streets of Kuwait City in his disguise as a mentally retarded Kuwaiti, while he assessed the effects of the first waves of Coalition airstrikes.

God, I hope this works, Kernan thought, limping on toward the smoldering enemy installations in the center of the city. Ahead of him the air raid sirens wailed, and the Iraqi anti-aircraft guns began their fruitless hammering once more.

*   *   *

Anatoly Vasilnikov sneered at the sight of Hassan al Ahwabi kneeling on the ground, facing south toward Mecca.

"You should be facing north toward Moscow," he said, "thanking the Soviet Union for these things."

He was gesturing toward the Scuds the men had dragged all over Kuwait and Iraq for months. They were slowly raising to a vertical position for firing.

The urgent order to launch them had arrived from Baghdad only minutes earlier on a secondary radio net the Iraqi high command had managed to restore. The erector/launchers had been driven from the underground bunkers where they were hidden, and were now in the previously surveyed firing positions from which they would soon be launched at the heart of Israel.

Hassan ignored the Russian's blasphemous comment and finished his prayer, imploring Allah to guide the missiles on an unerring flight to their targets. Then he rose and stood beside Vasilnikov, watching the missiles which now pointed almost straight toward the sky.

In a few minutes they would roar off the launch vehicles, bearing their deadly loads of nerve gas in a high arc to the west, then plummeting down into the population centers of the evil Jewish state.

It would be the beginning of the final Jihad, then. The Jews were sure to act, and that would herald the end of the coalition the misguided leaders of the Arab states had been duped into forming with the infidel armies of the West. The Arabs would see the error of their leaders' decision, and turn against them. The desert sands would soon be awash with the enemies' blood.

It was a brilliant plan that Allah had given Saddam, bringing the evil Americans and their western lackeys to Arab lands where they could be destroyed in a holy war. Hassan al Ahwabi felt blessed to have a part in its beginning.

He felt compelled to fall to his knees in thanks once more, and did so.

His prayer was interrupted by a flash of light, and he turned his head toward its source to see one of the missiles engulfed in a ball of fire. Stunned, he watched the second missile erupt, and then the third.

"No! No!" he screamed as the first missile toppled onto its side in the flames. Then the fuel in the second one ignited, and it roared into the air, twisting sideways before it exploded.

The third Scud's fuel ignited as well, and while the two missilemen watched in horror, it leaned in their direction, rose a hundred feet into the air, then began to tumble. It smashed to the ground near Hassan, engulfing the kneeling Iraqi in an inferno of burning fuel.

The Russian began running as soon as he saw the missile tumble in their direction, and he managed to escape the flames. He ran a short way more, but now he couldn't seem to breathe, and he stumbled heavily to the ground. A violent wave of nausea swept over him as he gasped for breath, his mouth drooling wetly. And then convulsions began to wrack his body, and as his vision dimmed to darkness, he realized that the nerve agent from the missile had reached him. It was the last thought that Anatoly Vasilnikov would ever have.

Two miles to the east, a little, pilotless aircraft buzzed on to the north, the transmitters in its belly still broadcasting their coded signals, unable to know that there were no detonators left to receive them.

Eighteen

18 January 1991

There is nothing that can be done to adequately prepare a soldier's family, when he's away, for the sight of solemn men in dress green uniforms walking up the sidewalk to their home—not even when they're friends.

Pat Healy's wife saw her husband's friends on the sidewalk, and before they even reached the door, she knew she was a widow.

Her mind began to swirl with a thousand memories, and she thought they would overwhelm her. She steadied herself on the desk beside her—his desk—and waited for the doorbell to ring. She looked down at the hand on which she was leaning heavily and saw the wedding ring that he had taken from Wayne Wilson and placed there. It suddenly seemed so very long ago.

Near her hand, in a silver frame, was his photograph, a proudly smiling father with his children on his knees. Beside it stood a small wooden plaque, a brass medallion in the center of it bearing the combat knife and triangular lightning bolt of the Delta Force logo. It had been presented to him at the end of his first tour in Delta, when he had left, at Wilson's request, to serve a tour as the first sergeant of one of his old friend's Ranger companies.

Beneath the Delta Force logo was a small plate etched with his name and dates of service with the unit, and with one simple word: "Thanks." It was, she knew, his most prized material possession.

There was a rosary on the desk, too, and when the doorbell rang, she looked at it, then at his photograph again.

"Oh, Pat," she whispered, "I loved you so."

And then she picked up the rosary and walked slowly to the door where her husband's friends waited quietly with their awful news.

*   *   *

Five and a half miles above the Saudi-Iraqi border, south of the town of Ash Shabakah, Iraq, an aging Boeing 707 aircraft was making slow figure eights in the black night sky. Crammed with sensors, electronic intercept gear and direction-finding equipment, and skilled airmen to operate them, the aircraft had been converted to an E-8A JSTARS battlefield surveillance system, capable of detecting vehicles, radio and radar emissions, and manmade heat sources on the surface of the earth far below.

Beneath the JSTARS, a few hundred feet over the desert just inside Saudi Arabia, a squadron of A-10 Thunderbolt attack aircraft, known affectionately by their pilots as "warthogs" because of their ungainly appearance, were orbiting lazily. They were waiting for the JSTARS to locate targets and vector them in for an attack.

A battery of four self propelled eight-inch guns were the first things the operators in the JSTARS saw moving on the ground below. As the artillery pieces pulled out of the schoolyard in Ash Shabakah where their Iraqi crews had hidden them at the beginning of the Coalition air offensive, one of the sensor operators detected them. He marked the vehicles on his computer screen and contacted the A-10 flight leader on secure voice radio.

The squadron commander, Lieutenant Colonel Taffy Hughes, U.S. Air Force Reserve, acknowledged the JSTARS radio call and weighed the decision he now had to make. Should he take the first mission for himself and his wingman, or let a pair of the younger pilots have a go? The aging skywarrior had flown scores of combat missions as a young Phantom fighter pilot over Vietnam more than twenty years earlier. Was it now time to sit back and let his young charges take the fight to the ememy?

No, not yet, he decided. He was their leader, and he would lead them. There would be plenty of targets, he was certain, before the just-initiated campaign ended. The others would have their opportunities. Anyway, the others were getting low on fuel, as they had taken off ten minutes before he and his wingman, who'd had to replace a circuit breaker in his instrument panel just before takeoff.

Hughes turned the remainder of the squadron over to his exec with instructions to return to base and refuel. He and his wingman, Lieutenant Les Knapp, broke and turned onto the heading the JSTARS indicated would take them to an intercept point with the target vehicles.

During the five minute flight to the target area, Hughes had time to reflect on his decision to remain in the Air Force Reserve after leaving the regular Air Force to fly commercial airliners for a living. He had joined United Airlines shortly after completing his second tour in—and over—Vietnam, only to quickly become bored with being an airborne taxi driver. So when a former comrade-in-arms contacted him with an offer to fly fighters on the weekends, he had jumped at it, eventually transitioning to the A-10 Thunderbolts when they were relegated to the reserves a short time after being delivered to the Regular Air Force.

Hughes had been made the squadron commander in July, just two weeks before Iraq's invasion of Kuwait. He began to take his reserve duty with deadly seriousness then, finding that his greatest challenge was to get the younger pilots to understand that the possibility existed that they might end up in combat over the Arabian peninsula. Then, in mid-November, the wing had been ordered to active duty and placed under the command of CENTAF, the Air Force element of General Norman Schwarzkopf's United States Central Command. The younger pilots' attitudes had changed immediately, and now, after honing their skills to perfection over the bombing ranges of Saudi Arabia, they were spoiling for a fight.

The tools with which they were equipped to do battle included a variety of ordnance, but the Thunderbolts' primary weapon, around which the whole aircraft was designed, in fact, was the 30mm chain gun, a rotating cannon which spat out superheavy depleted uranium rounds at a rate of over 600 per minute. These heavy, high-speed DU projectiles could penetrate any armor on the battlefield, and a short burst from the gun jutting from beneath the chin of the ungainly warplane spelled instant death for any machine in its sights.

For standoff attacks, the A-10s carried Maverick air-to-ground missiles, a television- or infrared-guided weapon which would fly itself to whatever target the pilot locked it onto before firing. The relatively slow, but highly maneuverable airplane also carried Rockeye anti-armor cluster bombs, which would separate after release from the airplane and rain scores of deadly shaped-charge bomblets onto targets below.

The voice of his wingman, Les Knapp, startled Hughes, rousing him from his almost reflexive flight toward the intercept point. Lieutenant Knapp—intentionally selected by Hughes to be his wingman because he was both the youngest and newest member of the squadron—announced in a high-pitched voice, "Eleven o'clock! Four tracked vehicles on the road there, headed south!"

Hughes glanced at the monitor on his instrument panel which was wired to one of the Maverick missiles slung beneath the aircraft's wings. The infrared TV camera in the missile's nose enabled him to see into the darkness ahead—an ingenious system which allowed the A-10 to be used for night operations. Until one of the pilots in Hughes's squadron had proved the technique to skeptical members of the AFCENT staff, it had been assumed that the Thunderbolts would be restricted to daylight attacks, since they contained no built-in night fighting capability. The only drawback to the technique of using the Mavericks as the airplane's eyes was that, once the missile was locked onto its target and launched, the aircraft was "night blind" again. For that reason, Hughes had made it squadron policy that, during night operations, one of the Mavericks would be the last piece of ordnance expended by each aircraft.

Now he turned the nose of his airplane slightly to the left and down, and spotted the enemy vehicles about a mile and a half ahead.

"Got 'em," Hughes announced calmly, arming the big rotating cannon as he did so. "Follow me in."

He nosed his airplane up to gain a bit of altitude, instinctively checking the instruments as he did so, then pushed the nose down toward the artillery pieces, aligning the crosshairs of the Maverick's camera on the front of the nearest one. From half a mile away, he loosed a burst of cannon fire. Almost immediately the front of the vehicle flew apart, and it careened off the road. Hughes turned hard to the right then, losing sight of the target as his young wingman bored in toward the enemy vehicles. Then Hughes turned back to the left to watch Knapp's attack.

"Goin' in hot!" the young Thunderbolt pilot announced, and swooped in toward the three undamaged vehicles with his cannon blazing, triggering a much longer burst of fire than was required. One of the self-propelled guns erupted in a huge explosion of orange flame, nearly engulfing the lieutenant's aircraft as he passed just above it.

"Ya-hoo!" Knapp called as he skidded his aircraft hard to the right, his cannon still spewing forth its deadly spittle.

Taffy Hughes watched in horror as his wingman's A-10 swung toward him with its gun still firing. Two of the rounds ripped into his airplane, one of them nearly severing the left engine pod from the fuselage. He managed to utter only one phrase before quickly grabbing the ejection handle which would catapult him from the titanium bucket of his dying airplane's cockpit into the dark night sky: "Sonofabitch!"

At a forward operations base near Ar'ar, in northern Saudi Arabia, six members of a US Army Special Forces A team sat on the open ramp of one of the 20th Special Operations Squadron's big HH-53H Pave Low III helicopters.

Along with its sophisticated navigation and terrain-avoidance avionics, the Pave Low also had onboard direction finding equipment to assist it in pinpointing the location of downed allied airmen for combat search and rescue, or CSAR missions.

It was for this CSAR mission that the helicopter and its crew, as well as the six-man Special Forces team members had been placed on alert at the beginning of the air offensive the previous night. The airmen who had just come on duty were Major Bob Leonard and his crew, who had led a flight of Apache helicopters into Iraq the night before to blind Saddam's early warning network.

Losses of allied aircraft were expected to be heavy, at least in these first few days of Operation Desert Storm. Some planners had estimated that the effort to gain air superiority in the skies over Iraq and Kuwait might cost the loss of as many as a hundred allied airplanes, and combat search and rescue operations were a high priority mission for both Air Force search and rescue elements and selected U.S. and British army units, namely Americans from the 5th Special Forces Group, and Britons from 22 Special Air Service Regiment. So far, the allied airmen had been extremely fortunate. Taffy Hughes was one exception.

As soon Hughes's wingman, Les Knapp, realized what had happened— that he had shot down his squadron commander—he immediately sent a mayday distress signal, which was picked up by the AWACS Airborne Warning and Control System aircraft managing the air battle over western Iraq. The AWACS crewmen immediately plotted the location of the A-10s and notified the Central Air Force CSAR staff in Riyadh of the situation. The CSAR staff further ordered the Combat Search and Rescue element near Ar'ar to scramble Major Leonard's Pave Low helicopter, and directed him to head for a rendezvous point with his escort aircraft.

Ironically, the escorts included a pair of A-10 Thunderbolts from the same air wing as the downed pilot, Lieutenant Colonel Taffy Hughes.

These A-10s would provide close air support to the rescue helicopter and its ground force, to keep any Iraqi reaction forces from reaching the downed airman. In addition, there would be a pair of F-15C Eagle air superiority fighters high overhead to preclude enemy aircraft from interfering with the rescue.

The flash of the propellant which ejected Taffy Hughes and his aircraft seat from the cockpit of his mortally wounded airplane temporarily blinded him. He saw nothing as his seat separated from him and his parachute snapped open to lower him to the dark earth below.

He hit the ground much more quickly than he thought he would, badly twisting an ankle as he did so. For half a minute he lay there, trying to comprehend what had happened to him in the last fateful minute. His vision was returning, and in the distance he saw a large pillar of flame reaching into the night sky. He wondered if it was the vehicle Lieutenant Knapp had hit before accidentally turning his cannon on Hughes, or whether it was the wreckage of his Thunderbolt, knocked down by that same long burst of fire. Incongruously, Hughes felt a deep sense of bereavement at the loss of the machine—as strong as he would have felt at the loss of a fellow airman.

He could hear the distinctive low moan of another A-10's rear-mounted jet engines somewhere in the distance—Les Knapp's bird, no doubt. He fumbled with the harness of his parachute, freeing himself from it before removing his emergency radio from its pocket and turning it on.

The little radio was capable of operating in one of several modes; it could emit an electronic beep either on the international distress frequency, or on other selected frequencies not normally monitored except by his own CSAR elements. It could operate in the voice mode on the same selected frequencies. And it could operate in the transponder mode, sending a response to electronic interrogating signals from friendly search and rescue forces.

Hughes switched the radio to the channel designated as the primary Combat Search and Rescue frequency for the initial phase of Desert Storm, and activated the beeper. Almost immediately, the CSAR coordinator aboard the AWACS aircraft somewhere in the dark skies above marked the location of Hughes' transmission, then responded by voice.

"Roger your beeper on channel Bravo. If you acknowledge this transmission, initiate authentication sequence now, over."

Hughes turned the beeper off, counted slowly to five, turned the beeper on once more for what he estimated to be ten seconds, off again for five seconds, then on once more. The purpose of doing this was to allow the CSAR elements to be certain the radio was being operated by an allied pilot, not the enemy.

"Your authentication is correct," came the voice from the AWACS controller. "CSAR en route. Activate transponder mode Alpha until arrival, except to report imminent capture."

Hughes complied with the CSAR coordinator's instructions, then replaced the small radio into a pocket of his flight suit.

His eyes were becoming accustomed to the darkness now, but he could still barely make out any features of the barren terrain surrounding him. He gathered the parachute in toward him and hobbled slowly in a direction away from the burning wreckage in the distance. When he reached a dip in the ground—it appeared to Hughes to be a shallow, washed out area—he dropped the parachute, then nestled into it, ensuring that the orange and white panels of the 'chute were beneath him, and the tan colored panels were the only ones exposed to sight. It was cold in the early morning darkness, and Hughes was thankful for the parachute to wrap himself in.

He drew his pistol from its holster, looked at it for a moment, then replaced it. There was no real need for the thing. If he was not rescued by friendly forces before he was discovered by the enemy, he would simply surrender and throw himself on their mercy. He was confident, though, that the American search and rescue forces would reach him soon, so he tried to relax, stay calm and warm, and await a call from them.

Overhead, he could hear Lieutenant Knapp continuing to circle the area. Poor, dumb son of a bitch, Hughes thought. Ah, well. Maybe his gun jammed on him. If not, and it was pilot error which caused Knapp to hit his plane, then Hughes had no one to blame except himself. After all, he was the one who'd been responsible for the rookie lieutenant's combat training.

At the forward operations base near Ar'ar, Bob Leonard's big Pave Low helicopter was lifting off to fly to its rendezvous with the A10s and F-15s which would escort it on the search and rescue mission.

Aboard the helicopter with its Air Force crew of half a dozen airmen were the six Special Forces soldiers who would conduct a ground search for the downed pilot, if necessary. As soon as he was clear of the Ar'ar control zone, Leonard switched to the search and rescue frequency and contacted the AWACS. The woman controlling the CSAR effort advised him that the escort aircraft were awaiting his arrival at the rendezvous point.

"Warthog Two is still over the area," she added, "but he's almost bingo. The rest of Warthog flight and the JSTARS have already had to break for home." Lieutenant Knapp's callsign was Warthog Two, and "bingo" was slang for "out of fuel."

Leonard's navigator in the seat behind him overheard the controller and said, "He'll have to leave before we get there, then. We're still forty minutes away from the search area."

Les Knapp used the burning Thunderbolt as a reference point to maintain his orbit above Hughes's approximate position. He was still shaking at the realization that he had shot his squadron commander out of the sky. Thank God Hughes had ejected safely. Until the AWACS reported that fact, Knapp couldn't even be certain that he hadn't killed Hughes. Knapp wished that he could do something to make up for the mistake, but knew he never could. He couldn't even attack the two remaining artillery pieces, because he didn't know just where, on the dark ground below, his commander's parachute had landed. The last thing he wanted to do was hit Hughes inadvertently—again.

So he just kept circling, watching the dying flames from the downed A-10, his guts grinding with remorse for the stupid accident he had caused. The investigation board would probably hang him. At the least, it would mean the end of his flying career, of that the was certain. Damn. He had wanted so much to do well, to have Hughes give him a good efficiency rating on his combat evaluation report so that he could apply for a Regular Air Force commission.

Knapp checked his fuel gauges again and saw that he had already burned up more than he should have before returning to base. But he decided to arm a Maverick missile so that he could use the television camera in its nose to scan the area for Hughes one last time before heading home.

He did so, then put the airplane into a shallow dive and pointed its nose at the burning Thunderbolt wreckage, watching the monitor on his instrument panel as the Maverick's infrared camera provided him a narrow view of the ground below. He was about to pull up when he spotted something moving toward the crash site—a vehicle of some sort. He was still several miles from it, so he kept the Maverick's camera pointed at the vehicle while it grew larger and more distinct on the monitor screen. It was a boxy, tracked vehicle. As he closed in on it, Knapp was able to see that it had four narrow tubes projecting forward from the front of its turret. On the rear of the vehicle's turret was a circular dish.

Knapp yanked the control stick over and slammed the pedal left as his radar warning indicator began to squawk in his ears. The highly maneuverable A-10 slid into a sharp turn just as a burst of tracers from the vehicle streamed past on the right of him. He had identified the enemy vehicle just in time. It was a Soviet built ZSU-23/4 self propelled anti-aircraft gun, its four 23mm cannons controlled by radar.

Taffy Hughes jumped at the sound of the four cannons firing nearby, and crawled out from beneath his parachute. He watched as another burst of tracers streamed up into the sky from half a mile away, searching for his wingman. Hughes pulled out his emergency radio and called the AWACS on the search and rescue channel.

"There's a triple-A position about a klick north of me," he told the controller. "They're firing at my wingman. Tell him to get the hell out of the area."

"Wilco," the woman's voice replied. She called Knapp and advised him of the downed squadron commander's report.

"Roger," Knapp said in acknowledgment. "You say he reports they're about one kilometer north of his position?"

"Affirmative."

"That's all I need to know," he said, ignoring her added comment that Hughes had said for him to "get the hell out of the area." If Hughes was a kilometer away, that was plenty of separation for an attack on the enemy weapons system.

Knapp slid the Thunderbolt into another sharp turn and climbed into the darkness as he headed back toward the anti-aircraft gun. He was six miles away when he nosed his airplane down again and began searching for the vehicle with the Maverick missile's camera.

"There," Knapp said aloud when he saw it. His radar warning indicator was sounding again, but he disregarded it. The enemy gun's range was much less than the Maverick's.

He laid the missile's crosshairs on the center of the vehicle, locked it on, and released the missile.

"Do your thing, baby," he said to the weapon as he put the A-10 into another sharp turn and headed home.

The missile guided itself unerringly toward the image Knapp had electronically locked into its memory. When it struck home, Taffy Hughes saw the target erupt in a bright flash. He covered his head as secondary detonations of 23mm ammunition filled the air with debris.

Les Knapp didn't see the missile's deadly work. He was too busy nursing his Thunderbolt home on the critically small amount of fuel left in its tanks.

By the time Bob Leonard's Pave Low helicopter approached Taffy Hughes's location, the burned out A-10 and twisted enemy weapons system were nothing but two bright globs of heat on Leonard's FLIR screen.

"I hear you coming, but I can't see you yet," Hughes announced over the CSAR channel.

Leonard turned his big chopper in the direction toward which the Pave Low's radio direction-finding equipment indicated Hughes's radio was located.

He spotted the downed pilot's infrared strobe light immediately. "There he is," he announced to all involved in the rescue effort as he made a pass over the flashing strobe.

"Bingo!" Hughes called as the helicopter roared past, thirty feet above his head.

Leonard and his crew began their landing checklist as the Special Forces men in the back prepared to exit the helicopter when it touched down. They would move to Taffy Hughes and assist him to the helicopter as they covered him from any enemy who might be pursuing him.

A minute later, the chopper settled to the ground a hundred feet from Hughes, and a minute after that, the Special Forces men had him aboard.

"We've got our man. Coming out," Leonard announced as he lifted the big bird off the desert floor. Twenty feet above the ground, he nosed it over to pick up speed. The smoldering wreckage of the enemy weapons system was dead ahead, and he was about to turn to avoid flying over it when he saw, on his FLIR screen, a man standing near it. He appeared to be waving a piece of cloth above his head.

His copilot saw the man, too. "Look at that!" he said over the intercom. "There's some son of a bitch down there, trying to surrender."

"Tough shit," Leonard replied. "We're out of here."

"Wait one," the leader of the Special Forces team said. "How 'bout putting us down and letting us get him?"

"I don't know," Leonard answered. "Suppose it's a trap?"

"Put us down a good way off, then," the soldier said. "Hell, we've got two A-10s up there. If they try anything funny, we'll bring them in! The guy may have some good intel we can use."

The Pave Low pilot thought for a moment, then said, "All right. Coming around left. We'll set down with the man at our nine o'clock, about 250 meters away."

The man was the only survivor of the enemy gun crew. The Special Forces men had him blindfolded, his arms bound behind his back, and aboard the helicopter less than four minutes later.

One of the American soldiers was trained in Arabic, and had been giving the prisoner orders in that language when the man said, "Hell, speak English, man. Your Arabic is terrible."

The Iraqi soldier, they soon learned, had lived in Washington, D.C. for six years. He claimed to be a conscript, forced into Saddam's army just weeks earlier, when he had come back to Iraq to attempt to convince his widowed mother to return to the States with him.

"Bullshit," one of the American troops said.

"Just look in the lining of my jacket," the captive said. "My passport's sewn into it. My green card's inside the passport."

The Special Forces men tore the lining open and discovered that their prisoner was apparently telling the truth. In addition to the green card, there was a picture of him standing beside his taxi at Washington National Airport.

He told the Americans everything he knew about the military situation in and around the town of Ash Shabakah, where he had been sent just after being taken from his mother's house and issued a uniform.

"We moved into a schoolhouse there as soon as the bombing started," he explained, yelling above the whine of the helicopter's deafening engine noise. "I was just a 'hey boy' for the anti-aircraft gun crew. The big artillery pieces that were parked in the schoolhouse with us were headed toward the border to shoot at some targets in Saudi Arabia. They were still in radio range when they got bombed. They called back to us and said that one of your planes had crashed."

The prisoner shifted uncomfortably on the floor of the helicopter, and one of the Special Forces men shoved a flak jacket under his face.

"Thanks," the blindfolded man said, then continued to babble the tale of what had happened to him.

"The lieutenant—the one who was in charge of the anti-aircraft gun—had this idea that we could drive out near the plane wreck and ambush your helicopter when it came after the pilot. They had just sent me over to get some scrub brush to use for camouflage when I heard them yelling something about a plane on radar. They shot a bunch of ammunition at it, and I didn't see them hit anything, so I thought, 'Oh, shit,' and got down under the bushes.

"I heard one of them yell, 'Here he comes again,' and a little while after that, the damn thing just blew up. I mean, it really went sky high. I was scared shitless.

"When the ammo finally stopped exploding, I went over to see if I could find anybody else alive. Hell, I couldn't even find a whole body. Then I heard your helicopter coming, so I said, 'Fuck it,' and got what was left of the lieutenant's jacket and started waving it."

He paused for a moment, squirming uncomfortably on the floor, and said, "Man, I'm lucky to be alive, you know it? I'll tell you, this goddam Saddam is nuts, man. How the hell's he ever think he can take on Uncle Sam without getting his ass kicked?"

Les Knapp was waiting for Taffy Hughes when the Pave Low landed half an hour later at the sprawling airbase where the Thunderbolt squadron was stationed. He saw the Special Forces men lead their blindfolded prisoner toward a waiting van, then saw Hughes emerge after shaking the hands of the aircrew who had come to his rescue.

"Might as well get it over with," Knapp muttered to himself, then walked to his squadron commander. He saluted and said, "Colonel, I...Hell, sir. I'm glad they got you out."

Hughes studied the young pilot a moment, scowling at the man who had nearly killed him.

"Lieutenant," he said, "that was a damn good job, finding that friggin' anti-aircraft gun and nailing it. If you hadn't stuck around, they'd probably have taken out the Pave Low with it, and killed all twelve men aboard."

Hughes broke into a grin, and slapped his wingman on the shoulder. "So, you get one big 'attaboy' for that. But just remember, it takes ten 'attaboys' to make up for one 'awshit.' What the hell happened? Your gun jam?"

Knapp hung his head, and said, "No, sir, Colonel. I just got excited and kept it triggered."

They were nearing the row of "warthogs" now, and Knapp's was the first one in line. Knapp's crew chief, assisted by the squadron commander's ground crewman, was pulling maintenance on the big rotating cannon that had blown Hughes out of the sky. The pair saw Hughes and Knapp approach, and turned toward them.

"Hey, Colonel!" the airman who had cared for Hughes's A-10 called, saluting his boss. "Welcome home! As soon as I get this thing checked out, I'll change the name on it to yours, and you can have another go at those raghead bastards."

"Not that one, Sergeant Stalnaker," Hughes declared. "The damn gun on it jams! Give me one of the spares."

The two ground crewmen eyed him strangely, and Stalnaker said, "But, sir, we just checked it out. There's nothin…" Hughes interrupted Sergeant Stalnaker, giving the crew chiefs an exaggerated wink as he repeated, "The damn gun jams, I said, chief."

The senior crewman elbowed Knapp's mechanic, and both enlisted men smiled at the pilots.

"Uh huh. Well, we got it fixed now, boss," Stalnaker said, then looked at Lieutenant Knapp. "But if I was your wingman, I'd be mighty careful. Your gun might be the one that jams next time."

▼

Nineteen

21 January 1991

There were still a few leaves blowing off the almost bare, old hardwoods of Arlington Cemetery when the blue clad soldiers of 1st Battalion, Third United States Infantry—the Old Guard—lifted the coffin onto the same honored caisson which had borne the body of another Irish-American, President John F. Kennedy, to be buried nearby.

The only noise was the wind, and the snorting of the riderless black horse, a pair of riding boots secured backward in the stirrups of his empty saddle.

Only a few soldiers were there other than the immaculately uniformed burial detail from the Old Guard, and those few wore Army Green and green berets. Most of Pat Healy's Delta Force comrades were still in Saudi Arabia, or deep behind enemy lines inside Iraq.

The former Secretary of the Army and his wife were there. It was he who had arranged to have the sergeant major buried with the full, traditional military honors he deserved. The silver-haired Virginian was like a godfather to the Delta Force, and more; his own son was serving with them.

Some of Delta's old-timers were there, too, drawn together as they too frequently were these days, to say farewell to one of their own.

One of them had stopped outside the chapel at Fort Myer before the service began. The burial detail seemed a bit too relaxed, and the old trooper saw their first sergeant standing nearby and went to him.

"First Sergeant," he said, "I'm sure you've had the honor of burying a lot of good men. But you'll never bury a better one than this one."

The first sergeant could see the military air of the man, despite the civilian attire he wore. He came to attention and asked, "Who was he, sir?"

Security considerations would normally have demanded a less revealing answer, but the old soldier looked the first sergeant in the eye and said, "A Delta Force sergeant major, killed on the way out of Iraq, First Sergeant."

The word was passed, and the Old Guard troopers' chins came up, and their precise movements became even sharper than they usually were.

Visitors to the sacred hillside stopped and watched, hands over hearts, as the flag-draped caisson wound its way slowly past row on endless row of headstones and down the hill. Their country was at war in a distant land, and they could sense, somehow, that this was one who had died there.

The sad but hope-filled words of the Christian burial service were said, the Stars and Stripes folded to a crisp triangle of blue and presented to the brave, young widow.

Seven rifles fired a volley with such precision that it sounded like one shot, then fired twice more.

And then, across the hallowed ground of Arlington, a bugle mournfully sounded its haunting, last farewell: "Taps."

Sergeant Major Healy's last formation was over.

One retired comrade stayed for a while, after the family and the others had left, to watch the coffin lowered into the grave. When it was done, he threw a handful of dirt into the hole. "'Well done, thou good and faithful servant,'" he said. "Well done."

.

He saluted his friend for the last time, then saluted the first sergeant of the Old Guard company. The other old soldier snapped to attention and returned the sharp salute.

Together, they turned and walked slowly up the hill.

*   *   *

"How many sorties?" Private Anderson asked incredulously.

"More than four thousand," Lieutenant Redmond replied to the driver of his Abrams battle tank.

The tank's gunner, Sergeant Peterson, said, "Hell, sir, the damn war's only been goin' on for four days. You mean to tell me the zoomies have been flying over a thousand sorties a freakin' day?"

"That's what I'm saying, Pete," the platoon leader replied.

The crew's loader, Specialist Begay, was nodding his head to show that he could confirm Redmond's statement that the Coalition air forces had flown more than four thousand combat sorties in the first four days of Operation Desert Storm.

"What you nodding at, Gibbs?" Anderson asked Begay.

Redmond chuckled at the nickname "Gibbs" by which Begay was now known by the whole tank company. With the strange logic by which nicknames evolve in the US Army, Begay—a native American from the Navajo nation—was initially called "chief." After he had whipped two soldiers at once to demonstrate his displeasure with that nickname, Begay had been referred to as "Rosso," which, in Italian, means "red," short for "redskin." When Begay thrashed another trooper after discerning why he was being called "Rosso," the men of Charlie Company next began to call him, "Mr. Washington," as in Washington Redskins.

Begay had accepted "Mr. Washington" as an adequate balance between respect and ethnic slur. But then a soldier whose name actually was Washington arrived in the platoon, so they had to find yet another name for Begay. Someone decided on "Gibbs," for Joe Gibbs, the Washington Redskins' head coach. Since it made almost no sense at all, it was quickly and irrevocably adopted.

"I heard it on the Voice of America myself," Begay said "More than four thousand sorties. The way I figure it, since every airplane carries, say, six bombs, that's something like twenty-four thousand bombs already dropped. If only half of them were aimed at Saddam's tanks, then that means twelve thousand tanks have been attacked."

"Why, hell, Gibbs," Anderson interjected, "he only had about four thousand to start with—right, sir?"

"That's what the S-2 claims," Redmond said, grinning at his crew's conversation.

"Well then," Gibbs Begay continued with his strangely simple logic, "that means each of his tanks has been attacked about three times, right? Now, if these bombs are half as smart as that Marine general doing all the briefings claims they are, then every tank Saddam owns has been hit one-and-a-half times. So the war's over, for all intents and purposes".

The other tankers laughed, and Sergeant Peterson said "Gibbs, you ought to be in charge of this operation. With logic like that, we'd be getting orders to go home any day now."

"Yeah," Private Anderson said, "back to Georgia. Back to all those Hinesville honeys just waiting there for Handy Andy to show 'em how much they been missin'."

"You going to start yakking about all those women you claim to have again, Anderson?" Gibbs asked. "The ones you never seem to get any mail from?"

"Women," Peterson said, and Lieutenant Redmond cast a concerned glance at him. He knew his gunner was married, but he had noticed that there never seemed to be a letter for him at mail call.

"You know, don't you," Peterson continued, "that if they didn't have pussies, there'd be a bounty on 'em?"

"Hey," Redmond said, "how'd you manage to get on the subject of women, Pete? I thought this conversation was about airstrikes."

But Peterson's mind was on his wife now, and the lack of news from her was gnawing at him. Without looking at the other members of the tank crew, he stood and walked off into the empty desert to be alone with his thoughts.

I guess they're all the same, Larry Redmond thought sadly as he watched his homesick gunner walk away.

The Coalition air campaign was exceeding all expectations of success, except in one area. The Scud missiles with which the Iraqis were playing a deadly shell game were having great effect—not much effect militarily, but a great deal of effect politically and psychologically, as they fell on Israel and Saudi Arabia.

Patriot missiles, already in Saudi Arabia, were immediately shipped to Israel. The ensuing duel between the Scuds and the Patriots which streaked up to intercept them, usually successfully, was the highlight of television news coverage of the war. Except for the controlled release of footage of the allies' most successful "smart bomb" attacks, and impotent anti-aircraft fire in Baghdad, the missile duel provided the only combat footage the frustrated journalists could acquire.

Like it or not, the conventional thinkers at Central Command finally had to come to grips with the continuing problem of the Iraqi ballistic missiles. Their current technique, which consisted of maintaining combat air patrols over the areas from which the missiles were being launched, simply wasn't working. True, the launchers were usually hit after the missiles were fired, but that was too little too late.

The CENTCOM staff turned to Major General Wayne Wilson and his US Special Operations Task Force to solve the problem.

Wilson had an immediate recommendation: infiltrate American and British special operations forces throughout the Scud launch areas. Their constant presence would enable them to saturate the area with reconnaissance patrols in search of the sites where the Scuds were hidden, and to maintain surveillance on likely launch areas. When they spotted any missiles or their supporting equipment, the Special Forces teams could immediately report it on their satellite communications, or SATCOM, systems. In addition, they could use the hand-held laser target designators with which they were trained to mark targets for fighters and helicopter gunships to attack with laser-guided munitions. And, in the event that no aircraft were immediately available, the ground patrols could attack the missiles with their own weapons to prevent them from being launched.

Wilson had asked that top of the line fighter-bombers such as the F-16 Fighting Falcons or F-15E Strike Eagles be assigned the mission of supporting his teams, but the AFCENT staff already had an almost endless list of critical, fixed targets for them to strike and "revisit," as follow-on attacks came to be known. So the mission was handed to the cumbersome looking old "warthogs" of Taffy Hughes and his Air Force Reserve A-10 Thunderbolt squadron.

Now Hughes and those of his pilots not on strip alert were standing in a hardened aircraft shelter, trading respectful glances with several groups of other men also standing there. They were the Army and Air Force special operations helicopter crews and some of the American and British special forces troops under Wilson's command.

Wayne Wilson stood before them.

"The reason that I've gotten you all together," he explained, "is to welcome the newest members of the USSOTAF team—Lieutenant Colonel Taffy Hughes and his Warthog squadron."

There were a few cheers and whistles, and Hughes waved a salute to the other groups.

"Now," Wilson continued, "there is no substitute, I learned long ago, for having the men on the ground and the men in the air who support them to get to know each other. That way, when one of them calls the other one with a desperate request for airstrikes or for search and rescue, or for information, or for any other reason, it's more than just two strange voices on the radio. When an airman or a soldier is able to put a name or a face with the voice, it becomes a man he's talking to, not just a radio."

Some of the men in each group were nodding in agreement, and Wilson said, "I see that a lot of you—the old farts like me, in particular—agree with me.

"The best way for those men to get to know each other is to spend as much time together as possible—to eat together, sleep together, drink together. But this is Saudi Arabia, so drinking together is a bit of a problem. And the fact that there aren't many women available for off duty social engagements makes me hesitant to recommend sleeping too closely together. So most of the camaraderie, I suppose, will have to be developed in the mess hall. The problem with that, of course, is that most of the ground troops are going to be out in Scudinavia, not in the mess hall."

The aircrews looked at the Special Forces troops with a mixture of awe and sympathy as Wayne Wilson continued his pep talk.

"Now, thanks to the kindness of Augie Busch, we've been able to overcome part of this problem..." He nodded to his sergeant major, Matt Jensen, who was standing in a corner of the shelter, near some tarpaulin-covered drums. Jensen pulled back the tarp, reached into one of the ice-filled drums, and hoisted a cold bottle of O'Doul's non-alcoholic malt beverage. Jensen had learned of the Anheuser-Bush contribution of ten thousand cases of the near-beer to the troops in Saudi Arabia, and he'd managed to get his hands on twenty cases for his men.

A loud cheer rose from all parties, and Wilson waited for them to quiet somewhat.

"So let's welcome Taffy and the Warthogs, and get to know each other. And I don't want to see anyone walk out of here until those drums are empty—unless its hand-in-hand.

"Dismissed!"

Had he not witnessed it first hand, Bill Kernan doubted that he would believe the accuracy with which the allies were attacking military targets in Kuwait City. With very few exceptions, the only serious damage inflicted on non-military personnel and installations as a result of the airstrikes was from the Iraqi anti-aircraft shells and missiles when they fell back to earth.

It made his job as the principal advisor to the resistance force much easier than it would have been, had the bombs been inflicting large numbers of civilian casualties.

Kernan spent several days in the center of the city in his disguise as a mentally and physically impaired Kuwaiti, sleeping and eating above the shop where he had previously stayed with Abdul. He was there when Abdul came to him with news about Saddam's latest response to the aerial attacks—environmental terrorism.

"They're filling the Gulf with oil," the Kuwaiti reported. "Hundreds of thousands of barrels of it."

"Oil? Where?" Kernan asked.

"At the tanker terminal," Abdul said. "They're pumping it out of the tankers that got stranded by the invasion, and they've opened the valves at the docks, too."

The CIA operative's brow furrowed as he tried to figure what the Iraqis could possibly stand to gain from such a senseless and environmentally tragic act.

He shook his head, then looked at Abdul. "Maybe they think it'll prevent an amphibious assault, or something. Why else would they possibly do it?"

"I don't know," Abdul said. "But we need to do something to try to stop it. It could mean the end of all life in the waters of the Gulf."

Kernan watched the resistance chief mentally struggling with the problem. He was no longer surprised to hear Kuwaitis expressing such concerns as the environment and democracy and women's rights. It shamed him when he remembered thinking that the Western world somehow had a monopoly on such concerns.

"What can we do about it?" Bill asked.

Abdul shook his head and sighed, then looked at Kernan. "I don't know," he said. "But at least we can go and have a look."

Dr. Francesca Singh finished the brief medical examination of her patient, then said, "Yes, Abir, it's just as you thought. You're pregnant, all right."

Abir closed her eyes. She and Bill had never even discussed the possibility of it, and she wondered if he had even thought about it. Certainly, he must have realized that it might happen. Or had he just assumed that she was taking birth control pills? What would his reaction be when he found out?

She looked up at Francesca with a forced smile and slid off the examination table to her feet.

Not far away, an anti-aircraft gun was firing, but the women paid little heed to it.

Abir's hand moved instinctively to her abdomen and pressed against it.

"I wonder if the war will be over by the time this child is born?" she said.

Abdul and Kernan stood near the seaside south of Kuwait City. A heavy carpet of thick, black oil undulated along the sandy shoreline, and here and there doomed cormorants struggled amid the muck in futile attempts to fly.

Bill Kernan spat into the oil in disgust. How could you fight something like this? What was the point of it? This wasn't war. It was senseless terrorism, pure and simple.

Behind them, some distance inland, the men heard a boom, and turned around to see whether it was an allied bomb, or another instance of an additional form of environmental terrorism they had discovered on the way out of the city. It was the latter. Another wellhead in the Ahmadi oilfield had been dynamited, the pressurized oil blazing as it shot high into the air. There were about a dozen wells afire, now.

Abdul turned back to the tanker terminal pier. "See that structure just this side of the shore end of the pier, Bill?" he asked.

Kernan turned around and saw where the Kuwaiti was pointing. "Yes," he replied.

"That's the key to cutting off the oil flow," Abdul explained. "The fail-safe valves are in there. They're connected to the valves all the way back at the distribution junctions in the oilfields. They won't allow oil through the lines unless they're electronically held open. If anything goes wrong here, the valves back at the junction boxes automatically close, shutting down the flow."

"I don't understand," Kernan admitted.

Abdul looked at the American. "You don't have to understand," he said. "All you have to do is believe me, and get the Air Force to bomb it. The system itself will do the rest."

"All right," Kernan agreed. At the start of the air war, he'd received a message stating that the CIA had been assured that they could receive immediate strikes through CENTCOM on targets they considered critical to their efforts.

"Then let me get back to my radio. I'll call for a strike on it right away, and I can pick up my rifle, too. I'll come back and watch the airstrike, and report the results."

"Your rifle? The silenced one?" Abdul asked.

"Yes," Kernan replied.

"It will be dangerous to try to bring it all the way down here from the villa. Why do you need it?"

Kernan looked back at the oilfield, where a huge column of black smoke from the burning wells was rising into the afternoon sky.

"Because, after I watch the strike, I'm going to pay a little visit to the guys who're doing that," he said, gesturing toward the sabotaged wells.

Abir had not seen Bill for several days, as he had been in the city center, reporting the results of bomb strikes against critical targets there.

He stopped by the little underground hospital long enough to kiss her and to ask, "How are you feeling now, my love?" She had been nauseated on several occasions the day before he left, and he suspected that she had eaten some tainted food.

"I've never felt better," she replied, smiling. She would tell him about the baby as soon as she got some time alone with him, she'd decided. "What are you going to do right now?" she asked.

"I've got to make a radio call and pick up something, then leave right after that," he said. His lover looked disappointed, so he added, "But I should be back here by daylight. See you then?"

Abir nodded, disappointment still showing on her beautiful face. Bill kissed her warmly and said, "I love you, Abir. I'll see you in the morning."

"I love you, too," she said as he hurried off to use his radio. "Be careful, Bill."

Once more her hand went instinctively to her abdomen, even though she knew it would be months before she'd feel the tiny child growing inside her.

The strike on the failsafe valve system at Kuwait's Sea Island oil terminal was delivered by a US Navy A-6 dropping a Paveway guided bomb.

Kernan heard nothing except the hissing of the flaming wells just inland—there were two dozen or so, now—until the bomb struck home. The valve system suddenly erupted in a giant flash, and a second later, the concussion nearly blew Kernan off his feet. When he looked back at the valve shed, there was nothing left of it but a mass of smoldering, twisted metal. He hurried over to it. Crude oil poured out of it for several minutes in a dwindling stream, then died away to a thick trickle.

"I'll be damned," he muttered to himself. "It worked." Then he heard a small explosion from the oilfield behind him, and turned to see another sabotaged wellhead ignite.

He returned to the pile of rubble near the oil-fouled beach where he had been awaiting the airstrike since shortly after dark. On the small, handheld radio he had there, he announced, "Beirut, Beirut."

Abdul heard his radio call and answered with the same codeword. Kernan knew his friend would pass on the message to Riyadh immediately: the airstrike on the failsafe valves at Sea Island terminal was successful. The flow of crude oil into the Gulf has been stopped.

Kernan slid the radio into his dirty robe. Then he untied the bundle of splintered wood he had carried on his shoulder earlier when he limped past the Iraqi checkpoint north of the terminal. In the middle of the wood was his suppressed .223 rifle, broken down into two parts and wrapped in dirty rags. He quickly assembled it, checked to ensure that the night sight was functioning, and loaded it. Then he moved stealthily across the road and into the oilfield.

*　　*　　*

"Look at this, Dave," Wayne Wilson said to his operations officer, Colonel Dave Ames.

Ames went to the general's desk and looked over his shoulder at the satellite photograph lying there. It showed several piles of twisted rubble lying on the ground, and splotches of blackened earth surrounding them.

"What is it?" Ames asked. Wilson answered by lifting the satellite view and pointing to several photographs beneath it. They were considerably more detailed, obviously taken by a reconnaissance aircraft at a much lower altitude. Ames picked them up and studied them.

"Scud launchers, huh?" he said. "Airstrikes?"

Wilson shook his head. "Nope. There haven't been any strikes put in where these were taken. And there aren't any bomb craters. We think they're the one's that had the chemical warheads. Looks like that drone of Rains's did the trick."

Ames smiled at him, then studied the detailed photos again. "Yeah," he muttered. "Yeah, you can see the three launch vehicles. And these two piles look like they used to be missiles."

"That's right," Wilson said. "And see the bodies lying around, some of them quite a distance away? Probably killed by their own chemicals, since there isn't any debris around them. The image interpreters seem to think the missiles had been erected for launching, and the fuel in them partially ignited, that's why they're a little way from the launchers."

"I'll be damned," Ames said. "That was a close one. Can you imagine what the Izzies might have done, if they'd landed in Israel?"

"I sure can," the USSOTAF commander replied. "As it is, they launched a long range missile out into the Med—a nuclear-capable missile—to show us they're dead serious about putting a stop to the damn things."

"Jesus," Ames said. "I guess we owe Sergeant Shumate a medal for this one."

"Yes," Wilson agreed. "And your buddy Rains deserves one, too."

"Well," Ames said, placing the photos back on his boss's desk, "the teams we have up in Scudinavia should be able to do some good. And the Warthog pilots are all fired up to shoot for them. By the time they drank all that O'Doul's together, you'd have thought they were long lost pals."

Wilson grinned. "Yeah, that was a good idea old Matt had. They got to placing so many bets on who was going to outdo whom, that the Scudders don't stand a chance."

"We better hope so, boss," Ames said with a look of deadly seriousness. "If the Israelis try to jump into this thing now…Well, I'd hate to think what it might turn in to."

Wilson nodded. "Those men out there are the best on the planet, Dave. If they can't do it, nobody can."

*   *   *

Bill Kernan felt—and looked—as if he'd literally been to Hell by the time he left the Ahmadi oil field south of Kuwait City. He was covered with soot and oily sand from his night-long effort to put a stop to the sabotage of the wells there.

He had failed to deter the Iraqis from continuing their senseless assault on the environment. But he had made them pay a price. Eight of the saboteurs lay dead in the oil field, killed by Kernan's whispering weapon during the hellish night.

Abdul picked him up north of the Iraqi checkpoint on the road from Ahmadi to Kuwait City. He was driving a beat-up old Land Rover he had gotten from somewhere, and he turned off the road shortly after picking Kernan up, driving across the sand to avoid Iraqi troops along the road.

"You look like hell, Bill," he said as they bumped across the furrowed ground where Iraqi tanks had made deep grooves in the desert floor as they moved south.

"That's the right word," Kernan agreed. Abdul was looking at him through the night vision goggles he wore to guide the blacked out vehicle across the desert.

They bumped along in silence for awhile, and the bone-tired Kernan dozed off.

Suddenly, Abdul suddenly slammed on the Land Rover's brakes and yelled, "Get out! Get out and run!"

The men flung open the doors of the vehicle and ran into the open desert surrounding them. Kernan had no idea why they were running, but he followed the sprinting Kuwaiti as quickly as he could, the muscles in his wounded thigh burning with pain at the unaccustomed strain.

Suddenly, two hundred feet behind them, the Land Rover erupted in a flash of flame and smoke, and the men dived to the ground as fragments whizzed overhead.

"Holy hell!" Kernan said.

"The laser," Abdul said. "I saw the beam move onto us with the night vision goggles."

Kernan hefted himself to his knees and looked at the wrecked Land Rover smoldering nearby, realizing how narrowly they had avoided being killed by the laser-guided bomb. The infrared beam was invisible to the naked eye, but Abdul had been able to see it marking their vehicle through his night vision goggles.

High above them, the weapons officer of a Navy A-6 Intruder fighter-bomber turned to his pilot and said, "Lucky sons of bitches. How the hell did they know they were about to get hit?"

"Don't know," the pilot said, "but I'll bet the bastards are on their knees thanking Allah right now. OK, wizzo, find us another target."

It was mid-morning before Bill Kernan limped tiredly in through the gate of Abir's villa. He figured he'd walked about ten miles. He was hungry and thirsty, and went straight to the kitchen.

Mara was there. She looked at the filthy American curiously and said, "What happened? Abir has been worried. And where's Abdul?"

Kernan pulled the little radio and his pistol from beneath his dirty robe and placed them on the table. His silenced rifle had been destroyed in the Land Rover.

"Abdul's all right," he said. "He went to the video shop to collect the reports on last night's bombing. We had a little problem with the Land Rover."

She handed him a cup of tea. "We got three more torture victims in last night," she said. "The Mukhabarat are getting more brutal every day now. One of them died. Just as well. They had ripped out his eyes, and cut off his penis and testicles."

Kernan looked at her. "What about the others, Mara?"

She sat down across the table and looked at him with eyes dark from fatigue. "Yassir," she said. "Abdul's son. They pulled out all his fingernails, and poured gasoline on his hair and set it afire. Doctor Singh is worried."

"Oh, Jesus," Kernan said. "Does Abdul know?"

"How could he? He was with you."

"Yes, he was." He drained the cup of tea, and Mara poured him another. "He'll be here soon," Kernan said. "I'm afraid of what he might do, Mara."

"Yes," she replied. "You must make sure he doesn't do something foolish."

Kernan wondered what a man could do after learning that his son had been tortured that might be considered "foolish." The Kuwaiti woman sensed his thoughts and said, "Something that will get him killed. He's too valuable to the resistance for us to lose him."

"Yes," Kernan answered, draining the teacup again, then standing. "I'm going to see Yassir."

"Not like that," Mara said. "You're filthy. Go and wash first."

"All right," Kernan said. "I will. Where is Abir?"

"She's there—with the boy. You'd think it was her own son, the way she's caring for him."

"Thank God her own children are safe in Saudi," Kernan muttered.

Mara nodded, her dark, weary eyes fixed on his. She looked as if she wanted to say something else, but didn't, so he left to get himself cleaned up.

Twenty minutes later, he walked into the resistance force hospital secreted in the villa of the absent Sheik al-Sabah.

Yassir was on the table in Dr. Singh's little operating room, where she was carefully removing flakes of dead, charred skin from the boy's head, face, and shoulders. His hands were bandaged, and strapped to the table to prevent him from touching his terribly burned skin. Tubes ran into his nose, and from two bottles into needles in his arms.

Abir was sitting there beside the table, and when she saw Bill walk in, she rose and walked to him. Tears fell from her already reddened eyes. He hugged her to him, then kissed her head and asked, "How bad is it, Doctor Singh?"

Without looking up at him, Francesca said, "Quite bad. We can't take proper care of him here. Apparently, he inhaled some of the flames. Even if we can keep him alive, the scarring will be terrible. I can't tell if he has his sight or not."

There was a gurgling moan from someone on a gurney in the corner, and Bill looked in that direction. Dr. Singh glanced over also, then went back to work on Yassir. A moment later, a deep, rattling sigh came from the corner. Once more Francesca Singh glanced at the patient on the gurney, then looked at Kernan.

"Cover her up, will you, Bill? She just died," the doctor said in a matter-of-fact way.

Kernan went to the lifeless body to cover it. He gasped when he looked at the dead woman's head. The top of her skull was missing, the purplish gray folds of her brain exposed to the air. The Mukhabarat had neatly sawed it off.

Bill fought off the urge to vomit, then returned to Abir's side. "What can I do to help?" he asked.

"Nothing, really," Francesca said. "I'm nearly finished here. Where's his father?"

"He should be here at any time."

Mara came in just then. "Abdul is in the kitchen," she said to Kernan. "I didn't tell him."

When Kernan walked into the kitchen, Abdul smiled at him. "You look a hell of a lot better than you did last night, but you still look tired." he said. "Did you get some sleep?"

Bill suddenly realized that he hadn't slept in two days. "No, not yet," he said.

"I got some damage reports from Basra and Umm Qasr," the resistance chief reported. "There was a news team from CNN in Basra. The Iraqis were trying to make them believe all the damage there is from American bombs, but actually, it's from the Iran-Iraq war. The Iranians pounded the place for months."

He handed Kernan a cup of tea he'd poured for him. "I also have another video tape of the Mukhabarat in action. I haven't seen it yet, but they said it shows the bastards pouring gasoline on a boy's head and setting fire to him."

Kernan stared at his Kuwaiti friend with eyes so full of sadness that Abdul sensed something terrible, and then he understood. The color drained from his face and he slumped into a chair.

"Y-Yassir," he said, and Kernan nodded.

"Dr. Singh is working on him now," he said, then made a sudden decision. "I'll get him evacuated to Saudi Arabia, Abdul. They can care for him better there."

Abdul nodded absently, not really listening. Rage was building inside him now, and his eyes had a fiery, far-away look in them. He was muttering something in Arabic, and the American was certain it was curses.

Then the tough Kuwaiti fighter dropped his head into his arms and sobbed. Kernan reached across to him and put an arm on his shoulder.

"I'm going to my radio to put a call in for the helicopter," he said. "I'll try to get them to come for him tonight."

Before Kernan made the call, he sat there by his radio, thinking just how he should word the request to have the young torture victim evacuated. The CIA station in Riyadh had already notified him that there would be no helicopter flights in support of the resistance until further notice. There was too great a chance, until the allied air forces virtually wiped out Iraq's anti-aircraft capabilities, of the low flying helicopter being shot down, or mistaken for an enemy aircraft and engaged by Coalition fighter escorts. And, with captured pilots being paraded before television cameras by the enemy, he was certain that the CIA would want to avoid the risk of Claude Owen becoming one of them. He knew Owen would be glad to make the flight, but doubted that the Agency would allow it.

No, they would never risk the flight for a single Kuwaiti patient, Kernan knew. But then he came up with an idea. He called the station and told them that the resistance had recovered a badly-burned man whom they believed was a missing Coalition pilot. He needed to be evacuated immediately.

"No," he responded when asked from Riyadh if he could identify the man by name. "The Iraqis got to him first," he lied. "They took his uniform, ID tags—all of that. The resistance ambushed the truck that was carrying him north of the city. I guess they were going to take him to Baghdad."

"All right," he was finally advised over the radio. "We'll let CENT-COM know. They'll want to fly in and get him, no doubt."

Riyadh advised their field agent to call back at midday to work out the details, then Kernan went to let Abdul know. He was gone.

The car bomb that exploded in the center of Kuwait City that day devastated the Mukhabarat headquarters there. The Iraqis correctly assumed that it was done by Kuwaiti resistance forces, and they began to exact revenge from the civilian populace almost immediately.

When Abdul saw the results of his act of rage, he realized that it had been a mistake. But it was too late to undo it, then.

Bill Kernan got the boy Yassir evacuated that night. When the Pave Low landed in the prearranged spot a few miles southwest of Al Jarah, Kernan went aboard.

"I'm afraid there's been a mistake," he yelled to the crew chief over the din of the helicopter's engines. "It's not a pilot—just a twelve year old boy the Iraqi's tortured."

The Air Force crew chief looked at the badly burned boy two other crewmen carried up the ramp of the helicopter as Dr. Singh removed the sheet shielding him from the dust.

He looked back at the CIA man in the dim red lights of the Pave Low's cargo bay. "I have a boy about that age," he yelled. He held out his hand for Kernan to shake. "Thanks for giving us the chance to get him out, sir. We'll take good care of him."

A minute later, they watched the Pave Low lift off the desert floor in a huge cloud of swirling dust and speed away to the southwest.

"At least that's one who'll get good care," the weary woman doctor said. "I'm afraid there's going to be a lot more who won't, because of his father's damned car bomb."

"Well, let's get going," Kernan said, pulling on his night vision goggles. He had been advised that CENTCOM would grant them a safe corridor to and from the landing zone, so that he wouldn't have to worry about another smart bomb attack on the vehicle. But sometimes not everyone gets the word, he knew, so he wanted to be able to tell if they were being targeted by a laser, just in case.

Abir decided not to tell Bill about their child—not now. He had enough to worry about, she explained to Mara and Francesca. And the way things were going, the war would be over soon, and she could tell him then.

The other women understood, and pledged to keep her secret.

✳   ✳   ✳

The war was indeed going well for the Coalition, in spite of some minor setbacks. The weather turned bad for a time, but soon the skies were filled with allied planes again, decimating the tanks and aircraft shelters and supply convoys of the enemy. After the infiltration of Wayne Wilson's American Special Forces teams and Sir Peter de la Bretaigne's British Special Air Service troops into western Iraq, the Scud attacks dropped off markedly. Most of the inaccurate missiles whose crews dared to surface from their hiding places were seen by the Special Forces men. They either destroyed them with their own organic weapons, or marked them for the prowling Warthogs to attack. The few missiles which the enemy did manage to launch were almost all intercepted by Patriots. Most did little damage.

Saddam's air force fared no better than his ground forces. A few Iraqi aircraft did initially rise to meet the allied planes. Without exception, they were quickly blown out of the sky. The others, being systematically destroyed in their hardened shelters by the Coalition's guided weapons, began to flee to Iran for safety. Those that made it, it soon became clear, would become Iran's air force after the war.

When Central Command became convinced that the enemy's intelligence capability was almost totally blind, and his armor sufficiently weakened from attrition at the hands of the Coalition air forces, the American and British and French tanks began to move. It was time to deal with Saddam's army on the ground—time to do to that army what the Chairman of the Joint Chiefs, General Colin Powell, had said would be done when he made the most eloquent statement of the war.

"First we're going to cut it off," he said. "And then we're going to kill it."

▼

Thunder

▼

Twenty

24 February 1991

They thundered across the rocky desert floor like some primeval beasts of old, led by a steel-toothed giant at the point of the herd. Had Bedouin tribesmen from earlier times seen them, they would no doubt have fallen to the desert floor to worship the things in awe.

Without slowing, the iron monsters belched smoke and flame from long, trunklike tubes, spewing lightning bolts of steel at the lesser beasts far out in front of them. The lightning struck home, and the distant enemy creatures erupted in flames as if they were dragons exploding from uncontrolled inner fires.

Inside the great steel herd that thundered forward were the men of Team Charlie, 5th Battalion, 64th Armor—a tank company team composed of three platoons of high-tech M1A1 Abrams tanks and an attached infantry rifle platoon in Bradley fighting vehicles. The sharp smells of burned propellent and diesel fumes could not mask the stink of fear that hovered in every vehicle—not even the onboard air conditioning systems and charcoal impregnated chemical protective suits the men wore could hide it.

This was to be the biggest tank battle in the history of the world, the men had been told.

Only a handful of them had ever been in actual combat before, and none in a tank battle. But every man in every vehicle knew what an anti-tank round could do to an armored vehicle, and to the men inside. An

explosion, jagged chunks and molten streams of steel, onboard ammunition igniting in an immediate flash of unimaginable heat, and almost
certain death by fire. Quick death, if a man was lucky. No wonder the
stink of fear was so prevalent.

Only one man among them all was totally without fear. Like many of
the others, he was anxious for the battle to develop. But unlike them, he
wanted it not as the beginning of the end—the first step toward home,
by way of Baghdad, if necessary. He wanted it because he believed that
this was the day for which he'd been created, the moment for which he
had so eagerly trained, so intently prepared.

First Lieutenant Larry Redmond had never been to war before, but
he was a warrior, and everyone who knew him—every private and sergeant, and every officer from general on down—knew he was a warrior.
And now his day had come.

His only regret was that this first battle was against an enemy who
was expected to employ chemical weapons, for that required him to
attack "buttoned up", hatches closed and sealed, his vision limited to the
narrow perspective of vision blocks and his infrared sight. Had their
been no chemical threat, he would be seated high in the commander's
cupola of the Abrams, exposed to the air from the waist up, surveying
the entire battlefield, dropping his seat and closing the hatch above him
only if the team encountered artillery fire. He didn't linger on that
thought, though, preferring to look at it as a greater challenge to
maneuver and fight his platoon buttoned up.

His voice came across the platoon and company radio nets with a
degree of clarity and calm and confidence that none of the other voices
possessed, his orders precise, timely and correct in every instance. His
confidence was so infectious that when his company commander's tank
struck a mine—disabling but not destroying it, and wounding only the
driver—and Redmond announced over the radio, "This is Charlie One
Six. I have command," his battalion commander and the other platoon

leaders knew that the team was in even better hands than before, and Team Charlie pressed on without hesitation.

The company executive officer, who would normally have been designated to assume command, was not the sort of officer inclined to lead men into combat. He was happy to be far to the rear of the battle, shepherding the fuel and ammunition vehicles of the company trains.

Lieutenant Redmond saw every target first, it seemed, and directed the appropriate crew to engage it. After they had destroyed a number of bunkers and trucks and armored personnel carriers which had the misfortune to stand in Team Charlie's path, they came upon their first tank. It was an aging Soviet-built T-55, 3600 meters away. Redmond took it for his own crew, directing Sergeant Peterson to engage it with a sabot round.

A discarding sabot projectile travels at a speed so great that by the time any enemy within its range sees the flash of light from the gun firing it, it is too late to do anything but have perhaps one fleeting thought of panic. There is not even enough time to think a brief prayer that it is headed for someone else. Traveling at nearly a mile per second, the sharp, depleted uranium dart possesses the kinetic energy of a meteorite. When it strikes an armored vehicle, it pierces the thick armor as an icepick stabbed into an aluminum can would do. And then the real damage begins, because as it enters the vehicle, its path deflected slightly, the dart-like projectile begins to tumble. Now the armor, meant to protect the crew, becomes a trap. It traps both the crew and the tumbling hunk of metal, which ricochets madly around inside the vehicle, ripping apart radios, ammunition, torsos, heads and limbs until its speed and energy are dissipated by its destructive fit of anger.

The projectile that Larry Redmond's gunner fired into the turret of the Iraqi T-55 tank more than two miles to his front killed only one of the crewmen initially, decapitating the gunner on one of its first violent ricochets. But a subsequent bounce ripped the tank commander's legs off at the knees, adding his boots and leg bones to the flying debris. The heavy dart blasted through several rounds of main gun ammunition, spraying the inside of the vehicle with propellant powder, then severed an electrical line, creating a shower of sparks. It was the resultant explosion, which also touched off the undamaged ammunition, that killed the driver and ended the brief suffering of the legless tank commander. It also caused the turret of the tank to be blown into the sky.

Redmond watched it lift into the air a short way, trailing smoke and flame, then crash back atop the tank's hull. It reminded him of films he'd seen of failed rocket launches in the early days of space exploration. He gave no thought to the enemy crew.

As the tanks of Team Charlie rumbled on they came upon what had been an enemy defensive position before an allied bomb strike had ruined it. Bloating bodies lay about, and many of Team Charlie's members saw their first dead men.

Still farther north, almost to the burning tank Redmond had destroyed, another bunker line appeared, defined by several white flags being waved from the bunkers. To Redmond's left rear, a Bradley opened fire with its 25mm chain gun, the rounds erupting near one of the surrender flags.

"Chain gun, cease firing!" he ordered over the radio. The firing ceased immediately, and he asked angrily, "Whose gun was that?"

When he got no answer, he again demanded, "Whose gun was that firing at the flag?"

"Mine, sir…Blue One," a voice said, and the lieutenant said to all of his team, "The next man who fails to honor a surrender flag is relieved. Blue One, halt, take the prisoners, and clear the bunker line. Blue Two and Three, press on with the rest of us."

They were nearing their first objective now, a slight, rocky rise a kilometer or so to their front. He checked the readout of his tank's GPS—Global Positioning System—which, with input from satellites high above them, pinpointed his position.

Yes, that was Objective Grant about a thousand meters ahead.

Redmond's mind shifted from fighting to fuel. The big gas turbine engines of the Abrams tanks sucked it up in huge quantities, and he wanted to make certain that his vehicles were kept as full as possible. Switching to the logistics net, he called the company executive officer to determine the location of the big fuel trucks that were to service his tanks and Bradleys. He learned that they were on schedule, about ten kilometers to his rear and continuing to move toward the initial objectives.

Team Charlie thundered on.

*   *   *

Far to the rear, well inside Saudi Arabian territory, Staff Sergeant Michelle Myers was at her radio intercept station, listening intently to the frequencies she had been assigned, trying to glean anything she could of value from the radio conversations of the Iraqi soldiers upon whom she was eavesdropping. As usual, she was getting nothing of value. That was partly a result of the fact that it was obvious the Iraqis—at least at the level of regiment and below, to which she was listening—knew little of what was going on themselves. Until the ground war began, that fact was, of itself, somewhat important; it showed that any orders being issued from Baghdad were not getting to the front line troops in a timely fashion. Another reason she was getting little "take" was because the old Soviet radios the enemy were using at that level were nearly useless, compared to the modern ones employed by most of the Coalition forces. But probably the biggest impediment to Staff Sergeant Myers's attempts to intercept anything of value was the fact that Arabic was a difficult language to learn in a year's time, even if one studied the correct dialect, which she had not. The year she had studied Arabic at the Defense Language Institute in Monterey, California, she had been made to concentrate on Egyptian Arabic, which bore little resemblance to the dialect used by the few men that she now heard on the radio.

The setup on the console of the mobile intercept van in which Michelle was working was much like a commercial scanner. She could set a number of assigned frequencies in the scanner's memory, and it would rotate through them until it picked up a transmission of radio waves on one of those particular frequencies. The scanner would lock onto that station until she pressed a key to release it, or until a preset number of seconds passed after the transmission ceased. Each transmission she heard was also automatically recorded on audio tape.

In addition to the Iraqi frequencies she had programed into her intercept scanner, Michelle had one American frequency which she had pirated from the division signal brigade a couple of days earlier, when she was picking up her section's excerpt of the Communications and Electronics Operating Instructions for the current phase of Operation Desert Storm. It was just, she told a friend of hers who had access to the frequencies of all the units the signal brigade supported—it was just that she wanted to check in every now and then to ensure that her brother's unit, 5th of the 64th Armor, was doing OK. The other woman saw no harm in Michelle's request, and gave her the frequency.

Getting the code tape required to listen in on the secure voice radio nets the American units employed was a bit more difficult. But she had done it.

The chief warrant officer who was the cryptographic materials custodian had, Michelle knew well, a fondness for booze. And among her possessions was a bottle of Wild Turkey, a commodity so rare in the forces deployed to Saudi Arabia that, had she merely wanted money, she could have sold it for hundreds of dollars. It had been in her section's repair parts trailer for months, where she had stashed it after receiving it as a birthday gift from one of the NCOs in the section, during a field training exercise back in the States. She convinced the crypto custodian that she wanted the code tape only because she knew her uncle, one of the division's tank battalion commanders, was to command the lead battalion during the coming ground war. She only wanted the code tape, she said, so that if some really hot intelligence was gained as a result of the intercept operations, she could let him know about it right away.

"Otherwise," she had told the warrant officer, "by the time it goes through channels, it wouldn't be of any use to him and his battalion. You know that's true. And besides, he gave me this bottle of Wild Turkey that I don't know what to do with..."

Michelle had programed one channel of the secure voice device attached to the van's FM transceiver—the radio she and the other two operators in the van with her used to talk to their headquarters—with Team Charlie's frequency and code tape. Now she turned it on. The speaker was just in front of her, so by pulling one of her earphones off, she could listen to both the Iraqis on the scanner, and Team Charlie's frequency.

There was hardly any radio traffic now on the radio nets she had been assigned—an Iraqi armored regiment and its subordinate battalions. She had no way of knowing that it was because nearly all the Iraqi officers in those units had fled the thundering assault that the 24th Division's Team Charlie was leading.

An American voice came across the speaker almost immediately: "The next man who fails to honor a surrender flag is relieved. Blue One, halt, take the prisoners, and clear the bunker line. Blue Two and Three, press on with the rest of us."

Michelle Myers smiled broadly. "Hello, Lieutenant Redmond," she whispered to the speaker. "I love you. Good hunting, bold warrior."

Michelle hadn't heard Larry Redmond's voice in two months, yet she knew it as soon as she heard him speak. It was as distinctive and clear and confident as she had remembered, and now, she knew, he was out there on the battlefield, leading the hunt.

It was hard to believe that it had been two months since they had met in Bahrain. She had written several letters to him during the first month after they had become lovers, explaining that she was sorry to have deceived him into believing that she was a Red Cross worker, asking his forgiveness and understanding. But none of them had sounded right—had expressed her feelings for him adequately. So she had destroyed them. And when the air war had begun, things began to move so quickly that she had not had time to sit and think through what she really wanted to say to him.

Anyway, now that the ground war was underway, he didn't need such problems to contend with. When it was over, she would find him, and tell him face to face what she had to say. In Baghdad, perhaps.

There continued to be very little radio traffic on the four frequencies Michelle's intercept scanner was tuned to—just a few desperate calls from enemy battalion radio operators looking for their bosses, or trying to get someone—anyone—at regimental headquarters. But the young woman seated next to her, Specialist Jane Pollock, was listening to four tank company nets, and she heard a great deal.

As Michelle heard Redmond's voice over the US frequency say, "This is One Six, nice shot, Three…Wow! You too, Joe! Keep on line, now…" she noticed Jane grasping her earphones and closing her eyes tightly, as if the volume was turned too high. Then Jane's hands moved over her eyes, and she shook her head back and forth. Michelle pulled her own headset off and went to her subordinate's console.

"You OK?" she asked the younger woman—just a girl of nineteen, really. "Something wrong?"

Jane handed Michelle the headphones, tears spilling over onto her cheeks, and Michelle pulled them on to listen.

Nothing came from them for awhile, until just after she heard, from the speaker over her own console, Larry Redmond's voice. "Gunners! Tank! One o'clock, uh, two eight hundred! You take him, One One!"

It was just a few seconds before she heard, over Jane's headset, a panicky voice in Arabic say, "They have fired another…" And then there was a sharp clang, followed in a split second by a hissing noise above which agonized screams could be heard, the terrible sound of helpless human beings waiting for the merciful peace of death to end their suffering. And then the headset went dead.

Michelle ripped the earphones off, eyes wide in shock, looking at the weeping young intercept operator beside her.

"Tank crews," the teenager mumbled. "You can hear them scream while they're dying, until their radios burn up. I just—I can't…" Jane buried her face in her hands and sobbed, and Michelle put her arms around her, fighting off an attack of nausea at the realization of what she had just heard. The younger soldier's whole body was trembling.

"You take a break, Jane, then take over my nets. There's almost nothing on them." And she suddenly knew why. "They're headquarters nets, and I guess those wonderful officers of theirs have bugged out and left their men behind to die. Those sons of bitches!"

Tears came into Michelle's eyes, too, but they were tears of anger.

She heard a new voice on Team Charlie's net declare, "I've got a turret to my right front…wait…about four thousand. I'm gonna stop and give the bastard a sabot."

"Roger," Redmond's voice replied matter-of-factly. "Get him!"

"Yeah! 'Get him,' is right, Larry," Michelle mumbled. "Get all the bastards!"

The Iraqi voice she heard this time said only, "Get out! Get out!" before the radio went dead. Shortly after that, though, she heard a voice in her ear say, in Arabic, "They're in range. The first one! Shoot the first one! That must be the commander!"

"Which one? Where is he?" another panicky Arab voice squawked.

"Right there! To your left front, you fool! Your left front!"

It took a second for Michelle's busy mind to fathom what was happening, and for a second after that she felt utterly helpless, fearing for her warrior's life. Then she bolted from her chair, grabbed the handset of the radio tuned to Team Charlie's net, and depressed the push-to-talk button.

"Your left front, Larry!" she yelled into the microphone. "They're getting ready to shoot at you! Left front!"

When he heard the voice in his ears Redmond was shocked, confused, and he said aloud, "Mickey!" He wondered, for a moment, if his mind had snapped. But his warrior instincts caused him to look through his vision blocks to the left front as he heard one of his tank commanders say, "I see him! Turret only, ten o'clock!" Then the voice went silent, and Redmond knew it was because the man was issuing his gunner target engagement orders over the intercom.

Redmond swung his Abrams tank's long, flat turret to his left front just in time to see the flash of the enemy tank's main gun firing. He knew it was fired at him, and thought, in the following half-second, must not be sabot or it'd be here. Then he felt his big beast of a tank rock sideways from an explosion.

Michelle grabbed the intercept scanner's headphones and thrust one to her ear just in time to hear the Arab tanker shout, almost incoherently, "I hit him! I killed him! Allah akbar!" The blood drained from her face, and she dropped the headset, staring at the console. From the American net came a new voice, full of urgency. "You hit, Six?…Larry, you hit?…"

"Sonofabitch! Right beside us! Anybody get him?"

It was Larry Redmond's voice, and Michelle dropped into her chair and finally breathed again. Then she heard another voice over the net—Cincotti's, she thought—say, "Roger that! One round HESH, without even slowing down. Who the hell was that broad on the radio, anyway?"

There was silence for a time until Redmond replied, "Cut the chatter. We're on Objective Grant, now. Move ahead another half klick to clear the ground, then we'll back into positions. Platoon leaders to my tank ASAP after that. We'll top off as soon as the trains pull in, SOP. Now, move!"

✳   ✳   ✳

"Here they come," Bill Kernan said to Mashid, one of Abdul's principal lieutenants in the Kuwaiti underground. They were out in the desert west of Kuwait City once again. This time, they were waiting for a Special Forces team to arrive from Saudi Arabia. The twelve Americans were bringing radios, laser target designators, and night vision equipment in with them. Their function was to coordinate the actions of the Kuwaiti resistance forces with the advancing allied ground forces. In addition, they would serve as ground controllers for airstrikes in support of the battle.

Mashid looked in the direction Kernan was scanning with his night vision goggles. At first he could see nothing, but then the dark shapes of a pair of Blackhawk helicopters appeared, silhouetted by the glow of distant fires from burning oil wells. The Iraqis were continuing to set them afire in retaliation for the devastation of their armed forces.

Kernan pointed an infrared-filtered flashlight at the approaching aircraft and signaled them with the Morse code letter "A" to indicate that the landing zone was clear. The lead Blackhawk signaled its recognition by flashing its infrared landing lights twice. Then the aircraft flared and settled to the ground fifty meters away.

The Special Forces team exited quickly, the Kevlar helmets on their heads and bulging rucksacks on their backs making them look deformed as they ran from the aircraft and hit the ground.

The Blackhawks lifted off just seconds after they had touched down. They had already made several quick touchdowns along the flight into Kuwait—decoy landings to confuse any enemy who might see them land. They would make several more on the flight route out, as well.

Kernan continued to flash the recognition signal until the team leader and one of his men, covered by the other ten, approached him.

He held his hand out to the desert-camouflaged men and said, "Hi, gents. I'm Bill Kernan. Welcome to Kuwait."

He introduced Mashid to the somewhat nervous men, then said. "I'm afraid we have quite a walk to get to the safehouse. We'd better get moving."

*   *   *

"Hell, maybe we taken out all of them," Al Schwarbacher said to his commander, Captain Jack Marsh. "We've already accounted for more than the damned intel weenies said they had out here to start with."

They were looking for the few remaining Scud missiles Saddam was believed to have in the western panhandle of his embattled country. But they had found none in the last several days, and none had been launched from the area during that time.

The soldiers weren't surprised. In the four weeks since they had been roaming the area while Taffy Hughes's Warthogs prowled the skies above, Marsh's team and the other special operations men in "Scudinavia" had found and destroyed dozens of the enemy missiles.

"Well, we've got to find at least two more," Lew Merletti said. "The Delta guys have one more than 5th Group's total, so far."

A squadron from the Delta Force, supplemented by an Air Force special operations combat control team, was searching an area to the west of where Marsh's A team and other teams from the 5th Special Forces Group were. Lieutenant Colonel Hughes and his A-10 pilots had been keeping an unofficial score of the numbers of Scuds each element had been responsible for finding, and reporting the tally to the two elements. This had resulted in some keen competition and, at the goading of the Warthog pilots, some pretty sizeable bets as to which group would end up with the highest total. The Warthogs had even given their comrades on the ground team names. The 5th Special Forces Group they called the Scudnuts. The Delta men and their Air Force combat control team were known as the Blue and Green Scud Hunting Machine, usually shortened to just "Machine."

Now the familiar voice of one of the Warthog pilots came over the handset of Jack Marsh's ultra-high frequency radio.

"Scudnut Five, this is Warthog Seven, over."

"Go ahead, Fartlog Seven," Marsh answered.

"Hey, I got a new score for you, buddy," the pilot reported. "Your teamies in Scudnut One just found three missiles in the hills up north. We took 'em out with thirty mike-mike. Looks like you're two up on the Machine, now."

"Hey, that's good news, Warthog," the Special Forces captain said.

"OK, we're headin' for the ranch," the pilot said. "It's steak night, don't ya know. Warthog One and his wingman are enroute to cover you. Adios from Warthogs Seven and Eight, out."

"Steak night," Jack Marsh mumbled. He and his men had eaten nothing but MREs—Meals, Ready to Eat, as the current combat rations of the US military were called—for the previous month. His stomach growled at the thought of a big, juicy T-bone, and he muttered, "'Meals, Ready to Eat,' my ass. 'Meals Rejected by Ethiopians' is more like it."

Twenty one

25 February 1991

The thundering herd under Lieutenant Redmond's command continued its charge to the north in a driving rain. They were not at the point of the 24th Infantry Division's mechanized spear during this leg of the race around the Iraqi flank, but it mattered little to Redmond. There were almost no Iraqi forces in this part of the desert, if the intelligence reports were correct. So he was content to let another battalion lead the charge for awhile. Team Charlie would take the point when the division turned east, and into the teeth of the vaunted Republican Guards divisions dug in there.

"Mud," Private Anderson said over the intercom as he drove Redmond's big tank through the sticky mess. "Who the hell ever heard of mud in the damn desert. You been doin' a damn rain dance or somethin', Gibbs?"

Gibbs Begay laughed. "Hell, yes," he replied. "I didn't want to see all those raghead prisoners die of thirst before they got to the rear."

"If we'd have known they were such chickenshits, we could've attacked as soon as we got over here," the gunner, Sergeant Peterson, said. "Could've whipped their asses and been back home by now."

The Iraqis were surrendering in droves as the Coalition ground forces swept over them. Having to deal with thousands of prisoners was slowing some units even more than the storm now sweeping across southern Iraq.

But these were Saddam's cannon fodder; the conscripts he had sent to the forward trenchlines to be sacrificed. They were intended only to hold up the Americans and their allies long enough to enable him to maneuver his better motivated, trained, and equipped Republican Guards divisions in counterattacks—the Mother of All Battles.

That mother plan had long since gone to hell, though—been blown to hell by the allies' devastating air attacks, and rendered meaningless by Schwarzkopf's superb deception plan. But those relatively elite divisions were still back there, battered but waiting.

"Don't get overconfident, men," Lieutenant Redmond counseled. "All we've run into so far is Joe Shit the ragman. When we get back on point and turn east, we've got several Republican Guards divisions to deal with. With T-72 tanks, not tired-assed old T-55s."

"Dead meat," Gibbs Begay said.

"We'll see," Lieutenant Redmond warned. "We'll see."

✶   ✶   ✶

Staff Sergeant Michelle Myers's radio intercept unit was moving, too—displacing forward in an attempt to stay within radio range of the charging combat units and the enemy they were attacking.

"We're getting low on fuel," her driver said. They were sitting in the cab of the truck on which the intercept van was mounted, following in the tracks of a column of combat vehicles which had passed earlier in the day.

"Well, just keep moving," she said. "One of the division supply points is supposed to be somewhere up ahead."

The driver leaned on the horn to get another group of surrendered Iraqi conscripts to move out of his path. The defeated soldiers responded by turning toward the truck and holding out their hands, begging for food and water.

"Out of the way, shitheads!" the driver yelled, gunning his vehicle toward them. They moved aside as the truck lurched past.

"Easy, Neal," Michelle said. "They're…" She was interrupted by a deafening ripple of explosions off to their right. The startled driver veered off the track and bumped over the berm of sand which had been pushed up beside it by the scores of vehicles which had passed before.

The noise was the backblasts from a battery of American multiple-launch rocket systems. Michelle watched as the big rockets raced in a high arc toward the northeast, trailing long tails of white smoke as they streamed toward their targets, miles away.

"Damn!" the driver said. "I'm glad those things are on our side."

He shoved the truck's transmission into reverse, but the wheels dug into the sand. After several unsuccessful attempts to back over the berm, the truck was hopelessly stuck.

"Neal," Michelle muttered, "you're just about useless, you know it? Get the shovel and see if you can dig the damn thing out."

Her section sergeant pulled up beside her in his truck.

"Stuck," she mumbled to him, shaking her head. "Think we can pull it out with yours?"

"Wait one," he said. He called the company headquarters on his radio for instructions. The company commander ordered him to continue on with the rest of the section. There would be plenty of recovery vehicles coming along eventually, he explained, and the rest of the section needed to keep going if they were to get close enough to the combat to hear the enemy on their intercept sets.

"Oh, great!" Michelle said. The real reason for her disappointment was that she would not be able to listen in on Team Charlie's net, to hear her lover lead his tanks in battle. "All right, Sergeant Harwood," she said. "We'll catch you when we can." The rest of the section pulled away, and she added, "Probably in Baghdad, by the time we get out of here."

*   *   *

Far to the east, Bill Kernan had managed to get the Special Forces team which had arrived the night before linked up with the resistance force elements in the southern sector of Kuwait City. There, they would report on enemy movements, direct airstrikes on lucrative targets, and coordinate the entrance into the city of the lead units of Coalition forces moving steadily north.

That the Iraqi units to the south were being routed was obvious. They were fleeing north through the city by the thousands, in total disarray. The resistance was receiving reports of widespread looting, rape, and the systematic destruction of the remaining key facilities in Kuwait.

The sky over the city was becoming increasingly dark from the huge columns of smoke as the vengeful Iraqis continued to ignite more and more oil wells.

The most disturbing report, though, was that the fleeing enemy were taking Kuwaiti citizens hostage as they retreated through the city toward Iraq.

Kernan was limping through the back streets in his disguise as a deranged Kuwaiti, headed for Abir's villa. From there, he would move with Abdul to the resistance forces along the highway leading around Kuwait Bay to the north. There, they would do what they could to rescue Kuwaitis being taken north as hostages by the enemy.

*   *   *

The thunderstorm through which Team Charlie had been attacking had turned into a sandstorm, and then abated. Lieutenant Redmond had refueled his iron monsters and moved to the front of the battalion.

Now, while the last of the companies refueled, he was studying a map of the terrain to the east with his fellow company commanders and Lieutenant Colonel Farrar, who commanded the combined arms task force built around the 5th of the 64th Armor.

"They're dug in all around the airfield, here," Farrar said to Redmond and the others. He was pointing to an Iraqi air base lying south of highway 8, which runs along the Euphrates river.

"At first light, division artillery will prep them, and we'll attack with Alpha on the north and Bravo on the south."

He looked at Larry and said, "Redmond, you'll be in the center— straight down the runway."

Redmond smiled and his eyes sparkled. "Yes, sir," he said, and thought, Hot damn! The point of the spear.

The battalion commander designated the attached infantry company as the reserve element for the attack on the airfield, then turned dissemination of the details of the operations order over to his operations officer.

When the briefing was completed, a time check of the officers' wrist watches signaling its finish, Lieutenant Colonel Farrar called Redmond aside.

"Larry, I've decided to leave you in command of Team Charlie for the rest of the operation. Your CO…well, let's just say that mine his tank hit did something to him other than just blowing the tread off. I was going to put him back with the company, but he, uh…I guess the concussion from the mine has scrambled his brain or something."

He studied his star lieutenant's face a moment, then smiled, and chucked him on the shoulder. "Anyway, I need my best commanders leading these troops when we hit the Republican Guards divisions in front of Basra."

Redmond looked the man in the eyes. "Thank you, sir," he said. "I won't let you down. We'll go through them like shit through a goose, as Patton used to say."

"Patton?" Farrar said. "Hell, son, even old Georgie Patton never moved this far, this fast. And Third Army never took so many prisoners in such a short period of time either. This is history we're making here, boy! Now, get on over there and brief your platoon leaders. You've got an attack to lead."

"We figured it out, Larry," Lieutenant Jim Locher said when Redmond returned to his tank where his platoon leaders sat waiting for him.

"What's that?"

"The woman who warned you about the Iraqi tank," Joe Cincotti said. "It was that girl you were with in Bahrain."

Redmond felt his face flush.

"Mickey," he said. "Yeah, I know. But how the hell could a Red Cross girl be on a secure net?"

He'd had little time to think about the bizarre radio transmission while they raced through Iraq. When it did cross his mind, it baffled him.

"And how the hell would she know you were about to get shot at by an enemy tank, right?" Locher said. "Because she's not a donut dolly, that's why, my man. She's a radio intercept operator."

"A radio inter...?" Yes, that must be it, it suddenly dawned on him.

"Remember before she gave you that, 'oink oink' bit?" Cincotti reminded him. "You said something about not messing with her, 'cause she might be an enlisted soldier, and we ought to look for a donut dolly."

"She must have heard you," Locher said. "And I guess she wanted to jump your bones so bad, that she figured she'd better come on to you as a Red Cross type."

"Yeah, maybe," he said. "Anyway, she's history." He unfolded the map he was carrying and said, "All right, men, gather 'round. We're leading the assault on this air base at first light."

*   *   *

Bill Kernan limped around the corner to the entrance gate of Abir's villa, then froze to a halt.

"Oh, Jesus," he said, yanking the .45 automatic from beneath his Arab robe and looking around. There was no one in sight, so he looked once more at the macabre scene which had shocked him.

A severed human head was shoved onto one of the wrought iron spikes of the villa's entrance gate. It was Abdul's.

He checked the pistol to make sure a round was chambered, then stalked into the villa.

He found no one until he entered Francesca Singh's improvised operating room. Abdul's headless body lay atop the table. Kernan wretched at the sight of a pair of eyeballs lying on the table beside it.

Something made a rustling sound in the adjoining room, and he moved to the door, pistol at the ready. He peered inside to see Mara cradling Francesca Singh in her arms.

Dr. Singh moaned, her head wagging from side to side. The sockets of her eyes were bloody and empty.

"Oh, Jesus," he said. "Where is Abir?"

"I don't know," Mara said. "I went to get bread. They came while I was gone."

"They took her with them," Francesca sobbed. "They made us watch them kill Abdul. Then they did this."

She gave an animal-like wail of grief, and Mara hugged her tightly.

"I'm going," Kernan said. "I'll call the Special Forces men to send a medic here."

He hurried to his attic hideout. It hadn't been disturbed. He pulled the encryption tape he'd gotten from the American team leader out of his pocket and ran it through the speech security device of his satellite radio. His hands were shaking so badly that he had difficulty doing it. Next, he set the radio on the correct frequencies to match the up and down links the American soldiers were using.

The Special Forces men agreed to send someone to tend to the injured doctor as soon as they could.

Kernan hurriedly put the radio away, picked up two boxes of ammunition for his pistol, and went out through the garage at the back of the villa. The sheik's Jeep Cherokee was gone. He guessed that the Iraqis had taken it to carry their loot and hostage north to Iraq.

"Good," he said aloud. If he could somehow cut them off on the highway to Basra…Then he remembered seeing a motorcycle lying in the street at the front of the villa. It had been years since he had ridden one, but perhaps it would run.

He rushed around to the front of the villa, pausing only long enough to remove Abdul's head from the gate and place it beneath the bushes just inside.

The motorcycle, he discovered, was out of gasoline, so he ran inside to the generators and took a can from there, then filled the motorcycle. He kicked the starter several times and the motor sputtered to life.

Bill Kernan sped away from the villa, headed for the highway north. He was far behind the Iraqis who had pillaged the villa, and he could only hope that they had stopped along the way for more booty or hostages. But even if he had to go all the way to Baghdad, he was going to find Abir, or die trying.

Michelle's truck was pulled out of the sand and back onto the road by a tracked recovery vehicle which was dragging a damaged Bradley to the rear.

She headed north again, driving the truck herself while Specialist Neal slept on the seat beside her.

There was a battle going on somewhere to the east; she could see an arc of white smoke trails from another salvo of deadly rockets being hurled at the enemy. A pair of Apache helicopter gunships roared across in front of her, headed for the battle.

Ahead, the trail veered to the right. As Michelle approached, she could see that it turned to bypass an enemy installation there. The twisted remains of a radar antenna, and the fins of what had apparently been air defense missiles stuck up out of several piles of burned debris.

There was an Iraqi soldier there, lying near the defensive wire surrounding the ruined air defense site. He was reaching pitifully out toward the passing truck, and Michelle saw that one of his legs was twisted grotesquely up behind him.

She looked in the side mirrors of the truck. There were no vehicles in sight behind her. Ahead, in the distance, was a plume of dust from the only other vehicle she could see.

"Damn," she muttered. The Iraqi was trying to crawl toward her, but his twisted leg made it almost impossible. She applied the brakes and stopped. The man was looking at her with pleading eyes and saying something in Arabic.

"Neal," she said. "Wake up and cover me while I see what I can do for this wounded Iraqi." Neal came awake and sat up.

"What?" he said, then saw the man she was pointing to. "An Iraqi? Fuck him. Let him die."

"Do what I say, Neal," she ordered as she climbed out of the truck. "Get your ass out here and cover me. He's a soldier, too, you know, just like you and I are."

She took the first aid kit from beneath the seat of the truck and walked toward the injured man.

Then there was a flash of light, and she was flung into the air. A mine, Michelle thought, and felt herself slam back onto the ground. Then she felt nothing, and her world went dark.

*   *   *

Bill Kernan sped through the streets of Kuwait City's suburbs on the motorcycle, dodging rubble and other vehicles. As he pulled onto the ramp leading to the Basra highway, a pair of Iraqi soldiers tried to flag him down, no doubt to take his motorcycle.

Kernan slowed and reached beneath his robe. He drew his .45 and shot the first one in the face, then shot the other in the back as he dived, too late, for cover.

He looked for the Cherokee in the chaotic traffic ahead. There were military and civilian trucks and automobiles, most loaded with loot and soldiers. But no Jeep Cherokee that he could see.

He passed one van with an Iraqi soldier driving. In the other front seat, another Iraqi was pointing a pistol at a frightened group of women and girls in the back of the van. Kernan slowed, fell behind the van, then pulled around the right side of it. He accelerated up to the front window and blew apart the head of the man holding the pistol, then shot the driver. The van careened left into another car, and Kernan gunned his motorcycle and sped on, not even glancing back.

He was almost to Kuwait's northern border with Iraq when he thought he saw the Cherokee in the traffic up ahead.

He strained to see past the vehicles in front, then suddenly had to swerve to miss a truck slowing down in front of him. The car behind him plowed into the motorcycle, knocking Kernan sprawling onto the road and tumbling to the edge of the highway. No one paid him more than a glance as they sped north in their desperate flight. He crawled off the shoulder, still trying to spot the Jeep wagon in the northbound traffic. It was only when he rolled over and sat up to look at his bleeding hands and knees that Bill Kernan finally noticed his left foot turned almost backward, jagged edges of bone sticking through the skin of his badly-fractured leg.

He looked to the north as the panicked exodus continued, knowing he could never catch them now.

"Abir," he whispered as he flopped back, the pain in his body equalling the grief in his heart. "Abir, I can't go on."

▼

Twenty two

26 February 1991

The attack on the Iraqi airfield south of highway 8 opened twenty minutes before daylight with a preparatory artillery barrage delivered by the 24th Infantry Division's big guns and multiple-launch rocket systems.

The ground shuddered with the awful fury of the barrage, and the horizon was filled with flashes both behind and before the waiting tanks of Team Charlie and their anxious crews—behind as the guns and rockets were fired, and before as they blasted into the enemy positions.

The tanks were still well back from the edge of the airfield, out of sight and out of range of the enemy forces there. Five minutes before the barrage was to end, the task force would begin their move forward. As the fire lifted and the smoke and dust from it cleared, the enemy would be engaged by the Abrams tanks at near their maximum range— well beyond the effective range of the Iraqi T-72s. They would be systematically picked off by the superior American armor as it moved against the objective.

"All right, remember now," Larry Redmond said to his platoon leaders over the Team Charlie radio net, "if we start receiving artillery fire from the Iraqis, we're going to charge right through it—and I mean all the way through it, right to the far end of the runway."

His sixth sense told him that the enemy would attempt to answer the attack with artillery fire once the American barrage subsided. He hoped they would. That would give him the excuse he needed to charge the airfield ahead of the companies on his flanks. They could sit back and pick off the Iraqis all they wanted to; if he had his way, his tanks were going to charge in and mix it up with the enemy—quickly overwhelm them with shock and speed and firepower.

"H minus one minute," the operations officer announced on the battalion net. The company commanders acknowledged the call in sequence, then passed the word to their platoons, and the engines' whine increased in volume as the drivers wound the big gas turbines up.

It reminded Redmond of a herd of bound dragons straining at their bonds—of snarling, wild animals held in check by some invisible god of war, waiting to be loosed.

And then the great steel beasts were freed to charge. They lurched forward, picking up speed as their objective, still well to their front, continued to shudder from the fury of the guns.

The artillery fire slowed, then ceased, and soon the light of dawn was visible through the lifting smoke ahead.

Redmond flipped open the hatch of his commander's cupola and raised his seat to get a better view of his charging team.

On the left, Cincotti's platoon advanced in perfect echelon. Ahead, Jim Locher's tanks, in a wedge, formed a point aiming straight at the airfield's battered control tower. Redmond knew before he even looked to the right that his old platoon, now commanded by his former platoon sergeant, would be moving in good order. It was. Behind him, he saw that the infantry platoon in its Bradley fighting vehicles was a bit bunched up, but moving well. The companies on his flanks were not moving as fast as Redmond's, and one of them called the battalion commander to report that he was falling behind.

Damn it, captain, Redmond thought, you're going to slow us down—take away the momentum of the attack.

But then three rounds of enemy artillery fire fell just ahead of Locher's platoon. "Good," Redmond said aloud as he saw it explode.

"Press on!" he called on the team net. "Keep moving. Press on through it!"

He called the battalion commander, Lieutenant Colonel Farrar, and declared, "We're receiving artillery fire. We're pressing on through it, now."

The next pitiful salvo of enemy fire landed well behind the team, but Redmond continued to implore, "Press on. We're almost there, now. Keep your interval, and keep up the speed. We're the shit, and they're the goose now, men."

They started engaging targets as they neared the airfield, shooting on the move.

"That's it, that's it," he said as he saw his tankers blasting anything that looked like a threat.

Lieutenant Colonel Farrar's voice came over the radio. "You're too far ahead Charlie," he said. "Slow it down some. Your flanks are getting uncovered."

Redmond responded by calling his platoons. "Cover your flanks," he ordered as Team Charlie stormed onto the runways of the Iraqi air base. "We're outrunning the rest of the task force. Get those turrets turned more to the flanks, Joe. And keep the machine guns firing. Make 'em keep their heads down!"

The enemy crumbled in the face of the thundering assault, running for cover as the Abrams and Bradley gunners poured fire into them. The tanks' big 120mm main guns were blasting crippled aircraft, armored vehicles, fuel trucks, and bunkers, and the team's progress was marked by pyres of flame and smoke.

He could hear the urgent calls of the battalion commander imploring him to slow the brutal attack, but Redmond ignored him. Any tanker knew better than to hold back when he had momentum, when he had the enemy in a rout. He'd finish his sweep across the objective, first. Then he'd halt Team Charlie's charge and wait for the rest of the task force.

They were nearing the end of the runway now. Off to the left, a road leading away from the air base was covered with fleeing enemy troops.

"Sweep the road, Charlie Two," he ordered Joe Cincotti. They were in a killing frenzy now, merciless warriors on a rampage of destruction. He saw Cincotti's hatch pop open, and the platoon leader swung the 12.7mm machine gun atop the turret toward the road and raked the fleeing Iraqis with a stream of steel.

"All right, find a place to get in defilade and halt," Redmond ordered. They had reached the far end of the base. It was time to reign them in.

"Team Charlie, halt!" he demanded again. "Blue, pass through and dismount," he told the attached platoon of infantrymen.

Reluctantly, the armored warriors slowed, then stopped. All except Joe Cincotti, who pressed on toward the road, his guns ripping the foe streaming down it toward the east.

From behind Joe, an Iraqi 23mm gun opened fire, its tracers flashing past his head. Cincotti dropped into the protective cocoon of his turret, then swung it around toward the source of fire. His gunner blasted the enemy gun to rubble.

Far down the runway, through the smoke and dust and flame, another Abrams tank commander saw Cincotti fire. Because the gun was fired back toward him, the other American assumed it to be the enemy. Seconds later, a sabot round slammed into the turret where Cincotti was. It blasted him with shards of steel, and tore the arm off of his gunner. Only luck left the loader and driver unharmed. They quickly abandoned the tank, dragging the wounded crewmen with them.

Redmond had heard the round slam into his platoon leader's tank, and now he ordered his driver to move there. As every one else did, he assumed the Iraqis had hit the tank, just as the Abrams gunner assumed his target was the enemy.

Redmond called Lieutenant Locher. "Take over, Jim," he said. "Give battalion a report. I'm going to get out and check on Joe. His tank just took a hit."

The driver was trying to staunch the flow of blood from the stump of the writhing gunner's arm. The stunned loader sat on the ground staring at Lieutenant Cincotti.

Joe was dead, his lifeless eyes staring up at the smoke filled sky, his head covered with blood from his mouth, nose, and ears. Redmond knew immediately that his friend was dead. He didn't dwell on the fact, turning his attention to the wounded gunner instead. A medic from the infantry platoon ran up, checked Cincotti quickly, and declared, "This one's gone." Then he moved to the soldier with the severed arm.

"I'll take over here, sir," he told Redmond. "You'd better call for a medevac."

"All right," Redmond muttered.

He turned back and looked at Cincotti.

"God damn it," he said, then knelt and closed his dead comrade's eyelids.

The loader was still staring blankly at Cincotti's corpse as Redmond stood and ran back to his tank.

✶   ✶   ✶

Master Sergeant Ike Kerstetter of the US Army's Delta Force raised his binoculars and made another sweep of the rocky hills to the north of him. There was no sign of the enemy anywhere, nor any indication that they had ever occupied the steep, barren hills or valleys of the area.

"Looks like a dry hole, Jerry," Kerstetter said to the young Air Force combat controller beside him.

Sergeant Jerry Bennett looked up from the map he was studying in the fading light. He was trying to find any areas within the team's reconnaissance zone that they hadn't yet patrolled, where the Iraqis might possibly have Scud missile launchers deployed.

He nodded his agreement with Kerstetter's assessment, then pointed to one spot on the map and said, "Unless they have something in this little bowl here, Ike."

Kerstetter leaned over the map and looked at it.

"There's no roads leading in there, though, Jerry."

"None that shows on the map," Bennett agreed. "But look at how flat this valley floor is. They could easily move down there from this secondary road 'way up to the north of us."

Kerstetter studied the map for awhile. The area was in the very northeast corner of the reconnaissance zone assigned to the ten-man detachment of which Kerstetter was the leader; half of one Delta Force troop, and two Air Force special operations combat controllers. The airmen, Sergeants Bennett and Lampe, were there to serve as the primary forward air guides for airstrikes on any targets the reconnaissance team encountered.

"Damn it," Kerstetter said. "I should have had that area checked out when we had some people over that way yesterday, Jerry. That's what I get for not looking beyond our recon zone on the map. I didn't see that road up on the north."

He looked at his watch. The team had split into two four-man reconnaissance elements and a command post manned by Kerstetter and Bennett. The recon elements were now well to the west and southwest. They were to patrol that area until about midnight, then return to the command post. From there, all ten men would be picked up by helicopter and moved to another recon zone further south.

"No time for the recon teams to finish up where they are and get up there before we get extracted. But I'll tell you what; we could go check it out ourselves."

"What about the satcom?" Bennett asked. The command post was responsible for monitoring the satellite communications link with Delta's forward operations base in Saudi Arabia, so that intelligence reports and requests for airstrikes could be relayed from the recon elements.

"Brauch has the spare with him," Kerstetter said. "I'll just tell him to take over the relay duties from his location for awhile."

"Sounds good to me," Bennett said. "I'm tired of sitting here on my ass all day, anyhow."

Kerstetter called the recon elements to advise them that he and Bennett were going to check out the area that had been bypassed earlier, then the soldier and the airman moved out to the northeast.

"This is some shit, ain't it, Jerry?" Kerstetter remarked as the two men started down the rocky hillside.

"What's that, Ike?"

"Here we are, a tired-assed old Army trooper and a young zoomie, takin' off on a two-man recon patrol hundreds of miles behind enemy lines."

"Hey," Bennett said, echoing a statement he had heard often from the Delta Force men, "nobody said it was gonna be easy!"

The combined arms task force of the 5th Battalion, 64th Armor sat at the airbase they had so rapidly overwhelmed in the early morning hours of February 26th. They had rearmed and refueled, and were now the brigade reserve. The brigade was turning north once more to seal off highway 8. When that was done, they would turn east again, and storm into the Republican Guards divisions sitting astride the highway on the approaches to Basra.

Lieutenant Larry Redmond was standing with the other company commanders and their battalion commander, Lieutenant Colonel Farrar, beside the Abrams tank in which Lieutenant Joe Cincotti had been killed. It was a very tense meeting. An examination of the tank and of what had occurred during the attack led Farrar to conclude that

Cincotti's Abrams had been struck by a discarding sabot round from one of the battalion's other tanks.

"A fine young officer is dead," the battalion commander said, "and one of his NCOs is crippled for life."

He studied the faces of his subordinate commanders, pausing to look longer at Redmond and at the company commander who had fallen behind in the attack, Captain Black. It was of one Black's tanks which had apparently hit Cincotti's.

"And why?" Farrar continued. "Because this is war—that's the primary reason. Clausewitz wrote about the fog of war, and I think we all know what he meant, now."

Most of the other officers nodded their agreement. The confusion of battle had proved to be greater than they would have thought possible, as they tried to keep their tanks and Bradley fighting vehicles in formation, and attempted to differentiate between enemy fire and the friendly guns cracking all around them. Everyone had seemed to talk on the radio at once as the commanders struggled to see what was going on and who was where through the restricted field of the armored vehicles' narrow vision blocks. And on top of that, the attack had taken place before sunrise, in limited visibility made even worse by the smoke and dust of the preparatory artillery barrage and the ongoing attack.

As often as they had been told about the confusion of combat, about "the fog of war," they had not been prepared for what they had encountered that morning.

Lieutenant Colonel Farrar looked around at the smoldering carnage. It had been a brilliantly successful attack. Aside from Cincotti and his gunner, the only casualties the battalion task force had suffered were minor wounds to several infantrymen whose Bradley had been hit by a rocket propelled grenade.

But that only made Cincotti's death and the maiming of his crewman by friendly fire that much more tragic.

"But the fog of war is no reason to be engaging our own forces—killing our own men," Farrar said. "If I had it to do all over again, I might be more deliberate about it. Damn it, the division commander has been telling us for months that the way to fight these bastards is to let our superiority in range and accuracy work for us—to sit back at our own max range and pick off the targets one at a time."

He looked around the airfield again, then back at his subordinates' faces. "On the other hand, if we'd done that in this instance, we'd still be back at the far edge of the airfield. And we'd never have seen the targets around all these buildings, and all the bunkers. If we hadn't just flat overrun them, shocked them with the speed and violence of our attack, they might not have hauled ass or surrendered so quickly. So, I don't know which would have been the best way—whether Lieutenant Cincotti would have survived if we'd gone in slow, or whether we'd have lost more men if we hadn't just rolled over them. We'll never know."

Now he fixed his eyes on the captains who had been on Redmond's flanks. "I do know this, though," he said coldly. "If you don't keep up with the attack, whether it's going slowly, or balls to the wall, things like this"—he gestured toward Cincotti's damaged tank—"are going to happen."

Captain Black, the commander of the company whose tank had killed Cincotti broke eye contact with Farrar, who shifted his gaze to Redmond.

He was about to speak again when the operations officer, standing on the ramp of the "high top sneaker"—the M-577 armored command vehicle used as his mobile command post—called to him.

"The brigade commander, Colonel. He's got some new guidance for you."

"Wait here," Farrar ordered the company commanders, and hurried to the command post.

None of the officers spoke for awhile. Then Captain Black broke the silence.

"I don't give a shit what he says, golden boy," he said to Redmond through clenched teeth. "I had defensive wire to get through, and deep sand on my axis of attack. We couldn't keep up with you hauling ass down the runway. And, God damn it, you knew it!"

His face reddened in anger and his fists were clenched, and he took a step toward Redmond. One of the other captains grabbed his arm to restrain him, but Black continued to stare angrily at Redmond and said, "If you hadn't been trying to be such a glory hound, Lieutenant fucking Patton, you wouldn't have gotten one of your buddies killed!"

He pulled his arm away from the other captain and turned to walk away, then turned back to look at Redmond, who said nothing, but stared icily back at him.

"I'll tell you one thing, Redmond," Black said, wagging an index finger at him. "If you pull that kind of shit again, I'll blow the turret off of your goddam tank, you got it?"

Larry Redmond watched him walk away, then looked at the other officers. The tankers from his battalion were staring at him with angry eyes. The infantryman whose company was attached to them was looking at the ground. Redmond turned away, walked over to a blasted Iraqi bunker, and relieved himself.

He thought about what Captain Black had said.

"Bullshit!" he muttered, then thought, What they did on the flanks didn't matter; there was no enemy out there. Or did it matter? If he hadn't gotten so far ahead, Cincotti's tank wouldn't have been taken for one of the enemy's. Maybe Black was right. After all, the battalion commander had called on the radio to tell him to slow down enough to wait for the others. But he had ignored the order. He glanced back at his friend's tank, then touched his shirt pocket and felt the letter Cincotti had given him.

Ah, Joe, he thought, I'm so sorry.

And then the reality of war struck home. He sat down crosslegged in the dirt, and placed his face into the crooks of his elbows. In his mind's eye, he saw his friend lying on the ground, staring up at the sky with lifeless eyes. He remembered the conversation they'd had that night, before the ground war commenced, when Cincotti had spoken as if he'd had a premonition of his death.

He saw the terribly mangled bodies of the enemy, imagined their horrible deaths as they were blasted apart, or burned to death in the unimaginable heat of burning ammunition and fuel. Where was there any glory in that? Where were all the high ideals of "defending one's country" or "guarding freedom" in a country half way around the world, where one greedy ruler had only seized the oil rich emirate of another?

Glory. His quest for glory was what had made him storm down the runway into the enemy. And it was what had gotten Joe Cincotti killed.

Someone was calling him, and he looked up. The operations officer was waving to him to join the other company commanders, where the battalion commander stood waiting with new orders.

He rose and walked to the group of officers. Black glared at him with hate in his eyes.

"All right," Lieutenant Colonel Farrar said, not noticing the tension among his subordinates, "here's your warning order: The brigade will attack tomorrow morning at 0400 Zulu—about 10 hours from now—east along highway 8, to destroy enemy armored forces between here and Rumaila. We're to be prepared to continue the attack toward the Basra-Kuwait highway. Task Force 4-64 will be on the right, 2-64 in the center. We'll be on the left, along the highway."

He looked up from the card on which he had made some notes. "We'll move out of here just after dark to an assembly area north along the road, then top off and get into our attack positions. We'll attack with Team Alpha on the left, Charlie in the middle, and Blue on the right." Looking at Captain Black, he said, "Bravo, you'll be in reserve. The S-3 will give a detailed order in one hour. Any questions?"

Black, relegated to duty as the reserve company for not being able to keep up with Redmond during the morning attack, he correctly assumed, was shaking his head slowly and glaring at the Team Charlie commander.

"Problem, Captain Black?" Farrar inquired.

"No, sir," Black muttered.

"Yes, there is, Colonel," Lieutenant Redmond said.

The others looked at him, and Larry said, "It wasn't Captain Black's fault that Joe got killed, sir. It was mine."

"What do you mean, Lieutenant?" Farrar asked.

"I mean I shouldn't have gotten so far ahead. I should have known that the flank companies, out in the sand, couldn't keep up with me. But even if I hadn't, I should have slowed down when you told me to. But I didn't. It's my fault, sir."

The battalion commander's face had reddened, and he glared at Larry through narrowed eyes.

"You mean to tell me that you heard me tell you to slow down, Redmond, and you just ignored it?" he asked.

"Yes, sir," Redmond said.

"God da…It wasn't that you just didn't hear me, in all the confusion?"

"No, sir. I heard you, but I…no excuse, sir."

Farrar shook his head in disgust, then looked at his operations officer. "Change one, S-3," he said. "Put Captain Black in the middle. Team Charlie will be in reserve."

He looked back at Larry. "And while you're back there, Redmond, you should do a lot of thinking. About Cincotti, and whether or not he'd still be here, if you could obey fucking orders. And about whether or not you're fit to hold a commission."

Farrar kicked the dirt at his feet, then looked at Larry again and mumbled, "I swear, if I had enough officers, I'd relieve your ass right now."

He looked the other officers over and noticed the smug smile on Black's face, then said, "Well, what the hell are you waiting for? Get back there and give your troops their warning order."

He watched Larry Redmond walk away, pausing for a moment to gaze at Cincotti's disabled Abrams, then striding purposefully toward the positions of his team's tanks and Bradleys.

"God damn it, Bill," he said to his S-3 officer. "It took some balls for Redmond to admit that. And you know what? If I'd had the momentum he had, I'd have probably done the same damn thing."

"Maybe so," the other officer said as they walked toward the command post. "But he still disobeyed your order."

"That's why he's in reserve this time," Farrar said. "But he's still the best company commander I've got."

*   *   *

"We're going to have to head back soon, to make exfil time," Ike Kerstetter said after checking the luminous dial of his watch.

"Yeah," Jerry Bennett said, "I know."

The Delta Force patrol leader and his Air Force combat controller had made the long trek up and down rocky hillsides to the bowl-like valley only to discover that it, too, was void of Iraqi military presence.

"Well," Kerstetter remarked, leaning over to shift his heavy rucksack further up on his back, "at least I feel better about coming over here and checking this area out."

"Me, too," Bennett said. "But I'd feel even better if we were to cross over and check the lower end of the valley leading in here."

Ike looked across to the far hill, which they would have to scale if they were to see beyond the curve the narrow but flat valley made a mile north of the bowl. He was bone tired from a month in the field—particularly from the fast march he and Bennett had just made up and down the hills. If they went across to check the other part of the valley, it would mean a tough hump up and down an additional hillside en route back to the command post.

The powerfully built Bennett seemed as fresh as when they had started, and Kerstetter said, "You're just trying to wear my tired old ass out, ain't you, Jerry? Why didn't you just stick to boxing, if you wanted all this physical punishment?"

Bennett had been an All-Air Force boxing champion before joining the 1st Special Operations Combat Control Squadron.

He laughed and said, "Nobody said it was gonna be easy, Ike."

Kerstetter chuckled and slugged his comrade-in-arms on the shoulder. "I heard that," he said, then started down the rocky slope in the darkness.

"Hang on just one minute," Bennett said. "I've got to take a dump, and I mean right now."

"Good," Ike replied without slowing. "Go ahead. Last one there is a rotten egg."

The Air Force sergeant did his business and passed the aging Delta Force master sergeant just as he started up the far hillside.

As Bennett strode easily past the puffing Kerstetter, Ike said, "Hey, hang on a minute, Jerry. I have to pee."

"Well, have at it then. I'll see you at the top."

"No, you don't understand, man," Ike joked. "I want you to hold it for me."

Jerry continued on up the hill as he said, "Hold it? You mean find it, don't you?"

"Ah, you damn chitlin' eater," Ike mumbled. "Everybody knows that bit about you black dudes being so well hung is just a myth. Why, Congress ought to investigate you for fraud!"

"They ought to investigate the Army for keeping tired old farts like you on active duty. Now, get on up this damn hill."

Ike almost caught up with the airman several times before they reached the top, but he knew Bennett was just waiting for him. Still, just before the pair made the crest, he tripped the younger man, and Bennett fell to his hands and knees and slid a short distance back down the hill. Ike pushed quickly to the top.

He was lying there on the ground when Bennett got to the top, gasping for breath and holding his night vision goggles out to Bennett.

"Jesus Christ, Jerry," he puffed. "Take a look down there."

Bennett surveyed the terrain below through the goggles. There was a long line of vehicles on the flat valley floor below—missile erector/launchers.

"Oh, my Lord, Ike," he whispered, dropping to the ground beside Kerstetter. "There must be at least twenty Scuds down there."

It was well after dark by the time Bill Kernan managed to drag himself, on bloody hands and knees, toward a group of buildings a quarter of a mile east of the highway. He had twisted his foot back around and tied his Arab headdress over the bone protruding from his ankle, then splinted it with a piece of automobile debris from the roadside. He'd been unable to find his pistol.

The pain in his leg throbbed and burned so badly that he thought he would pass out, but he dragged himself all the way to the nearest building and thumped on the door with his bloody fist.

There was a noise from inside and the door flung open. In the eerie glow of light from dozens of oil wells burning in the distance, he saw a man holding a rifle. The man was asking him something in Arabic.

"I don't speak Arabic," Bill said. "I'm an American."

Seeing how badly he was injured, the man said something else to Kernan and hurried away.

He returned a few minutes later with someone else. "You say you're an American?" the new arrival asked, kneeling to study the face of the injured man.

"Oh!" he said as he recognized Kernan. "It is. It's the American named Bill! I'm Mahwan. I met you with Abdul a month ago, in the video shop."

The men carried Kernan to another of the buildings. There were a half-dozen more resistance members there, gathered around a diagram illuminated by a small oil lamp.

"We have been killing Iraqis as they passed on the highway near here," Mahwan explained. "But they attacked our position with an armored carrier. We lost two men, and had to run for it. We were just trying to decide what to do next. What happened to you?"

Kernan struggled to answer him, but became incoherent, and then passed out from pain and exhaustion.

✳   ✳   ✳

"Uh, Coyote Two Kilo, say again the number and type of targets," the USSOTAF base radio operator said to Kerstetter.

"Soccer Base, this is Coyote Two Kilo," Ike repeated, "I say again, we have two four Scuds. Twenty-four, goddamnit. Two dozen Sierra Charlie Uniform Deltas. Are you ready to copy the coordinates?"

"Good God a'mighty!" the base station radio man exclaimed. "Send the grid, Coyote!"

The coordinates were passed immediately to the AWACS managing the aircraft over western Iraq, and relayed to the A-10s patrolling the panhandle.

The Warthog squadron commander, Lieutenant Colonel Taffy Hughes, had just arrived on station with his wingman, Lieutenant Les Knapp, when he received the incredible report that twenty four Scud missiles had been spotted. He quickly called the pair of A-10s that he and Knapp had just relieved.

"We heard the transmission, 'Hog One," the flight leader reported to his squadron commander. "We're on the way there now, but we won't have long to hang around. We're getting low on gas."

"You can recover someplace closer than home base," Hughes said. "Land on the road, if you have to. But get back up here. We're going to need your ordnance."

"Roger that, 'Hog One. Wouldn't miss it for the world."

Hughes switched channels and began trying to contact the ground team that had reported the huge battery of missiles, callsign Coyote Two Kilo, but he was still too far away to reach Bennett's UHF radio.

Bennett was trying to reach the aircraft, also to no avail.

"Warthog Lead, Warthog Lead, Coyote Two Kilo on uniform," he kept repeating, as Kerstetter watched the long line of missile carriers maneuvering onto level areas of the valley floor below.

Kerstetter glanced overhead. The stars which had clearly been visible before were only showing through the clouds here and there now.

"How much longer, Jerry?" he asked. "It looks as if the weather's going to hell again."

"Don't know," Bennett replied, glancing skyward. "I can't raise them yet. You're right about the weather, though. If they don't get here soon, it may be socked in by the time they do."

Kerstetter peered down at the valley floor through his night vision goggles. He counted the missile carriers once more. This time, the count was twenty six. He reported the new total to USSOTAF headquarters on the satellite radio. He also reported the worsening weather conditions.

The word about the large number of Scuds had spread through the headquarters like wildfire. As soon as Major General Wayne Wilson heard the number, he hurried to the operations center. Now he stood near the radio, considering the disturbing report.

Twenty-four—now twenty-six—ballistic missiles. How had so many been missed by the patrols on the ground and in the air? He recalled what he'd heard one briefer say when asked why the allies were having so much problem finding the things: "It's like looking for a fire truck in Texas," the man had said. And one that the firemen are trying to hide from you, at that.

Twenty six. Why had the Iraqis brought so many of them together? And then it dawned on him: they were going to salvo them at Israel all at once. The Patriots would never be able to get them all—not even a fraction of them. They'd rain down on Israel in one last, desperate attempt by Saddam Hussein to draw Israel into the war and destroy the Coalition.

Wilson didn't believe the Coalition could be easily torn apart now—not when the liberation of Kuwait was so near at hand, and the allies were in the midst of a gaining a stunningly quick and complete victory. But the American intelligence community's assessment of what the Israelis might do if a large number of missiles landed on their territory was frightening. They had already sent a message by successfully testing a long range missile of their own over the Mediterranean. It was well known, now, that Israel had produced a large number of tactical nuclear weapons. The assessment of many of the intelligence community professionals was that they would use them—especially if any of the missiles landing on their territory contained chemical or biological warheads.

Wilson turned to his weather officer. "He said the weather's worsening?"

The meteorologist nodded, and pointed to his latest satellite photographs. "This cloud bank is just about over him now, I think, sir."

"How long until the A-10s get there, Dave?" he asked his operations officer, Colonel Dave Ames.

Ames looked at the Air Force lieutenant colonel who was his assistant for air operations, who said, "About eight or ten minutes, General."

"All right," Wilson said, his voice filled with urgency. "Get with CENTAF—General Horner, if possible. Tell him the situation and that we've got to have some all-weather fighters up there immediately—right now. And get a Pave Low and a flight of Apaches scrambled and on the way there. The Pave can lead them straight in through the clouds. Do it."

"Wilco, boss," Ames said, although he wasn't optimistic about getting any aircraft diverted quickly; they were all committed to support of the ground battles raging in Kuwait and eastern Iraq.

"Give me the team leader," Wilson said to the radio operator.

The radioman called Kerstetter, then passed the handset to Wilson, who didn't bother with the use of formal callsigns on the secure voice radio.

"Ike, this is Wayne Wilson. Get your team in close enough that you can engage those damned missiles with your organic weapons, if you have to. If they erect them for launch before we can get any airstrikes in, do what you can. I know it'll be risky, but we've got to keep the things from launching. It's important, you copy?"

"Roger that, sir," Kerstetter replied. "But there's only two of us here, and all we've got are M-16s and hand grenades. The rest of the team's heading this way, but they won't be here for over an hour, at best. We'll do what we can with what we've got though, over."

"What's the weather now?" Wilson inquired.

"Almost total cloud cover," Ike answered. "But Bennett just made contact with the Warthogs. They're five minutes out."

"Roger, Ike," Wilson said. "Thank God you found the things. Now you've got to make sure the A-10s get 'em."

"We'll try, General," the Delta Force soldier said.

Bennett was verifying the ordnance the A-10s had aboard and describing the target and surrounding terrain to the pilots. He glanced overhead, and said, "I don't know if you'll be able to get in, though, Warthogs. We're getting completely socked in here."

"Hang in, Coyote," Hughes said. "We'll think of something."

"I don't know, Ike," the airman said to his team leader, gesturing skyward. "They'll never get down through that stuff."

"You feel like fighting?" Kerstetter asked.

"What do you mean?"

"I mean, the biggest prize fight of your life. If we get down there near them, just in case they get ready to launch the things before we can get airstrikes in, maybe we can put a few rounds in each one. It probably won't knock 'em out, but at least it'll do some damage."

Bennett stared in his direction. There were twenty-six launchers down in the valley, and each had a crew of eight men—more than two hundred Iraqi soldiers. And Kerstetter was proposing that they go down there and attack them with two men.

"You son of a bitch, Ike, you're crazy," he said after a few seconds. Then he stood, picked up his rucksack and rifle and said, "Well, let's go."

The A-10 Thunderbolts of Hughes and Knapp had made their aerial rendezvous with the pair of aircraft they had intended to relieve, and arrived over the valley just as the men started downhill.

"Damn, Coyote," Hughes said over the radio to Bennett, "It's dark as a well digger's ass down there. I've got an IR camera on my Maverick looking, but I can't see a thing through the soup."

"Copy, Warthog," Bennett said. "Hang around. Maybe we'll get a break in the clouds. We're moving down closer to the targets."

"OK," Hughes answered. "I'm going to look real hard at the map. Maybe I can figure out a way to get down under the stuff without plowing into a hillside."

Dave Ames hurried back to Wayne Wilson's side. "OK, sir," he said, "CENTCOM's launching four A-6s from the Saratoga, over in the Red Sea. They'll be there in, oh, thirty or thirty-five minutes."

"Good job," Wilson said. He knew the A-6 Intruders were capable of the precision bombing of targets they couldn't even see by using their radar to "see" the ground below. The valley where the Scuds were would be easy to pick up on radar. He called Kerstetter on the satellite radio.

When the heavy-breathing master sergeant answered, Wilson said, "We've got two sets of A-6s on the way there, Ike. When they check in, give them the best grid you can for a first drop, then adjust the other strikes from there, over."

"How long?" Kerstetter puffed.

"Three zero minutes,"

"Too late, General. They're starting to erect the damn things now. The A-10s are here, but they can't see anything. We're moving on down, out."

There was dead silence in the operations center when Kerstetter's report came over the speaker, broken only by the voice of Dave Ames muttering, "Oh, my God."

"Hey, Coyote, I've got an idea!" Taffy Hughes called to the men on the ground far below him.

"Send it," Jerry Bennett replied.

"Point your LTD straight up at the clouds. Maybe I'll be able to spot it. If so, you can give me a direction and distance from it to the Scuds."

Bennett grabbed Kerstetter, "Hang on," he said in a stage whisper. "The Warthogs have an idea. It might just work."

The combat controller dropped his rucksack and dug into it for his laser target designator. Normally, the LTD's infrared beam was employed by pointing it directly at enemy targets to illuminate them for laser-guided munitions. But Hughes's idea was to see if the concentrated beam was strong enough to penetrate through the clouds, so that he could locate the team below with the infrared camera in the nose of his Maverick missile.

Bennett handed the laser target designator to Ike. "Lie on your back, point it straight up, and illuminate," he said.

Kerstetter did so. He was wearing night vision goggles, and he could see the infrared beam when he turned the LTD on. It made a bright dot on the cloud bottom.

"OK, it's on, Warthog," Bennett said over his ground-to-air radio.

Hughes, well back from the location and above the clouds, pointed his aircraft in the general direction of the valley and nosed it down. He saw nothing, so he made a slow flat turn to the left, then back to the right.

"I got it!" he called as he saw a bright spot on the cloud tops on his cockpit-mounted monitor. "I've got it, Coyote. Give me a heading and distance from where you are to the target."

Behind him, the other three Thunderbolts aligned themselves with their squadron commander's aircraft, strung out in a long, straight formation.

On the rocky hillside below, Sergeant Bennett was pointing his compass at the center of mass of the enemy vehicles. "If you fly straight over the LTD on a heading of, uh, three zero eight degrees, the center of the target is about four hundred meters beyond it, over."

Placing Ike and himself on the bomb target line was dangerous business, Jerry Bennett knew. But it would give the pilots a better chance of hitting the missile launchers than they would have if he'd required them to attack on a line offset from the mark the laser made on the cloud cover.

"Three zero eight degrees, four zero zero meters beyond your mark," Hughes repeated.

When he heard Bennett's "Roger, roger," he warned the pilots behind him, "All right, make sure you don't drop anything short, guys. The team's right on the attack heading."

He made a wide circle, the other Warthogs maintaining their positions well behind and above the aircraft in front.

Hughes acquired the spot of light from the laser with his Maverick missile camera, lined up on it on a heading of 308 degrees, and started in.

"Coyote, Warthog's comin' in hot with thirty mike on heading three zero eight."

"Roger," Bennett acknowledged. "You're cleared in hot." "Keep that thing steady, Ike" he warned, peering at the Scud missiles in the valley below through night vision goggles. About half of the missiles were now pointing straight toward the sky. Most of the others were on the way to the vertical, as well. The sound of the approaching aircraft was clearly audible, now.

There was a sudden series of cracks directly over Ike and Jerry's heads, and Bennett saw the rounds slam into the hillside on the other side of the valley.

"Long and left," he called immediately, "Nose down five degrees, and five degrees right, 'Hog Two,'"

"Right five, down five," Les Knapp acknowledged. "Comin' hot, Coyote!"

He had been on the exact glidepath as Hughes when he got Bennett's correction, so he turned slightly right and pushed the nose of his A-10 down. Just above the cloud tops, he triggered the big, 30 millimeter rotating cannon in the nose of his airplane, and held it for two seconds. One hundred and forty depleted uranium slugs streamed through the clouds to the ground below. A handful of them slammed into two of the Scuds, and one of them erupted in a huge ball of flame.

The flash of the explosion was visible through the cover of cloud, and the pilots heard Bennett's jubilant voice.

"Target! All right, Three," he called to the next pilot, "can you see the burning Scud?"

Warthog Three said, "Yeah, I can see the glow through the clouds."

"OK, most of the missiles are strung out from there to the north for, shit, half a mile."

"Roger," Warthog Three replied. "I'm about bingo on fuel, so I'm going to pickle the whole load, ground."

He dove straight at the flame, firing his cannon as he pulled the nose of the airplane up, then dropped his bombs.

Several more missiles and carriers ignited amid the line of explosions from the bombs.

"Right on!" Bennett called.

"This is Warthog Four," the next pilot said. "Plenty of light down there now, ground. Want my load the same place?"

"A little more north," Bennett answered. He could see figures scurrying around in the light of the flaming wrecks that Warthogs Two and Three had caused.

"Four, roger. Coming in hot."

The next salvo struck most of the same area, but also took out an additional missile. About half the Scuds were destroyed or damaged in the first pass.

Hughes had Three and Four make another pass to empty their cannons, then sent them on their way to the nearest air base, as they were critically low on fuel. Then he led Les Knapp in on several more attacks. There were only a few Scuds still untouched by the time they'd expended their ammunition, but the clouds were beginning to break up here and there.

And then the carrier-based A-6s appeared overhead. The six Intruders made short work of the remaining missiles. By the time they departed, another pair of A-10s was waiting overhead, but there was nothing for them to do.

At the United States Special Operations Task Force war room, Major General Wayne Wilson called the Central Command commander-in-chief, General Norman Schwarzkopf. He reported the astonishing results of the attack on the missiles his men had discovered the enemy preparing to launch at Israel.

"Give them a message for me, Wayne," the burly four-star said. "Tell them I said, 'Congratulations. You just kept Israel out of the war.'"

By the time the message was relayed to Kerstetter and Bennett, they had left the area to avoid discovery by the surviving Iraqi missile crewmen they saw fleeing the carnage into the surrounding hills. They linked up with the remainder of their team, and were awaiting extraction from the recon zone.

"Why, that's mighty kind of the old Bear," Ike said when Wilson passed him the CENTCOM commander's message. "Pass him a message from me and Jerry, will you, sir?"

"Roger, send your message," Wilson said.

"Tell him we said, 'Scudinavia pacified. What next, General?' over."

Twenty Three

27 February 1991

Emotion is contagious—especially that of a strong leader, whether he is the leader of a football team, a religious congregation, a family, or just about any other group of human beings. This is particularly so of a military unit, and most especially a combat arms unit at war.

The mood of Team Charlie, Task Force 5-64 Armor, could well be described as a blue funk in the early morning hours of Wednesday, February 27th, because that was the mood of its commander, Lieutenant Larry Redmond.

A combination of things had led the soldiers of Redmond's outfit into this mood: the death of one of their platoon leaders and the maiming of his tank's gunner; the sinking in of the realization of the terrible destruction they had wrought on the enemy during their blitz into Iraq, especially at the airfield they had so mercilessly assaulted; and the fact that there was more dangerous combat ahead.

But mostly, it was the sullen, listless mood of their commander which had infected them.

Redmond's mood was caused by all those things, to some degree. But it sprung mostly from a sense of disappointment. He was disappointed in himself for having ignored the order of his battalion commander.

Suppose he had acknowledged the call, but informed Lieutenant Colonel Farrar that he had momentum, that his troops were destroying almost every enemy position during their rampage down the runway?

Had Redmond told him that, wouldn't Farrar have allowed the team to continue its overwhelming assault, and warned the other commanders to be careful not to engage Redmond's armor well out in front of them? If all that had happened, wouldn't Joe still be alive?

He was disappointed, too, that none of the other company commanders had stood up for him during Captain Black's verbal assault. Would none of them have attacked so vigorously, if they'd been in his position, and had the enemy scattering in disarray before them? Perhaps not, but did that make him wrong?

And he was disappointed that his admission of ignoring the order had caused him to be threatened with relief.

But mostly, Redmond was disappointed that his tank company team had been relegated to battalion reserve during what might well be the biggest tank-on-tank fight since the second World War.

The tactic that seemed to be preferred by most of the division was to sit as far away as possible and pick off the enemy one at a time. It was a sound one, he had to admit, for dealing with most of the Iraqis encountered so far in the brief war. They had dug their armor in so deeply, according to intelligence reports and what little he had seen, that they were really nothing more than pillboxes.

But that just made Larry's mood even more sour. In that sort of deliberate shootout, the leading companies would do all the shooting. It was unlikely that the reserve would need to be committed.

A great chapter in the history of tank warfare was about to be written, and it appeared that he and his men were going to be sitting on the sidelines.

"Have I got time to take a leak, sir?" It was the voice of the driver of Redmond's tank, Private Anderson, over the intercom.

Without even looking at his watch, Redmond said, "Sure, go ahead." The lead companies weren't due to cross the line of departure for another fifteen minutes or so.

Team Charlie was in a column on highway 8. In front of Redmond's tank was Jim Locher's platoon. Behind was the platoon of attached infantry in their Bradley fighting vehicles. At the rear, in team reserve, was the platoon Redmond had commanded, now led by his platoon sergeant. The remaining tanks in the platoon which had been Joe Cincotti's had been detached from Team Charlie, and were now with Team Blue, the infantry company team.

Redmond climbed out of the commander's cupola, stood atop the turret, and urinated over the side. Just in front of Jim Locher's leading Abrams, he could see the red glow of lights through the open door at the rear of the battalion commander's M-577 command post vehicle. What was it Farrar had said only a little over a day before? Something about leaving Redmond in command of the company, because he needed his best leaders when they hit the Republican Guards in front of Basra.

"Damn it, Redmond," he mumbled to himself. "One stupid mistake…" Well, it was still a long way to Basra.

He climbed back into his seat and reconnected the communications cord to his combat vehicle crewman's helmet. Gibbs Begay was talking to the gunner, Sergeant Peterson, on the intercom.

"Anyway, Sergeant Pete," Begay was saying, "I told the son of a bitch that if he'd been with us, he'd know the difference between an M-1 and a goddam T-72. I shoulda just whipped his ass."

"Well, in all that shit, anybody could have mistaken him for the enemy, Gibbs," Peterson responded.

It was obvious to Redmond that the men were discussing the friendly fire incident that had killed Cincotti.

"Bullshit," Redmond said. "Nobody in this crew, or any crew in our old platoon, would have mistaken an Abrams for a damned Iraqi tank, and you know it!"

The other crewmen went silent. Their company commander was obviously in a foul mood.

The task force began its attack a few minutes later. It seemed to Redmond that it took forever for the units to deploy from their attack positions into battle formation, and even when they got going it was maddeningly slow.

Lieutenant Colonel Farrar began imploring them to pick up the pace a few minutes later. The lead teams finally did so, but barely.

After a few kilometers of the accordion-like stop and go effect which occurs at the rear of any slow moving column of vehicles, Anderson—Redmond's driver—said, "Stop, go. Stop, go. Get the lead out of your ass and start attacking, dammit."

"Yeah," Gibbs Begay said. "If we was in the lead, we'd be in fuckin' Baghdad by now."

Larry Redmond said nothing, but he smiled to himself.

*   *   *

Taffy Hughes had rearmed and refueled his A-10 Thunderbolt, and was back over Scudinavia for what he figured would be his last Scud hunting patrol. He had been informed by USSOTAF that his squadron was to be relieved by combat air patrols of all-weather A-6 Intruder fighter-bombers from the carrier battle groups steaming in the Red Sea.

He was making one last circuit of the ground reconnaissance teams he had come to know and respect during his month-long tour in support of them.

He was in radio contact with Jack Marsh's patrol from the 5th Special Forces Group.

"Well, Scudnut Five," he said to Marsh, "looks like your pals in the Blue and Green Scud Hunting Machine are going to take the MVP trophy in this little war—especially old Coyote Team. They're more than twenty up on you, after that little tea party in the hills up north."

"I hear you, Fartlog One," Jack Marsh replied. "But we think the three chemical Scuds we took out should count ten times what their generic Scuds count. The way I see it, we're still ahead."

"Yeah, well, you'll have to work that out with the head scorekeeper. Tell you what though, old buddy, it's been a pleasure shooting for you. You guys can put yourselves on my bar tab any place, anytime. Take care, now."

"All right, head Wart," Marsh said. "Thanks a bunch. I hope we'll meet again…Where you going to be sowing your wild, depleted uranium oats next, or can you say?"

"Uh, over south of Basra, from what I gather," Taffy Hughes said. "Apparently Saddam's boys are all trying to get home to momma up there. They say it gives the term 'target-rich environment' a whole new dimension."

"Well, good hunting, Warthog Leader. Give 'em hell," Marsh said.

"Roger, Scudnut. Keep your head down. Fartlog Leader, out."

*   *   *

The lead elements of the Coalition ground forces reached Kuwait City early on the morning of February 27th.

One of the first medical evacuation flights out of the partially-liberated capital was requested by the Special Forces medic who had gone to Abir's villa to care for the sightless Dr. Singh. Also on the flight was the CIA agent who had requested their presence there, Bill Kernan. He had been taken to the villa by the resistance force men whom he had contacted after his motorcycle wreck on the highway to Iraq.

As the helicopter lifted off from a landing zone near the villa, Kernan stared out and thought, I'm in Hell. I haven't died yet, but I'm already in Hell.

There were fires—huge fires—in every direction. A pall of smoke so thick that it seemed impenetrable hung over everything, and soot rained down like black snow.

To the north, the horizon which wasn't lighted by oil well fires twinkled from allied artillery and airstrikes. Kuwait was free, for all practical purposes, and Iraq's fleeing forces were all but smashed to pulp.

Bill Kernan didn't care.

He had finally found the one person he felt he could love after years of struggle and killing and searching for some reason in it all. But she was gone. He looked to the north again before the medevac helicopter turned south. He could see the tracers and bomb flashes and flaming wrecks all along the highway leading north. Somewhere in all that carnage, he was certain, were the remains of the only thing he cared for.

Tears of pain—not from his injuries, but his heart—spilled from his eyes, and he whispered, "Abir."

$$* \qquad * \qquad *$$

The much-heralded Republican Guards divisions of Saddam Hussein's army, which six weeks earlier had been the world's sixth largest, withered and crumbled in the face of the Coalition blitzkrieg.

Hammered by weeks of bombing by B-52s, with their thunderous hailstorms of exploding bombs, and picked to pieces by the "smart" munitions of the allied air forces, they now found themselves being routed by tank assaults, Apache gunships, and sudden storms of artillery and rocket fire.

Most of them wanted no more of it. Along highway 8, they tried to flee with what remained of their battered divisions north across the Euphrates river into what had once been known as the Cradle of Civilization. But the Euphrates bridges were gone, smashed to rubble by guided bombs.

The way west was blocked by the Screaming Eagles of the 101st Airborne Division, whose lightning-fast air assault had put them on the banks of the Euphrates just hours after the ground assault began.

In western Kuwait, the American VII Corps had smashed into the Iraqi divisions there. A thousand Abrams tanks had reduced most of the enemy armor to smoldering rubble, and many of their crews to carrion for vultures.

The survivors of the massive tank assault who had not surrendered were fleeing in disarray, north for Basra.

The United States Air Force met them there, and slaughtered them.

The attack by the 24th Infantry Division in the north was also faring well. At Tallil airbase, the 197th Infantry Brigade was rooting out the enemy, capturing more than a thousand men. The remainder of the division roared east along highway 8, blasting the fleeing Iraqis to shreds. Among the burning rubble were more than fifty T-72 tanks, most destroyed aboard transport trucks as the Iraqis made a futile attempt to haul them off to fight another day.

Not all of the Iraqi tanks were in flight, though. Northeast of Rumalia, one tank brigade had managed to stay intact.

Hidden beneath a heavy blanket of oil well smoke by the shifting winds, they escaped detection by the Apaches—and destruction by their Hellfire missiles —as the helicopters screened the 24th Division's northern flank.

With a rare opportunity to blunt the Americans' rampage through Iraq, the enemy brigade launched a counterattack.

They opened their attack with artillery fire. It was answered in short order by counter-battery fire from the Victory Division's guns, but not before it caused the Americans to button up and slow almost to a halt.

One enemy airburst found Lieutenant Colonel Farrar's command vehicle, and though its armor shielded the men inside, the antennae were carried away, and his orders to press on went unheard and thus unheeded.

Lieutenant Larry Redmond didn't drop inside his tank and button up. Instead, he surveyed the battlefield ahead. He was the first to see the line of enemy tanks appear. They came up out of the low ground south of the broad river, and took the leading companies of Farrar's task force on the flank from less than a kilometer away.

The taste of battle filled Redmond's mouth, and his melancholy mood evaporated, replaced by the warrior spirit for which he was better known.

He called on the battalion radio net to warn the other companies as the enemy opened fire, then ordered his own crews into action.

"Gunners, enemy tanks, left front!" he warned, then barked out battle formation orders. "Flank left and form a company line. Charlie Two, swing around to the north. Blue platoon take the center. Charlie One, get on line from here to the left! Move, move!"

As his tanks and infantry fighting vehicles deployed into attack formation, he called the battalion commander, but got no response.

"I'm swinging left to hit them from the flank," he said, but there was so much traffic on the net, he wasn't certain he was heard.

Before the other companies could bring their guns to bear, the Iraqis slammed their T-72s into reverse and backed down into the defile from which they had appeared.

Larry Redmond knew what they were doing. They would reload, dash forward again into alternate firing positions, and, with only the turrets of their T-72 tanks exposed, send another volley of gunfire into the lead American companies from close range.

His tanks raced into the low ground with the enemy, their turrets facing east, and Redmond said, "Let's go! Let's take it to 'em! This one's for Cincotti, men. Don't let the bastards come back up."

The company flanked back to the east and tore into the enemy, surprising them as they came back up to fire another salvo into the task force on the road above. Closing fast and firing on the move, Redmond's tanks and Bradleys were taking them apart, the T-72's guns still pointed toward the south.

Explosions blasted turrets off their hulls and set ammunition and fuel ablaze as the Abrams' guns took their awful toll. Some Iraqis tried to swing their guns to bear on Team Charlie's armor, but the American gunners saw them, and blasted them to rubble. Others dashed back down into the low ground, although few made it. Several Iraqi crews flung their hatches open and, arms in the air, begged for surrender.

Lieutenant Colonel Farrar, the battalion commander, was back on the air now. "Flank left, Alpha!" he ordered. "You've gotta move down there and get the goddam things. And make sure you don't engage Redmond's tanks!"

Larry called Farrar and said, "This is Charlie Six. Shall I keep counterattacking, over?"

"Roger, roger, Charlie Six," Farrar replied. "Good work, boy. Take it to 'em!"

Redmond began to maneuver his team to the north to stay on the Iraqis' flank, but before he could attack again, Farrar called and halted him.

The fickle desert wind had blown away the pall of smoke under which the Iraqis had hidden, and a swarm of Apache gunships appeared. Farrar decided to let the Hellfires finish the destruction which Redmond had begun, and continue the attack of his task force toward Basra.

When the task force reached the last of the day's objectives and halted to rearm and refuel, Lieutenant Colonel Farrar went in search of Redmond. He found the lieutenant standing beside his tank in the midst of an onion field.

"Well done today, warrior," he said, reaching his hand to shake Larry's. "I didn't know what the hell was going on at first—my antennas got blown away. If you hadn't moved on the bastards' flank, I'd hate to think what they might have done."

Redmond only nodded.

Farrar looked around at Team Charlie's crews. Half of them were busy pulling maintenance on their vehicles while the others remained at their guns, ready for action.

Private Anderson crawled out of the engine compartment of Redmond's tank and saw the task force commander.

"Hey, Colonel," he said. "I guess old Charlie Company earned their pay today, huh, sir?"

"Roger that, soldier," Farrar said, smiling. "Damn good work."

Gibbs Begay was up on the hull of the tank drawing silhouettes of T-72s on the tube of the big 122mm main gun with a Magic Marker—symbols of the enemy tanks the Abrams crew had destroyed. He paused and looked down at Farrar.

"That mean you're going to let us get back up front where we belong, Colonel?" he asked.

Farrar looked at Begay, then at Redmond, and back at Begay again. "There's a couple of Republican Guards divisions dug in between here and Basra," he said. "You sure you want to take the point, Gibbs?"

"Hell, yes, Colonel," Begay answered. "You got anybody who can do it better?"

He had heard no such indicators of high morale from the crews of other companies. Nor had they been as well organized as the crews in the onion field, half of them pulling maintenance while the other half remained ready for action.

Farrar grinned, and said, "I guess not, Gibbs," then looked at Redmond. The young lieutenant looked so much older—so much more tired—than he had just days before. But he still had fire in his eyes.

"'Shit through a goose,' eh, Larry?" he said.

"Yes, sir," Lieutenant Redmond replied. "Let us up there, and we'll go through Baghdad like Grant went through Richmond."

*　　*　　*

Lieutenant Les Knapp pointed the nose of his A-10 Thunderbolt down toward the jumble of cars and trucks ahead of and below him, and triggered the fighter-bomber's big rotating cannon. The burst of 30mm rounds slammed into several of the vehicles, causing some to careen into those already destroyed by earlier airstrikes. As he pulled up, Knapp could see people darting away from the wrecked and burning vehicles.

"They're trying to swing left up along the bottom slopes of the ridge now," he heard Taffy Hughes, the Warthog squadron commander, say over the radio.

"Warthog Three, roger," the lead pilot of the next pair of Thunderbolts responded. "We'll put a stop to that shit with Rockeyes."

The next two A-10s swept over the half-dozen cars and trucks which were attempting to bypass the mass of smashed vehicles now blocking the highway leading from Kuwait City to Basra. Each aircraft released a pair of Rockeye cluster bombs, and as Knapp made a climbing turn to set up for another strafing run, he saw the line of explosions from the bomblets run across the escaping vehicles. Two of them burst into flames, and again Knapp saw figures running from the target vehicles. One of the running men was aflame.

"Anybody carrying scatter mines?" Hughes asked.

"Affirmative. Warthog Seven and Eight," another pilot replied.

"OK, Five and Six, hold it high and dry," Hughes ordered. "Seven and eight, lay your mines left and right of the highway at the front of the pack there."

"Seven, wilco. I'll take the left, Eight; you take the right."

The two aircraft swooped down and released their munitions alongside the traffic jam of Iraqi wrecks, scattering strings of aerial-delivered mines in the desert beside the highway to prevent more vehicles from escaping the carnage.

As they pulled up, the pilot of Warthog Eight said, "Hey, there's a whole bunch of 'em hiding in that big culvert up near the front of the vehicles."

"Roger, we'll take care of 'em," Taffy Hughes answered, then said to Knapp, "Follow me, Warthog Two."

Lieutenant Knapp followed Hughes as he swung his airplane out to the east of the highway, then made a turn back toward it.

"OK, I've got the culvert in sight," Hughes said. "You still have a Maverick, don't you, Les?"

"Uh, roger that," Knapp answered.

"Do you see the culvert?" Hughes asked.

Knapp turned his aircraft almost on its side and looked out of the canopy toward the front of the tangle of smashed vehicles. There was a big culvert beneath the roadbed there, and he could see a group of people huddled inside it, and others running for safety toward it.

"Yeah, I've got it," Les said.

"OK, make a racetrack and put your Maverick in there," the squadron commander ordered. "I'll follow you in."

Oh, my God, no, Knapp thought. He didn't mind attacking Scuds and tanks and bunkers. But these were people, not equipment. They were already out of the war, trying to escape in cars and trucks and vans, and even on foot—any way they could.

As he set up for his run at the target, Knapp armed his Maverick and aligned the crosshairs of the missile's camera on the opening of the big culvert. It was packed with people. A wave of nausea swept over him and he mumbled to himself, "I can't do it."

He moved the crosshairs up onto a Jeep Cherokee on the highway above the culvert, launched the missile, and watched it fly to the already disabled wagon and explode.

"Aw, shit," he heard Lieutenant Colonel Hughes say, "you missed, Les. I'm going in hot."

As Les Knapp pulled up and turned, he looked over to watch his wingman's attack. Hughes blasted the end of the culvert with a long burst of cannon fire, and Knapp could imagine the big depleted uranium rounds slamming into the mass of humanity inside, tearing off arms and legs and ripping bodies apart. He nearly vomited into his mask.

Another of the A-10 pilots said, "This is Five. They're running out of the other end," and Hughes said, "All right, Five and Six, you nail them. Everybody else hold it high and dry."

Knapp slid his airplane in behind his squadron commander's and watched the Thunderbolts of Warthogs Five and Six swoop in for their attack.

About a dozen people were running out of the west end of the culvert, and Warthog Five dropped a bomb in their midst. His wingman followed him in, diving low to the ground before leveling off and filling the culvert with another long burst of 30mm DU fire. Les Knapp looked away, not wanting to witness the result.

To the rest of his flight, Taffy Hughes said, "All right, we'll make one more run on the highway to unload what we have left, then return to base and rearm."

The A-10s bore down on another group of vehicles still moving north into the lengthening column of wreckage, and blasted them to rubble.

Hughes led the attack and as he pulled out, looked back to see Knapp cut loose with a burst of cannon fire into the mass of vehicles which had already been destroyed. He watched as the rest of his pilots ripped into the fleeing enemy, then said, "Well done, Warthog flight. All right, let's head for home, rearm, and get ready to get back in the air."

▼

Twenty four

27 February 1991

"Compared to what we're about to face," Lieutenant Colonel Farrar said to his assembled company commanders and platoon leaders, "the fighting we've done so far has been a cakewalk."

Farrar saw some of the officers glance nervously at one another, and some looked down at their feet. He noticed that Lieutenant Redmond's nostrils flared, his sparkling eyes fixed steadily on his battalion commander's.

Farrar turned toward the maps taped on the side of his armored command vehicle.

On the west of the map was an orderly line of blue symbols denoting the 24th Infantry Division's maneuver units, including Farrar's own; Task Force 5-46. On the east were clusters of red symbols showing the last known positions of the Iraqi Republican Guards units south and west of Basra.

There were many more red symbols than blue ones, although they were not as neatly aligned.

Lieutenant Colonel Farrar pointed to the arc of enemy unit symbols nearest the American positions and said, "There are the remnants of three enemy divisions..." He stopped in mid-sentence, stroked his stubbled chin as he thought a moment, then said, "No, 'remnants' is too weak a word. There are the reorganized elements of three Republican Guards divisions, here southwest of Basra."

He eyed his subordinates and saw Redmond's steady gaze still fixed on him.

"Their problem is, they've got no place to go. The bridges across the river are down and the Air Force is bombing the hell out of anybody who shows up trying to get across. And, unlike the units we encountered earlier, their officers haven't all bugged out on them.

"So, to paraphrase what the Chairman of the Joint Chiefs said, we've got them cut off. Now we're going to kill them."

There was more nervous shuffling within the group, but again Farrar noticed the Team Charlie commander standing steady and attentively.

"All right," Farrar said, pointing to the acetate overlay his operations officer was holding, "this is how we're going to do it..."

The operations officer aligned the transparent overlay with the map and taped it in place.

There were a series of boundary lines and blue arrows running from the friendly unit symbols to the enemy ones, with blue ovals around the clusters of Iraqi forces.

"First, the big picture," Farrar said. "An air and artillery prep of the objectives will commence at H-hour minus forty minutes. At H-hour, the division will attack with 1st and 2d Brigades up, and the 197th in reserve. As you can see, our brigade's attack will be up here where we are, on the north."

The task force commander pointed to the northern sector of the map, where one of the blue arrows split into three smaller ones.

"For our attack, this is what I've decided to do: Alpha and Bravo will attack straight ahead."

He looked at the captains in command of A and B Companies to make certain they were paying attention.

"You'll engage the enemy at maximum range. Fix 'em. Pick 'em off. Keep their heads down, and move in on them slowly but steadily."

The captains nodded, but Redmond wondered why Farrar wanted them to attack slowly and methodically again, instead of using the speed and shock and violence of action of which the tank battalion was capable, to overrun the enemy positions and scatter them. He glanced at the map and saw that the northernmost attack arrow curved north of the enemy positions, then into their flank, and he understood what the task force commander had in mind before he even said it.

"Redmond, you'll go balls out around the flank, down in the low ground, then flank right and roll the bastards up, with the infantry right behind you."

Farrar paused a moment to let the basic element of the plan sink in.

Larry Redmond felt the gaze of the other tank company commanders on him. He looked over at them and wondered what they were thinking. They were probably wondering whether C Company was being given the toughest job as a result of Redmond having previously disobeyed an order of Farrar's, or because Farrar had more confidence in him than his other commanders. Redmond hoped it was the latter reason, but either way, he was glad the toughest mission was going to him.

Farrar's voice interrupted his thoughts. "Now, what's the danger in that, Captain Black?" he asked.

Black moved his eyes from Redmond to the task force commander and said, "Target identification, sir. When Charlie Company comes up, we'll have to make certain that we don't engage them."

Black's company was the one on the north of the straight-ahead part of the attack—the one most likely to mistake one of Redmond's tanks for the enemy as Charlie Company attacked into the enemy flank from the north.

"Exactly," Farrar said, then looked from him to Redmond, then back at Black again. "Can you handle it?"

"Yes, sir," Black answered, glancing around at his platoon leaders.

Black's lieutenants were nodding their agreement, and Lieutenant Colonel Farrar thought, They're relieved as hell that they're not in Redmond's platoons, driving into the midst of the enemy positions.

"We can handle it," Captain Black said.

"All right, then," Farrar said. He looked at the commander of the attached infantry company. "Jones, you'll be right behind Redmond. Once he sweeps over the objective, you'll come behind him and clean it up. There'll probably be a lot of prisoners."

Captain Jones said, "Yes, sir. But suppose Redmond gets bogged down before he can get across the objective? What do you want me to do then?"

Farrar nodded. "Attack through him and root them out," he said, then looked at Larry and added, "He's not going to get bogged down, though."

Redmond was certain, then, why he'd been assigned the most difficult task, and a slight smile curved up at the corner of his mouth.

"OK," Farrar said, "the S-3 will fill in all the details in a minute."

The lieutenant colonel studied the group of grubby soldiers, their hands and faces blackened by the charcoal linings of their chemical protective suits and the oil and smoke of their war machines and the battlefield.

They can do it, he thought. They're Americans, and they've been blooded now. They'll do it, and they'll do it well.

"This is the big one, men," he said to them. "This is the Iraqis' last chance to try to bloody our noses. But we're going to roll right over the sons of bitches, by God—right over their asses and into Baghdad."

*   *   *

It was only mid-afternoon, but the sooty blanket of smoke from hundreds of burning oil wells had drifted south now. It made it seem as if the sun had already set at the airbase where Lieutenant Colonel Hughes's A-10 Thunderbolt squadron was being rearmed and refueled.

Hughes watched the bomb loaders swarming around his airplanes, hanging Maverick missiles, Rockeye cluster bombs, and aerial mines beneath the stubby wings, and reloading the big 30mm rotating cannon in the nose of each plane with rounds of DU—depleted uranium.

He walked into the double-wide trailer which served as a ready room for the pilots where they waited for word of their next mission.

"Same target for the next sortie, guys," he said to the six pilots sitting there.

A couple of them shook their heads and one said, "Jesus. When are the grunts going to get up there so we can get back to killing tanks and Scuds?" The man's question reflected the feeling most of them had about the slaughter they were perpetrating on the highway south of Basra.

On their first sortie, they had caught what appeared to be an organized enemy unit of military trucks and armored personnel carriers trying to escape the overwhelming assaults of US Marines from the south and the Army's VII Corps from the west.

The Warthogs had demolished them, blocking much of the highway with wrecked vehicles.

The squadron's second sortie to the area, though—half of the aircraft were still up there—had been a different matter. There were scores of vehicles of every description, crammed with people making a desperate attempt to flee in the face of the Coalition onslaught. They were defenseless, and the squadron's cluster bombs and cannon fire were annihilating them as the Iraqis continued to pile into the carnage like cattle stampeding blindly over a cliff.

There were reports that they were taking Kuwaiti citizens with them, and the pilots wondered how many of the bodies littering the highway and the desert beside it might be those of innocent civilians.

Taffy Hughes noticed that his wingman was the only pilot of the half-squadron flight missing from the ready room.

"Where's Lieutenant Knapp?" he inquired.

"Sitting out behind the trailer, last I saw of him," one of the pilots replied.

Hughes looked at his watch and said, "OK, be ready to launch in about, uh, twenty minutes," then stepped outside into the sooty air.

He walked around to the back of the trailer and found Les Knapp sitting on the ground smoking a cigarette.

Knapp glanced up at him, then looked back at the ground. He said nothing.

"Let me have a smoke, Les," Hughes said.

Knapp looked up and said, "I thought you quit?" but drew a pack of Merits from the pocket of his flight suit and handed them to his squadron commander.

"I did," Hughes said, looking up at the smoky sky. "But with all this damned secondary smoke from the oil well fires, what's the use?"

He took a cigarette and leaned over as his wingman lit it for him, then handed the pack back to Knapp.

"Where's the next mission?" the lieutenant inquired.

Hughes took a deep draught of smoke, exhaled it, and said, "Same place."

Les Knapp tossed his cigarette away, wrapped his arms around his knees, and laid his head on them. After awhile he said, "I'm not going back up there."

"What?"

Knapp lifted his head and looked at Hughes. "I'm not going back up there, I said."

"What the hell do you mean by that, Lieutenant?" the squadron commander asked, glaring at his subordinate.

"Just what I said. It's senseless slaughter, and I'll be God damned if I'm going to have any part in it."

Hughes threw his cigarette down and squashed it with his boot. He said, "The hell you're not! You'll damn well fly wherever I tell you to, and you'll bomb and strafe whatever I tell you to!"

Knapp narrowed his eyes, but said nothing.

"You missed your targets on purpose, on that last run, didn't you? And the culvert, too?" Hughes asked angrily.

Knapp's expression didn't change as he sat in silence looking at his commander.

Hughes nodded knowingly, then kicked at the ground and said, "I ought to whip your ass, Knapp!"

Les got to his feet, the muscles of his jaw flexing and his hands balled into fists. He stood half a head taller than Taffy Hughes, but was not nearly as muscular.

Now Hughes shook his head slowly. His anger was subsiding into disappointment in his young wingman.

"First you shoot me down, then you refuse to fly for me," he said softly.

"Sir," Knapp said, his voice choked with emotion, "that's unfair. Shooting you down was an accident. This is premeditated murder."

"Murder?"

"Yes, sir," Knapp said, his hostile stance dissolving into a stoop-shouldered posture of despair.

Taffy Hughes looked at the blackened sky, then back at Knapp.

"For Christ's sake, Les," he said, reaching out to place a hand on the lieutenant's shoulder, "the people we're attacking up there are the ones who raped Kuwait—literally raped it. They're the murderers. They're the bastards who did this," he said, pointing up at the pall of smoke above them. "And now they're trying to escape the punishment they deserve—they deserve, God damn them—for what they've done."

Hughes removed his hand from Knapp's shoulder, and the younger man said, "But, sir, what about the reports that they have hostages?" He hung his head and added, "I just wonder how many of the people in that damned culvert were innocent civilians."

Hughes ran his hand through his curly gray hair.

"Les, this is war," he said. "And war is a terrible, messy thing, at best. Don't you think the people who're ordering us back up there have considered that there might be some hostages in that mess? How do you think the poor bastards feel who called for the strike on that target in Baghdad the other day—the one that turned out to be a shelter?"

"No worse than the ones who hit it," Knapp mumbled in reply.

"Maybe," Hughes said, nodding his understanding of Knapp's point. "Maybe. But you know we wouldn't be told to go back up there if there wasn't good reason to."

He placed his hand on the shoulder of the younger pilot again. "Look, Les," he said, "there's been more emphasis placed on avoiding civilian casualties, more honest effort to avoid them in this war, than in any conflict in history. And we're succeeding. But they can't all be avoided, especially when the enemy is using civilians the way they are. If they succeed with this 'human shield' idea, what do you think the bastards, and others like them, would do next time? Huh?"

Knapp just stared blankly at him, so Hughes stirred the dirty sand with his toe, then looked at the young officer and said, "All right, I'll let you sit this one out, Les. The rest of us will go fulfill our commissions— go uphold the oaths we swore when we accepted them." He was staring at Knapp's insignia of rank and his pilot's wings, and nodding.

"And we'll accept the responsibility for what we have to do. So, you just make up some excuse for me to give your wingmen, and I'll pass it on to them for you, OK? And I won't even report your refusal to fly to the wing commander. But hurry up, will you? Because the rest of us are getting ready to go do our duty."

Knapp nodded slowly, then looked at his aging mentor with moist eyes. "All right, I'll fly, Colonel," he said. "It's my responsibility to. But I don't like it."

"Who the hell does, Les?" Hughes said sympathetically.

Lieutenant Knapp shook his head, then turned and walked around the trailer and out toward his heavily-laden bird of war. His commander watched him, then heaved a heavy sigh.

He's scarred for life, now, the gray-haired Air Force lieutenant colonel thought. His mind drifted back to his days in Vietnam, and he remembered a napalm strike on a village there, and he thought, We are all scarred. Then he, too, walked toward his bristling Thunderbolt.

*   *   *

Larry Redmond was sitting in the onion field, leaning against his tank and reading his little Bible by the dim red light of his penlight.

He had prepared his operations order for the coming attack and briefed his troops, then made a final coordination visit to the commander of the infantry company who would follow him into the enemy flank. The rest of Redmond's crew were on the other side of the quiet Abrams, trying to get some sleep before the dangerous assault.

Someone approached out of the darkness and said, "Redmond?"

He recognized Captain Black's voice, so he switched off the penlight and stood up.

"Yeah, I'm here," he said softly.

"Got a minute?" Black asked.

"Sure."

"Look," Black said, then cleared his throat. "Uh, you've got a hell of a tough mission tomorrow."

Larry waited for something more, but after a few seconds pause, when Black said nothing else, he said, "We can handle it."

"Yeah, I know," Black muttered.

There was silence for awhile before the captain spoke again.

"You've got a good company, Larry. A lot of spirit, of, ah, aggressiveness. You're doing a damn fine job of commanding it."

Redmond wondered if he really meant that—wondered what he was really trying to say. "Thanks," he replied.

Again there was a period of silence before Black broke it.

"Look," he said, "I just want you to know that I'm sorry about Cincotti—I really am. I, uh, it was my troops' fault."

This time Redmond broke the silence of a long pause.

"It was my fault, not your troops'. I'm the one who disobeyed the order."

"No," Black retorted, "that's no excuse for shooting one of our own guys—for fratricide," Black said.

"Well, he was firing back toward your company," Redmond said. "It was a mistake—a reasonable mistake. Shit happens."

"Yeah," Black sighed, "shit happens. But it's not going to happen again, not if I can help it."

"I hope not," Larry replied honestly.

"I just don't want you and your crews to worry tomorrow," the captain said. "Not about my guys, anyway. You've got enough to worry about, going smack into the middle of the bad guys' positions."

Redmond considered what his fellow company commander was saying, and thought, He means it. We don't have to worry about friendly fire—not from his tanks. That's why he's here, saying these things. He felt a great sense of relief, and realized that he had, indeed, been subconsciously afraid that he might lose someone else to fire from Black's guns.

"Shit through a goose, sir," he said to Black. "With supporting fire from you guys, that's how we're going to go through the bastards."

"Yeah, I know you will," Black said. "Well, I just wanted you, you know, not to worry about what I said to you earlier. I, uh, I'm sorry. We'll watch out for you tomorrow."

"Thanks, Captain Black," Larry said.

Black took a step away, then turned back to Redmond and tapped him on the chest with his right hand.

Redmond understood his purpose and took the hand and shook it firmly.

"I'm glad we're on the same side, Larry."

"Yeah," Redmond replied. "Me too."

"Well," Black said, "guess we'd better get some sleep."

"Right. And thanks, Captain Black."

The captain said, "See you tomorrow," then walked off into the darkness.

"Roger that," Lieutenant Redmond called after him. "On the objective."

He watched Black's dark silhouette disappear, then sat down and leaned back against the big battle tank.

Decent of him, he thought. Now we're a task force again.

Charlie Company's officers had been the least well-liked group among the officers of the 5th Battalion, 64th Armor Regiment.

The former company commander and the executive officer were disliked because they were weak. This opinion of them was vindicated when they had found excuses for not assuming command of the company from Lieutenant Redmond—the captain after having suffered briefly from concussion when his tank struck a mine shortly after entering Iraq, and the XO because he'd made it plain to Lieutenant Colonel Farrar that he preferred to remain in the rear and handle the company's administrative and logistical duties.

The company's platoon leaders, on the other hand, were disliked by some, although respected, simply because they were damned good.

Their platoons invariably outshone those of the other lieutenants in the battalion in tank gunnery, field maneuvers, and maintenance. Most realized that it was largely a result of Redmond's leadership and innovative training techniques, a fact which did little to endear him to his peers in the other companies.

Because of the weaknesses of the officers in C Company headquarters, Lieutenant Colonel Farrar had paid what some felt was an inordinate amount of attention to Lieutenants Redmond, Locher, and Cincotti. But he had done so with good reason—he didn't want them to lose their motivation, their striving for excellence, their aggressiveness of spirit.

Most of the aversion of the battalion's other officers to those in Charlie Company had dissipated, though. Thanks primarily to Redmond, it now ranged from grudging respect to outright awe, for Team Charlie had destroyed three times as much of the enemy and his equipment as the rest of the task force combined.

They had also suffered its only member killed in action, Lieutenant Joe Cincotti.

Poor Joe, Redmond thought. He was such a fine officer, and a good guy. He'd also been Larry's best friend.

Damn, he thought. I haven't written a letter to his family yet.

The personal letter from the commander of an American soldier who had been killed in action to the soldier's family is one of the most sacred responsibilities that combat arms commanders have.

Redmond patted the pocket which held the letter Cincotti had written and given to him to mail in the event of his death. He'd have to remember to give it to the battalion adjutant in the morning.

He thought of Joe's girlfriend, Beth. Joe had said that he'd sent a letter to his father for her, in case he was killed, hadn't he?

Larry decided to write her a letter, too. It wasn't a requirement of command to write letters to girlfriends. But it was the responsibility, Redmond felt, of friends.

Beth was a good girl. She didn't understand anything about the Army, except that Joe loved it, and was a good soldier. But that was enough for her.

Larry thought back to the R&R in Bahrain, and to Mickey, and to what she had said. It had been such a pleasant surprise to hear a woman share his beliefs, particularly his belief that Saddam's army needed to be dealt with promptly and mercilessly. The task force—Redmond's own company, in particular—had done so, so far. And by God, they'd do it even better tomorrow, now that they'd felt the sting of battle, and had tasted victory.

Mickey. Yes, he decided, she must be a soldier, not a Red Cross lady, as she had claimed. An NCO, he guessed, judging from her age and attitude.

He wished Mickey knew how he was performing in combat—that she could have seen him in action at the airfield. Maybe she'd heard him, or at least heard the enemy he was routing from there. After all, she must have been listening to them, intercepting their communications, when she warned him about the enemy tank about to fire on his. Yes, that must be it; his fellow platoon leaders must have been correct when they speculated that she was a radio intercept operator. He hoped she'd be listening tomorrow.

Why hadn't she been forthright with him about who she really was?—especially after their lovemaking, and the discovery of each other's desires and the joy and sharing of all their senses—their very beings. Why hadn't she written? Was she married, or was it something else?

Well, it doesn't matter, he decided. After they got to Baghdad and ended this thing, he was damn well going to find her, and find out.

But first there was tomorrow. He closed his eyes and conducted the attack in his mind: the air and artillery preparation of the objective, ending with smoke to screen the flanks. The other two tank companies moving on line and engaging what targets they could see at long range. His own company dashing in a column of platoons around the left flank of the enemy positions which were the objective for the attack, down in the low terrain north of them, toward the swamps of the Euphrates.

He would have to make certain that a third of his tanks kept their guns oriented north to protect his left flank during the move. He'd reminded the commander of the infantry company following him to do the same.

They would flank right when they got north of the enemy, and attack out of the smoke with three platoons abreast—fast, violently, mercilessly.

The infantry behind him could serve as his reserve—he'd already discussed it with their commander.

Surrendering Iraqis would be bypassed by Redmond's company, their positions marked with yellow smoke grenades by his tank commanders so that the infantrymen could locate and collect prisoners.

Charlie Company's rapid, violent assault would sweep quickly across the entire task force objective, smashing any enemy in its path who failed to surrender immediately.

Thank God Captain Black had come down to see him and alleviated his worry about his tanks being engaged by friendly fire. But he was still concerned about it. In the chaos of battle, it was always a danger.

I know what I'll do, he thought. He had a big, three-by-five foot American flag in his Abrams. If he hooked that onto his antenna and stayed up front with his lead tanks, there would be no mistaking them for the enemy.

Like the old battle flags of regiments in wars long past, he thought. Yes, he liked the idea. His troops would, too. And Mickey would also, if she could see it.

He was cold and tired, he suddenly realized, and shivering. He needed to get what sleep he could, so he climbed up onto the hull of the tank to get his sleeping bag.

"Lieutenant Redmond?" someone called from the ground in a stage whisper. He didn't recognize the voice.

"Redmond here," he said. "Who's that?"

"Colonel Farrar."

Larry hopped off his Abrams onto the ground, thinking, I hope to heck there's no change in the plan. When he was standing beside his battalion commander, he said, "What's up, sir?"

"You all ready for the attack tomorrow?"

"Yes, sir. Everything's set. I'll go over it with the troops once more when I get them up. They're really beat."

"Yeah. Give 'em as much rest as you can," Farrar said. "They've earned it—your troops, especially. They're good men." Farrar started to add, "because of you," but didn't. He knew some of his other officers felt Redmond was his "colonel's pet" or "golden boy," as he had overhead one of them say, so he was trying not to show favoritism.

Favoritism, he thought to himself. If that means the one who gets the tough missions, then they're damned right he's my favorite.

"They're all good men, Colonel," was Redmond's response. "This is the best damned battalion in the Coalition."

They both believed Redmond's assessment and allowed themselves a few moments of silent pride. Then Larry said, "Captain Black came down awhile ago, sir. Just wanted to assure me that I didn't have to worry about fratricide."

"He's a good commander," Farrar replied and thought, *the second best I've got.* He avoided saying it for the same reasons he hadn't praised Redmond earlier in their conversation.

The ground to their east suddenly sparkled with a long line of flashes, then the ground beneath their feet shook and there was a thunderous rumbling.

"B-52s," Farrar announced. "Taking some of the fight out of the units on our objectives."

"I hope they don't tear it up so bad that I can't get my tanks across it," Larry commented.

Farrar smiled to himself in the darkness. *Typical Redmond,* he thought.

"You may not have to cross it," the colonel said.

"Sir?"

"Well," Farrar said softly, "I haven't made it known yet because I don't want the troops to build up any false hopes. But the brigade commander told me awhile ago that there may be a cease fire coming."

"Cease fire?" Redmond said. There was a hint of disappointment in his voice.

"Yes. Looks like they've had enough. If it does happen, it'll probably be early tomorrow morning."

"What do you think, Colonel?" his C Company commander asked.

Another long line of flashes lighted up the eastern horizon from a flight of B-52s pounding the Republican Guards again. The ground quaked once more, then the sound of sixty tons of bombs exploding thundered in the American warriors' ears.

"Thunder in the desert," Lieutenant Colonel Farrar said. He looked around at the tanks of Redmond's company, then back at the enemy positions. "Yeah, Larry, I think they're beat. I think they've had enough."

Redmond thought so, too. Saddam Hussein would agree to a cease fire and try to salvage what little of his military he had left. Even if he didn't, the B-52 strikes would take all the fight out of his vaunted Republican Guards.

"We ought to finish them off while we have the chance, though," Larry said.

Farrar thought about it. "Maybe," he said. "But they had the sixth largest army in the world when Desert Storm started. It's been whittled down to about fiftieth, by now, I'd guess. He's no real threat anymore."

"I wish I could be so sure," Redmond started to say, but still another rippling B-52 strike landed on the enemy positions. Again, the Cradle of Civilization trembled, and the sound of manmade thunder rumbled up the Euphrates Valley.

That's it, Larry thought. It's over. Even if the attack went in the next morning, he would see nothing but surrender flags on the objective.

"Well, at least there won't be any more friendly casualties," he said, and thought of Joe lying lifeless on the airfield. "Thank God for that."

"Yes," his colonel agreed, "thank God for that."

After awhile he said, "You've grown up, Larry."

Redmond considered the comment before saying, "I guess combat does that, doesn't it, Colonel?"

"Colonel Farrar?" a voice called softly from nearby. It was the operations officer.

"Yeah, Chuck. Over here."

The major appeared from the darkness and said, "It's over, sir. The official word just came down."

"Oh shit, oh dear," Farrar said jubilantly. "We won!"

"Yes, sir. We won. Cease fire at 0800."

Farrar smacked Larry Redmond on the back, then said to the major, "Let the other company commanders know, will you, Chuck?"

"Don't you want to let them know yourself, Colonel?"

"No, Chuck," the commander of the 5th Battalion, 64th Regiment of Armor said. "You did all the planning for this task force; you can be the one to let 'em know the plan worked."

"Thank you, sir. It's an honor," he said, and moved off toward Captain Black's tanks.

The other two tankers, Farrar and Redmond, stood beside the big American main battle tank, savoring the heady taste and smell of victory.

There were flashes from the west a few moments later, out where the Victory Division artillery was laid in. Then the deep booms of heavy guns firing reached their ears, and soon after, more explosions on the battered enemy's positions.

"Our redlegs getting their last licks in," Farrar commented. "Well, Larry, I'd better get back to the CP and see what we're supposed to do next."

There was cheering now from over in the vicinity of Bravo Company, and Redmond said, "I'll let my troops know, sir."

Farrar reached out, found the lieutenant's hand, and shook it warmly. "You're a real warrior, Lieutenant Redmond," he said, his voice choked with emotion. "I'll go to war beside you anywhere, anytime."

"I'd follow you into hell, sir," Larry answered, his throat also tight with the feelings of the moment.

Farrar let go of his hand and disappeared.

Larry climbed back up on the tank and found his big American flag. He was tying it to the antenna of the Abrams when the sound of cheering and whistling began to grow from the infantry company, not far away.

It woke Gibbs Begay, who sat up in his sleeping bag. "Lieutenant Redmond," he called. "What the hell's going on?"

"The war's over, Gibbs!" he yelled. "We did it!"

The other members of his tank crew heard him, and jumped up from their sleeping bags. Larry leaped off of the tank, and as the word spread through Charlie Company, 5th of the 64th Armor, the four soldiers who had fought the war together in Redmond's Abrams hugged and cheered and wept, and then they danced around their tank together in the Iraqi onion field.

▼

Twenty five

28 February 1991

News of the cease fire had also been flashed to the American and British Special Forces teams elsewhere in Iraq, but they would have to wait to celebrate the stunning 100 hour victory. They were ordered to maintain their vigil in the Scud launch areas, and to remain prepared to direct airstrikes on any of the missiles they discovered.

The Warthog pilots of Taffy Hughes's squadron resumed armed patrols over the area in their A-10 Thunderbolts, as well.

Several of the reconnaissance and surveillance teams—those which had been in the field the longest—were replaced by fresh teams, though, and one of those replaced in the pre-dawn hours of February 28th was Captain Jack Marsh's A team from the 5th Special Forces Group.

The commanding general of the US Special Operations Task Force, Major General Wayne Wilson, was there to meet them when they arrived at the forward operations base.

Wilson had two other people with him to greet the team when they landed. One of them was Barbara Marsh, whom Wilson had arranged to be flown up to meet her husband.

When Jack Marsh saw his wife standing beside the landing zone in the glow of the portable lights illuminating the base, he dropped his rucksack and went to her.

They embraced and kissed briefly, and then he held his wife at arms' length and looked at her pretty face.

"Welcome home, soldier," she said.

He hugged and kissed her again before he asked, "How'd you manage to get up here, honey?"

"General Wilson," she replied. "The casualties were so light, thank God, that most of us never even saw a battle casualty. My CO was happy to let me go."

They hugged once more, then Jack turned and pointed to one of his teammates. "See young Shumate, there? He saved your life."

She looked over and saw the Vietnamese-American walking toward an older man.

"Saved my life?" she asked with a quizzical expression. "What do you mean?"

Jack Marsh dismissed from his mind the horrible vision of his Army nurse wife dying in a chemical Scud attack. "Maybe someday I'll be able to tell you," he said.

Walter Shumate, Sr., had a broad smile on his face as he saluted his adopted son and said, "Good job, boy."

The young staff sergeant returned the salute before he hugged the legendary old soldier and asked, "What the hell are you doing over here, Dad?"

"Heard there was a war on," the retired sergeant major said, twirling the ends of his handlebar moustache. "Can't keep an old war horse out of a war."

The younger Shumate grinned and shook his head in amazement.

"Actually," his father said, "Colonel Ames sent for me. Said they didn't have anybody over here who knew the right way to build an FOB." He looked at the defensive wire around the forward operations base and added, "He was right, too. They had the damned engineer pickets facing the wrong way."

Ames had, in fact, gotten the elder Shumate there. The retired Special Forces veteran had a civilian job with the Special Forces School, so it wasn't difficult to do.

Sergeant Major Shumate had done a lot to see that Dave Ames was brought up properly when he was a young Special Forces officer. So when Ames learned that the younger Shumate was in the theater of operations, and when he recalled how much it meant to his own father and him to have served together in Vietnam, Dave wanted the Shumates to enjoy that same experience. The much-respected old soldier and his capable son certainly deserved it.

The two Shumates walked together toward the operations base and the older man said, "General Wilson tells me he's putting you in for a medal for rigging those Scuds."

"Nothing to it, Dad," young Walt said. "Anyway, this wasn't a real war, like Korea or Vietnam." His father had served well in both those thankless conflicts.

"Bullshit, boy. You won this one," the old man said, then chuckled and added, "even though it is the first war I ever went to that I never had a hangover or a case of the clap."

His son laughed and elbowed his bawdy namesake, then the elder man twisted his moustache and said, "Actually, I did win the Vietnam war."

"What do you mean, Dad?"

The retired sergeant major put his arm around his son's shoulder and said, "I got you, didn't I, boy? Yeah, I won."

Major General Wayne Wilson had shaken the hand of each of the proud but tired warriors as they got out of the helicopter. Now he watched them saunter easily into the forward operations base.

They had done it again, these good American soldiers, they and the Navy Seals and the Air Force special operators of his elite command, and the half million other young Americans in the Gulf. They had won.

They always did, when the politicians allowed them to, and always would.

Thank God America's people had supported them this time, for that was all the really good ones wanted in return.

The country was awash with American flags and yellow ribbons, and, like Wayne Wilson, with pride in every one of them.

He looked at the empty helicopter, then turned and watched the men disappear into the debriefing tent.

He would gladly have given his life if Pat Healy could have been among them.

*   *   *

Company C, 5th Battalion, 64th Armor, commanded by First Lieutenant Lawrence Redmond, Jr., spent the last hours before the cease fire in the onion field beside highway 8 west of Basra, Iraq.

The battalion chaplain was there, preparing to conduct a sunrise memorial service for Second Lieutenant Joseph Cincotti.

Several miles away, the commander of a nearly-defeated Republican Guards artillery battery decided to unload his few remaining guns by firing them at the Americans along the highway to his west. It was a foolish and fatal act—his last.

His battery's rounds were less than midway in their trajectory when they were picked up by the 24th Infantry Division's counter-battery radars. The radars tracked the rounds, computed their source, then computed the firing data necessary to engage the enemy guns with counter-battery fire.

The American artillery commander showed no mercy. He responded to the Iraqi's puny display of defiance with a salvo of 155mm and eight-inch gunfire, and twenty-four rounds of accurate and devastating rockets from the division's multiple-launch rocket systems.

The ground where the enemy battery stood was blasted to moon-scape, and the guns and crews were obliterated.

But the Iraqi rounds were not without effect. Two of them landed in the onion field, and although one did no damage, the other landed twenty meters from Lieutenant Redmond and his crew.

Gibbs Begay's belly was ripped open by a jagged shard of hot shrapnel, and Redmond took a smaller piece in the meat of his calf. The other two crewmen were untouched.

Redmond, knocked off his feet by the blast, was at first unaware that he'd been injured. He yelled "Incoming!" and jumped to his feet, looking quickly around for his crewmen in the near dawn to see if any of them had been hit.

Sergeant Peterson and Private Anderson were scrambling under the protective armor of the big Abrams, but Specialist Begay was down. He was holding his gut, writhing in the dirt and moaning.

Redmond made a move to run to him, but fell heavily. It was only then that he became aware of his wound.

He didn't bother to look at it, but crawled quickly to Begay on his hands and knees, calling, "Medic! Medic!" as he did so.

Begay's abdomen had been ripped open, and his guts were spilling out of the long gash as he tried to hold them inside.

Redmond quickly examined his loader for any other wounds he might have suffered. Except for minor cuts on the face and arm, he found none.

"You'll be all right, Gibbs," he told the young soldier as he tore open a battle dressing and placed it loosely over the exposed glob of slick intestines.

He heard the whoosh whoosh whoosh of artillery rounds passing overhead and froze for a second, listening.

"That's outgoing!" he yelled to the men lying beneath the nearby tank. "Get out here and help me with Gibbs!"

There were flashes of exploding artillery and rockets on the enemy positions to the east, and he thought, Good. That should be the last we hear from those bastards.

The medics arrived at his position in an armored ambulance shortly after that and took charge of the badly injured Gibbs Begay.

Only then did Redmond sit back and examine his own wound. There was a jagged hole in the meat of his calf.

"Anybody else get hit?" one of the medics was asking, and Larry said, "You'd better take a look at this, I guess."

The medic examined the wound, put a field dressing on it, and said, "OK, buddy, we'd better get you into the ambulance."

"Just patch it up," Redmond said. "I can't leave. I'm the company commander."

"Sorry, sir," the man replied, "but we have to medevac you."

"I'll be all right. Just do what you can to fix it up here," he said.

Lieutenant Colonel Farrar arrived and seeing that his C Company commander had been wounded said, "Redmond? Damn, you got hit!"

"Just a scratch, sir," Larry said.

"We've got to medevac him anyway, Colonel," the medic explained, just in case it's a germ round."

"What?" the injured lieutenant said.

"A biological warfare round. We have to put all artillery casualties in the isolation facility, just in case."

"But that's ridiculous," Redmond replied. "If it was a biological round, it would infect everybody near it, not just the wounded."

"Hey, sir," the medic said. "I don't make the rules—I just follow 'em."

"Get going, Larry," Lieutenant Colonel Farrar said. "Let them check you out and sew you up. It's all over now, anyway."

"Ah, damn it," Redmond muttered, but got to his feet. The wound was hurting him more all the time. Maybe it was a good idea to get it properly cared for, so that he could get back to duty in a hurry.

He looked around in the growing light. About half the company was standing around gawking at the casualties and the crater made by the enemy artillery round.

"Get back to your tanks, damn it!" he said, angry at having to leave them. He spotted Jim Locher and said, "Lieutenant Locher, take charge of the company."

Locher said, "Yes, sir," and saluted, then to the men around him ordered, "All right, men, you heard him. Move out. One round will get us all."

Redmond hobbled to the ambulance with the help of Farrar and the medic.

"Well, Lieutenant Redmond, that's a Purple Heart to go with the other one," the battalion commander remarked as Larry crawled into the tracked ambulance.

"Other one?"

"Yeah," Farrar said, "Other one. I'm putting you in for a Silver Star for the way you defeated that Iraqi counterattack."

2 March 1991

"Jesus Christ, what a mess," Claude Owen said as he saw the tangle of wrecked and burned out vehicles through the windshield of his little helicopter.

His passenger shifted uncomfortably in the back seat, trying to get the fiberglass cast that ran from his hip to his toes on one leg situated so that he could peer at the highway below.

"Slow it down now, will you, Claude?" Bill Kernan asked. "See if you can spot a Jeep Cherokee down there in all of that."

There were several US Army engineer machines moving in the rubble. Some were trying to clear a path through the mess so that Coalition vehicles could pass.

Others were digging trenches beside the highway. Owen could see men carrying bodies to them.

He slowed the Defender and dropped it down to a hundred feet above the ground. Some of the men below looked up at it, saw the freshly painted inverted "V" on its bottom and sides, and went back about their grisly work.

Owen spotted the Cherokee toward the front of the wreckage. He didn't recognize it as a Cherokee at first, it was so badly mauled, and lying on its side.

He brought the Defender to a hover. Yes, that was a Jeep Cherokee, all right. It had taken a direct hit from something big.

He looked at the remaining vehicles ahead in case there were other Cherokees there, but there were none.

"There it is, Bill," he said to Kernan, turning the helicopter sideways so that the other CIA man could see it. Owen heard his friend's breath escape as he spied the twisted wreck.

"Set down near it, please, Claude."

"OK," the pilot responded. He settled the little chopper down onto the highway in an open space the engineers had cleared, then looked back at Kernan.

He was sitting motionless, staring at the burned out wreck sixty feet away.

"Shall I shut down?" Owen asked, and Kernan mumbled, "Yeah."

When the engine and rotors stopped, Kernan sat and stared at the wreck for a long time, then said, "Do me a favor, will you, Claude?"

"Of course," his friend replied.

Kernan handed him a piece of paper with Arabic numerals on it. "See if the license plate matches this, will you?"

"Sure." Owen climbed out of the pilot's seat and walked to the back of the vehicle. The numbers were barely legible, but they matched those Kernan had given him.

He looked back at his friend and nodded his head. Kernan returned the nod.

Owen looked inside the vehicle. There were no human remains in it. There were no bodies lying nearby, either. They'd already been taken away.

He walked back to the Defender and said softly, "There's nobody inside."

Again Kernan nodded, still staring at the wreck.

An American Engineer Corps lieutenant walked up and said to Owen, "You'll have to move your helicopter, sir. We've got to keep this lane open."

"Right," Owen replied, then asked, "What happened to all the bodies, Lieutenant?"

The engineer pointed to a huge mound of dirt beside the highway.

"In there," he said. "Most of 'em came out of the big culvert under the road there." He gestured toward a wadi running out from beneath the highway.

"Any women, Lieutenant?" Kernan asked.

"Are you guys reporters?" the Army officer inquired.

"No," Owen said, tapping the Coalition symbol—the inverted "V"— on the side of his helicopter. "CIA."

"Oh," the engineer said. "Yeah, there were a few women. Some of the bodies, we couldn't tell what they were."

Kernan's lower lip quivered and he inhaled deeply through his nose. There was a strange mixture of odors in the air—of death and oil smoke and perfume.

The CIA men were silent, so the soldier said, "You should see what these son of a bitches had with them: VCRs, TVs, jewelry, chandeliers. Very few weapons, though. Didn't have room for 'em, I guess."

"What's that smell?" Claude Owen asked. "It smells like perfume."

"It is," the engineer said. "They were stealing that, too."

Bill Kernan suddenly realized, incongruously, that Abir had never smelled of perfume when they were together.

He stared at the mounded dirt of the mass grave until the engineer lieutenant said, "Uh, sir, I need to keep this road clear."

"OK," Bill said. "Thanks, Lieutenant. Let's go, Claude."

The engineer moved clear of the rotor blades, and Owen cranked up the helicopter. As it built up RPMs, he looked back at his friend's pale, drawn face.

"Bill, old buddy," he said, "I'm really sorry, man." Kernan looked at him with hollow eyes, and said nothing.

▼

Calm

▼

Twenty six

2 March 1991

Lieutenant Larry Redmond had sent a message to the headquarters of the 5th Battalion, 64th Armor Regiment, advising his unit that he was ready for release from the big hospital in Dhahran, and requesting transportation back to the battalion.

He received a reply from Lieutenant Colonel Farrar stating that the Commanding General, 24th Infantry Division, was coming to the hospital that afternoon to present awards of the Purple Heart to the members of the division there who had been wounded in action. He advised Redmond that the division chief of staff said he could fly back on the general's aircraft after the awards ceremony.

Good, Larry thought when he read the message. I can be with Gibbs and Joe's gunner when they get their Purple Hearts.

He had visited the two men at their beds on the surgical ward several times. The gunner was terribly despondent about the loss of his arm, but pleased to hear that the battalion—Charlie Company, in particular—had done so well in combat. Redmond had refrained from telling the soldier that his wound was the result of friendly fire from one of the battalion's own tanks. That could come later.

Specialist Begay was in good spirits, in spite of the fact that his gut was still laid wide open—something about peritonitis, the doctor had explained to Redmond when he inquired about his men.

Larry made his way to the surgical ward a half-hour before the commanding general was due to arrive.

His two wounded subordinates had been moved to a different part of the ward, one of the nurses explained, so that all of the Victory Division's troops would be in the same area for the ceremony.

Redmond limped through the double doors leading to the area and spotted Gibbs on a bed in the corner.

Several of the soldiers—including the gunner—were sleeping, so he spoke softly to Begay.

"How you doing, Gibbs?"

"Oh, I'm fine, sir. They finally sewed me up. Now I can go home."

"Hey, that's great," Larry said.

"Yeah. Hey, you're styling in that nice, clean set of chocolate chips," Begay remarked.

The hospital supply sergeant had issued Redmond a new desert battle dress uniform—referred to as "chocolate chips" by the troops because of the splotches of brown in the pattern.

Redmond ran his hand over his closely-cropped hair. "Haircut, too," he said. He nodded toward the sleeping gunner and said, "How's he doing today, Gibbs?"

"He'll be all right. They said they're going to give him a new arm that's as good as the real thing. So, the general's coming to give us all a medal, huh, sir?"

"Yep," Redmond said. "I don't feel like I deserve it, though. Compared to you guys, I just got a scratch."

Begay surveyed his lieutenant again and said, "Well, it'll look good on you when they make you a general."

Redmond chuckled and said, "Yeah, sure."

"Hey, that sergeant over there is getting two medals," Gibbs said, "a Purple Heart and a Soldier's Medal, so the chaplain told me."

He was gesturing to a bed across the aisle, and Redmond looked, noticing the bandaged stumps of the soldier's legs sticking out from beneath the sheet.

"Walked into a minefield," Begay continued. "Went to help a damn wounded Iraqi, and stepped on an AP mine."

Redmond didn't hear Begay's explanation. He had looked up beyond the stumps to the face of the sleeping soldier.

It was Mickey. At least, it looked like her.

He stood frozen for a moment, staring at the pretty face, then he limped to her and whispered, "Oh, my God." Yes, it was Mickey, all right. He reached out and touched her cheek with the back of his hand, and her eyelids parted slightly.

"Mickey," he said with a choked voice. "Ah, Mickey."

Her eyes widened, then closed tightly, and tears spilled from them.

He brushed the tears from her cheeks, then leaned over and kissed her gently on the lips, and her eyes opened again. She said hoarsely, "Larry, Larry, I'm so sorry that…"

He put his finger to her lips and said, "Shhhh, don't talk now. There'll be plenty of time for that later." He took her hand in his, and for a time they just looked at each other, until tears began to spill down her cheeks again, and she closed her eyes.

"Damn, sir," Begay said, watching curiously from across the aisle. "You know her?"

"Know her?" Redmond said. "Yeah, Gibbs, I know her. I know her all right."

He felt Michelle's hand grip his tightly, and he leaned over and kissed her softly again. Then he looked over at Gibbs Begay and said, "You remember the woman who warned us when we nearly got taken out by that T-72?"

"That was her?" Begay asked, and Redmond nodded. "Well, I'll be damned," the gunner said. "Kiss her again, for me, Lieutenant. She saved my life, too."

✱   ✱   ✱

4 March 1991

"What are you going to do, Bill?" Claude Owen asked his friend.

Kernan had barely spoken since their flight to the carnage on the highway below Mutla Ridge two days before. Now he was going home on an Air Force Nightingale medical evacuation aircraft, and Claude had driven him to the hospital. There, they had required him to change into surgical pajamas for the flight before Owen took him out to the airfield.

Kernan stared at the black, smoke filled sky, then looked at his pilot friend.

"I don't know. Get healed up and think about it, I guess."

"Staying with the Agency?"

"Fuck the Agency. I've had enough, Claude."

They watched the ambulances pulling up beside the Nightingale.

"You, uh, you want me to do anything about her—you know, try to find out what happened, or anything?"

Kernan shook his head slowly and said, "No, there's nothing to do."

He thought in silence for a minute, then said, "Yeah, there is, actually. Make certain those assholes at the station take care of Doctor Singh. And Abdul's boy, Yassir. I checked up on them while I was getting this fixed," he said, tapping his leg cast. "But I mean afterward—don't let them just dump them for the rest of their lives. And check on the other women— Mara and Sanaa—if you get a chance. Do what you can, will you?"

Owen nodded. "I will."

The wounded were being loaded aboard the aircraft, and one of the crewmen was waving to Kernan to get aboard.

He looked at Owen and held out his hand.

"Thanks, old rotorhead," he said. "Call me when you get to Virginia."

"Hey, we'll do this all again sometime," Owen replied as he warmly shook his friend's hand.

"I doubt it," Kernan said coldly. Owen had never seen a man's eyes so full of sadness.

Kernan took his crutches and hobbled off toward the Nightingale.

They made him lie down strapped onto a stretcher for the flight, and he couldn't see outside when they took off.

The airplane accelerated down the runway and lifted off, and when it broke through the blanket of smoke from the oil well fires—there were more than seven hundred of them—the interior of the airplane brightened markedly.

"That's better," the wounded soldier lying beside Bill said.

Kernan looked over at the man and saw an American Indian smiling at him.

"How you doing, trooper?"

"I'll be OK—back in my tank before you know it. The Victory Division—5th of the 64th Armor."

Kernan returned the smile and said, "You guys did a hell of a good job."

"Thanks," the soldier said, holding out his hand. "I'm Gibbs Begay."

Bill took the hand. "Bill Kernan," he said.

Begay surveyed the long-haired man a moment and asked, "Air Force?"

Kernan smiled. "Civilian," he replied. "Defense Department paper pusher."

"Scud get you?" Begay asked.

"Nah. Wrecked my motorcycle, of all things."

Begay snickered, then said, "Sorry. I know it's not funny."

An Air Force flight nurse was making the rounds, checking the charts and condition of each patient.

Begay was asleep by the time she got to him. She checked the clipboard attached to his litter, changed the bag of intravenous fluid running into his arm, then lifted the sheet and looked at the bandage.

When she got to Bill, she read his chart, then said, "Hello, Mr. Kernan."

"Hi."

"How does the leg feel?"

"It's fine."

She rolled the sheet back. "Let me check those gunshot wounds," she said as she pulled the loose-fitting top of his pajamas off his shoulder.

"They're all healed up," he said.

"Yes, the shoulder looks good," the nurse said, then unsnapped his pajamas at the inside of the thigh.

"Ummm, pretty nasty one," she said as she examined the wound that Abdul had cauterized. "All that's from a gunshot wound?"

"Well, it had to be cauterized," Kernan said.

"Cauterized? In an American hospital?" the nurse asked.

"It wasn't in a hospital. It was done by a friend, to keep me from bleeding to death."

She pressed the ragged purple oval of a scar with her fingers and asked, "Does that hurt?"

"No feeling at all," he said.

She wrote a note in his records, then moved to the other side of his litter and pulled back the curtain screening the patient beside him. Kernan looked over and saw that it was an attractive looking young woman.

The nurse examined her chart, then lifted the sheet at the bottom of the woman's litter.

Bill noticed that her feet were missing, then glanced at the pretty face again before looking away, thinking, Oh, God, no.

"You're Sergeant Myers," he heard the nurse say to the footless soldier. "They told us about you. You're a very brave woman."

Brave, hell, Michelle thought. Do they think I would have gone after the man if I'd known he was in a minefield? It was a careless act which had changed her from an attractive young woman into a legless freak, she felt, and telling her a thousand times that it was brave couldn't change that.

"Stupid would be more like it," she said to the nurse.

The fact that losing her feet made her feel freakish disturbed her even more than having to leave the Army did. She loved the Army, and had a deep sense of pride in serving her country as a soldier. She had been on Operation Just Cause—the Panama operation—and was proud of her part in that. But Desert Storm had been so much more meaningful to her, especially when she was listening to Larry's attack and found the opportunity to warn him of danger. It made her feel so good—as if she were there with him, somehow. And then she had come upon the wounded Iraqi…

Thank God Larry had shown up at the hospital. Had it been luck, or fate?

He had been so good to her. He seemed to dismiss the loss of her legs as if it were something as minor as a new hairdo, and that had been a great boost to her devastated morale—much more of a boost than the Soldier's Medal the division commander had pinned on her.

But she wondered if Larry really meant the things he'd said, or if it just an act of pity, of sympathy. Could he really be serious when he said that he was in love with her?

Several news organizations had satellite telephones up at Safwan, where his battalion was now, and Larry had convinced some of the journalists to allow him to use one to phone her at the hospital several times. Each time, he had ended his brief call with, "I love you, Mickey. I really do."

But could he possibly mean it, and was he really serious about wanting to spend his leave with her when he got back to the States? Or was it only that he remembered their passionate lovemaking that long night in Bahrain? How could it ever be the same, now that her once beautiful body was scarred, her legs nothing but ugly stumps?

She wondered all these things, and the severed nerves in her ankles made it feel as if her feet were itching—a cruel reminder that she had none.

Tears dripped down her cheeks, and the man beside her said, "Are you all right, miss?"

She looked at him and wiped her tears, trying to manage a smile.

"I've been better," she said.

"Shall I call for the nurse?"

"Oh, no. I'm all right. The nurse called you Mr. Kernan, didn't she?"

"Bill."

"Michelle," she said, then changed it to the name she'd adopted in Bahrain. "Mickey, to my friends."

After a moment of silence, she said, "Uh, you're a civilian?"

"Yeah. DOD paper pusher."

"A paper pusher with gunshot wounds?"

"Oh, they're old wounds," he said, then tapped the leg cast. "I laid a bike down and turned my leg around backwards the other day."

Old wounds? Who are you kidding? she thought. She had seen the fresh scar on his shoulder, still scabbed over in places, when the nurse examined it.

CIA, Michelle decided.

They returned to their own thoughts, staring at the top of the aircraft fuselage.

Kernan remembered the nurse saying, "You're a very brave woman," to Mickey. He wondered how the girl had lost her legs. Was it that Scud attack that had hit a barracks and caused so many casualties?

He had also heard a story about a female soldier stepping on a mine when she went to the aid of an enemy soldier. Maybe Mickey was that woman, he thought, looking over at her.

God, the things I've learned about women these last few months. He still found it difficult to comprehend some of the things he'd seen done by Abir and Mara, by Sanaa and Francesca Singh. And women like this one beside him.

Abir. The image of the Jeep Cherokee amid the carnage at Mutla Ridge, and the mass grave beside it, returned to him.

Why? Why, when we had finally found each other?

Bill Kernan sighed deeply, and Michelle noticed, and wondered why. Thinking about a woman? A wife at home, perhaps, or one he'd left behind in Saudi Arabia? It was that sort of a sigh.

"Where's your home, Bill?" she asked.

"Virginia. Yours?"

"Fort Stewart, Georgia. Or at least, it was."

Not Pennsylvania, where all the Scud victims were from, Bill thought, then said, "I don't mean to be nosy, but you're the young woman who went to help a wounded Iraqi soldier, aren't you?"

"Yes," she said. "Stupid mistake."

He looked her in the eye. "No, it was a very kind and brave mistake, perhaps. But not stupid."

She forced a smile and said, "Thank you."

Their conversation turned into a discussion about the war in general terms, but both Bill and Michelle avoided discussing their part in it.

After awhile, Begay awoke and joined the chat. He was more than happy to talk about his part in the brief war, and the things Company C, 5th of the 64th Armor had done.

"Like my tank commander—hell, company commander, now," Gibbs said to Kernan. "That's Lieutenant Redmond—Mickey knows him, don't you, sarge?"

He winked at her knowingly, then rattled on. "He's, like, a big Patton fan, see? And he was always saying, 'We're gonna go through 'em like shit through a goose,' y'know? And we did, man, just like he said. We sure did. He got hit the same time I did. Not as bad, though. Old El Tee Redmond. He's my hero, man."

Gibbs looked beyond Kernan to Michelle, and said, "But, hey, you're my other hero, Sergeant Mickey."

They discussed the amazing success American technology had enjoyed in the fighting, and what an advantage it had given the allies. That part of the conversation turned out to be mainly a lesson from Gibbs Begay on the invincibility of the M1A1 Abrams main battle tank.

The trio spoke of the outpouring of support of the American people for their troops, and the two wounded soldiers described the scenes they had seen on the hospital television of the jubilant celebrations in Kuwait's liberated capital.

Bill Kernan seemed strangely detached during this part of the conversation, and Mickey noticed, and wondered why—whether it had anything to do with the gunshot wounds he'd suffered.

Their chatting died away then, and they dozed or kept their thoughts to themselves for the rest of the long flight to Sigonella airbase in Sicily.

At Sigonella, they were transferred to a larger C-141 Starlifter for the flight from there to Andrews Air Force Base, just outside Washington, DC. Gibbs was placed on a different part of the aircraft from the other two, but Bill and Mickey ended up on neighboring litters again.

The two had established good rapport, based more on a sense of mutual respect and values than anything else.

At one point during the seemingly endless flight across the Atlantic, Bill asked, "What are you going to do with your life now, Mickey?"

She thought about it for a time before answering. She had been thinking desperately about that since she had finally come to the realization that she was maimed for life, and could do nothing to change it. Sometimes those thoughts turned to daydreams, but she gave Bill the answer she usually arrived at when she thought realistically about her future.

"First I'm going to get a new pair of feet. And learn to use them," she said. "Then I'm going to use my GI bill benefits to go to school—find a new career. I don't have any idea in what field, though."

"You could always use your radio intercept and Arabic language skills with some other agency of the government," he said. "You'd get veterans' preference, you know."

Like your Central Intelligence Agency, she thought. But she didn't particularly like the field, especially working at a fixed base. And her Arabic actually wasn't very good.

"Oh, I don't know," she said. "I don't think I'd really like it, except in the Army."

"Marriage, maybe?" Bill said.

"Humph. I've got a lot to do before I even think about that. I, uh, let's just say that I came from the kind of home that makes you think you never want to get married."

Michelle's parents had been miserable, both before and after their divorce when she was a little girl, and they had both taken much of that misery out on Michelle. It was the reason that she'd joined the Army as soon as she graduated from high school. And since then, she'd seen too many good relationships seemingly ruined by marriage.

"Anyway," she said, trying to do so without making it sound like self-pity, "I'm not sure it would be fair to burden some guy with a, uh, double amputee."

Kernan's forehead wrinkled and he said, "Don't even think things like that, Mickey. Any man who'd feel that way wouldn't be worth having, anyway."

"Well, I'd still feel like I was a burden, especially when I got older—not that marriages last that long, these days. Are you married, Bill?"

"Divorced," he said. "A long time ago."

"See what I mean?" she said. "Do you think you'll ever remarry?"

He smiled at her. "Is that a proposal?"

She laughed for the first time since she had stepped on the mine. "Heck, no! Who'd want to marry a civilian who gets shot while he's pushing papers, and can't ride a motorcycle?"

She saw him respond with a brief smile, then he averted his eyes and stared absently at the ceiling of the airplane, a mask of despondence covering his face.

He was remembering the motorcycle wreck, and the sight of the Cherokee disappearing into the northbound stampede out of Kuwait City. And then the image of the burned and blasted vehicle and the nearby mass grave below Mutla Ridge entered his mind.

He closed his eyes, and his face became clouded with torment, Michelle noticed. He was obviously deeply disturbed about something, and she started to ask him if he wanted to talk about it. She decided not to; if he wanted to talk, he would.

Anyway, she thought, what's he got to be so upset about? At least he has his legs...

Michelle immediately admonished herself for her self-pity, although her feet suddenly began aching badly. The doctors had warned her that it would happen—that her nerves would make it feel as if the missing feet were in pain.

A flight nurse came by, so she asked for something to kill the pain, and got it. She was asleep almost immediately.

Bill Kernan's pain was not physical, nor so easy to assuage.

It was made worse when the aircrew passed around some newspapers and magazines they had brought from the States two days before. Inside one of them was a story about the slaughter on the highway south of Basra. It included a photograph of several dozen of the shot up, bombed out vehicles the Air Force had destroyed.

The photo had been taken before the bodies were removed and buried.

If only I'd been there when the bastards came to the villa, Bill Kernan thought. Or if she had left on the helicopter with her sons, as she was supposed to have done.

If, if, if...

*   *   *

7 March 1991

Jane Parry inhaled a stream of smoke from her cigarette, exhaled, stubbed it out, and pulled her bathrobe more tightly around her. She picked up her glass, took a sip from it and said, "A penny for your thoughts, Yank."

Dave Ames, seated in the other metal chair on the balcony of the hotel room, drained the champagne from his glass, then refilled both their glasses from the bottle on the table between them. It was the champagne Jane had gotten them for Christmas. They hadn't gotten around to drinking it that night, so she had saved it until they could be together to celebrate the success of Operation Desert Storm.

He looked at her, then reached over and took her hand in his. "We should have gotten the bastard, Jane," he said.

She knew he was talking about Saddam Hussein. And, as a member of General de la Bretaigne's inner circle, she was aware of the top secret mission that had been mounted in the last hours of the war to rid the world of the Iraqi dictator.

The best calculations of allied intelligence had determined with reasonable certainty that Saddam had spent most of the war hiding in a deep, hardened bunker at al-Taji airbase a short distance outside Baghdad—a bunker which had already withstood several accurate attacks by 2,000 pound bombs.

Two options had been briefed to the Coalition leaders for eliminating the enemy commander-in-chief.

The first, espoused by de la Bretaigne and the US Special Operations Task Force commander, Wayne Wilson, had envisioned a raid by Delta Force and SAS commandos in American special operations helicopters. As they had successfully done at the enemy air defense radar sites in the moments preceding the war, they would attack the bunker and root out its occupants. But such a raid would have risked a relatively high number of Coalition casualties.

The US Air Force had a less-risky plan. They had hurriedly constructed a pair of laser-guided 5,000 pound bombs with delay fuses which would enable them to penetrate and destroy the formidable target. They could, they convinced the Coalition leaders, eliminate Saddam with a minimal risk to friendly personnel.

The air raid was chosen. The bunker was struck, and it was destroyed. But the charmed—or secretly-informed—tyrant was not there.

"Well," Jane Parry said, "the fat lady has sung now. Maybe next time they'll choose your plan."

Dave Ames drained his glass again, and repeated his lover's words.

"The fat lady has sung. Maybe next time."

He stood up, stretched, and looked at her.

"What about us, Jane?" he said.

"What do you mean?"

"I mean, what about us?" He leaned back against the balcony rail and studied her. "Why don't you come back to the States with me?"

She stood, went to him, and wrapped her arms around his waist, resting her head on his chest. She had frequently thought about the possibility of living with him—perhaps even marrying him—since they had found each other again. And she had decided, in the end, that such an arrangement bore the risk of losing the passion they had come to share. What, after all, was the spark that ignited the fire of their love? It was the stolen moments, the chance encounters, the bitter taste of missed opportunities that made the times they were able to share all the sweeter.

No, she would not risk the loss of that, she had decided.

She kissed his mouth lightly and looked at him, and he could see in her eyes what she was thinking. And he understood.

"Well," he said, "I think I just heard the fat lady sing our song."

"No," she said, taking his hands and placing them inside the front of her robe, "You just heard her warming up. She doesn't sing until the morning."

▼

Twenty seven

9 March 1991

Staff Sergeant William Allen, United States Army Reserve, sat at a field table sipping coffee beneath a tent just outside of Safwan, Iraq.

Allen was in a foul mood. He had been ever since November, when he received orders to report to his reserve unit, the 96th Civil Affairs Battalion.

He looked at his watch. It was five minutes to eight on the morning of the 9th of March. There was no reason for him not to start processing the long line of people who were waiting in the morning chill, except for his disdain for them and for his job.

"Well," Allen said to the female soldier seated next to him, "another day, another lousy couple of bucks."

The woman continued filling in the printed cards in front of her with the date and Allen's signature block, passing each one over onto the growing stack on the sergeant's table.

There was a bilingual Kuwaiti seated on the other side of Allen to serve as his interpreter. As usual, Allen ignored the man.

He scratched out some figures on a tablet and said to the woman, "Humph! Twenty thousand goddam dollars. Do you know I've already lost about twenty thou' by being over here in this godforsaken armpit of a place, Julie?"

The female soldier glanced at Allen in disgust and thought, Sorry prick of a used car salesman. With his demeanor, she figured he'd be lucky to sell one lousy heap of junk a week.

"So you've told me," she muttered, thinking, Every damned day, you've told me. "What are we waiting for?" she asked. "Let's get started."

Allen looked at his watch again. Three minutes to eight. He stood and said, "The hell with 'em. Let 'em wait. It's not eight o'clock yet," and went to get another cup of coffee from the messhall.

He returned with a full cup five minutes later and sat down at the field desk. He brought no coffee for either of his assistants.

"All right, Sayed," he said to the interpreter, "let's get this shit over with."

They were a miserable lot, the line of refugees Allen and the others were processing. They were dirty, cold, and hungry, and some had wounds and open sores.

As each one came forward and was questioned—through the interpreter, unless they happened to speak English—Allen classified them into one of several categories: those requiring medical attention; those with papers identifying them as Kuwaiti citizens; those claiming to be Kuwaiti, but without papers to prove it; and Iraqi refugees.

Once Allen classified them, they were directed to one of the four tents behind Allen's for further processing.

The disgruntled staff sergeant usually made some snide aside concerning each of the refugees to the other American seated beside him in the tent.

When a one-legged boy limped in on a crude pair of crutches, his first comment was, "And what the hell's your name, son? Tiny Tim, I suppose."

The female clerk glared at him and said, "Is that really necessary, Sergeant Allen?"

His response was, "Is it really necessary for us to be here dealing with this scum?"

She glared at him again and shook her head, deciding that, at the first opportunity, she'd lodge a complaint about Allen with the company commander.

The boy was sent directly to the medical tent, and the next refugee was waved forward to the tent.

"Umm," Allen said, "here's a sweet one.

"Name?" he asked the woman, her face dirty but beautiful beneath the grime.

Without waiting for the interpreter, she said, "My name is Abir bint Hamad bin al-Sabah."

The interpreter stood immediately, examining the woman's face.

"What's with you, Sayed?" Allen asked. "You know this broad?"

The Kuwaiti interpreter glared at him. "That's Madame al-Sabah to you, sergeant!" Sayed replied. "I think you'd better go and get your major."

10 March 1991

"Madame al-Sabah," the young American officer said to the attractive Arab woman in Western dress, "I'm Lieutenant Redmond. I'm going to escort you on the flight down to Saudi Arabia."

"Please, just call me Abir," she said, and offered her hand to him.

He shook it and said, "Yes, ma'am."

"Would it be possible to land in Kuwait City for a few minutes?" Abir asked. "You can land the helicopter on the grounds of my villa."

"Uh, ma'am, I was told that we were going to Dhahran."

"Yes," Abir said, "but I need to stop for a few minutes in Kuwait City."

"Well, I'm not sure it's considered safe enough. The Emir hasn't even gone back yet, you know," Redmond responded.

He had been instructed to escort the woman on the Blackhawk helicopter he was taking from Safwan to Dhahran. He had to go to the hospital there to have his leg wound checked, and to deliver some of the

Iraqi documents the task force was still unearthing from the positions the enemy had formerly occupied.

She was some sheik's wife, he had been told, so he had also been appointed as her escort officer for the flight.

"I'm quite sure it's safe enough for me, Lieutenant," she said. "My villa was a hospital for the Kuwaiti resistance forces."

Redmond gave her a look she took for one of disbelief, so she said, "I was taken as a hostage by the Iraqis when they were fleeing Kuwait. We barely made it to Basra ahead of the bombing on the highway. I was only released the day before yesterday."

"I see," Larry said. "Pardon me a minute, then, ma'am. I'll have to square that with my higher headquarters and the aircrew."

He limped over to the civil affairs company command post and returned two minutes later.

"All right, Mrs. al-Sab…"

"Just 'Abir,'" she interrupted.

"Abir, then," Redmond said. "It's all set up. I was told it would be all right to stop at your villa, but not for more than ten minutes."

"Thank you. That should be enough time," she said, smiling faintly. "I saw you limping, Lieutenant Redmond. Were you wounded in the war?"

"Oh, just a scratch, ma'…Abir."

"Kuwait owes you Americans a great deal," Abir said. "I was pleased to hear that the allied casualties were so few," she said, then paused before adding, "and that the Iraqi casualties were so heavy."

He gave her a look of strange surprise, so she said, "If you'd seen what they did in Kuwait City, you wouldn't look at me like that."

Redmond nodded. "I heard about it," he said. "I can understand your point."

He stared at the ground, thinking about Joe and his gunner, and about Mickey. 'So few casualties,' she said. Yes, but not few enough.

Abir was nothing at all like the handful of Saudi women he had encountered, nor as he had expected Kuwaiti women to be. Her Western clothing, alluring beauty and manner, her flawless English—it all made him very curious about this wife of a wealthy sheik.

He'd been told to treat her as he would the wife of a general officer, yet here she was insisting on being called "Abir," and declaring that she was glad the Iraqi casualties were heavy.

One of the Blackhawk pilots came out with a map. In order to file a revised flight plan, they needed to know the location of the villa.

Abir studied the map for several moments, then pointed to the villa and the garden at the back of the compound.

"You can land in the garden, here," she said.

"OK, ma'am," the pilot said. "We'll be ready to load up in a couple of minutes."

Damn, Redmond thought, looking over her shoulder, she can even read a map!

"Where did you go to school, Lieutenant Redmond?" Abir asked, just to make conversation while they waited for the pilots.

"The Citadel. It's a military school."

"South Carolina, isn't it?" Abir said.

"Yes. You've obviously spent a lot of time in the States."

"Some," she replied. "I got my degree from Columbia University."

"Columbia? Wow."

Abir smiled. She liked this young American officer. He triggered fond memories of some of her fellow students at Columbia—the Southerners, in particular.

"Are you married, Lieutenant?" she inquired.

"Please just call me Larry, Abir," he said. "No, I'm not married—not yet."

"Engaged to be married, then."

"No, not yet. But I've decided who I'm going to ask to marry me."

"Absence makes the heart grow fonder," she quipped. "How long have you been away from her?"

He grinned. "Just a few days," he said, pleased to have someone to whom he felt he could talk about her. "She's a fellow American soldier."

Abir smiled at his use of the phrase. Larry shook his head and said, "She's really a remarkable girl. She, ah, she got pretty badly wounded during the ground war."

"Oh, I'm terribly sorry to hear that, Larry," Abir said. Her tone was one of genuine concern.

"Yes," he said. "She stepped on a land mine when she went to the aid of a wounded Iraqi."

"Oh, no. She must have been badly wounded, then."

"Yes. She lost both of her legs at the ankles." He sighed, then added, "But it could have been a lot worse. She's still alive, at least."

Abir was gazing at him with a look of sadness. "Thank God for that," she said.

It struck Redmond that the God this remarkable Kuwaiti woman referred to was the same one that every Muslim, Jew, and Christian worshipped.

"Yes," he said. "Thank God."

The pilots waved them onto the helicopter then, and Redmond assisted Abir aboard and helped her get strapped in.

Soon after they took off and headed south, Abir noticed Redmond and the crewmen looking out of the helicopter at the ground below with expressions of awe, and she leaned over and looked out, too.

They were flying along the highway past Mutla Ridge, and the seemingly endless tangle of wrecked vehicles destroyed by the American airstrikes. She had nearly been killed down there by those same bombs.

The Iraqis had come to the villa that afternoon in a stolen van half-filled with loot. After they beheaded Abdul and gouged out Francesca's eyes, they looted the villa's remaining valuables, as well. They missed one safe in Abir's chambers, where many of her jewels were hidden, but they took almost everything else of value that they could carry in their van and the sheik's Cherokee. They had merely beat Abir with their fists, then bound and gagged her, and threw her in the van. Then they headed north for Basra and Baghdad.

They saw some airplanes—strange, moaning things of an ungainly shape—swoop down and attack the concentration of vehicles behind them, and after waiting for the Cherokee full of loot to catch up to them in Basra, they finally gave up on it.

They were getting ready to leave again when an Iraqi major came up to the van. When he saw the Kuwaiti woman, he took her away from the murderous looters. The government wanted to round up all the Kuwaitis they could, the major explained, and keep them safe to use as human shields.

Thank God they hadn't raped her, at least, although she heard them discussing it on the trip north up the highway.

She'd been thrown into the cellar of a battered building with scores of other Kuwaitis, and the next morning someone noticed that all the bombing and shelling had gone quiet. A few days later, the guards just disappeared. The Kuwaitis simply walked out of the building and started south.

Abir shuddered, and looked out of the window of the helicopter. They were flying over an oil field now—Rumaylah, she guessed correctly. Scores of burning wells were pouring black, sticky smoke up into the sky.

The Blackhawk descended through the pall of smoke, turning midday into nightfall, then came to a hover above the back garden of the once-elegant villa. The helicopter slowly descended and settled to the ground.

Abir looked desperately about for Bill Kernan. He wasn't there. She saw two other Americans, though—uniformed soldiers. One of them ran to the pilot's window and spoke to him, then looked in the back at Abir and Larry, and nodded.

The helicopter engines shut down, and the two Americans helped her out of the Blackhawk.

"Ma'am," one said, "I'm Captain Howard Genet, US Army Special Forces. We've taken over this compound for military purposes. What is it you want?"

Larry said, "Sir, I'm Lieutenant Redmond, 24th ID. I'm Madame al-Sabah's escort officer. My orders are to bring her here and let her take a few minutes to get some of her things, then take her on down to Dhahran."

"I see," the captain said, then turned to the other Special Forces soldier. "Go get Mara to come identify her," he said.

"Mara? She's here?" Abir asked. "Thank God! Is Bill Ker…"

Mara came out, and when she saw Abir, her dark face lighted up in a brief smile. The women hurried to each other and embraced, then spoke in Arabic.

"We thought for certain you were dead, Abir," Mara said.

"Bill?" Abir asked. "Where's Bill?"

"He went after you…"

"Oh, God. He's not…?"

"He's all right, Abir. He broke his leg, but he's all right. The resistance brought him back. The Americans flew Francesca and him to a hospital."

Tears of relief fell from Abir's eyes as Mara continued. "He was here about a week ago, in the little helicopter. They went to look for you again. They found the Cherokee. It had been bombed. They thought that you'd been killed."

Mara wiped a tear from her own eye, then said, "He left a telephone number in America, just in case we learned something."

Abir took her dear friend's hands in her own. "Is the jewelry still in the bedroom safe?" she asked.

"I don't know," Mara said. "I haven't checked."

"Well, let's go see. If it is, Mara, we're going to America."

"America?"

"Yes."

"What about your sons?" Mara asked. "The Sheik will never allow you to take them with you."

Abir's eyes saddened. "I know it. But even if I stayed, he'd almost never let me see them—you know that."

"Are you still carrying the baby?" Mara asked.

Abir pressed her hand to her abdomen and said, "Yes. He's still in there."

Mara surveyed her former mistress's face. It was bright with hope and love.

"Yes, you should go, and go now, while you have the chance," Mara said. "But I am going to stay."

"Don't even think of it, Mara. Don't. Nothing is going to change here, don't you know that?"

"I've got to try, Abir. For Abdul and Francesca and all the others, I've got to try."

"No, Mara. Please."

"Yes. I must."

Abir nodded, her eyes sad again. "And Sanaa?"

Mara shook her head slowly. "She won't leave, either."

The women walked hand-in-hand to Abir's chambers. She opened the small safe behind a bedside table. The jewels and passports were there.

Abir removed the box of jewelry, opened it, and took out several necklaces of gold and precious jewels. She held them out to Mara, who started to refuse, then took them. She had no money, or anything else of value.

"When you finally realize that nothing's going to change here," Abir told her, "bring Sanaa and come to the United States."

Mara looked at the jewelry, then at Abir, and said, "We'll see."

"I have to go," Abir said.

"Yes. You'll let me know how things turn out?"

"Of course, dear, dear Mara."

When the helicopter took off again and cleared the dreary mantle of smoke, Abir's sparkling eyes and bright mood made Redmond wonder what had changed her so quickly.

"You look much happier, now," he remarked above the engines' whine.

She flashed him a smile and said, "Yes, I am."

Then she opened the box she had brought from the villa. She took out a gold ring with a large, emerald-cut diamond, and held it out to Redmond.

"This is for your wife-to-be," she said.

"Oh, I couldn't, Abir," he said. "That's mighty kind of you, but I can't. We're not allowed to accept gifts."

"You can't refuse. It's not for you, it's for her."

"No, honestly," he said. "The same rules apply to her."

"But she was wounded, you said, Larry. Won't she be leaving the Army?"

"Well, yes, once they get her squared away," he replied.

"All right," Abir argued, "just ask her to hold it for me until then, when she can accept it as a gift from me."

Larry thought about it. What the hell; it's for Mickey. He'd check with Colonel Farrar to see if accepting it for her was legal. If nothing else, he could return it, or make it a gift to the regimental silver collection.

"All right," he said. "I guess you can give it to her for a wedding present, if you really want to."

He took the ring, looked at it, then put it in his breast pocket.

"Thank you very much, Abir. You'll have to give me your address, so she can write to you," he said.

"Yes," Abir said above the engine noise, "so she can send me a wedding invitation."

He smiled and nodded, then closed his eyes and leaned his head back against the bulkhead of the Blackhawk, thinking.

Had it really only been six months since he's left Charleston aboard the roll-on, roll-off ship crammed with Abrams tanks and Bradley infantry fighting vehicles?

It seemed as if that was a lifetime ago, some moments, and only yesterday at others.

It had changed him immensely. He felt now as if he must have been nothing but a little boy when he left the States. But he was a man, now, he knew.

All he could ever remember wanting was to be a soldier. When he had left the Citadel with honors and a commission as a Second Lieutenant of Armor, that dream—that goal—changed to one of leading a tank platoon into battle.

He had trained hard for it, damned hard, and the Fates must have been pleased, because they had allowed him, in ideal tank country, to lead not only a platoon, but an entire tank company team—the Fates and Lieutenant Colonel Farrar, anyway. And Major General McCaffrey, the Victory Division commander.

It hadn't been nearly as long or difficult a war as he had expected. He might have been disappointed by that fact, were it not for Joe's death, and the wounding of the other tankers, and of Mickey.

Thank God there would be no more—not this time. And he would continue, he knew now, to train his men hard, for the rest of his career, so that whenever and wherever they were called upon to fight next time, they would not only win, but would survive. They were too important to throw away, to risk unnecessarily by allowing them to go untrained.

The next one would not be so quick and so relatively easy; it couldn't possibly be, of that Larry Redmond was certain. But he would be there; he was also certain of that.

He thought of the romp across Iraq, and the assault on the airfield. Of the Iraqi counterattack he had spoiled, and of the attack that never went in.

He remembered Mickey in Bahrain, and lying wounded in the hospital, and he recalled what Farrar had said to him one night in the officers' club at Fort Stewart, now so long ago:

"There are two things which turn boys into men, Redmond," his battalion commander had said. "Women and war. If you're lucky, you'll know both."

▼

Epilogue

5 December 1991

The leg feels good. Everything feels good, in fact, Bill Kernan thought as he jogged along North Carolina's narrow route 12.

He didn't have to worry about traffic; the fourteen-mile long road on Ocracoke Island was nearly deserted this time of year. Even when the ferries landed—the only way cars could get to the fragile barrier island—there were just a few of them.

The little village around the harbor near the southern tip of the island was on its lazy winter schedule. Only the old Island Inn and two motels were open, competing for the rare visitor who made the long trip for a day or two of solitude on Ocracoke's nearly deserted beach.

Howard's Pub was open much of the day, but the 3/4 Time Saloon was closed until 6:00 PM, when the Ocockers—the native islanders, many of whom were descendants of the notorious pirate Blackbeard and his crew—were finished with the day's toil. Except for the fishermen and a few who earned their livings building summer homes on the island, Ocracoke's inhabitants had drifted into what they called an "ocracoma."

Bill was approaching Parkers Creek, an indentation in the soundside marsh where a sandy trail led through the brush and across the dunes to his favorite spot on the beach.

He had left his Chevy Blazer there, and he saw that another car was parked behind it.

Kernan sprinted the last fifty yards to the cars, then stopped and checked his watch.

Good run, he thought. He reached inside the Blazer for his windbreaker, noticing that the other car was a rented one.

He started along the path, and his professional eye caught the sight of new footprints on the sandy trail leading through the dunes toward the ocean—a man in street shoes, he surmised.

It struck him as an intrusion that someone else would be at "his" spot, when there were sixteen miles of beach on Ocracoke, and no more than a handful of people on it. His whole purpose in moving to the island for the winter was for the solitude it offered. The only time he had left the Outer Banks in months had been to go down to Fort Stewart, Georgia, to see Mickey Myers marry Captain Larry Redmond.

He climbed through the sea oats up the last high dune behind the beach, the sound and smell of the ocean and the cold breeze blowing across it engulfing him with their delightful freshness. As he crested the dune, he was treated to the sight of a pair of dolphins surfing down the face of a breaking wave, and he envied them.

He crossed the top and looked down, then stopped and broke into a broad smile. The intruder was his old friend, Claude Owen.

He was sitting on the blanket with Abir, watching the baby playing in the soft sand, discovering the feel of it with her little fingers.

He trotted down the steep face of the dune, thinking, There sits everything I love.

"Rotorhead!" he called, and Claude turned, saw him, and stood, a broad grin lighting his face.

"Old Conan," the pilot said, and the two friends hugged while Abir watched, smiling at the sight of them.

Owen turned and nodded toward the baby. "That's a mighty pretty little girl you've got there, Bill. Pretty name, too—Mara Francesca."

Kernan looked at his daughter, and then at his wife. They were his whole world now, all that mattered to him—they and the friend who now stood there beside him.

"Yes," was all that he could think to say in reply.

"You're a hard guy to find, Bill Kernan," Owen said, then added, "I don't blame you, though."

Bill nodded. "Yeah. I guess I should have let you know."

He was going to send his old friend a note eventually, letting him know where he and Abir were, and inviting him to come for a visit. But not yet. He wanted to be alone with Abir and their child for awhile longer, enjoying the peaceful little world they had discovered together, where the struggles of the past could be forgotten.

"How did you find us, anyway?" he asked Owen.

His friend's smile melted and his eyes became serious, and Kernan knew the answer.

"The Company sent you, didn't they?" he said, suddenly feeling betrayed.

Owen sighed and nodded. "Yes. They want you to come back in," he muttered.

Kernan looked at his wife and child, then back at Owen. "Yeah?" he said, hostility rising in his voice. "Well, you can go back and tell them this for me—tell them I said…"

He stopped and looked at Abir. Her face had taken on a blank expression, as if her mind had shut down. She reached out and drew her baby daughter to her.

"Let's take a walk," Bill said. He knelt and hugged his wife, then kissed her forehead and the baby's.

"Be right back," he said, and Abir nodded, her dark eyes full of worry such as he had not seen since those terrible days in Kuwait. They seemed so long ago.

The two men walked slowly up the beach on the hard sand near the water. A gulf had suddenly formed between them, and they both sensed it.

After awhile, Owen said, "Don't shoot the messenger, Bill."

Kernan looked over at him. "Sorry, old friend," he said. "You're right. I'm glad they at least had enough sense to send you, not somebody else."

"What shall I tell them?" Owen asked.

There had been a time when he wouldn't even have had to ask, when all that had to be said was, "We need you," and Bill Kernan would have gone without question. But no longer.

"Tell them to go get fucked," he said.

"All right. Well, that's that, then. I had to ask."

Kernan spotted a scotchbonnet shell and picked it up, examined it, then tossed it into the surf.

"So, how long can you stay, Claude? We'd love to have you spend a few days—there's plenty of room."

"Thanks, but I have to get going, Bill. Maybe when I get back, though."

"What's the job, anyway?" his old friend asked. "The same one they want me for?"

"Yeah," Owen answered, shoving his hands into the pockets of his jeans and glancing at the clouds. "I don't know exactly what it is. Something to do with Saddam and his WMDs—weapons of mass desruction, apparently."

Kernan stopped and looked out across the empty ocean.

Somewhere out there, over the broad Atlantic and the Mediterranean Sea beyond, the madman still plotted, still gathered his evil means for some insane end which the world—perhaps even he, himself—had not yet come to know.

Bill Kernan looked back toward his precious wife and child and wondered if their world would ever be safe.

From the north, a pair of aging Navy A-6 Intruders streaked past offshore, low and fast.

Claude glanced at his watch, then at Bill. For a long moment, the men looked deep into each other's eyes. And then, without a word, they turned and walked back down the beach toward Bill Kernan's wife and baby daughter.

▼

About the Author

L.H. "Bucky" Burruss, author of MIKE FORCE, A MISSION FOR DELTA, CLASH OF STEEL, and the soon-to-be-released ALL THAT MATTERS, is a retired Army lieutenant colonel and native Virginian. After earning a degree in history and English, Burruss enlisted in the army and spent two tours in Vietnam with the Special Forces, then assisted the late Colonel Charlie Beckwith in forming the 1st Special Forces Operational Detachment—Delta (Delta Force). He served as deputy commander of the ground force during the Iran hostage rescue attempt and as Delta's deputy commander during the seizure of Grenada. He is a frequent contributor to the *Philadelphia Inquirer* and other publications. He is married to the anthropologist Rachele D. Burruss and is the father of five children. When not writing, he is a muleskinner in Wyoming, a fisherman on the Outer Banks of North Carolina, and a homeschooler of his youngest child, Carmella.

Printed in the United States
25652LVS00003B/95

9 780595 120253